Books by Gwen Hunter

In the DeLande Saga:
BETRAYAL
FALSE TRUTHS
LAW OF THE WILD

———

In the Rhea Lynch, MD. Series:
DELAYED DIAGNOSIS
PRESCRIBED DANGER
DEADLY REMEDY
GRAVE CONCERNS

———

Stand-alones:
ASHES TO ASHES
SHADOW VALLEY
BLOODSTONE
BLACKWATER SECRETS

Law
of the
Wild

Third in the DeLande Saga

GWEN HUNTER

BellaRosaBooks

LAW OF THE WILD
First USA Edition
Copyright © 2005 by Gwen Hunter

ISBN 1-933523-11-5
Library of Congress Control Number: 2005909761

Also published as:
Law Of The Wild – Great Britain, Hodder & Stoughton, hardcover, 1997
Law Of The Wild – Great Britain, Hodder & Stoughton, paperback, 1998

Printed in the United States of America on acid-free paper.

Cover painting and interior graphics by Joyce Wright – www.artbyjoyce.com
Book design by Bella Rosa Books

To Bobby Benson Prater, my dad.

For all the late-night debates around the kitchen table.

For making me fill in all the holes in my arguments and support all my hypotheses.

For making me think and use my mind.

For telling me my mind and my arguments were my greatest weapons.

For teaching me to fish, to repair the boat motor, to mow the grass.

For not making me do only "girl things".

For forcing me to accept responsibility even when I would rather run away.

For all this and more,

With love,

Gwen

Acknowledgments

Thanks to:

Bobby Prater for sharing bayou lore and for being available at every moment to answer dumb questions.

Betty Louise Cryer for helping with the research on Lake Charles and Saint Patrick's Hospital.

Joyce Wright for proof-reading and suggestions and great cover art.

Mike Prater for solving those dreadful computer problems.

Rod Hunter for finding the perfect word when my brain wouldn't work.

Beth McKnight for typing when my fingers were just too tired.

Suzanne Horton for bringing the files up to date.

Randy Crew—warrior, pilot, fellow author—for the crash course in helicopters . . . pun intended.

Jeff Gerecke, the perfect agent.

And last—but not least—to my editor at Bella Rosa Books.

Law
of the
Wild

Prologue

Mara was born into a race of slaves.

After all this time, after all she had seen and begun to understand, she could finally admit that simple and salient fact. In the modern-day world, this world of personal freedom and privilege, DVDs and satellite dishes, war by push-button and remote control, she was a throwback to another time—bred for the use of a man, as were all the women of her Louisiana clan.

She was born a LeMay. A breed apart from the rest of the world, different in mind and body, emotions and spirit, conceived from the genes up to be shackled, owned. Chattel to the DeLandes.

The Eldest DeLande of New Orleans had a strange power over the LeMays, an enchantment that bordered on wizardry. To the women of the LeMay clan, the DeLande males were a fascination, an enticement, a beguilement that could not be refused, though legend had it some had tried over the centuries. The DeLandes ruled them, owned them, possessed them. In the eyes of a DeLande Eldest, the LeMays were their entitlement. An inheritance. A birthright. The family ties lay intertwined for centuries.

Mara had seen it herself as a child—had seen the way they could captivate and entrance—and she had seen what was left when that power was broken. She had watched her mother for years as Rosemon waited for her man, her DeLande protector, to call for her. Watched as she wasted away, growing pale and lifeless, drab and passive. Watched as she came alive when she finally heard his call, changing from submissive and unresisting, to passionate and fiery in the space of a heartbeat.

Mara watched her mother the night her man died.

He was Andreu, called the Eldest, a title of power and respect among the DeLande Clan, that strange and powerful family who had ruled Louisiana for centuries. Mara knew him as the green-eyed master of her mother's sensual enslavement. The father of her half-brothers and sisters. A man of secrets and prestige, holding the power of life and death, joy and misery, passion and indifference, all in the palm of his hand. He could destroy with a word. Comfort with a glance.

The night he died, Rosemon had been lying supine, her head thrown back, her eyes glazed, skin flushed with passion, in thrall to him, though he was miles away and perhaps not even aware of her at all. In some bizarre manner Mara had never understood—never would understand—Rosemon was linked to him and lost to her children.

It was late, cold, and wet in this land that was never dry, this land of bayou and swamp, miasmic gasses and cypress, predator and prey. Fog wisped in through the windows, pale tendrils touching Rosemon's skin as she locked on to Andreu, communing and captivated. Sharing his life as she had been bred to do. And Mara watched, curled in a corner, gnawing her lip, jealous and frightened as always.

And then Rosemon screamed, threw back her head, the tendons in her throat stretched taut. Screamed as if she were dying and faced a hell unimaginable. Clawing her throat and chest in blood-red welts, she crawled, crab-like, on to the floor. Cowered in the far corner. Hidden, Rosemon whimpered, eyes wide and staring, mouth open, as her throat bled from the violence of her own nails. And then the seizures started.

She had been nearly catatonic ever since. Silent. Staring. Compliant.

Mara hated her for her little death. But she hated the DeLandes more.

We are DeLande by blood but not by name. That was the maxim by which LeMays lived. It had been a way of life for over two hundred years. A life of freedom and safety in the wilds of the Badlands of Louisiana and Texas.

LeMays were DeLande only by bloodlines, not by marriage, not by custom, and never by mores. LeMays were free from DeLande dominance, free to live as they chose in swamp and bayou.

The DeLande Eldest guaranteed that independence, and at least one LeMay woman in each generation secured that freedom with her body. In the last generation that woman had been Rosemon, Mara's mother. In this generation that woman was to be Mara. Unless Momo set her free.

Mara hated it, this life of slavery promised to her. And she would fight it with the last drop of life in her body. Yet, though she could admit it to no one—not even Momo—Mara had lived all her young life in terror that she would one day meet a DeLande and lose herself to him as her mother had lost herself to Andreu. And a worse fear . . . that she would no longer care.

Chapter One
The Badlands—A Trap

She tossed her hair back over her shoulder, irritated that it was no longer in its braid. It was too long, too straight, too black, and some day she would disobey Momo and hack it off with a skinning knife. Would cut it short, above her ears, boy-style.

Momo would shriek and wail and proclaim disaster over Mara's life and future, her shrill voice sounding like wildcats mating on high ground. She would wring her hands and cry to her saints, and big tears would run down her face like rain down cracked window glass. She would make a fuss because the day Mara cut her hair, she would be free. That day, she would be grown.

Twisting up her skirt, Mara pulled the fabric through her legs, tucking the hem into her waistband, creating makeshift short, baggy trousers, exposing her legs. Balancing her cane pole on a stump, she freed both hands to re-braid her hair, and tied it off with a length of twine pulled from her pocket.

Unencumbered, she waded deeper into the bayou, mud to her ankles, water to mid-thigh, and untangled the fishing line from the brambles collected there. Perch and catfish were attracted to the brambles to feed and lay eggs. Mara had seen a three-footer in the shallow water just yesterday at sundown, and was determined to hook him.

Yesterday, he swam past in lazy superiority, flaunting himself. Today, it was if he could read her mind. As if he knew her intent to catch him, skin him, and serve him up crisp and fried golden brown, to Momo for dinner. He stayed hidden.

She was using the pole just to occupy her hands and mind, the real work done by the trot-line—the catfish line—she had strung over the bayou. Eighty feet of number 18 nylon twine was tied off to a sapling on either bank. It was sturdy cord, 165-pound test-line, just in case she caught more than one monster fish. Mara had tied ten loops in the twine at various distances, and dropped 18-inch stringers from each. On two, she had tied weights, short lengths of cast iron pipe buried in the muddy bottom, keeping the trot-line in its proper place. The other stringers were hooked with 3/0 Eagle Claw hooks, and baited with worms or crickets or a slice of Momo's whole-hog sausage, all treats for even the most finicky catfish.

If she caught the granddaddy catfish, it would likely be on the trot-line, not the single hook caught in the brambles beneath the dark water. Statistically speaking, the trot-line was her best bet for success. But it was so boring.

Freeing her line, Mara clambered back up the muddy bank, settling herself on the rounded stump of the huge oak at her back to re-bait the hook. It was sundown, finally, blue herons soaring past to roost nearby, gators slapping the water as they slithered off the banks to hunt, mosquitoes swarming up from some watery hell to feast on her blood, a breeze from the gulf blowing in damp and almost cool, and the sky turning a vicious red that bled into the water like a great wound. It was her favorite time of day.

Tossing a wriggling worm back into the water, its body threaded with the fish hook, she smeared insect repellent on to her skin and waited for her supper to bite. The world darkened around her and daylight died. Bullfrogs sang a basso harmony. A cat screamed in the distance, sounding like a woman in agony. Bats flitted and dived after insects. Mara narrowed her eyes, watching warily. She didn't like bats. Ugly things. Rats that could fly. Careful to monitor their movements, she rested her head back against the bark.

Behind her, a twig snapped, the sound sharp and clean.

It is never silent on the bayou; the sounds of wildlife are a constant accompaniment. Mammals and insects, reptiles and amphibians, birds and fish, all intent on their next meal, carry death up the food chain making a mutable hum of background noise, a varying clamor. Even the plants contribute to the insistent cacophony as wind rustles leaves and dead branches break off and fall. A thousand sounds she knew by heart and scarcely even heard.

But this one was different. Mara held her breath, listening.

Twigs that break off, tend to fall and land in underbrush or water, settling with a tiny susurration of sound. Twigs are stepped on, don't.

Moving slowly, she slid her hand along the root stump where she sat, and found her gun, its worn butt sliding into her hand as if it had missed her touch. She rested the bamboo rod on the aged wood.

With a single motion, she dropped to her belly. Rolled. Extended her arms. Bracing her body, she scanned the low foliage.

There were three of them that she could see, dark shadows widely spaced among the tree trunks. Moving, crouched, man-sized.

They hadn't seen her yet, but they had seen her airboat, *Jenny's* tall fan-cage painted in the yellow and black tail bands of a Japanese hornet, the powerful engine cool to the touch. They knew she was here. They knew who she was.

And Mara knew what they wanted. Shock, like a jolt of icy water, drenched through her. *She knew what they wanted.* She *knew*. A flush, hot and burning, steamed through the sensation of cold. She shouldn't *know* anything. She should simply be afraid.

A crow cawed in the distance. Bat wings whisked by her head. Not thinking, Mara aimed the Colt. Squeezing gently, she pulled off a single round, shattering the music of the bayou. She could hear his scream over the roar of the shot. He dropped, a bullet in his thigh. She could feel his fury. His pain. His fear. Her heart twisted and thundered in her chest.

The one on the left had seen the muzzle flash. A Colt 9mm makes a cannon flash in dim light. He ducked behind the wide, twisted bole of a leafless chenier and emerged a moment later in a different place, carrying a shotgun.

Mara had lost the one on the right. Not good. The bayou was to the left. The one with the shotgun had nowhere to go. The one on the right had plenty of room to maneuver.

Rolling again, she came up beside the old tree where she was protected on all sides, by the tree in front, by the bayou behind. Her heart hammered, her breath came too fast. Too loud. Louder than the sounds of the men. Again, she aimed and fired, this time taking her target in the abdomen, low on the left.

His scream of pain was more than an auditory reflex. She heard it reverberate through the swamp and through her mind as well, a psychic impulse that left her shaken. She had hurt him badly. She knew it. She *knew*.

Mara clutched the tree. Blinded. And then, suddenly, she felt them move away. She didn't *see* them leave. She never left the safety of the tree that was both her protection and obstruction. She just *felt* them leave, her eyes wide in the falling darkness.

The one on the right was HoBoy, and he just followed orders. The one she shot through the thigh was DeMarc. And the one seriously injured was her cousin, Tether. He was one of her clan. And he was a traitor.

Heavy silver clinked against fine china as footmen moved with choreographed precision down the long table, removing the roti settings from the guests. Priceless Limoges china, smeared with the greasy remains of quail and stacked with small bones like piles of twigs, vanished, exposing fine linen beneath. Elegant conversation was exchanged to either side. Discreet laughter whispered the length of the room.

The setting sun cast fiery shadows across the long table as coffee was poured and a trolley laden with confections rolled down both sides for the guests to chose between a half dozen luscious desserts. There were local politicians, a former Texas governor, her hair in a bee-hive, three bankers, one from Tokyo, two from Germany, an artist, a drunken writer, and the winner of this year's British Open. And, of course, there was family, moving elegantly among them, guiding conversation, eliciting information, titillating and seducing. Always seducing. After all, these were DeLandes at their best.

Miles watched it all with hooded eyes, the guests to either side of him forgotten for the moment, his mind blank, his quiet anger carefully shielded as he watched a red-haired cousin cajole a smile out of the man across from her. Further down, a red-headed second cousin flirted with the woman to his side. Beautiful, each and every one of the DeLandes. Utterly and completely beautiful. And most of them were broken or depraved within, thanks to the lifestyle that came with the looks and the grace and the very name itself. Miles frowned slightly, distracted.

The butler appeared at the head of the table, his mien stiff, haughty, and affectionate all at once. He bowed behind the host's chair and whispered in Miles' ear, "The Grande Dame has suffered another attack, just an hour ago, sir. I have taken the liberty of having her physician summoned, and upon his orders, have administered a dose of Haldol. Any other orders, Mr. DeLande?"

"Yes, Jenkins. Ready the Cessna," he said, speaking of the twin-engine aircraft in the hanger at the back of the estate, "and pack me a bag. Jeans, boots, survival gear."

Jenkins lifted a brow in that supercilious manner that had held sway over the estate for two decades. It was his only indication of surprise. "Destination, sir?"

Miles grinned finally, black eyes like sooty torches, throwing back the light. "Don't know yet," he said. "Somewhere in the Badlands. I think the Grande Dame's attack was the result of an injury to one of *us*."

"You found another, sir?"

"I think so. I couldn't pinpoint the location, but I have a general idea of the territory."

"Very good, sir. And I'll have Cleo reschedule your appointments for the rest of the week."

"Thanks, Jenks."

"My pleasure, sir. My pleasure."

Miles turned his attention back to the crowd before him. His sister Angelique was laughing into the eyes of Raul Gastineau, an artist from the South of France. Gastineau was the art world's newest sensation. His medium was construction paper cut into tiny triangles and pasted on artist's board, or some such nonsense.

Angelique, scarlet hair seeming to burn in the crimson light of sunset, bent forward, her low-cut dress gaping, revealing far too much to be merely accidental. Angelique had always been attracted to the artistic type and Miles could hear the warm purr of her voice as she put her hand on Gastineau's arm. Her laughter melted away, eyes grew wide, lips parted. Raul's eyes rested on them, fascinated. Snared by the art of seduction perfected.

She was good at it, Miles' sister, practiced at seduction and temptation, the destruction of marriages and of good men. She considered it her calling, as others are called to the ministry, or to the mission field, or to some selfless occupation. She went about it with the dedication of the true believer, leaving heartache and misery in the wake of dozens of affairs.

If the devil ever advertised for a female lieutenant whose specialty was to lure the tempted but undecided, Angelique would snap up the job in a heartbeat. She had even made an attempt or two on Miles himself in the last year, appearing in his suite in the middle of the night, naked and inviting. The ties of blood between them had been only an added attraction, from her point of view.

Until he became Eldest, incest had been a DeLande family tradition, a custom going back for centuries. Some Eldests had insisted upon the practice, mating brother to sister, parent to child. During kinder times, the ritual matings had been optional rather than obligatory. Throughout the reign of the Grande Dame such matings had been forced. Angelique believed they should be again. Miles wanted the matings abolished.

Miles watched his sister preen, a sheen of sweat and imported oils glistening on her skin. Her pulse beat like the heart of a trapped bird as she slid her palm along the artist's thigh.

Down the table, Gastineau's wife watched the little tableau of Angelique and her husband in the prelude of passion. Her face was furious and embarrassed all at once. Angelique cast slanted eyes at the wife and smiled her triumph.

Miles sighed. He would have to do something about his sister. And soon.

Chapter Two
Badlands—New Knowledge

"You play with you food, Mara. You quiet. All dis good food and you got nothin' to say?"

Mara pushed the small strips of fried catfish across her plate, lining them up like soldiers marching through the vegetables. Fried okra, peppered summer squash and thick slices of deep red tomato, the color of a setting sun. She had cooked it all, and nothing was what she wanted. "I wanted to catch the three-footer."

"That not why you so mose."

"Morose."

"Mo-rose. You gettin' too much learnin'. What mo-rose mean again?"

Mara stood and picked up her plate. "Sullen. Sulky, glum, gloomy, moody."

"That you, yes, all they things," Momo agreed, her French accent slipping from strong to weak as it did when she indulged in intimate conversation with family.

Mara cleaned up the kitchen, storing the leftover food in the small fridge set on the back porch. It was over thirty years old, almost as old as Rosemon, her mama, and painted a hideous shade of green, where the rust allowed the color through. It ran on power created by the generator, alternately freezing and thawing the food, depending whether anyone remembered to crank on the new gas-powered version that had recently taken the place of the worn-out one.

"Tell you Momo why you so unhappy, Mara?"

She rinsed the glasses in the washbasin and tossed the water out the front door into the bayou. It fell with a splash, muting for a moment, the bullfrogs' terrible clamor. Down the bayou, lights twinkled from the Torres' houseboat, tied up at an abandoned electrical piling. Music, rough and coarse, reached her through the stand of cypress, bouncing off the water in tinny rhythms. Laughter, just as coarse, followed. Slowly, she turned.

"Three men found me on the bayou while I was fishing," she began.

Momo tilted her head, the glare from the oil lamp flashing off her spectacles as she waited for Mara to continue. The bullfrogs recommenced their primal melody, drowning the distant sounds of humans, while Mara wandered about the room. She dried the dishes and put them away. Wiped off the scarred table. Adjusted the wick of the lamp. Her hands were trembling. She wondered if Momo saw the tremors.

"It was near dusk," she continued finally. "I heard a twig snap." She couldn't go on for a moment, some unknown emotion rising in her like a sudden flood. A violent swelling of bayou waters after a random cloudburst far upstream. Rampant, uncontrolled violence surged through her, a major torrent, sweeping all before it.

Tears trembled at the corners of her eyes. Her heart beat like a child on a toy drum, a rough uneven cadence. "I knew what they wanted," she whispered. "I knew who they were and how long they had been watching me, and—" Mara broke off suddenly as two tears fell.

She wiped at her cheeks viciously, dragging at her skin. Mara had always hated scenes, perhaps because Rosemon had indulged in so many when her Andreu was alive. Using the dish towel, Mara dried her face, roughly.

"I *knew*," she whispered, the word as potent as a shout. "I knew."

Momo held out her arms and Mara crossed the room to drop at her side and bury her head in the ample lap. Momo's skirts smelled of talcum powder and sunshine and starch and a hint of lavender from the sachets in her closet. Familiar smells of Momo's skin and clothes, dependable and steady, unchanging for all of Mara's life. For long moments, she hid her head in the cotton dress as Momo stroked her hair and murmured the French patois of a long-ago youth. Comforting sounds, liquid syllables that calmed the strange

11

emotions washing through her. Syllables that proved Momo was here, the one constant in her life. The emotion, whatever it was, roiled away and was gone.

Finally, Mara eased back and began to speak. "I shot one. In the leg. And the other in the stomach. He screamed, Momo. He screamed, a man dying. It was awful, his pain." Momo mumbled something inarticulate, her fingers making little spit-curls of the hair around Mara's ears. "It was Tether, Momo, and he wanted to hurt me, I knew it. And I don't understand *how* I knew it," she whispered. "I don't understand."

The peculiar emotion returned at the edges of her mind, circling like Croak, the black crow Momo had befriended when she healed him of a broken wing three years past. He would glide outside the house a dozen times a day, a shadow in the sunlight, waiting for Momo to call to him, still greedy for a free meal and the touch of his mistress' hand.

"Mara, what you feelin' is fear. And you can't be 'fraid of fear," she added, tapping Mara's head twice with her nail.

Mara laughed, tasting the word on her tongue. *Fear. Yes*. With the naming of it, it seemed to recede, as if Momo had chanted some spell. Like Croak, the fear seemed to perch and study Mara as she studied it. She had felt fear dozens of times. Fear of a hungry gator. Fear of a sudden storm, its waters blocking the way home. Fear of Rosemon and her new, empty moods. This was a different kind of fear. A powerful, debilitating fear that had a life of its own.

She had hurt a man. *He might die*. And inside herself some strange . . . thing had taken over. Yet, her fear was separate from that realization, set apart, distinct.

Mara sat on the floor, her head on a level with Momo's waist, and when she turned her head, her chin brushed Momo's knees, rubbing against the old, starched cotton of her long skirts. A water roach, two and a half inches long, crawled across the floor and disappeared into a crack between two boards. Automatically, Mara noted the spot to spray later.

"Mara, what I'm thinkin' now?"

"That you love me. And that God let you live too long just so you could."

Momo chuckled, and brushed Mara's hair back, her hand gentle. "You think it easy, dat you know Momo's mind?"

"What do you mean?"

"You think other folk live inside each other head, know each other thought like you and me do?"

"Well . . ." Mara didn't know where this conversation was headed, but already she didn't like it. Not at all. It smacked of DeLande witchcraft.

"They don't do it, no, Mara. And now you be growin' up, you mind be . . ." Momo made a stretching motion with her hands, like pulling taffy.

"Expanding?" Mara supplied.

"Yes, 'spandin'. Dat de cat eat de cabbage," she said happily, using the old saying that meant 'that's a fact'. "And growin', you be hearin' sound o' other minds, de babblin' o' dey spirit, like de tricklin' sound o' water runnin' de bayou after summer storm. Other thoughts you be hearin' soon, too, not just mine, an' you close kin. I be tellin' you long time, '*Watch fo' this*,' and you not be hearin'. It come now, Mara, like hurricane in gulf, an' you no be stoppin' it. You got DeLande blood." Momo nodded, the light on her spectacles alternately revealing and obscuring her black eyes.

"But I'm not a DeLande," Mara said stubbornly, in her tone the resonance of an old argument. "Not in the ways that count. I'm a half breed! I've never been like the others, like Rosemon and Lucien and Cady. I've always been *different*." Momo started to speak but Mara overrode her words. "Rosemon always said I would be different. Her *normal* child. She promised me I wouldn't be like her. She *promised*," Mara said fiercely.

Ignoring the last complaint, Momo said, "You most half DeLande. Dat enough. In you, more than enough. Tonight, when Tether scream, he let loose with all he spirit, send he pain, he anger, all through bayou with you name in it. You hear because you DeLande. I hear. DeLande in New Orleans hear it too, most sure," Momo shrugged. "Tether never have no control anyway."

"You heard?"

Momo nodded again, her eyes like black diamonds sparkling on black velvet. Her lips were compressed as if she heard Mara's next comment before she asked.

"You heard, and you knew all that happened, and you didn't say anything? All this time?" Mara got up from the floor and found the Raid. Taking careful aim, she sprayed the crack between the boards, concentrating the poison where the roach had disappeared. Anger, as intimate as the fresh spit-curls in her hair, stirred in Mara. Momo always did this. Waited for her to speak when she already knew everything there was to know.

Momo's lips pressed together even tighter. "You not make you DeLande blood go way, Mara. You no can kill it, jus' like you no can kill all de roaches. Maybe you make dem hide some little bit, kill four, three, two, but you not kill dem all, not never. You no stop bein' a DeLande, jus' like Momo no stop bein' DeLande. Rosemon, she alway 'bellious, fightin' what has to be. She no have the sight like you Momo, not even befo' Andreu die. She not *know* what you be."

Mara put away the bug spray, her anger dying, as the sharp scent of poison cut through the hot grease smell of supper. "I don't want—" She stopped, remembering the sound of Tether's scream. Its texture. Its vivid pulse.

She laid her head against the cupboard. The slick blue enamel was almost cool against her skin, in this place where nothing was ever cool for long in the summer. The bright pigment was grayed out by the night. Mara traced the raised panel of the cupboard, edges blunted by the many coats of blue paint layered on it over the years. Momo loved blue. Everything in her cabin was blue except the small refrigerator on the porch. Electric blue, cobalt blue, heather blue, aqua, teal, lapis lazuli, and baby blue. Even Momo's clothing was blue: blue floral dress, navy cotton slip, a faded blue and pink shawl, so old its mended sections were larger than the whole ones.

Mara heard again the scream in her mind, felt it as it raced along her nerves. It was seductive, that connection.

"Yet, I thinkin' things be some different now," Momo mused from her rocker.

Mara raised her head. The enamel was already warm and damp against her skin. "What did you say?"

"I be thinkin' 'bout what you say las' time we talk, yeah."

14

"Argued, you mean?"

Momo grinned, her pearly dentures a flash of white against her deep olive skin. Her smile created a hundred fine wrinkles not visible only a moment before. "Had us a row, we did, las' time we dis-cuss DeLandes."

"I was younger. More emotional. And besides, you provoked me," Mara said, still ashamed of her outburst, though it had been over two years ago. Momo hadn't mentioned the incident since, and it had sat between them like a cat, toying with a mouse.

"Bad temper on you Mara. Half-wild, like you daddy."

Mara jerked at the mention of her father. He was a taboo subject. Off limits. Rosemon's secret sin that everyone knew about but never spoke of. Momo went on as if she hadn't uttered the forbidden words, *your daddy*.

"Like you say then, things be different now, yes." Momo lifted her rosary and the charm she wove each month by the light of the new moon. The relic and the fetish, hanging together, would have been incongruous anywhere but here in no-man's-land. The place some called the Badlands. The thirteen miles of hell.

Here, they belonged together, like darkness and light. Day and night. Holiness and mortal sin.

The rosary with its crucifix was over two hundred years old, its origins lost in antiquity. Constructed of black and pink pearls strung together, it was centered by the bleeding Christ, an ivory effigy dying on a solid gold cross.

The charm was the feathers of three birds—the crow, the white egret, and the blue heron—twisted together and dipped in the blood of a chicken, tied with a lock of Momo's own white hair and hung on a gold chain.

Together, they dangled in the flickering light of the lamp.

At the door, a huge pale green moth beat against the screen, its wings a feathery flutter of sound, mimicking the beating of a heart in distress. "Long time back, I be young like you is now. Firs' come into mah power." Momo's eyes were gentle in the lambent light, remembering. "De world not like now, no. Century new then, but de old ways still de same. Dis be power, den," she said, twirling the gold chain, its bloodied feathers beneath. Her voice was a satiny melody, French and English pronunciations intertwining, the tone of voice she used when she spoke an enchantment and captured the soul of a beast or a man.

"Den dis be power." She lifted the gold crucifix to dangle the bloodied Christ beside it, twin talismans that Momo had clung to all her life. "Dese things part of de spirit world—call o' demon, whisper o' dead saints." She dropped the rosary and the amulet. They fell from the light into the dark folds of cloth at her waist.

The moth at the door trembled, its wings a raw, agitated sound.

"Now? Now power is dat." She pointed at the laptop, its screen dark. "An' dat." She pointed at Mara's shelves of books, the row upon row of encyclopedias, histories, biographies, moldering in the damp air. "Knowledge, Mara. Dis de power de new century." Her voice was sad suddenly, a melancholy timbre, mesmeric. Mara leaned in closer, drawn, as always, by the authority of her words. The moth beat harder, the sound of its wings distressed and tormented, as if it wanted to escape and could not, held to the screen and the faint light of the lamp by some force greater than itself.

"I be one hun'red 'n twelve year old, and de world be different now. Different fo' you. If you take a man, it be new thing from when I take my DeLande protector. Different from when you mother take her man, Andreu. When you take a man, you be choosin'. Yes or no, it be *you* choosin'." Momo inclined her head, and her spectacles seemed to flash with an inner fire. "I have spoke." The final words fell with the decisiveness of a pronouncement, a benediction—or a curse.

Mara shivered, a silent *frisson* crackling through her, kindred to the thrill of distant lightning. A heady feeling, like stolen wine at a fais-do-do, thrummed through her. *I have spoke.*

Mara was seventeen. She had been fighting to hear those words all her life. "I can choose?" she whispered. Her words breathed through the night, tremulous, timorous, shaking like the moth, still beating at the screen.

Momo said, "Yes. You choose you man, Mara. You choose." The moth fell away as if exhausted.

"You rub face red, yeah. Put some mah cream on you face. You make wrinkles too soon, like you Momo, less you pampers you skin. I still young and I got wrinkles too much," Momo cackled

16

with laughter at her witticism. *Still young.* To Momo that was high
humor.

"I got take care o' you—" Momo stopped mid-sentence, tilting
her head to one side. A slow transformation began, and Mara
moved closer, watching her change. Her mouth gradually went
slack, her full lips parting. Momo washed her hands together
slowly, languidly, as if she sat in the bath in the cool of the
evening.

It was like watching the unknowable, the incomprehensible,
take place. Momo called it *listening*, the trance-like state that gave
her power over kin and clan, and over most of the Badlands for
miles around. Momo's eyes fell out of focus, staring at a distant
landscape only she could see.

It happened often, this sudden shift in her attention, this other-
worldly awareness. Common, and yet dark, mysterious, the earth
power of another age, a mystical era, long lost to time and history.
Lost everywhere but in a few pockets of mystical places and
mysterious bloodlines—the Aborigines of Australia, a few tribes in
Africa, the DeLandes of New Orleans, and here in the Badlands
with the LeMays. Ancient ways, ancient power, collected in the
person of Momo, Mara's great-great-great grandmother.

Though she never told her, Mara hated it when Momo went
away like that. Especially since the night when her mama's
protector had died and Rosemon slipped into a similar state,
seemingly listening forever for the Andreu she had lost. They had
never spoken of it, despite the fact that Momo surely knew Mara's
feelings. Momo knew almost everything.

She took Momo's unresisting hands in hers, the skin old-lady
soft on the palms, work callused on the fingertips and along the
inside knuckle ridge. Watching Momo's face, Mara checked her
pulse as the old woman wandered in whatever timeless place she
visited. It was steady and slow, the muted beat of a strong heart.
Mara hated it when Momo *listened*, yet there was within her a
fascination as well. She had always loved the tales Momo told
when she returned.

A kin woman had had a girl baby. A couple conceived a child.
Someone died . . .

Old knowledge. Old as the Celtic race from which the Cajuns had descended. Old as the African lore brought in by slaves chained in the bowels of slave ships. This power that Momo claimed was passing in favor of modern knowledge, modern power. But Momo was still a powerful force, a strong soul. Her pulse was steady. Her eyes moved beneath closed lids. A small frown puckered her brows.

Momo was a spiritualist according to the ancient ways. A mystic. For five generations a DeLande by blood and full of DeLande power, *but* with the added strength of the first of the LeMay line, the pregnant black slave who'd escaped into the Badlands with the wealth of her DeLande masters, the woman originated their clan.

Suddenly Momo's eyelids fluttered. Her lips pursed. "Mara, get shotgun," she whispered slowly. Her voice was parched, like the rustling of old leaves and dry bones. "Men come down bayou." She paused. "Four or three. Dey come fo' you."

Mara was moving before the words consciously registered, her hands on the worn, hickory stock of the shotgun. By the time Momo finished speaking, she had checked to see that it was fully loaded with three shells, removed the safety and shoved the 9mm into the waistband of her skirt, dropping an extra clip of ammunition into a pocket. She doused the lamp. Moving to the front door, Mara stared out over the bayou. Into night, dark and full of sound.

"Why do they want me, Momo?" she asked, never doubting her words. Momo had never been wrong. *Never*.

"DeLande blood. DeLande power. And fo' Tether. What you done to him." Her voice was growing stronger as she spoke. Behind her, Mara heard her move to the washbowl and the ancient pump handle that serviced the cabin. The handle squeaked, an archaic, mechanical sound. Water splashed.

Mara stared into the dark, straining for the sound of men and a boat. Upstream or down? Momo hadn't said. They came without a motor. Without running lights.

The scent of slow-moving water and roach spray mingled uneasily in the air. A fish jumped, landing with a splash that scattered moonlight into ripples.

In the dark behind her, Momo drank. Mara felt her relief more than heard her swallow. They were closely linked, mind-to-mind, a strange swirl of connection that let them feel certain things together, know certain things in concert. Momo had done this, created this pathway between them. Momo the witch. Few words were needed.

Mara shivered at the strangeness, feeling her skin tense and rise, the hair along her arms lift. And she knew, somehow, that this communication she had taken for granted for so long was the same thing she had feared for so many years. This bizarre communication was the DeLande gift and the DeLande shackles of slavery.

It had happened before, this close linkage. The night Rosemon's protector died, and she had tried to tear out her own throat, Momo came to Mara, mind-to-mind, and told her what to do. How to bind her mother's hands and shove a cloth in her mouth to keep her from chewing out her tongue.

The close communion had happened even before that. There was the time an alligator had overturned Mara's *bâteau*—her flat-bottomed boat—before she had the airboat. Momo had told her to swim away from the bayou bank instead of toward it. Climb the vine-covered tree growing up out of the black muddy water. Momo had promised that help was on the way. How the old woman had known that there were more hungry gators waiting in the shallow water at the bank of the bayou was one of the mysteries of Momo. She had never explained.

"It be de same when you mama come into her power. She be younger than you. Twelve. T'irteen. Same age as you sister Cady when she come into her gift. Rosemon come into it full up and strong. Reckless. Wild as swamp panther. Men smell her mind on de air, open like flower at dawn. She call out to dem with woman's heat from her little girl mind."

Momo moved in the blackness of the house. Mara strained again into the darkness, seeing nothing except the flickering lights of fireflies and the glimmer of illumination from the nearby houseboat. Shadows were darker strips of blackness on the night. Downstream, the Torres' party was in full swing, the music and high pitched laughter coating the dark night, a fog of unfamiliar sound. She waited for Momo to continue or not as she felt inclined.

It was a story Mara had heard often before, but sometimes Momo let something new slip. Some little sliver of the story never heard before. Hearing it again kept Mara calm. Certainly Momo knew that. She was a devious old witch. Outside, the night was unchanged, yet Mara knew Momo was correct about the approaching men. It wasn't open to question.

"Men come fo' you mama. For Rosemon. Three, two time. Callin' fo' her. Try to take her. I kill two men befo' Andreu come."

Mara jerked her gaze back from the bayou. This was something new. Momo had killed?

"Dey bury out back. Both dem. Andreu come. Keep others away. All but you daddy, who a fool, soft in de head. Powers of de Eldest keep Rosemon safe from dem."

Out front came a splash, soft and muffled. The even softer sound of a bâteau sliding up a muddy bank downstream and back again into the water. A silky splash of oar, the grate of wood on oarlocks. Sounds Mara would never have heard unless listening for them. Straining for them.

A strange tension began to thrum through her veins, beating with the pulse of her heart. It might have been a single note, vibrating within her chest. Strung taut and tight as a wire, plucked only once.

Momo had known. Momo always knew. Yet, until she heard the evidence with her own ears, Mara hadn't *really* believed.

"One come over water, take boat to de front," Momo whispered, her mouth close to Mara's ear. "Two roun' back, on land."

Without comment, she passed Momo the shotgun. The old woman took it in practiced hands and settled into an arm chair, a heavy piece of furniture, low to the floor and sturdy. One positioned with a perfect view of the deck-porch, and an unobstructed view of the back. A chair Momo would never have sat in but for an emergency. Momo liked change, she said, and rockers always changed, moment to moment. But she did not want her chair to change upside down with the recoil of the shotgun blast.

Supporting the shotgun on the blue painted arms of the chair—black now in the darkness—she waited.

Mara moved to the back door, silent as a cat, sliding through the kitchen, past the long table and its benches. Opened the back door. Moonlight marked the foliage out back, lush and luxuriant. Lantana and climbing rose. Gardenia, blooming with its rich scent, heady in the night. Jasmine. Bulbs of every description which were Momo's passion. Tomatoes and chilies, ripe and ready for picking, still carrying the daytime heat, adding a spicy undertone.

The mixed smells had a sound, similar to the tension feverishly growing in her. Mara could hear the soft whisper of men moving in the darkness. Long moments passed, and nothing happened. No one appeared. The sounds died.

Mara could have moved away from the house, into the shadows. Into the vegetable garden, or the long stemmed gladioli and day lilies that grew in extravagant profusion in untamed borders, their tall green stalks and thick, sharp-edged leaves circling the back of the cabin, ringing the porch, like a voluptuous bouquet on the wrist of an aging, one-time beauty. She could have hidden there, waiting for them. Taken them from behind.

Yet, she remembered Tether's scream, the feel of it. And her own near-paralysis. And then, there was Momo to consider. To protect.

Anywhere else in the nation, a woman in danger would simply have picked up the phone and dialed 911, called for help. But this was bayou country, the heart and soul of no-man's-land. Here there was no phone. No 911. No law but the law made here. The law of the strongest. Here there was no security for the unwary or the foolish. Or the slow to act. There was the maritime radio, of course, to call for family, the only help that existed in times of trouble, but by the time that kind of help could arrive, the danger would be over. Mara understood that.

She drew her 9mm. It was warm from the heat of day and the contact with her skin. It settled, a living thing, into the palm of her hand, as if it were a willing servant prepared to be used. It and the single barrel 12-gauge shotgun were the only things she had from her daddy, the nameless man who had seduced her mother and given her a girl child.

Mara had cleaned and reloaded the weapon the moment she entered the cabin. Before she cleaned the fish. Before she changed her clothes and washed the mud from her body. Before anything. As if she had known she would need it, soon. She shuddered, the bizarre vibration within her again, a febrile heat.

A shadow, darker than the ones around it, moved from the back of the shed and around the outhouse. A second one moved a moment later, from tree to tree. They were flanking the house.

She caught a feeling, a peculiar awareness from them, almost a scent, or a taste. They had orders. They were to bring her to someone. And they were to kill Momo.

A sudden acid rage drenched through Mara, a flood of fury and heat. *Kill Momo*. "No," she whispered. She lifted the 9mm, checked the safety and aimed.

Mara squeezed off a shot. It broke the night into a hundred pieces, fracturing the darkness, puncturing the silence. The shadows dropped. Disappeared. She could feel no pain from either. She had missed.

In the aftermath, she seemed to hear a steady thump, like the sound of helicopter blades, whump-whump-whump. Or the fierce beating of her heart.

"Fire you gun again, Mara," Momo said softly. Or perhaps Mara heard the sounds in her mind, scented them almost, like the chilies and the gardenia. Something was happening to her. Inside of her. Something— "Two, four, three time, fire you gun. De one in front come." Covering fire. Momo wanted a covering fire to draw their attention.

Without question, Mara fired, aiming at places where the shadows had moved, but lower. Hoping to hit one. Wanting to hit one. They meant to kill Momo. *Kill Momo!*

Mastered by an uncontrollable fury, a violent rage that boiled till her hands shook, she emptied the clip, all nine rounds, blasting into the night. Moving instinctively, her hands quick and adept, she released the magazine and inserted the new one. Eyes searching the flowers, she probed the night.

Nine shots left. Mara swallowed. Momo had said to fire up to four times. Would she need the other rounds? The ones Mara had wasted in her rage? Her fear? Momo had taught her better. Momo had taught her control.

In her mind Mara could hear Momo chuckle. It wasn't the aged chuckle from a weary, careworn throat, but a different tone. A younger timber. "Don' worry, Mara. He'p come now." Momo laughed outright. Momo was *having fun*!

And then she heard it—the steadily increasing power of the helicopter blades, cutting through the night air. Searchlights swept the ground out back, moving in a zigzag motion, a careful pattern, as if the one wielding the light knew where to place it.

Kill Momo! Kill!

The sound reverberated in her mind, a shriek of maddened hostility and intent. *Mara was a secondary target. They were here for Momo!* And Momo was laughing. *She had known.*

The stabbing light from above fell on a man, prostrate on the ground. Mara shifted her aim and fired. He howled and rolled into the shadows, his cry like a razor raked over the rawness of Mara's mind. She pulled away from his pain, trying to breathe past the agony.

The other man hesitated. She could feel him in the darkness. Found him with her next shot, hitting him in the shoulder, shattering his collarbone. *He knew who had shot him. He could see her in the glow from the helicopter.* He too pulled back.

She could feel them both, retreating into the night. There was a pickup point not far downstream, a place where they were to meet if they became separated. She could see it in her mind, a curve in the bayou, just down from where the Torres had tied off their houseboat. A dark and muddy bank touched by moonlight, overhung by cypress branches draped with moss.

Behind Mara the shotgun boomed, a cannon-like roar. And again. Momo stood like an avenging angel, the shotgun barrel blowing a twisted fog of smoke. The old woman danced in the moonlight and laughed, shouting with a feral glee. "DeLande. DeLande. De Eldest come!"

In front of her, a man crawled across the deck, his hands covered with blood, black in the moonlight that poured in through the open front door. Then bathed in the harsh light falling from the hovering craft. Leaves swirled, Momo's skirts billowed in the artificial breeze and she threw back her head, swaying, looking younger by three-fourths of a century. The thunder of the helicopter was a roar of wind and power. And over it all Momo's voice, pealing out, shouting, "DeLande! DeLande! DeLande!"

Chapter Three
Gator Bait

A gibbous moon hung suspended over the cypress trees, their gray moss a slow-moving, old man's beard. Crickets chirped a sharp chorus to the bullfrogs' hymn. The Torres' party had gone silent, the houseboat's lights extinguished, laughter stilled.

The helicopter had vanished as if it never existed. And with it the awful mental activity that had tied Mara to the attackers' minds.

Exhausted, worn beyond the simple, terrible events of the last hours, she sank slowly to the floor beside Momo's rocker. Mara was still holding the 9mm. Momo's arms still cradled the shotgun. The rocker treads made a soothing hollow cadence on the uneven floorboards. When the old woman breathed out, the sound was heavy with meaning, though Mara could read nothing from her mind. *Nothing*. The same *nothing* that was normal. That was all Mara wanted of life—to feel nothing from the people around her. *Not* to be DeLande.

Four men. She had shot and wounded four men. And felt nothing but this awful tiredness. She closed her eyes.

On the front deck, the body of Bush Guidry lay, a bleached-out, lifeless thing, pale and still. The moonlight reflected off the pool of blood spreading beneath him, shining blackly. Splats echoed softly as it trickled through the slats and hit the bayou water ten feet below. A louder splash of gator tail proved they had responded to the bloody invitation.

"Mara," Momo said. "De boat he come in. It still out dere?"

After a moment, she stood, clicked the safety on the 9mm and placed it on the table. It made a loud clatter in the quiet cabin. She pushed open the screen door and walked out on the deck, stepping over the pool of reddish-black blood. "Yes, ma'am. It's tied off below." It was indeed a small flat-bottomed affair, equipped with a motor for fishing, a cooler, rods, tangled nets, a tackle box. The boat had oar locks, with oars still in place. A faint scent of stale beer wafted up from it. Crushed cans were littered in with the fishing supplies, Bud, Miller Lite, and Schlitz in the moonlight.

"I too old, too tire', to bury him," Momo said. The rocker stopped and the old woman joined Mara on the deck, her body once again moving with the graceless shuffle of the very old. Mara tried to push away the memory of her standing in the glare of the helicopter's intense light, arms lifted high, screaming, "DeLande! DeLande! DeLande!" She had been a picture of another Momo for that instant, a Momo from a different time, a different place. The vision of her standing, somehow appearing young, slender and beautiful, hovered at the back of Mara's mind, taunting.

She wanted to ask Momo about what she thought she had seen, wanted to pursue the strangeness of it all, but she couldn't. Not tonight. Perhaps not ever. *DeLande and LeMay witchcraft . . .*

"Jus' too old, yeah. So I do next bes' thing." Momo lifted the boat hook from its supports on the side of the cabin. The boat hook was a handmade, twelve-foot-long tapered pole, a blunt iron hook on one end. With the ease of long practice, she snagged the boat's tie-off rope, untied the loose knot holding it to the deck piling, and retrieved the end of the rope. Using this and the boat hook, she maneuvered the bâteau into place below.

"Roll damn-fool Bush Guidry in he own bâteau, Mara. Maybe he float downstream to he people. Maybe gator get him. Maybe Momo don' care if they do."

Mara looked at the body and shuddered. Nausea rose in her throat.

"Use gaff, Mara. No you hand," Momo said gently. "Hurry. Gators restless, yes."

She could hear them below, bumping the boat, the pilings, splashing with long tails. Gators didn't hunt like most predators. They didn't have to. They were opportunistic killers, laying in wait for prey, pulling down the thirsty and the hasty and the careless.

And the dead.

It was odd that so many had gathered below. It smacked of Momo's power, as if the old woman had called to them and they had come. The sick feeling grew, an acid taste. She swallowed it down, hard.

"Mara—"

"Okay, Momo. Okay." She lifted down the gaff. It was made much like the boat hook, but shorter in length, and with a bigger, sharper hook. Handmade from cherry wood and cast iron, the gaff was six feet long and had a dozen uses, from removing non-poisonous snakes from one's path and lifting large fish from the bayou, to hooking interesting looking debris up from the muddy water. Mara had once even used it to skewer a twenty-two-pound water rat that had climbed the deck piling looking for a likely place to have her young. She wasn't cruel by nature, she just hated water rats. But this was the first time she had ever rolled a body with the gaff.

He didn't want to roll. Dead, Bush Guidry clung to the deck, his body heavy and unyielding, an ungainly, slippery bundle of flesh and cloth. She rolled a foot, a leg, an arm, and then put her weight to his shoulder and hip, her feet sliding in his blood. An inch at a time, Guidry approached the edge of the deck.

When the sweat was clinging to her like a thick layer of goose fat, Guidry rolled and fell. His body landed with a dull, empty sound. The boat rocked and threatened to turtle over, before it righted itself and settled in the muddy water. From below, a gator thumped the wooden bottom, jostling the craft. Using the longer boat hook, Momo reversed the boat and shoved it into the slow current of the bayou. It moved with a slight wake, bisecting the reflection of the moon on the still surface. The small vessel rocked again, its passage disturbed by the curious gators or some underwater obstacle.

Momo snagged a two-gallon bucket with the business end of the boat hook and lowered it into the bayou, raising it with strong arms that had always belied her age, and now belied her claim of exhaustion. Setting the bucket on the deck, she lifted it by hand and doused the deck, diluting the blood smeared there. Mara took the boat hook from her, bringing up three more buckets of bayou water before Momo pronounced it sufficient.

"'Nuff. I clean de shotgun, you clean de handgun. Den we both bathe. I tire'."

"Momo?"

"Yes, Mara."

She replaced the boat hook on the wall, and the gaff below it. "Why don't I feel anything? I mean, why don't I feel bad about shooting . . ." Her words trailed off. Mara wasn't quite certain what she was asking, only that something didn't seem right, something inside. She had read about people who shot other people. She read all the time, the way hungry people eat—ravenously. She had read that they always felt something afterward. Mara didn't. She felt nothing, not even an emptiness she could explain away as shock.

Momo sighed, old eyes picking her out in the moonlight. "DeLande blood, Mara," she said as if that explained it all. And went back into the house, her loose shoes shuffling on the decking.

Using the rest of the water in the bottom of the bucket, Mara rinsed off her shoes, removing the last traces of Guidry's blood, and stowed the bucket below the gaff where its rim rested against the wall of the cabin in an ancient ring of rust. She looked back downstream. The Torres' party had started back up again, though a little less boisterous than before. There was no sign of the bâteau. She followed Momo back inside.

The smell of cordite and blood hung heavy on the air in the cabin. Momo picked up the shotgun and went to the back porch where she turned on the generator, the refrigerator, the fans overhead, and the lights. They went to work.

Silently, they cleaned the weapons. The generator's roar blanked out any communication but hand signals. A point to the can of linseed oil. A chin tilted to the cloth rags. All traces of the night's work removed. Not that there would be police descending to question them about anything. Law enforcement had never been welcome in the Badlands.

The last enforcement type who'd wandered into the Badlands had been a game warden out to stop alligator poaching. He was discovered three days later, his body hanging from the top limb of a one thousand-year-old cypress tree, his feet dangling over the shallow water, which was thick with young alligators.

The warden had been shot, several times. Any one of the bullets would have killed him.

Ten years before that, a Texas Ranger had come looking for an escaped felon. He never returned to his headquarters. Nobody spoke of him much.

So, no cops would be descending on the cabin to ask questions, but Guidry's friends might drop by. The women might need help. And they'd surely need the guns.

The generator roared on through their baths, the second bath for Mara tonight, but her blood-splattered skin and clothes required it, the smell of blood and death adhered to her like another layer of flesh. They took turns standing over the drain in the corner of the cabin, the privacy curtain drawn closed. The electric pump shot cool shower water down over them and homemade soap made thick suds in the washbasin. Bath and rinse water drained out of the cabin on to Momo's garden, watering her bulbs. The chair-toilet for night and bad weather use was a perfect seat while they combed out and dried wet hair.

Toward midnight, they shut off the generator and silence was restored. Darkness returned, seeming thicker now for the earlier abundant light and noise. By lamplight, Momo poured out glasses of homemade scuppernong wine, and they sipped in the late-night hush. The moon had moved on, high overhead. The breeze had picked up, stirring through the cabin, taking with it the heat of mid-day and the cooking smells and the scent of boiled linseed oil and cordite from the fired weapons.

In her night clothes—an old T-shirt and a pair of men's boxer shorts—Mara sat beside Momo in the two-seater padded rocker. Her lids were heavy. The cloying sweetness of the wine coated her mouth. She tilted back her head and closed her eyes.

"DeLande blood," Momo said, her voice musing and soft.

Eyes still closed, Mara cast back, searching for the threads of their last conversation. Taking a sip of wine, she asked, "You mean the blood, the DeLande gift, is the reason why I feel so little after shooting four men?"

Momo grunted. "DeLande blood. It give power to hear an see inside mos' people. It give quick mind and strong body like a swan."

"Graceful," Mara supplied, her eyes opening as if they had a will of their own. The wine was potent, rushing through her veins to her head like the wind in the trees.

Momo grunted again. Mara could hear the utter weariness in her voice, in the wide spacing of her words, in the sound of her breathing which was fast and shallow, unlike her usual slow respiration and steady speech.

"DeLande blood make strange thing happen inside. Make DeLande man and DeLande woman feel some heat fo' one another. Heat stronger than other one who not DeLande."

"Other people?"

"Yes. All dis good. Dis gracefulness like a swan, dis heat, dis strong. But DeLande blood take away some great thing too. Much feel." Momo paused. "What de word, Mara? Mean to feel fo' de sick and de po' and de orphan?"

"Compassion," she whispered, understanding suddenly. "Compassion."

Momo nodded. "DeLande feel nothin' too many time. DeLande make decision, do what dey will. And dey no care if other hurt. Jus' no care. End justify mean. Dey call it 'bottom line'."

"I didn't care," Mara whispered. Tears gathered at the corners of her eyes as so many of the unfathomables of her life fell into place. "And my mama—" The words stuck in her throat and she stopped, appalled. "Rosemon didn't care when—" Mara stopped again, unable to go on, and drank down her wine. Instantly it rushed to her head, making her dizzy as she rocked. She laughed, the sound ringing and mocking, like the harsh cry of Croak when he stole something that a human wanted.

"Rosemon didn't care when she left us to be watched by Cousin Tether and went off with Andreu. And Tether would beat Devora and Lucien and Cady and me. She didn't care!"

"DeLande blood. Dey both full-blood DeLande, got much power, my Rosemon and her man. Too much heat. Nothing' else in de world when dey together. DeLande gift, DeLande curse."

Mara stood and went to the kitchen. Poured herself another glass of the hearty wine. Momo said nothing about underage drinking or Mara's sudden preference for alcohol. Recorking the bottle, she replaced it in the bottom of the cupboard and made her way back to the rocker.

"I don't want DeLande blood," she said.

Momo sighed. She had been doing that a lot tonight. It was a sound born of years of arguments, too many disagreements. Frustration. Exasperation. The old woman reached out to her, opened Mara's mind like a book and stepped inside.

Mentally, Mara shook herself. Her skin felt hot and chilled at the same time, as if she had a fever and the shakes, and her mind was suddenly an engine with the throttle stuck, operating at breakneck speed, fast and full of understanding. "Wide-ass open", as her brother Lucien would have said. It was a strange sensation, like being drunk or high or watching the way Rosemon's skin would glow and her eyes become sultry and passionate when she was close to a man.

Mara drank down part of the second glass of wine. She could hear Momo's thoughts, taste her despondency, feel her melancholy, touch the somber sadness that rode the old woman's mind tonight. The bleakness of her spirit was because of Mara. She could heal Momo's mind with a word, she knew. Cheer her. Bring her spirits back to their proper bright blue color. Mara drank another sip of wine and laughed again.

"Okay, Momo. I may not want it, but I've got it. So. How do I *not* turn into Rosemon?" Mara's laughter faded. "How do I not let the DeLande gift turn into the DeLande curse? And how do I avoid being bonded to one of them like my mama was?" She looked up at Momo, her face serious now. "I may not be able to help what I am, but I can control how I use it."

Mara was paraphrasing Momo, speaking words the old woman had often uttered when she was rendering judgment on a member of the LeMay clan. Momo was big on self-determination and personal responsibility, though she had never phrased it precisely so.

After a moment, Momo smiled. Mara couldn't see her lips move in the dark, but she could feel the flow of thoughts and view the changing colors of Momo's mind. "Jus' like any gift, Mara. You use it or it use you. You control it or it control you. It you life Mara. How you live it alway up to you. Good or bad, you life alway you own.

"You can't help what others do to you, no. But even if you slave or you in jail, you still have you freedom here." She touched her chest, tapped her head. "You sick, you still have youself. How you live you life is you decision, alway, Mara. Give Momo you glass."

Mara placed the nearly empty juice glass in Momo's outstretched palm, and stood. The floor of the cabin, warped and bowed by the years of humidity and heat, was even less level tonight for some reason. The hills were higher, the valleys lower. Funny, Mara seldom noticed the uneven floor.

She found her bed, the big feather mattress on the tall carved oak frame that had been Momo's in the twenties.

As her thighs touched the edge of the soft mattress Mara paused.

"Momo?"

"Um?"

Mara looked down at the coverlet, twisted her fingers in the crocheted weave. "The helicopter. Who was that?"

Momo shuffled across the floor behind her. A soft "whoosh" sounded and the room went completely dark as the old woman blew out the lamp. "Eldest. Come for you," she said finally.

"But I can choose?"

"I have spoke, chile. I have spoke."

Pulling the mosquito netting close around the bed, Mara settled into the sheets and pummeled the down pillow into the shape of her neck. Slumber rushed in, soft and welcoming as the mattress below.

At the edge of sleep, she heard a voice, Rosemon calling over the radio, "Who is he? Tell me. Who is he?" Rosemon, who had not moved under her own power for years. Dreams. Strange dreams.

Then Momo calling, speaking softly into the radio, "Lucien, come, you. We in danger. Bring you gun, all dem. Bring help. Come morning, before de sun think to shine."

The sound of a child, unable to sleep. *On the radio? Or in my head?* DeLande gifts. DeLande curses. Mara had fought against both all her life, denied them with all her being. She *wasn't* like her brother and sisters. They knew it. She knew it. Yet . . . there were the voices. Raised and soft, passionate and cool.

The voice of a man soothing the fevered skin of his lover. Dreams. Heated dreams.

The jangle of the Torres' party downstream, as an apparently empty boat floated past. Fear. Drunken dread.

The agony of two men huddled on the bank of a bayou, waiting for help that was dead, and floating slowly toward them. Drunken dreams. Too much wine. *Surely it was all just dreams.*

The groggy thoughts of Tether, as he woke from anesthetic. *Hatred. He hated her. Hated Rosemon.*

A strange mind drifted into view. It was cool and smooth, with the feel of polished marble, the green of veined stone. It was a beautiful mind, but flawed. Blackened at the edges and laced with fine cracks, a carved statue subjected to great heat. Fragile and sooty and touched with old pain.

Someone had tried to heal it once, and done a good job. Mara could do better. In her drunken state, she reached out and touched the stone, the mended places, still cracked beneath the roughly applied plaster. A patchwork of mortar and love. A gift.

Mara's fingers found a damaged place and pressed, palm of her mind against the broken stone. Heat roiled out from her touch, and the stone bubbled, melded and filled in the crack. Liquid stone and love on the soul of this injured one.

A hand gripped hers and held tight. "Who are you?" Beautiful voice of this one's mind. Incredible power. She had made it stronger with the healing. Her gift. Her decision.

With a strength she hadn't known she possessed, Mara pulled away. Back. Down into sleep and the softness of her feather bed and Momo's quiet snores from across the room.

Forgetfulness. Fog of drunken dreams.

Chapter Four
Mauriceville Motel—A Greeting

The lighting was nearly non-existent, a single 40-watt bulb behind a dusty shade. At least the room had an air conditioner. It rattled and resonated and had an awful squeak, but it blew out cool air in a constant breeze.

Boots on the floor, hat on the rickety table, Miles stretched out on the bed nearest the door. Wearing jeans and an old flannel shirt over his sweat-stained T-shirt, he looked the part of a young carpenter at the end of a long day. He stank of exhaust fumes and sweat, and though there was hot water in the minuscule shower, he was too tired and too wired to wash. Too tired from the late hour, the violence he had witnessed and participated in. Too wired from the contact with the strange mind he had encountered as he ate and rested.

Beside him on the bed were the remains of his meal. Traces of salmon tartar, roast duckling with raspberry sauce, mushrooms sautéed with fresh tarragon and white wine, a spinach salad, and an empty bottle of wine. With one hand Jenkins had handed him the satchel of clothes and supplies he had requested while at the dinner table. With the other hand he'd placed a wicker picnic basket just inside the door of the Cessna. His only comment had been, "Hope you have a lovely time, sir. When you are settled, I'll have a Chef's assistant and your man join you. You may be going to the ends of the earth, sir, but at least you can live well."

"The Badlands are only half a state away, Jenks, not the ends of the earth," Miles had said.

Jenkins sniffed, his eyes fixed on the distance. Even shouting at the top of his lungs, he managed to sound superior. "They do have a certain reputation. River Rats and poachers. Not exactly the Hapsburgs, sir."

Miles grinned, his hair blowing in the gusts from the engines. "I'll be fine, Jenks. I'll remember to brush my teeth and wash behind my ears and eat my green vegetables."

"And to dodge bullets, avoid stepping on poisonous snakes, and come back in one piece, I hope," Jenkins asked, his voice droll.

"Absolutely." Miles placed a hand on Jenkins' upper arm and squeezed. "I'll be careful, Jenks. And I'll bring you home a present."

Jenkins sniffed again, but Miles could see the pleasure in the butler's eyes. "Do take care, sir."

Jenkins had been with the DeLandes for thirty years, and in Miles' youth had been a footman and a shoulder to cry on. His own safe haven in the horror of the DeLande Estate, a true taste of home in the midst of the tyranny of the Grande Dame and her schemes. Why Jenkins had stayed on after he discovered the peculiar lifestyle of the DeLande family had never been discussed between the two of them, though Miles knew it wasn't the money, but rather the tender affection they had shared, like father and son. Almost. It was perhaps the only long-term, normal relationship Miles had ever known.

Jenkins had recognized that, surely. Realized he filled an empty place in a young man's aching heart. Known that he was the sole point of stability around which Miles walked, day by day. And yet, their affection had remained unspoken, and Miles knew that would never change.

His hunger satisfied, he rolled over to close the silver tins of food, and to secure the picnic basket's leather straps. In the corner was a small package, wrapped in lavender paper. It wasn't much bigger than a ring box, scarcely noticeable in the poor light, amid the open food tins, the sterling tossing back a glare that hid much.

Miles stared at the small package. It was meticulously wrapped, the tissue creased and folded just so, the tape that fastened it all together turned under so no ends showed.

No card. No note.

Not Jenkins' style.

Miles went to the other bed and lifted a lightweight Kevlar bullet-proof vest over his head and across his torso. Velcro fasteners molded it to his body. It was custom made and would stop almost anything a handgun could fire. He had worn it earlier as he watched anonymous DeLandes in the Badlands shoot at one another in the darkness. Though it wasn't designed to withstand explosives, Miles hoped it would offer some protection.

Pulling up his briefcase, he dialed in the combination. In one of the pouches in the top was a pair of latex gloves. Beside them was a set of lock picks and a box of ammunition to go with the 9 mil semiautomatic handgun packed in his luggage. There were other toys in there as well, including a cell phone and a laptop that beat anything currently available in the industry. Miles could take along anything he needed from home, including the convoluted lineage of twenty generations of DeLandes.

Donning the gloves, he returned to the lavender package and carefully lifted it out. Just as carefully, he peeled back the edges. Tissue and tape on one side. Tissue and tape on the other side. Moving slowly, Miles lifted back the paper. Beneath, was a plain white gift box made of sturdy cardboard.

Sweat broke out beneath his arms. Miles knew he should call for help, have an explosives expert flown in, let someone else take the risk. He couldn't. Innocents had been hurt in this struggle before, two in the last six months. This was his battle. His war.

Moving with all the stealth and grace bequeathed to him by his bizarre genetic history, Miles slowly, steadily, lifted off the top. There was no soft click and sudden flash of light. No hiss of toxic gas. No sound as the top came free. The box was empty.

In sudden comprehension, he flipped the lid over. The enraged spider had crawled out in the second it took him to understand. It was nestled into the palm of his gloved hand, perched on the inside of a knuckle, long jet black legs bent and poised, her bulbous middle lifted for a strike. A large red hourglass marked her torso.

Faster than the black widow, Miles flicked her away, followed her trajectory, and crushed her with a boot grabbed from beside the door. He exhaled sharply. Banged down the boot again, mangling the spider. And again, until it was only a dull gelatinous mass in the carpet fibers. Rolling over, Miles sat on the floor a moment, a hand to his head, the boot still clutched in one tightened fist, white knuckles visible through the latex glove. In a single smooth motion, he stood up and looked into the lid where the black widow had hidden. In a familiar tiny script were the words: "*A gift, my dear. Thinking of me? Love, the Grande Dame.*"

Laughter barked out, an angry sound. Miles grabbed up tissue, box and lid. Crushed them into a tight ball, knuckles grinding. The spider hadn't been a deadly trick, just a nasty one. And hardly what an average young man would expect of a gift from home.

Thinking of me? "Not if I can help it, Mother dear. Not *ever* if I can help it," he murmured.

Chapter Five

A Lesson in Math

Mara pushed back the mosquito netting, tarnished brass rings at the top clinking softly as the netting bunched. Suspended from a brass hoop over the center of the carved bed, the netting protected her from pesky bites and dangerous diseases. Malaria, once all but wiped out in the deep South, had made a comeback in recent years. Encephalitis was rife, too. West Nile. All unpleasant repercussions to a bite. The netting meant they could leave the windows open at night and the repellent in the bottle. She crawled out of bed.

It was just before dawn, the sky a purple, featureless plain, the day's heat not yet promised in the cool of predawn. Momo's voice murmured from the deck. A boat bumped gently. Other voices responded, Lucien's among them.

Quickly and silently, Mara dressed, pulling on a long, tiered skirt and loose peasant blouse. Both were faded by the sun and too many washings. They had been Rosemon's in the days of her youth, floral shades of bright pink and yellow on the turquoise background. Lively tints against Mara's brown skin.

Indian brown skin, the last gift of her father who had been full blooded Apache. Or Cheyenne. Or some other American Indian tribe. Rosemon had told her several different things over the years on the rare occasions when she would speak of him.

The elastic at the neck opening was stretched and the blouse hung off Mara's shoulders. She didn't bother with shoes.

She threw open the door and flew into Lucien's arms. He clasped her around the waist and whirled with her once, laughing, his booted feet dangerously close to the edge of the deck.

Lucien's laugh was a boisterous roar that startled Croak into flight. The crow didn't like laughter. A black feather fell at Momo's feet and she bent to pick it up, her face severe. Mara knew a crow feather was a bad omen. She didn't particularly want to hear Momo's interpretation of it. Not with her half-brother here for a visit at last.

Lucien set her down. "I heard you last night, little sister. For the first time. Your mind is like popcorn, open for a flash and then gone."

Mara frowned, her pleasure spoiled. "Momo says I can't stop it, but I don't want it." She stamped her bare foot on the decking, not caring that this conduct was left over from the hot-tempered youth she claimed to have left behind. With Lucien, she could be herself, entirely herself. "I don't want the DeLande gifts or the DeLande curse either." She stamped her foot again. "And I certainly don't want the DeLande Eldest. I just want to be me."

Lucien laughed again. He laughed at everything, green eyes sparkling like emeralds, white teeth flashing. Of all her half-brothers and -sisters, he was the most beautiful, and the one Mara loved most dearly.

"So? All children have peculiar understanding and strange powers of communication. Open minds. Even children not of DeLande blood and heritage are like us LeMays. You can't fight reality, MaraNo," he said, calling her by her childhood name. "Life gives us what she will, and it's possible she's finally opening your DeLande mind."

She stamped her foot again, this time bruising her heel. Lucien shook his head, his eyes tender. "I looked at your mind, Mara, in the moment before you slept. It is . . . wonderful," he said, his hand touching her face. "Like a warm pearl nestled between the breasts of a sensuous woman. Alive and provocative and aroused."

Mara pushed his hand away, and though she liked the way he described her mind, she wouldn't admit to it. She had been having the "DeLande argument" with her family for too long to give in now when she felt so different. She had been a DeLande by blood all her life. But being truly DeLande in mind and spirit was another matter altogether. A thing to be feared.

"To you everything is sex," she said crossly. "And my mind

would *never* nestle in the breasts of a woman."

Lucien laughed again, the sound bouncing off the water and echoing into the distance. "I was describing *your* breasts, Mara. *You* are the sensuous woman—"

"Enough," Momo said, still holding the black feather, her face thoughtful and stern. "We talk inside. Eat. I hongry. Mara, I got de eggs. Grits water boilin'. Coffee perkin'. Lucien set de table."

He threw up his hands. "Women's work! Never."

"You eat, you work. I no Rosemon, spoilin' you 'cause you got Andreu' face on you. We got talk. Come." Momo turned and shouted down off the deck. "Hello, de boat! Come. Bring you gun. Momo hongry."

Mara stepped to the edge and admired Lucien's boat. It was a royal blue beauty, sleek and fast, a brand new bass boat. She didn't ask how he had come by it. Although her brother had money of his own, he had a bad habit of appropriating the possessions of others. He did it for fun, and though he claimed he was only toying with his victims, and that no one ever got hurt, one day that would change. One day someone was going to pull a gun and shoot Lucien, turning his game deadly.

This particular item of his fancy was a nineteen foot, Ranger Bass Boat with a 150 horsepower outboard motor and a permanently mounted trolling motor. It had tall swivel seats for two at the bow and amidships, and a padded bench seat spanned the back that would easily seat two large men. James and Enoch Welch had piled their weaponry there. It was an impressive sight. James climbed the ladder and reached down for the weapons handed up to him by Enoch.

They had six shotguns, four rifles, and at least a dozen handguns, all neatly boxed or sheathed in leather carrying cases. There was enough ammunition to start a small war. Mara thought of Momo's crow feather and shuddered in the early light. Without a word of greeting to the Welch boys, she turned and re-entered the cabin, leaving them at work on the deck.

In a library in Silsbee Texas, Mara had read that the Badlands today were like the Appalachian Hills of the thirties. There was no law except in the small towns dotting the swampy area, few schools, no arts or civilization. Just clan territory, clan warfare, and survival of the meanest, strongest, and most vicious.

The Badlands was little more than a thirteen-mile-wide stretch of bayou and swamp between the Sabine and the Neches Rivers on the Louisiana/Texas border. It extended north from the Gulf of Mexico for one hundred miles and enclosed over a million acres of decimated cypress swamp, toxic dumping grounds, and River Rats, like the LeMays.

It was a clandestine society. Though only the LeMays referred to the family groups as clans, the makeup of Badlands' society was distinctly clannish, with a family leader and a closed but mobile community. Momo was the leader of the LeMay clan and had been for nearly a century. In this section of the Badlands, her word was law and her power absolute. Here, Momo was queen, and if she wanted Lucien to do women's work, he would. And smile about it.

Mara whipped egg whites to a froth and folded in the yellows, chopped onions, and multicolored peppers of differing potency, and shredded cheese for omelets. Under the noise of the generator, Momo and Lucien talked, trying to determine who was behind Tether's attack on Mara and the more virulent attack on Momo. While they talked, they worked, Momo making biscuits and Lucien setting the table as ordered. The Welch brothers were setting up their arsenal at the various windows, and rearranging furniture for easy access. Before they sat down, the brothers even went outside to clip back Momo's extravagant flower garden so no section of the yard was obscured.

They were preparing for a war.

The men moved with the quick economy of the well-trained warrior, and the special grace that bespoke DeLande heritage, graceful and smooth.

Mara kept her eye on Enoch as he worked. He was the younger of the two brothers, blue-eyed and blond, his hair hanging in a ponytail to the middle of his back. He had always been impressive to look at, but not much to talk to. He'd dropped out of school in the sixth grade and the truant officers were loath to track him down.

Unlike Mara, Enoch had elected for no at-home schooling; his brain had atrophied, but his body and face had developed spectacularly. He had muscular arms and a broad chest, slim hips, well-shaped thighs and a long, lean face. A face and body Michangelo would have coveted. As long as she didn't try to talk to him, he was a delight to have around.

The Welchs were both hired help and family. Back several generations, a LeMay had married a Welch who had been traveling through and decided to stay. The Welch branch was part of the clan, though distant. They shared a minute drop of DeLande blood, but had few of the DeLande attributes.

Like Tether, who had been paid to attack Mara, the Welchs were available to the highest bidder in the constant internecine warfare of the Badlands. But unlike Tether, they had never hired out against Momo and the LeMays. They were money-hungry but never traitors.

Several times in the first hour after Lucien arrived, while Mara was cooking and the men were working on positioning their weapons, Enoch turned suddenly and caught her staring. His neck reddened beneath his deep tan and his breathing sped up. Oddly, so did Mara's in the moment before she shifted her attention to some mundane task like folding linen napkins or handing Lucien juice glasses. Her skin was sensitive with a strange prickly feeling, an inexplicable warmth spread through her, as uncomfortable as an August noon.

The third time their eyes locked, Enoch jerked, looked at Lucien, and quickly went back to work, turning his back on Mara. Lucien tilted his head, a faint smile on his face, his brows raised in polite inquiry. But it wasn't polite. There was hidden laughter in the deep green of her brother's eyes.

Before they sat down, and before Momo turned off the generator to make talking easier, Mara pulled Lucien aside, shoving him out on the back porch beside the washer and dryer, in the nook beside the cat food dishes. He was laughing that irritating laugh, so softly she couldn't hear the sound, but could only feel it against the palm of her hand, vibrating deep in his chest. She doubled up a fist and hit him squarely in the belly; the sound ooofed out of him in audible chuckles.

"What's so damn funny?" Mara hissed, careful to speak below the sound of the generator so Momo wouldn't hear her cuss. "And what are you doing to poor Enoch? Trying to scare him off? I thought he was your friend!"

Still laughing, Lucien drew her off the back porch into the waist-high flowers. He didn't bother to watch for snakes and Mara was too mad to give the ground even a cursory glance. Though Momo had a proscription against hitting, even in fun, she hit him again. "He's family!"

Lucien pulled her close, no doubt so her jabs would pack no punch. "No, MaraNo," he whispered into her ear. "I'm not trying to frighten Enoch away. As you say, he is family, after all. I'm just trying to even the board, so to speak."

"What's that supposed to mean?" she snapped, and almost stamped her foot again, but the heel was bruised from the front deck. Lucien was her favorite, but he was also the most infuriating person she had ever known. His effect on her temper had grown over the years, and had worsened dramatically since he grew up and moved out on his own. She shook herself away from his grip, but he pulled her back close instantly, his mouth laughing and voice secretive at her ear.

"Your mind, MaraNo. And the obvious appreciation you have for his tight little bottom." Grinning, Lucien watched her face as the blood drained away only to flush up again hotly.

"What?" Mara was horrified, knowing what he meant before he explained.

"Have you ever been in a room with a person and they poison the air with their private feelings? Anger, frustration, jealousy? Love? Without saying a word, they project their feelings at every person who happens by. They can make someone smile or spoil someone's day at a glance. These are ordinary people, MaraNo, not DeLandes. DeLandes and LeMays do this too, of course, but with greater intensity, and to greater effect."

Lucien's eyes were serious now, but he kept his grip on her upper arm and around her waist as if he thought she might pull away or hit him again. "You are opening, MaraNo, at least this little bit. Opening as a woman opens to men. You call to them to make them desire you and they have little strength to resist.

"Enoch is not a very bright man, and unless you want him in your bed tonight, you must let me interfere or else find a way to control your desire for him."

All the resistance went out of her in a rush, and embarrassment flooded in to take its place. Mara leaned into Lucien, hiding her face in his shoulder. "He . . . He knew, didn't he?"

"Every LeMay for miles around knows, Mara. You are a LeMay, and even if you are not yet as strong as Momo has predicted you cast desire far and wide, as all women do." Lucien pushed her away from the protection of his shoulder and looked into her face. Though he was only twenty-two, he had fine, delicate wrinkles at the outer edges of his eyes from constant laughter and his life in the sun.

"I don't know what you will be, MaraNo. Perhaps even Momo doesn't know. But you are particularly powerful as a projector of your feelings, sister-of-mine. Perhaps even as strong as I, and I am a child of the Eldest." He shrugged, an expressive gesture like old Banoit, Delice's husband and Rosemon's step-father. "The gift sometimes works that way. Something to do with genetics and recessive traits. You could ask Uncle Tomas when he comes next summer. He has been studying our bloodline at that school of his. Says the gift can skip a generation or even die out. Or, as Momo claims of you, appear with great strength in a half-breed."

She searched his face. It was truthful, as pure and guileless as the seamless expanse of his mind. Mara nearly fell when she realized he was giving her access to his mind, but he steadied her, standing there in the sharp, long leaves of lilies and gladioli. Inside Lucien was a strong mind, an opaque place, like jade, full of light. And then the glimpse of his soul was gone, closed to her.

He smiled at her confusion. "Like a newborn babe instinctively turns its head from a too-bright light, you will discover the reflexes that protect your privacy from the peering eyes of other LeMays. And even the DeLandes in New Orleans, should you meet up with one someday." Lucien's eyes twinkled at his whimsey, and he sounded like Momo in that moment. Very French, very eloquent, full of DeLande lore. A teacher, though she had never perceived that talent in him before. "Think of turning away, or closing your eyes, and you will discover the ability, buried deep inside you. A part of your own gift."

Mara looked away. It was still a gift she didn't want. Lucien smiled and touched her cheek.

"Mara, if it makes you feel better, I never detected a gift of any kind in you until last night, and I have never heard of a strong mind opening this late in life, no matter what Momo says. As for Enoch, think of something else, MaraNo. Practice your multiplication tables or something. He'll feel nothing of your interest in him."

"I hate math."

"Exactly," Lucien said, returning to his characteristic laughter.

Mara punched him in the arm and pushed through the lilies, leaving him in the flowers. The heady scent of Momo's roses blended with the blooms of bulbs and surrounded Lucien there in the yard, the sweet, spicy scent a counterpoint to his joyous, sunny spirit. Even facing a battle, he seemed contented.

Mara re-entered the cabin and went in to breakfast which was ready for serving. She had work to do and math problems to focus on. Ignoring Enoch, she concentrated on the ordinary tasks of Momo's household.

Chapter Six
Searching

Miles woke with a start, his heart dancing a syncopated beat. *She was gone*. The dream faded—if it had been a dream—easing away like an old memory.

The room was dark, but through the crack in the drapes the sun was a red ball perched on a pink cloud. The scent of old cigarettes drifted from his rented pillow, leftover smells of garlic and fish floated up from the picnic basket. The odors mingled with the moldy smell of the bathroom.

With the supple strength of youth, Miles rolled from the bed and stretched up to the ceiling panels over his head. Grunting, he flexed stomach muscles and biceps, deltoids and quads, leaning first one direction then the other, tensing and releasing. He was still in his travel clothes; the stink of old sweat and night terrors clung to him. It was a thoroughly vile morning. Forcing himself alert, he headed to the shower.

Half an hour later he was in the rented helicopter, strapped in, watching the pilot power up. Flying was one of the things Miles did well, one of his personal loves, like classic cars and racehorses and short haired, mongrel dogs. But today, on this search for possible renegade DeLandes, he needed all his concentration focused on the ground below. He didn't have time for gauges, dials, wind conditions and the feel of the craft. He needed all his faculties free. Or he needed Andreu here, back from the grave, to explain who these DeLandes were, how they got here, and why there was no official record of them in the genealogies back home.

With a jerk, the helicopter lifted off. It was a Bell Jet Ranger, small and sleek with a relatively sharp nose, a little larger than the average traffic helicopter, or helo, as aviators called them, the make often seen on TV and in movies when cops search for criminals from the air.

Miles put on his head-set, part of the communication gear which doubled as ear protectors, and positioned his lip-mic so he could communicate with the pilot, J.T. "Fly to this GPD coordinates," he said, pointing to a series of numbers. "This will take us back to the same locale as last night's gunfire." He held up a map so J.T. could see the numbers scribbled in the margin. "Give me a search pattern at one thousand feet. Refuel when necessary, then take us back up. At a later point, we may do a tighter pattern at seven-fifty or five hundred feet."

A search grid was a flight pattern 1000 meters on a side, which would allow general coverage of ten square miles in just over two hours. Miles wanted to chart this area of the bayou looking for DeLandes and finish up toward noon.

J.T. nodded. "Will do." His eyes never met Miles' as the engine sound changed pitch and the helicopter gained altitude. Perhaps it was only a typical, laconic, West Texas response, but Miles was accustomed to a more gracious New Orleans rejoinder. One with a "sir" attached. He grinned at himself and shook his head. If Jenks could see him, he would ask if Miles' clothing was comfortable, a polite way implying he was getting too big for his britches. Being Eldest tended to make a man pompous.

Like the Bell Jet Ranger, the pilot was hired. Since the gunfire last night, Miles was paying hazard pay, and still J.T. wasn't exactly congenial. However, the DeLande helo had been delayed on its way from the estate, and patience wasn't a DeLande strong point. He wouldn't wait. Miles was willing to put up with an unfamiliar pilot's cussedness to begin this search immediately.

"You want to find the people shootin' at each other last night, you might be huntin' more 'n' one day, Mr. DeLande," J.T. said over his mic, his voice a scratchy drawl. "Them River Rats scatter like a pack of dogs when there's trouble."

Miles exhaled hard, the irritation lost over the poor quality radio. "Let's just give it a try, okay?"

J.T shrugged, and the bird surged forward, toward the Badlands.

"You got a death wish, I could name easier ways a dying. 'Course, none so private. You want to die in solitude and never let your kinfolk know you're gone, the Badlands is the place to do it, I reckon. Just do me a favor, mister. Don't try and take me with you."

It was the single longest speech Miles had heard J.T. utter. In honor of it, he said, "I'll try to do my dying alone, and many years in the future. These coordinates, please."

J.T. nodded and powered the small helicopter eastwards.

Chapter Seven
Old Wounds

The generator was silenced and the meal dished up on Momo's fine china plates as the five of them settled at the long table. Momo, Lucien and Mara used the good sterling silverware, James and Enoch each used stainless-steel forks, shoveling in omelets, grits and biscuit which they had stirred into a mash. The brothers were silent as Momo talked.

"Don' know who behind Tether and Bush Guidry. They no tell me. They no know, maybe."

"They have to know who paid them to attack you, Momo. There are no secrets, not from you. And although Tether's talent has always been wild, he's never been an easy man to fool." Lucien sipped strong black coffee from a Limoges cup, took a small bite of buttered biscuit.

"He not hisself. I can no get in he mind"

"Still under the influence of anesthetics?"

"Dat so, yeah. No see him clear. Mara, mo' grit, please," Momo said, passing her plate.

Mara spooned up the white, ground hominy and added a dollop of homemade butter before passing the plate back. She didn't want to involve herself in this DeLande-style discussion, with its talk of reading minds and gypsy talents, but these were her people, in danger because of her. "So who is it likely to be?" she asked, trying not to sound sulky. "Who might want Momo dead?"

"Ol' man Thibodeaux, yes. Or de young Jaffe, take over fo' Louis when he pass on dis year pass."

"Paulito," James said, around a mouth full of egg and grits.

"Paulito Jaffe."

"De same. He alway hate LeMay family. An' Momo de mos'. Paulito want Rosemon fo' hisself when she ready fo'a man. He brother want her more. Miko he brother name."

Momo sipped her coffee and poured in a generous helping of cream before speaking again. "Miko come fo' Rosemon, him and he frien', one night before Andreu come. Dey not come home to Jaffe place nex' day."

Lucien lifted a brow, laughter bubbling beneath his bland expression. The Welch brothers glanced at one another. Even Mara paused, her fork hanging in mid-air, waiting for Momo to continue. The old woman sipped again, this time adding a thimbleful of sugar to her coffee with a silver spoon. Carefully she stirred and tasted. Lucien's amusement emerged in a grin at what might be Momo's tactic to control the conversation, or might simply be age catching up with her. Either way it would be rude to notice. Hastily, he drank down his coffee.

"Dat why Paulito want revenge, maybe. Miko no come home."

Enoch glanced at Mara, then strode to a window where a .38 and a .45 stood ready with two boxes of ammunition. She could almost hear his thoughts, even without the DeLande talent she was supposed to share. The Jaffes were a big clan, quick and mean as snakes. If Paulito declared war, the LeMays would need more help.

Without being asked, Mara poured Enoch more coffee and Warmed Lucien's. The sudden tension at the table was heavy, like the prickly threat of heat at mid-morning or the warning rumble of far-off thunder.

Mara wondered if Miko was a new story, or one of the men Momo had buried out back. At a warning glance from Momo, she quickly did a five-times-nine and a six-times-seven to blank her mind. It worked, but Mara hated it. She hated being DeLande in the smallest detail. Hated being in the presence of people who suddenly left her no privacy, no secrets, no personal refuge. She just wanted to be . . . whatever she would have been had she not been DeLande and LeMay on one side.

Enoch looked up, his blond brows coming together in confusion. Mara realized she was projecting again, and having trouble controlling it. She gulped a mouthful of coffee, burning her mouth and choking.

Lucien laughed at her. "You swear well in your mind, Mara," he said. "But math is easier than pain for control."

She ignored him, drinking down the cool cream meant for the coffee. It coated her mouth, easing the burn.

"Ol' man Thibodeaux down with de cancer."

James swallowed a huge bite of biscuit. "Way I hear it is, DeMarcy is taking over. DeMarcy got a reason to want you dead, Momo?"

"Gold," she said. "DeMarcy think I got gold in here. Think it since he little boy and I buy shrimp boat fo' Banoit. DeMarcy not too bright," she added blandly.

Carefully and dutifully Mara did an entire row of sevens up to twelve and did not look at the cobalt blue china cabinet where the family fortune resided: a modest stack of gold ingots and bearer bonds and cash, the latter two protected in freezer bags with little silica gel packets inside to draw out the moisture.

Momo met her eyes, dentures shining, the wrinkled face innocent and approving. Mara moved on to the eights and drank more hot coffee.

"DeMarcy and Paulito, then," Lucien said. "Any chance they might join forces?"

"Might, yes. But no matter. DeLande come. He a powerful Eldest. We safe."

"Who's he coming for? Mara? Or is he not of Andreu's line? Cady's ready for a man. She's been talking about it for the last year."

"I will be no man's brood mare," Mara said instantly, her voice hard and intense. "LeMays may have been bred for the DeLandes in the last century, but I have no intention of living by some outmoded and archaic standard of, of, of . . ." she stuttered, refusing to look at Lucien; she knew he'd be laughing, ". . . of bondage."

Even with Lucien, this was an old argument. Years old. Momo and she had been having it since before Mara came to live in the cabin, years before Andreu died and Rosemon started acting so strange. A family argument, debated with the same phrases and the same tone, and for the same reasons. Mara would not be like her mother. *She would not.* "Besides, Momo said I could choose for myself," she finished.

Momo confirmed the statement, but when she spoke, her words disagreed on a different level. "Mara, I say dat thing de same," Momo said, her voice a raspy, tired wheeze, "till I see my man fo' de firs' time. Then my eye light up like a torch in de night and I do what my heart say, no my head. You be de same, Mara. You be de same."

Without a word, Mara rose from the table and went to the back door, her jaw clenched against the words she wanted to say. She didn't have to do math problems to shield her mind now. Anger was sufficient. Gripping the doorjamb, she stared out over the vegetables, yesterday's roses, and the remaining day lilies. The lilies and morning glory were lifting their trumpet blooms as the sun rose higher in the sky.

". . . *like a torch in the night* . . ." The words had haunted her for years, through childhood rebellion and gawky adolescence, through teenaged crushes and the interest of older men outside the LeMay clan. And though she claimed, still, that she would give her body to no man as his plaything, his sensual slave, the words hung there in her memory, a warning or a promise, the sound of their syllables intense and seductive and full of threat. *Like a torch in the night.*

Her thoughts flicked to Enoch and away. *Like a torch in the night.* Mara didn't burn for a man, never had. Rosemon had burned for a man since she was thirteen, most any man, anywhere, anytime, but especially for Andreu, her protector. Her DeLande.

And look where it got her. Tied to a bed with Cady, Mara's younger half sister, watching over her, her mind lost and wandering.

Mara didn't want a DeLande. She *didn't.*

But part of her wondered what it might mean to burn like a torch in the night. Wondered what it might be like to be so tightly bound to a man, mind-to-mind, that she would never stray. Except at his command.

A tomcat, battle scarred and imperious, prowled across the far edge of the yard, his shadow blending into the leaves of an overhanging willow. Andreu had been like that, proud and vain and completely fulfilled in his own power as Eldest. A purebred tomcat, half-wild, king of his domain.

There was a way out of all this. The airboat was fully gassed and stocked with provisions, water for several days, hand-held maritime radio for emergencies, sleeping bag, matches, ammunition, fishing supplies, clothes, tent. Money hidden in the side pockets of the hull.

Mara's own weapons were not included in the arsenal James and Enoch had positioned about the house. She could simply take the guns and run.

She did a set of nines up to thirteen and started in on the fours. Mara didn't know if her thoughts could be discerned, hidden among the anger and the numbers, but she wasn't taking any chances. These thoughts were sacrilege. *She could leave the Badlands*.

In the distance, the soft thump of helicopter blades reverberated against the dawn. If Momo was correct, it was an Eldest. The Eldest Mara had been bred for, providing that one of Andreu's sons had secured that position of power.

She could refuse him.

Or she could run.

Her fingernails sank into the soft wood of the jamb. Rot had set in beneath the layers of paint. If she ran, *who would take care of Momo*?

The memory of the mind Mara had encountered last night on the verge of sleep hovered, teasing. Cracked green stone, smooth and cool to the touch. Had it been a dream? Had it been the mind of an Eldest?

The sound of the helicopter faded. The silence that was never true silence descended on the bayou. Slap of gator tail on dark water. Gator roar. Chirp of bird and buzz of insect. Hiss of snake. Another of Momo's cats, this one a female heavy with young, climbed the porch steps and growled at Mara, demanding entrance. The cat was about to deliver, her thick tail waving in agitation, regal and begging. A strange blending. A womanly composite. Mara opened the door. The cat ran quickly to Momo and jumped into her lap. Mara didn't have to turn to know this. All Momo's cats delivered their young in her lap. It was unnatural and aberrant behavior, yet the cats always came to her. Mara had even seen wild cats come to her for a difficult delivery, as if they knew they would find help from the old woman.

The male cat lurked in the far shadows, another female at his side. Typical man.

"So where were you last night when uninvited guests came calling?" Mara asked them softly. "Cowering in some corner?" The female yawned and stretched, her limbs moving in sensuous deliberation, a delicious, hedonistic pull of muscle and sinew. It was the way Rosemon had once moved, as if the motion of her body was her greatest pleasure.

Rosemon, called so by all her children. Rosemon, not Mama. By Rosemon's command.

Conversation picked up behind Mara, voices muted. The click of metal-on-metal as someone checked a weapon. Without looking back, she bent to lift a basket and walked into the sunlight. It was already 85 degrees in the early light, and the chili peppers had only just begun to smell hot and potent. Pulling a round dozen, she added two cucumbers, two bell peppers, and five tomatoes with tight red skins. They should have been picked yesterday. Mara picked two kinds of lettuce and snap beans and early squash before kneeling to pull weeds.

There were insects to kill, clothes to wash and fold and iron, and the mousetraps to reset with peanut butter. If Mara didn't accept the Eldest, and if she didn't run, this would be her life forever. Cleaning and cooking and menial labor, unchanged and unremarkable. Dull. She lifted an overripe tomato and tested its skin. Pulled it from the vine.

The world had heated to a slow steam by the time she went back inside, the day's smells expanding and mingling in the pressure cooker that was bayou country. Dead fish and stagnant swamp water. Lilies everywhere, growing in Momo's garden and up out of the slow moving water, blooms full of perfume. The house was dark when she entered and Mara paused just inside the door, the basket beneath her left arm. Listening, she waited as her eyes adjusted to the inner gloom.

Around the table sat the men, Old Banoit's homemade beer in

mugs before them. The beer was warm, served in room temperature mugs, brewed with Badland's heat in mind. As her eyes adjusted, Mara picked out Momo sitting in one of her rockers, a basket of mending on her lap. One of Mara's many-tiered skirts was in her hands, her nimble fingers repairing a ripped seam.

"Mara?" Lucien asked.

She crossed the room to the sink and looked at him over her shoulder. He was a pale glow in the shadows, his golden hair shining in the gloom.

"We've been talking, and I want your opinion." His voice was tense and strained, perhaps even a bit ashamed.

Mara dumped the vegetables into the sink, protecting them from bruising with the palm of her hand. She didn't answer, and Lucien continued.

"Since a cousin is involved, and since whomever is trying to kill Momo has money, what do you think about a LeMay having hired Tether?"

A LeMay. One of our clan. The name that had hovered on the fringes of her thoughts came to her as she stood there in the indoor gloom. A dark, malignant name. A name out of her own past. Mara pushed the empty basket away. "Kenno," she said softly. Quickly, to cover the sound of the syllables, she pumped water into the washbasin, the mechanical noise loud in the awful silence.

"Kenno," Momo said, under cover of the splashing water. "Kenno, back from de dead."

Chapter Eight

New Plans

"We're getting low on fuel, Mr. DeLande. We have enough to get back to Mauriceville, but you might want to wrap it up soon."

Miles nodded absently, not looking up from the graph with its grid coordinates in his hands. He made a notation and added a question mark in one segment and scratched his head, sweaty beneath the headset. The grid pattern covered a little over ten square miles of swamp, water, and land, charting a section of the known course of Elephant Bayou and the swelling of the waterway that was called Elephant Lake.

The lake started small as Elephant Bayou trailed down from the Anglina National Forest. A tapered, ropy bayou, deeper than most, it emptied into the lake which was roughly body-shaped—large midsection with four stumpy limbs all on one side, and a head that could be considered to have massive ears. Elephant Bayou drained on toward the Gulf of Mexico in an undulating route, vaguely trunk-like. The shape of the lake was discernible only from the air and Miles found it interesting that the name had been chosen prior to the time of flight.

Even more interesting was the number of DeLande type minds he had encountered in the morning hours. At the thought, he added another mark to his graph. They were scattered over the landscape along the muddy banks of the bayou, these clear, crystalline minds. They were powerful in the way only his family's minds could be. DeLande minds. Cross-linked, conjoined, the shared consciousness of genetic bonds.

The DeLandes had been carefully bred for generations. Under

the control of a Grand Dame or an Eldest, the bloodlines had been twisted back upon themselves countless times through deliberate inbreeding, all for the purpose of creating DeLande mental traits and controlling the family fortune. The fortune was in his hands now, since the deaths of his elder brothers. The mental traits were his to blend as well since the mind of the current Grande Dame had begun to decay.

The traits of a typical DeLande mind were varied and complex. Most common was the ability to "see" another mind, especially a DeLande mind, communicating mind-to-mind, reading intent and purpose. Less common was the ability to read the thoughts of non-Delandes. Some few could determine the state of a pregnancy—the health of the mother, the sex and health of the fetus just days after conception. There were DeLandes who could read weather patterns and DeLandes who could start fires with a glance. And the rare DeLande who could see into the past or the future, though there had not been a DeLande seer for a century or more.

Miles himself had the rarest trait. He was a null, meaning he could not be scanned or read, or even detected by another DeLande unless he wished it.

The DeLande bloodlines and traits were jealously guarded and hoarded, chronicled in the genealogical histories now stored in the DeLande Estate Library under lock and key. Nowhere was there a mention of such large numbers of renegade DeLandes. Nowhere except in the whispered rumors of aged aunts and uncles, and in the legend of the Eldest's private files—the Legacy.

Miles was Eldest by default, not by design. He had not been schooled to be the next Eldest by his brother Andreu. He had not been the next in line. He was simply the only one left alive after a series of accidents involving his brothers and their heirs. Accidents not of his making, though perhaps he could have prevented some of them.

Miles smoothed the paper in his hands. DeLande legends. Renegade minds as powerful and capable as the strongest DeLande but living and breeding free. *And he had found them.*

They called themselves the LeMay clan or the LeMay family. There were almost a hundred weak minds, similar to DeLande stock, but not of a direct line. Some were so weak they were only intuitive or mildly prescient. If they were DeLandes, they were bred out, the connection to the family generations old. Like blood mixed with water they were thin, useless, and without power.

There were however, twenty-four clear, distinct minds of the first order, strong and powerful DeLande type minds. Most were perched on a bluff, a place of high ground, overlooking Elephant Lake near the animal's tail. Most of the minds he encountered there were young, though several were older and growing clouded.

One mind he inspected was injured, dormant. When he tried to scan it, it had suddenly come alive, reaching for him. Grasping, desperate tendrils of need, weakened and wounded, had wrapped themselves around him and tried to pull him inside, tried to meld with him. Tried to follow him away. Very few minds had ever detected him. It was disturbing that this injured mind had seen him so clearly.

Several other long-lost family members had seemed to perceive him as well, growing warm and alert before he could pull away. And then there was that strange presence he had felt several times in the last hours. He was certain he had been followed all morning from a distance, a mind taking peeks at him from time to time, curious and excited, yet un-revealed. A powerful mind, cloaked and mysterious. Stronger than he. And still Miles didn't know who these people were, nor how they came to be in Badlands territory.

"We have one more section of the lake to check." Miles held up the graph. "Here. Near this stand of cypress we passed over earlier. I think you can put me down there and head home."

"Like hell," J.T. drawled. "I ain't puttin' one of my passengers down anyplace. And sure's hell not down in Elephant Bayou. What goes in down there, don't come out. Not in one piece."

Miles replaced the graph in the clipboard on his lap. "That's pretty much what you've said about *every* place we've flown over all morning."

J.T. took his eyes off the landscape. "That's 'cause it's pretty much true, mister," he said, accenting the last word as if he was speaking to a fool with more money than brains. "And I don't intend to put my bird down where River Rats can get their grubby little hands on it. Got it?"

Miles smiled slightly. "In that case, consider your hire over. I have a dinner engagement at the cabin at these coordinates in a little over an hour. I'll need you to radio ahead to the airfield and inform my transportation that we are inbound. November 11962 is to be ready for immediate takeoff.

"And they are to have twenty pounds of ice and three cases of beer, domestic brands, and two bottles of my favorite red wine on hand. A nice selection of pâté and cold boiled shrimp would be appreciated, if they can find it in Mauriceville," he added, his voice affable, even courteous.

J.T. looked up from his instrument panel, brows raised in a "you got to be kidding" expression. But he keyed the ICS—the internal communication system—to external frequencies, using the VHF radio, and passed the message along to the tower in Mauriceville. The helicopter banked ten degrees, held a moment, and rolled out, heading back to the airfield even as he spoke. Miles settled back in his seat.

Timing would be tight, but they could make it. And it would be more appropriate to arrive at the cabin bearing gifts. He was fully aware of his social position with these distant cousins, however they came to be. And he was even more aware of the quiet presence hovering in the back of his mind, watching and waiting. He wasn't certain, but it was possible the watcher would be at the cabin to greet him.

Closing his eyes, Miles listened to the radio chatter, the sound of the chopper, and his own dark thoughts. There was no record of Badlands kin in the DeLande family tree. he was certain that the Grand Dame was unaware that these wild-kin even existed. In her current mental state, she was unable to screen her mind from him at all. She no longer had great secrets, only small ones like the black widow spider, an occasional use of poison, and gossip that was stronger than arsenic. She hadn't known about this group of family, he was certain.

That left the Eldest's records—the Legacy—the legendary journals, memoirs, and prophecies of the male leaders of the family. They were supposed to be passed down from one Eldest to the next as a way of maintaining power. But Andreu had died unexpectedly, as had Richard, and McCallum.

Until today, Miles had no idea that the records were a reality, and he had no idea what his not having them might actually mean to his power base. With the discovery of renegade DeLandes—family unknown to him—Miles had to rethink family lore and myth.

Old rumors and ancient family legend claimed the Legacy was part history, part future, both diary and oracle. With it, DeLande Eldests had steered the path of the family's fortunes for centuries. With it, Eldests had preserved political and financial dominance in a world characterized by illusion and corruption.

Depending upon which uncle one asked, the Legacy was either a gift from heaven or a vengeance from hell. It gave advice to one willing to be led. It offered a path to riches for the Eldest who interpreted it correctly. Or it led to certain damnation. Some claimed it told each Eldest whom to kill.

Becoming Eldest was easy. Remaining Eldest was the hard part. Over the centuries, only half a dozen Eldests had lived a full life span. Of those who did, almost all were despots and tyrants, ruling by might and force and a cruelty only another DeLande could truly comprehend. Being Eldest was a dangerous position. Exiting the position was almost always via death.

In the distance, a black crow rose into the air, its beak parted in a silent, raucous cry. It dived toward the helicopter as if in warning, its eye red and full of malice. Miles watched the bird's extraordinary antics until the Bell Jet Ranger outdistanced it, heading back to his base.

Chapter Nine
Memories

Momo completed her handiwork on Mara's skirt, flattening the mended seam, stretching the cloth between her bony fingers. She was in a half *listening* state, her experienced hands busy with a life and purpose of their own, while her eyes were dreamy, half closed, unfocused.

Momo was *listening* with a purpose, searching out Paulito and DeMarcy, touching all the minds she could to find an intention or design that included her own death and harm to the LeMay clan. She was also searching out the mind in the helicopter from last night, the mind that had shed light on the attackers on the ground. Literally. She was convinced an Eldest was in the helicopter, and that he was about to pay a social call on the LeMays and stay for dinner. And try to claim Mara, according to the old custom. Yet, she wouldn't discuss this Eldest with any of them. She ignored Lucien's questions as she had Mara's, and turned her mind inward and away.

While she listened, she searched for Kenno.

The first time Mara saw Kenno, she came upon him in the woods, her feet silent in the wet, marshy ground. Concealed by giant pines, she watched him, his back to her, his hair in wet tangles down his spine, flames from a campfire dancing before him. Dry deadwood crackled and spat. He had skewered a cat and hung it over the flames. She would never forget the agonized screams of the animal as it burned.

Mara remembered him as a big man, six-foot-four in his bare

feet, heavily muscled and fair-skinned with blazing blue eyes and a mane of reddish blond hair worn long to his shoulders. Twin lions were tattooed on his upper arms, sinking their claws into his flesh, mouths open in silent roars. He was handsome and virile and powerful. And thoroughly predatory. A man without remorse or conscience or morals of any kind, a man bound by the DeLande curse of violence and sexuality. When Mara was twelve and still living with Rosemon at Red Bluff with her siblings, he attacked her mama.

Mara had been swinging in a hammock, a biography of Truman open on her undeveloped chest. A Co'Cola perspired on the low, plastic table beside her, her daddy's 9mm lay resting on its side, cooling from a recent target practice. It was a torpid day with nothing happening anywhere. Even the fishermen who occasionally cruised by the bluff had stayed home. Mara was bored to tears.

Rosemon was stretched out on the dock taking the sun, her body oiled and sleek and brown as Mara's own. She was naked. Rosemon always took the sun that way, her clothes in an untidy heap on the dock, her lush body draped across a lounge, face turned to the sky. Oblivious to the effect she had on passing boatmen, unexpected guests or even her own children, Rosemon browned in the sun. That was Mama. Primal, earthy, totally willful.

And so beautiful, she took one's breath away.

On top of her piled clothes was Rosemon's .38, ready as always for protection or warning. The weapon was old, one she had claimed as a teenager and kept always by her side. She had used it twice that Mara recalled, once to scare off raiding nutria or water moccasin or some such pest, and once to rescue Devora from a gator. She was familiar with her handgun and was a fair shot, but didn't handle the weapon daily. The gun wasn't an extension of her arm or her will. Not in the way Mara would later learn to make of her own weapons.

Mara must have dozed in the heat, because the airboat was rounding the curve of the bayou before she realized it was there, the noise of the exposed automobile engine was a stunning roar. She had never seen an airboat before. It was a sled-bottomed contraption with an incongruous-looking cage mounted on back containing a huge propeller that powered the bizarre vehicle.

President Truman landed in a heap of bent pages on the ground.

The airboat was black and brushed aluminum, the shallow-draft hull skimming the surface of the bayou like a seagull searching for prey. Without slowing, the airboat changed course toward the dock, thundered up the bank, and beached itself as the engine died.

Kenno sat on the solitary seat, his upper body bare, his eyes locked on Rosemon. There had never been a silence like the one that followed. They stared at one another, Kenno's eyes were molten glass, his big body tight with an emotion Mara didn't understand, but instinctively feared.

He came off the airboat, moving with the ease of the lions on his arms, a hunter in the wild. With a single bound, he gained the dock, boots thundering hollowly. Rosemon reached for the gun. Leveled it at his eyes.

Mara never saw him move. With a single strike that blurred reality, Kenno attacked. Knocked the .38 away from Rosemon. Backhanded her across the face with a blow Mara could almost feel.

Somewhere far off, Lucien screamed, a bellow of rage and pain. He was coming, but he was on the other side of Elephant Lake, in the swamp that was one of its legs.

Kenno fell across Rosemon, his knee between her thighs.

Mara reached to the table where the Co'Cola was warming in a puddle of condensation. As if watching someone else, she saw her hand close around the grip of her gun. Thumb off the safety. And suddenly Mara was standing over Kenno, the barrel of the gun hovering over his body.

Rosemon made a little mewling sound. Blood trickled from her split lip. Her cheek was abraded and raw. Her eyes bewildered.

Kenno's hand was on her breast.

Mara pressed the barrel to the base of his spine.

"There's a round in the chamber," she whispered, the sound like a faraway jet engine in her head, the words a dull clamor that meant nothing. "If you move, I'll cripple you for life."

Kenno stilled.

"I'd rather shoot you in the head and be done with it, but you might shift at the last second and I could hit Rosemon. So I'll settle for crippling you. If you understand, you can nod."

Kenno nodded, the motion jerky.

"Good. Now take your hand off my mama. Slowly. And put it on the dock." Her voice sounded so strange. A hoarse rasp of sound, a peculiar, almost defiant tone, unlike Mara's usual brooding and quiet self.

Kenno did exactly as he was told, his body quivering under the strain of supporting himself over Rosemon's body. Mara could see his throat move as he swallowed. See the sweat trickle down his neck and drip off the end of his nose and chin to splatter on Rosemon's breast where his hand had rested.

Lucien's bâteau spluttered around the edge of the bluff, the engine a puny sound after the power of Kenno's airboat. He was still a long way off. Minutes away.

"Mama, *call* Andreu," Mara said. "Now."

Rosemon's eyes locked on hers, a shocked expression, panic swimming in their depths. Her refusal was plain. She had never *called* Andreu, reaching out to him in the way of LeMays and DeLandes, the dark and incomprehensible way of mind-to-mind communication. It was her place to await his summoning, not *call* out to him.

"Do it, Mama. He said you could *call* him only in an emergency. This is an emergency. *Call* him, Mama, and then *call* Momo. We'll need her." Mara pressed the barrel deeper into Kenno's spine. The grip of the 9mm was sweaty. "Kenno broke the rules. Momo will have to judge."

Kenno's back spasmed with her last words.

Closing her eyes, Rosemon obeyed, her fear unleashed, her mind crying out. Even Mara felt it then, a little, and her mind was locked up tight, her power only a possibility. Lucien felt it. Kenno felt it, she knew by the way his body tensed. All with DeLande blood felt it for miles around. Andreu in New Orleans on a business trip, heard her cry, and without the slightest hesitation, walked out of a meeting and headed west.

Mara held Kenno in place until Lucien and her cousin Emory both arrived, weapons drawn, faces fierce. Only then did she step back.

When Kenno rose from Rosemon's body, his hands locked behind his neck, he turned his head and looked at Mara. Fierce eyes burned her through the tangled tendrils of his hair. Blue eyes, wet with hatred, expressed surprise at her size and unquestioned youth. Mara stepped back, fearful and trembling. His eyes marked her, scoring her soul with malevolence. Mara understood that Kenno could kill her without a second thought. Intended to kill her. Soon. His teeth flashed in a smile as he read her terror.

Kenno had been dealt with according to Momo's strictest judgment. The sentence was harsh. He was beaten until he could no longer stand, then was branded on the left cheek with a symbol of Momo's power—the triangular shape of a black crow's feather. Even after all these years, Mara could smell the stench of burned flesh and hear Kenno's cry of rage and pain.

Stripped of his possessions, he was banished from the Badlands, a sentence like unto death for a LeMay. LeMays, like the DeLandes in Vacherie, had always remained close, needing the touch of similar minds, needing the security of family bonds and family contact with a desperation that approached addiction. In the space of that afternoon, Kenno had lost his home and his security.

He had committed the unpardonable. He had attacked Rosemon with the intent of rape. He had used violence against a LeMay, a woman bonded to a DeLande Eldest. Rosemon, his own half-sister.

This was the DeLande curse, the need for violence against kin. The need to dominate those of common blood. Perhaps it came from being open and vulnerable to all other DeLandes, exposed and stripped raw, without secrets, powerless, violated moment-by-moment, yet, so addicted to the close communion that there was no freedom from it anywhere. Perhaps that is what created the DeLande curse—that need to both strike out and to control.

Delice, Kenno's and Rosemon's mother, had been the woman of an Eldest, the consort of Louis DeLande, until he tired of her, or so it was said. Rosemon was the child of that bonding. Kenno was the child of another man, the child of rape, or so it was said, or perhaps the child of Old Banoit. Mara wasn't certain of his paternity.

Kenno, a half-breed like Mara, had fallen prey to the DeLande curse. He had used violence against kin and been banished for it. Mara had never thought Kenno would return to the Badlands. The sentence had been for life. Forever.

If he had come home, it would be to destroy them all.

Chapter Ten

Preparations

The table in the kitchen was twelve feet long and nearly three feet wide, with long hand-made benches to either side and an armchair at either end. Table and benches were solid hardwood, polished swamp hickory with a deep gray-brown sheen. The armchairs were mismatched, stiff backed, upholstered chairs that once belonged to Momo's mother. Layer upon layer of dry-rotted upholstery fabric had blurred the chairs' original lines, yet there was still something regal about them. Even the bright blue cornflowers covering them now didn't hide the chairs' distinguished origins in some elegant eighteenth-century French shop.

Momo directed the setting of the table with lace linen, her best silver, brass goblets and china. She personally cut flowers for the bouquet that centered the long table and gave explicit orders to the Welch boys to bring back a dozen big blue shelled crabs and as many catfish fillets from the bayou out front.

"No bone," she demanded. "No bone one." The rest of them Momo ordered around like her personal servants. Which in a way, they were.

She hummed and rocked the morning hours away, stroking her cat and making the occasional suggestion that amounted to a royal decree. The cabin was swept, dusted, sprayed for bugs, deodorized, and polished. The bedding was changed, dirty sheets and towels dumped in the washer on the back porch. Lace doilies were draped over every chair back, and all the silver was brought out and polished. Every surface visible to the naked eye, and most that weren't, was cleaned and burnished.

With little warning, Aunt Lillybloom and her two daughters, Freesia and Lantana, arrived, decked out in their Sunday best. Lillybloom was a spinster fallen from grace, a LeMay who had borne two daughters out of wedlock.

The illegitimacy would not have been an issue had Lillybloom mated with a DeLande or a LeMay, but she had found an outsider to couple with, and that without permission from Momo. And she had done so more than once.

In her mid-fifties, Lillybloom was a buxom, earthy woman, carrying the smell of fresh baked bread about her like a perfume. Her maiden daughters were carbon copies of Lillybloom, except they had their own teeth, a few less pounds, and less pronounced Cajun accents. Mara could understand Freesia and Lantana, at least enough to be cordial.

Using the old radio, Momo had summoned the LeMay women to cook and serve the meal she had planned for the Eldest. The first meal in years with an Eldest in attendance. Lillybloom was all a-flutter in her excitement, calling friends on the radio between the preparation of various dishes to boast about her part in this historic occasion. Bright Cajun chatter filled the cabin, dispelling the gloom that had settled over it since Enoch and James put weapons at every window and took up watch.

At this rate, the old maritime, fixed-mounted Triton which the LeMays used to contact one another, would need recharging sooner than usual. The radio's power supply was old, the battery needing to be replaced last year. Momo was known to be a parsimonious old witch, and as usual had insisted the unit had longer to last. With Lillybloom's summoning, the Triton was getting a workout it hadn't had in years.

By eleven a.m., the cabin was spotless, the meal prepared, and five mewling kittens had made their way into the world, birthed on Momo's lap, cradled on an old threadbare towel. The last thing she needed was another batch of kittens, but Lucien and Mara were wise enough not to think so where she could hear them. The Welch brothers didn't know enough to have an opinion about anything, even cats, and the LeMay spinsters were too busy to care.

At eleven-thirty, Momo turned on the generator and all the

overhead fans, blowing the cooking smells and heat out the open windows. The sky was overcast in preparation for an afternoon shower, the temperature dropping into the 80s almost as if Momo had ordered up a cool-spell for company.

At noon, she sent Mara to bathe and change. Hot and sweaty and shaking with an ominous mixture of excitement, anger, and fear, she pulled the privacy curtain around the little bath area, stripped and sat on the shower seat. Cool water drenched her. Her trembling worsened.

If Momo was correct, and an Eldest was coming, the old woman might still have plans for her. Plans she had resisted for years. Mara had no intention of becoming like her mama, living for some man, bonded to him heart and soul, existing only for him.

Momo had told Mara she was free to choose. *Had Momo told Rosemon the same thing?* Perhaps the promise of freedom was just a ruse to keep a LeMay woman compliant and calm until an Eldest put his hands on her and claimed her as his own. Mara took a dozen deep breaths. The cabin made a slow spin about her as she apprehended the danger she faced. That she could lose herself in some man . . . *like a torch in the night . . . .*

Yet, she couldn't run. Not now. Not today. Kenno was out there. Or he might be. The certainty she had felt when she first considered the possibility had faded, the way the far bayou bank blurred behind a curtain of rising fog. Yet, even as her certainty waned, her fear waxed, shining and luminous as a full moon.

Fear beat against her mind as the water beat the heat from her flesh. She could run, if she was brave enough. She could dress, take the guns from the arsenal in the cabin and walk out back, down to the shore and the airboat tied down beneath the lean-to.

Kenno's airboat. The one Rosemon gave to her after Mara saved her from his attack. Repainted, outfitted with new seats and a storage chest for fishing equipment, would Kenno recognize it as his own? Would he know she used it everyday? Or would he simply pluck from her mind the attachment she felt for the fast little craft? The pride she experienced each time she climbed aboard.

The airboat was Mara's. She had earned it the Badlands way. By taking it from another.

Kenno would know. If Kenno was waiting.

Shivering set in as the cold water poured over her and the clouds continued to build. After soaping with Momo's homemade butter soap, Mara rinsed, daubed herself lightly with Momo's vanilla scented jojoba oil, and turned off the stream of water. As the generator roared, she patted herself dry, stepped to her bed and dressed in the clothes she found lying there. There was a faint tremor in her fingers. She heard again the cry of the tortured cat blazing in the fire.

Momo had laid out Mara's favorite dress. It was royal blue crinkled silk, a floral print with multiple tiers to the skirt, and a loose smocked waist, the smocking done in navy to match the embroidery along the blouse's neck and arm holes. Delicate work stitched in silk thread by some cousin or other in return for a favor or charm conjured up by Momo. The blouse was billowy with a fine, soft hand to the fabric, the silk donated by other kin as payment for a fetish or amulet or love potion. Barter, Badlands style.

Mara wore the dress for special occasions, the yearly fais-do-do on Big Cow Bayou—the huge party at harvest time—and to funerals and weddings. And apparently to meet an Eldest DeLande.

With Kenno out there somewhere—maybe, perhaps, or maybe not—Mara didn't know how to refuse.

Silk boxers and a silk and Lycra chemise went against her skin, the dress over her head. Mara had grown since the last time she wore it, and filled it out more thoroughly than before. The bodice was snug against her.

As she moved, the scent of vanilla wafted against her skin like the silk, an erotic aroma. Mara counted the two times multiplication tables, then the threes as panic rose and sifted through her veins. She forced her breathing to slow, fighting the terror that had two names. *Kenno. Eldest.*

She reviewed all she had ever heard about the DeLandes and their peculiar relationship to the LeMays. It wasn't much.

DeLandes were wealthy beyond understanding, powerful in the way only DeLandes and LeMays could be. But unlike LeMays, DeLandes had inbred heavily over the centuries, brother to sister, parent to child, producing strong mental capabilities in some offspring, and gross deformities both mental and physical in others.

DeLandes were the root of LeMay stock, through Cecile, a pregnant, mulatto slave who had escaped into the Badlands, in 1794, carrying the son of an Eldest and enough DeLande wealth to provide for the LeMays for decades. It was Cecile's son Vaschon who had begun the process of bonding a LeMay daughter to a DeLande Eldest in exchange for more wealth and for freedom from DeLande lifestyles and dominance.

The DeLandes had abided by the original contract negotiated by Vaschon for over two centuries, the Eldest DeLande accepting a virgin LeMay as consort, bonding with her, providing for her and the children she would produce for as long as they lived.

If this Eldest was Andreu's direct stock, Mara was promised to him. If he was of another line, her half sister Cady would be offered up. Cady was fourteen. Mara shivered again, knowing an Eldest wouldn't care about her disinclination or Cady's youth. There was talk about the DeLandes and their preference for young women. Always had been.

Dressed, she brushed back her wet hair and braided it, starting at the crown in a French braid, pulling her hair tight against her skull. She would have worn the gold hoops laid out by Momo, but her fingers trembled so that she couldn't find the pierced holes in her lobe and she couldn't line her lips with color. Instead she powdered her face and added a hint of blush before drawing back the privacy curtain.

In bare feet, Mara stood, staring at the gleaming floor, waiting for Momo's reaction. For Lucien's reaction. For Enoch's.

Without even glancing in the mirror by Momo's bed, she knew she was beautiful. Not like Rosemon, lush and sensual, golden and provocative, but dark and somehow mysterious.

Over the noise of the generator, she heard Lucien suck in his breath. Felt Enoch turn sharply away. Her skin began to burn. Her breasts tightened as if cold water ran across them still. Clenching her fists, Mara picked up the men's reactions. The air was charged with heat, a tension that left her breathless.

She didn't want this DeLande Eldest. Yet, she had nowhere to run. Bred for generations for the DeLandes, Mara was about to be presented to one. An Eldest. Within the hour, if history was a reliable indicator, she could be bonded to him, wanting only him, desiring only him. And she might no longer care.

Her only hope was Momo's promise that she could choose, yet, suddenly, as her breath came fast and shallow, Mara understood that vow. She understood how Momo could promise that it was her choice. Momo believed Mara would choose her DeLande even over the desires of her own heart for freedom, for a life of independence. She would choose because she had been bred to choose. That was the power of the DeLande bloodline. That was reality as Momo understood it.

And now, there was Kenno and the message in his eyes the day she saved Rosemon from his attack. He wanted Mara dead. *But he wanted her in his power for a long time first.*

The generator went silent. As its sound died, it uncovered the steady rhythmic approach of a helicopter, blades beating fast, like the throbbing of a terrified heart.

Mara's nails cut into the soft pads of her palms. A pounding pain pulsed through her. Tears gathered in the corners of her eyes. She had planned for this day all of her life. Had planned to run away and hide until the Eldest lost interest or another LeMay was chosen. Now she was caught. Trapped. *Nowhere to run.*

The helicopter was directly overhead, stirring the damp air into whirling eddies of debris, leaves ripped from cypress, willow, live oak, a spray of water kicked up by the powerful blades. Momo and Lucien left Mara standing in the center of the cabin, a china doll on display. The front screen door opened and closed behind them.

Two tears fell and rolled slowly down her cheeks, forced out between closed lids. Mara's lips were trembling, out of control.

Suddenly an arm encircled her waist and she was lifted off her feet, pulled against a man's chest. Breath whooshed out of her. Enoch's bright blue eyes met hers. Close.

"I prob'ly won't have another chance, me sha," he said, using the Cajun endearment. "So I reckon you'll just have to forgive me."

His tongue caught her two tears in quick lapping motions, warm, then cool-damp on her cheeks. His blue eyes crinkled in a half-smile, and with no more warning, he kissed her.

Heat surged up from inside, melted in from his body. Vicious, primitive heat. LeMay to LeMay heat. Need and want and an unfathomable pain that was hunger and desire and passion. His tongue met hers.

Mara's arms crossed behind his neck, pulling him closer, lifting herself against him. His arms tightened, the fingers of one hand against her scalp, tangled in her braid. A hand slipped beneath her dress and caressed her skin. His flesh was hot under her palms. Face rough with unshaven beard, back smooth, corded underneath with muscle. The heat enveloped them as like minds read and gave at once. *He wanted her.* There was no breath, just a twin pulse of—

"And allow me to introduce my sister—Mara Noelle LeMay."

Lucien's laughter penetrated the heat of her mind. In shock, she pulled back, her mouth open, blistered and swollen with Enoch's kiss. Momo and Lucien stood inside the door, Momo's eyes blazing, Lucien's amused as always.

Enoch removed his hands from beneath her silk dress. Mara slid to the floor, cool, cool, cool, against the hot soles of her feet. Enoch stepped away, leaving her swaying and bemused.

Mara met the black-on-black eyes of the Eldest. His mind reached out and encircled hers, tasted the passion she was emanating. Cool green stone, heated by the touch of her mind. He smiled. "Miles Justin DeLande. At your service."

Mara sucked in a breath. She didn't see him cross the room, but he was suddenly beside her, tall and lean, a dark angel pulsing with power. He took her hand, icy flesh against her moist palm. Without taking his eyes from hers, he kissed her hand. A shock ran up her arm, a flash of lightning, traveling over her skin in an instant before settling low in her stomach a heated spiral of pleasure. His lips moved against naked skin as he spoke again.

"The pleasure, Mara, is entirely mine."

71

Chapter Eleven
A Torch in the Night

The room felt hot, though the sun remained hidden. Undercurrents Mara couldn't trace seemed to eddy through the room, strong pockets of emotion swirling between Miles and Momo, Miles and Lucien, Miles and Enoch. And occasionally between Miles and her. Emotions strange and unfamiliar, odd glances, uncertain tones, curious body language that she sensed but couldn't seem to interpret or ignore.

To protect herself she counted. By threes to one hundred, then by fours—mathematics blocking out the unwanted thoughts and the fear and shame of that awkward moment in Enoch's arms. Above the undercurrents, there was conversation of a different sort. Voices joined in casual dialogue.

"Eldest, taste you dat catfish. Lillybloom cook bes' in bayou, all dat ham wrap around and dat sauce. Some good, yeah? Fine cook, she." Momo, acting hostess.

"Momo, let me slice you a taste of this tasso ham. My chef, Deschamps, had it flown in especially for today." Miles, genial and watchful.

"Yeah, dat some good pig you got, Eldest. Lillybloom not cook any better."

"On the contrary, Lillybloom would give Deschamps a run for his money in the best of restaurants. Delicious meal."

Genial conversation above the emotional cross-currents for the first two courses. And then the strain began to show. Uncertain pauses marked the speech of the diners, the social discomfort the lowly often feel around those they consider to be their social betters, and the distance family can place between themselves and an outsider. Silent, Mara watched.

"Beer's not bad, DeLande. Don't drink much Coors except in restaurants. Needs to be kept cold and ice ain't 'xactly common where we live." Enoch, respectful and surly at once.

"We can't expect Miles to drink like us, cousin. Old Banoit's beer wouldn't be good enough for an Eldest," Lucien said. "I'm sure the Eldest prefers a European brand name and a frosted mug."

"Oh, and his finger in the air," Enoch said, sticking a finger up as he drank.

"I think it's supposed to be the little finger, Enoch," Lucien said.

He exchanged the obscene gesture for his pinkie. "Like this, Cousin Lucien?"

"I think so. But it probably means the same thing. In French."

Miles laughed, seeming to enjoy the mild insults directed his way. "Nice boat out front," he said very polite, and then he smiled, innocent and mischievous, joining in the game. "Is it stolen by any chance, cousin?"

"Twice," Lucien said, laughing, enjoying the restless social discord. "Nice chopper."

"It's a Sikorsky S-76," Miles said, turning black eyes on Lucien's green. Seeing interest there he added, "It's a bit like a Learjet with rotor blades, big and sleek, twin-engine, and in this case specially modified for bayou travel with pontoons as well as wheels." With a shrewdly treacherous grin, he said, "You don't fly, by any chance?"

"Nope. And don't make a habit of stealing from family. Cousin."

"Glad to hear it. Have another beer, cousin?"

"Much obliged, Eldest. Much obliged."

"I see a distinct family resemblance, Cousin Lucien. How far back did you say the LeMay and DeLande bloodlines mix?"

"I didn't say, Cousin Miles. I didn't say."

"So you didn't, Cousin Lucien, but perhaps you might."

"Long time, Eldest," Momo said. "Over two hundred year. Long, long time. Mind you manners, Lucien boy."

Laughter around the table.

Miles had an easy laugh and a casual elegance in the way he handled the silver or lifted a brass goblet to drink. Even his response to the barbed comments was refined. He didn't act like an Eldest, though Mara had only Andreu's stilted cynicism to measure him by. He didn't dress like an Eldest, either. Jeans and T-shirt, silver tipped western boots instead of Andreu's Italian suits. Not like an Eldest at all.

Mara turned away from the words and the riptide of emotions flowing around the table. Turned away from Momo's black and angry stare as the family matriarch shot her disapproval from man to man. *This a special time. Don't spoil it, you,* she seemed to be saying. No one was listening to her. Instead, Mara watched Croak outside the window as he tormented a young gator, blue jay style. The alligator was sunning itself in shallow water, its body close to the surface soaking up the ambient heat. Croak flew at its head, pecked or clawed once and swept away with a crow-cry of victory.

It was similar to the attack Lucien was leading on Miles. Mara wondered if the gator would soon have enough and spin suddenly at Croak, devouring the black bird in one bite. She wondered if Miles was as dangerous as the gator.

Lifting a spoonful of iced dessert to her lips, Mara held it there, her mouth open, mind busy and blank at once, retreating from the awful reality of this meal. Perhaps that was why she heard the call, the soft rattle of white noise, the buzz of sound on the family channel. Momo had turned down the Triton so the meal wouldn't be disturbed. Yet Mara heard it, delicate and intense. Familiar. And she understood.

It was a weak cry, full of terror, wordless anguish. "Rosemon," she whispered. Mara's heart began to race, a suffocating rhythm, quick and uneven. She dropped her spoon with a clatter. Turned to the radio beside the door, "Kenno has Rosemon."

The silence that fell at the table was instant. A silence peculiar to the LeMays. A *listening* silence, mind-to-mind. Soft, crackly words came over the Triton.

"I have Rosemon and Cady. I will exchange them for the Eldest, and for Mara."

In her mind she could hear Kenno laughing, low and mocking, half memory, half prophetic. Her fingers dug into the table, nails denting old wood. They had expected Kenno *here*, if he was to come at all, to fight on family terms. On LeMay home ground. Foolish, foolish thought.

A sharp click sounded in the hot room. Enoch aimed a gun at Miles. A small pearl handled .22. Easily concealed, seldom deadly, but aimed at Miles' midsection. The Eldest's brows lifted.

"Looks like this won't be a quick visit after all, cousin," Enoch said. "Looks like you'll be sticking around."

"Looks like," Miles agreed softly.

"And it looks like I'll be needing your Sikorsky, too," Lucien said sadly.

"I thought you didn't steal from family."

"I don't make a practice of it, but Rosemon's my mother, and Cady my sister, so I'll just borrow your Learjet-chopper for a while."

"I see. And Kenno?"

"Rosemon's half brother," Mara whispered. Miles looked at her. Briefly Lucien told him the old tale, cutting through the details with the bare outlines of the attack and the judgment Momo had passed over Kenno.

"So that's why he wants Mara. But why me?"

"Because you're the Eldest," Mara whispered again. "And he's older than you are." Before the punishment, Kenno always fancied himself the LeMay Eldest, and now he had a chance of becoming the DeLande Eldest as well.

The expression on Miles' face changed, altering in some near imperceptible manner. His countenance remained the same on the surface, yet beneath, where the muscles and nerves touched and twined, it hardened like the wood Mara still gripped beneath the table.

"He wants my place. He wants to be Eldest." It was a statement, cold and bare, harsh as the cry of a small dog pulled beneath the surface of bayou water. Behind the words was pain and fierce desire, an icy passion and glacial need. Miles fought to become the Eldest. And he would fight again. Mara shivered beneath his gaze.

To be the DeLande Eldest was a powerful position in Louisiana. It meant handling the vast resources of DeLande wealth. It meant control of politicians, judges, bankers, financiers and government officials. Men DeLande wealth had bought, men DeLande wealth had helped to become elected, or helped to obtain the unobtainable. It meant having one's finger on the pulse of power in the state, the nation, and the world. It also meant total control of the other DeLande family members.

The Eldest controlled the conjoined DeLande finances, a power unequaled in the world. It meant some control of the DeLande breeding program, which, over the centuries had produced the peculiar mental and physical traits of the DeLandes.

Being Eldest was an inherited position, one that automatically fell to the eldest living male DeLande descending through the first Lamont DeLande in the 1700s, though DeLande roots wove their way through the centuries prior to that time. Yet, a weak DeLande, even one descending from an Eldest himself, could lose his rights if a stronger male came along, legitimate or not. Being Eldest was a bit like playing King of the Hill. The strongest most often won.

And it was the Eldest who controlled the LeMays.

There was precedent for an illegitimate DeLande taking the position away from a legitimate son of an Eldest. There was precedent for taking the position by force. Even by murder. The times when force or murder had been used had always resulted in great evil for the DeLandes. Depravity seemed to come upon the family like a malignancy, to grow from within like a deadly disease that takes over its host and slowly sucks all the life out of it.

Momo had often said that was what happened when Andreu came into his power, because he assumed the position of Eldest through the murder of his father. The evil that lurked at the heart of the DeLande gifts, the curse, took over, and the Grande Dame became consumed in it. But then, Momo was always looking for the ultimate payoff, the cosmic climax of the battle between good and evil where the evil man was rewarded with evil and the holy was rewarded with crowns of glory. That was Momo through and through—a believer in Divine Compensation.

She nodded, spectacles shining, drawing Mara's eyes to her own, sorrowfully. "Kenno want. And I fin' crow feather drop at mah feet. Much danger. Kenno . . ."

"Intends to kill me and take over the DeLandes," Miles said again flatly. He pushed against the table and stood, his eyes on Lucien. "Well cousin, you can tell your lackey to put away his toy. It seems your battle is now mine." He looked from Lucien to Mara, his black eyes hard as polished stone.

"My men can remain behind, guarding Momo and Mara. I'll pilot the Sikorsky myself if someone else can track Kenno from the air," Miles said.

"I can," Lucien said, standing. "And Enoch and James will help once we locate him. Say you can put that chopper down *anywhere*?"

"Pretty much. She's specially rigged for land or water. As long as there's enough open space I can set her down."

The two men faced one another across the table: Lucien tanned, blond and green eyed, blazing like a sun; Miles, paler, dark-eyed and intent, a black hole that seemed to engulf the light. There was something here. Some dangerous competition between the two men. Some future pain.

"Enoch, provide Cousin Miles with the weapons of his choice, then load up water and supplies for three days, Lucien said. "Momo, Lillybloom, I'm sorry about the lovely meal. You taught me better than to eat and run, but—"

"You talk too much, boy. Lillybloom, pack dese men supper from leftover."

Mara looked up at Lucien. Though he was not laughing at the moment, his whole face was alight with some dark humor she had never seen before. A battle hunger as all-encompassing as his laughter.

Mara swallowed down the fear that threatened to choke her. She forced her hands to relax, to fall limply in her lap. Momo was watching. Mara started counting again, hoping the numbers would protect her from the penetrating gaze. The men were moving through the cabin, gathering supplies, assembling weapons in piles. Momo and Mara were alone at the table, eyes locked.

Mara stood, her silk dress catching on the bench at her back. Fingers trembling, her mind jumbled with numerals and their relationships to one another, she bent and worked at the trapped threads. The fabric was oddly speared by an ancient splinter. The wood of the bench was so old it looked and felt petrified. It was strange that a splinter should appear just now and catch her clothes. The thin silk tore, another garment for Momo to mend.

Around her, weapons clinked, the sound of metal against metal ominous in the cabin. Water scudded into the bottom of gallon-sized plastic containers.

Strange men—Miles' men, who had waited in the helicopter throughout the dinner—entered the cabin, the floor echoing with the sound of their footfalls. The generator roared to life, obliterating the lesser sounds, and still her fingers worked at the last threads caught in the old wood. Finally the dress came free.

Whirling, Mara turned and stepped from the bench. Met Miles' gaze only inches away. Heat burned from his body, steamy and sensual. He had been there for long moments, watching her. He was holding her weapons—the 9mm semi-automatic Colt and the 12-gauge Winchester with matching customized grip and stock that had belonged to her father. As if she were the wood in his hands, Mara could feel the pressure of his fingers, long and—her knees went weak. "Stop that."

Miles almost smiled. He had the most beautiful lips, and laugh lines at either side that curled just so as he whispered, "When I kiss you, will you lose yourself in me as you did with Enoch?"

Heat rushed through her like a summer wind . . . *like a torch in the night.* "You haven't kissed anyone in so long, do you think you'll remember how?" she said, the first words she thought, staring up into his eyes. The beautiful smile faded. Surprise flickered once at the back of black eyes, and pain. Mara felt it, bleak and empty. Lost and alone, the cracked green stone of his soul.

"I have no intention of being any DeLande's slave," she said, attacking to cover the shock she felt at being able to wound him.

Miles smiled slowly. "I don't want a slave. I just want you."

He hadn't intended to say the words. Mara felt his surprise as if it were her own. The heat in the space between them flared like a furnace. It would scorch her if they touched.

"I want my weapons," she whispered again, eyes still on him.

Miles placed the handgun and the shotgun carefully beside her and stepped away. Moments later the men were gone, the generator silenced, and Mara stood alone in the cabin, weak as molten wax. Out front, the Sikorsky whined, the sound growing in volume and intensity. The big blades began to turn, just visible through the windows between the bodies lined up on the deck: Momo, Lillybloom and her spinster flowers, the two men Miles was leaving behind. Over the noise of the helicopter, Mara heard Lucien shout, "Momo, stay by the radio. Miles has a maritime in this thing. You contact us if you need anything."

Whirling, Mara ran for the armoire that housed her clothes. Ripped off the silk dress that felt too hot, too damp, from the touch of his mind. *A torch in the night.* It was why LeMays were bred for them, this mutual need. Pulling on an old dress, older than she was, and new sneakers, Mara stuffed a change of underwear, a skirt, a pair of jeans and two T-shirts into a floral duffel. Jeans were the devil's clothes according to Momo, who insisted all her clan women wear dresses. She added a comb, soap, a first aid kit, antiperspirant, shampoo and two towels. An extra pair of sneakers. Grabbing the guns, still warm from his hands, she ran out the back door, past the ugly rusted refrigerator.

Out front, the helicopter began a soft whump, whump, whump of sound as the blades turned faster. *Helo. He called it a helo.*

The sound of the blades covered the sudden roar of the airboat's engine. Before the Sikorsky lifted off she was gone, math problems littering her psyche. She was running away, far and fast. Running away, until a silent scream pierced the walls of her mind.

Chapter Twelve

Jenny

Mara had named her *Jenny* the day the boat came to her, envisioning the sleek little vessel as she would be, once painted the yellow and black of the Japanese hornets that nested in the ground near Rosemon's house. Now, foot on the accelerator pedal, Mara gunned the engine and the airboat shot forward, her hand on the rudder stick.

Oak and tallo trees, young cypress and magnolia, flew past. Banking and turning, Mara cut across a spit of land, firmer than it looked. Was airborne an instant before the hull touched down again, jarring. The engine and the huge wooden propeller that thrust her into the wind were powerful at her back. The airboat was a roller coaster ride, as unpredictable as death.

Mara could hear Momo calling over the hand-held radio at her side, hear the fury in her tone. Momo, who was never really angry, was raging and fearful. Lucien called as well, demanding her return.

With her free hand, she jerked up the handset, depressed the button on its side. "Kenno has Rosemon," Mara screamed at the sky and the helicopter that followed her, tracing her path up the lake. "And he's got Cady. He's touching her!" she screamed, knowing somehow her sister's fear, feeling her struggle. Angry tears fell, dashed by the wind. Cady was crying as well. Mara *knew* it. "Cady's afraid."

Cady was fourteen, as beautiful as Lucien, red-haired and blue eyed, but soft, gentle. Not ready for a man, though she dreamed of one who would come to her one day. Kenno was touching her as he maneuvered his big airboat east, out of Elephant Bayou, over swampy earth. He was hurting her, and Cady was broadcasting just as Lucien had said in his explanation, tinting the very air with her horror and her fear, abject terror screaming out over the bayou. In the way of the LeMays and the DeLandes, she was calling out as the airboat headed east toward the Sabine River and fast flowing water. And Mara *heard* her.

Over the Triton, Mara heard Kenno's whispery voice, "Running man. Running man."

She knew, suddenly, his destination, pictured it clearly in her mind. It was as if he wanted her to know. Taunting her to find him, to take back the LeMay women before he had time to harm them. He was drawing them east, into territory not claimed by the clan.

Mara dropped the handset. It clattered to the floor and bounced with the vibration of the water rushing beneath the hull. Using both hands, she pulled the rudder stick hard left, banking against the faint current to avoid some obstruction barely visible beneath the water. Wind whipped her face and clothes, burning like steam.

She pressed the accelerator hard to the floor, passing between old stumps of cypress raped from the water decades ago. She was following a trail left by the sledges of loggers, curving at dangerous speeds through the slow moving water. She knew where Kenno was going. She *knew* it.

Lucien called to Kenno over the radio waves, shouting to him, demanding his return, commanding him to keep his hands off the women. Kenno laughed, his voice so soft it was little more than the static of empty air.

And then the silent scream that was Cady fell mute. It vanished from Mara's mind in a single instant, wiped away as if it never existed. The picture of Kenno's destination was gone as well.

As she swerved through a hub it occurred to Mara that she was losing her mind. *Or that her mind was DeLande, just as Lucien and Momo claimed.* The hub, a clear space in the swampland that had been left by a logging platform, opened into little Bayou Hache, one waterway opening into another as man shaped nature to his needs.

If Kenno was found, it would be on his terms, his ground. He would call to the LeMays no more. And Mara understood another fact. The men in the helicopter had not understood Kenno's whispered words. Mara was the only one who knew where Kenno was taking Cady and Rosemon.

Lucien screamed out his anguish over channel 16; Momo, *listening*, tried to calm him and search for Kenno's mind at the same time, her voice thick with worry and buried beneath static. Miles tried to calm them both, saying his helicopter was faster than an airboat, that there was no way Kenno could outdistance them. That Mara should return to the cabin and wait for them. "This is no place for a woman," he shouted. Babble of voices and phrases, half understood, gurgled over the radio.

But no one knew where they were going. No one but Mara had understood the cryptic remark.

And perhaps that meant that it was happening just as Lucien and Momo had said. Perhaps her mind was expanding, becoming DeLande, both gift and curse. She felt the acrid taste of failure in the back of her throat. She would never get away now. And she might be too late to save Cady. Behind her and above, the helicopter slowed and circled, buzzard-like, its blades beating the tree tops.

Removing her foot from the accelerator pedal, Mara bent, picked up the radio handset, and pressed the talk button. As the airboat slowed in the water, she shouted into the radio, silencing all the chatter with one statement. "I know where he's headed," she said. "I know." They all fell still, silent. "I know where to find them. Do you?" No one spoke. "I won't go back, Lucien. Cady's hurting. She needs me, not a helicopter full of more men. And Rosemon. What will you do with Rosemon without me there to help?" she demanded.

"Kenno said he would exchange Cady and Rosemon for Miles and me," she shouted again. The airboat had slowed to a crawl, the fan in the cage at her back scarcely turning though the big engine was still loud and raucous. "Miles and me. If I'm not there, he'll kill Cady without a second thought. Besides, if you want to know where he's headed, you'll let me go."

She could imagine the conversation between the men in the craft overhead. What bargain would they offer to placate and appease her? Mara eased her foot down on the accelerator a bit, gathering speed, moving north against the current of Bayou Hache. Little "hatchet bayou" was a narrow cut of water that ran along the Sabine River, sometimes a part of it, sometimes independent. Too small to be on any map, it was part of LeMay territory, and Mara was safe here.

To the left, rotting splinters of cypress poked up through the water. Snakes slithered beneath the surface, hunting, spearhead shapes ducking down. Mara used the respite to put on sunglasses, a wide-brimmed hat that tied beneath her chin, and the ear protectors she should have been wearing all along. Pulling out the bottle of sunscreen, she rubbed the white cream into her exposed skin. They were taking their time up there. She tried to act unconcerned, knowing they saw her every move.

The radio crackled again, easier to understand now that the ear protectors blanked out most of the sound from the unmuffled Ford engine at her back. "Where has he taken them?" Lucien asked, his voice fierce but controlled.

Mara lifted the handset. "You won't try to send me back?"

"No." He was furious with her and angry with Miles, backed into a corner and forced to compromise. Lucien had never been very good at compromise. She smiled, careful to keep her face angled away from the slowly circling helicopter.

An alligator, about two and a half feet long, slid into the water from a narrow spit of land, the splash of his tail hidden beneath the mechanical sounds of boat and helicopter. "Do you remember the deep water at the head of Sang Bayou? The place where the water turns that blood-red color?"

"Yes."

"Just north of it is that bluff—"

"Running Man Tree," Lucien interrupted. "I heard something about the 'running man'. He meant the tree."

Well, so much for her being the only one who heard Kenno. "Yes," she said simply, knowing there was more to it than that, and understanding the symbolism the tree might hold for Kenno. A running man who had come home. Knowing that Lucien would make the connections in his own time.

"Go home, Mara."

"You promised."

The radio crackled in her hand, then went silent. Overhead, the Sikorsky veered and picked up speed, gaining altitude. The sound of its engines and the beat of its blades vanished before the helicopter did, lost beneath the roar of the Ford engine at her back. Mara headed north toward Sang Bayou and the man who wanted her dead.

Sang Bayou and Running Man Tree. "Blood Bayou" and a tree out of legend, a tree that, according to tradition, had sheltered outlaws for over two hundred years. Outlaws and a running man, like Kenno himself. Mara shivered, wishing that she could feel Cady's mind, just for a moment, in the way of the DeLandes. To know that her sister was still alive and that she wasn't walking into this ambush for the sake of her sister's body alone.

Mara didn't ask herself why she didn't consider the safety of Rosemon. She tried not to think of her at all.

Miles pressed the trigger on the cyclic stick to the first indent, opening the ICS for communication between the helicopter's occupants. "This bird can outpace anything on the water. We should reach Running Man Tree before Kenno. Can you get a fix on him?"

"No. He's shut up tighter than anyone I've ever scanned for, and Rosemon isn't much help. She's . . . drifting. But she just passed beneath a bridge, which could put her about . . . here." Lucien lifted a detailed map of the area's bayous and roadways, his finger on State Road 62.

"If we're headed in the right direction."

"You think it's a feint?"

"Could be. Why tell us where he's going when we have faster transport? Why not give us an incorrect location? By the time we find them, Kenno's entrenched and we're flying in blind."

Lucien nodded, thoughtful, studying the land below them. "He could be at the tree by now. I've been at Momo's for hours. Kenno could have taken them anytime.

"I understand why he wants me, now. But why Mara?" Miles asked, his voice scratchy over the airwaves.

"You like my little sister, do you?"

"Beside the point. What matters is why Kenno wants her."

"She told you the story of Kenno and Rosemon," Lucien said, "but she left out two important parts."

"And?" Miles banked the Sikorsky, following the winding bends of the little bayou, watching its curving path for an airboat holding two women prisoners.

"She's the one who held a gun on him until we could get there. She was only twelve and 'bout four feet tall."

"Ouch."

"You should have seen his face when he turned and saw her. The great Kenno brought down by a skinny kid with a sexy grown-up voice."

"She has that. You said two reasons?"

"When Momo pronounced the LeMay judgment on Kenno, part of the punishment was a brand. A small, black crow feather beside his left eye. Brand was applied, and then while it was still sizzling, Momo rubbed ashes and grease into it. Turned it black. Permanently."

Miles sighed.

"I'm getting to it. You DeLandes are so impatient."

"About Mara? Please?"

"Impatient but well bred."

This time Miles didn't sigh.

"Well, it was Rosemon's job to apply the brand. And when she was too upset to do it, Momo said Mara had to."

"Did she?"

"Eyes steady and lips like a wire. She didn't waver, didn't break a sweat, didn't flinch. Stared Kenno in the eye the whole time. It was downright scary."

Miles could see the scene as Lucien spoke, the incident shocking in the memory of this volatile young man who was more than half DeLande. Then Lucien shut him out.

"That's why she lives with Momo," Miles said softly. "Because she has no feelings. No emotions."

"Not like normal people. The DeLande curse. A fine bunch of sociopaths we breed up, don't you think?"

Chapter Thirteen
Left Behind

Jenny skimmed the water, banking and turning on a dime as Mara took the shortcut to Sang Bayou. The four cylinder engine was impossibly loud, the wind hot and wet, sour with swamp smells, the scent of rotting vegetation and the occasional dead animal. She slowed twice more; once to rub on more sunscreen, reposition her sunglasses and retie her hat, once to check and stow the weapons. She had left them loose in the bottom when she roared away from Momo's.

The clouds which had protected the luncheon from noonday heat had vanished as a wind out of the west, out of the desert, whipped them away. Blue-gray sky peeked through, found the vision to its liking, and took over.

The sun beat down on Mara, a physical and spiritual heat, like the remembered heat of the flame the night Kenno was branded. Awful smell. Awful sound, the sizzle of human flesh. The memory of his eyes and his wounded-animal cry had been with her forever.

Mara shook away the thought. Water boiled just ahead as snakes mated or something died, fighting for its life, pulled beneath the surface. She went over the spot full throttle, then eased back a bit.

Running Man Tree was too far north to go there often, though Lucien had taken his sisters once or twice. Legend claimed two world renowned criminals had sheltered beneath its boughs back when it was alive, and oak leaves had waved like hair above the flailing, arm-like branches.

Jean Lafitte, pirate and slave trader, had spent an uneasy night beneath the tree, four slaves chained at its base. And Dillinger, wounded by a woman he had failed to satisfy, recuperated for a week, living off the bayou's bounty until he was well enough to move on. Slavery and scorned women, the very things that created the LeMay clan.

Ahead, the bayou stopped. Tree down. An abrupt end of spreading limbs and living leaves.

Instantly Mara slammed the rudder stick hard left. Cut speed. There was no brake. Water level was low, banks high. The bow hit hard, cut into mud, lifted. Mara fell forward into the bow. Sludge caught the rudder for an instant and *Jenny* whirled, slid back into the water facing downstream. Mara was shaking, breathless, bruised beneath her arm where she fell on the raised edge of bow. She dragged herself back to the driver's seat as the airboat stopped.

Gingerly, she sat down, hearing Lucien's voice in her memory as he warned about airboats. "The greatest danger in running an airboat is needing to stop suddenly. The drag of water on a sled-shaped-hull is the only way to slow down. Glide time for an airboat with a two-inch draft is too long for emergencies." The bayou was narrow here. Too narrow for speed.

Mara could have—should have—strapped herself in. With shaking fingers, she pulled the black nylon belt across her thighs and clipped the steel buckle. Lucien had installed old automobile seatbelts years ago, insisting she would need them one day. She hated it when he was right.

Mara took a deep breath as she coasted. Glancing back, she looked at the obstruction that blocked the narrow bayou. Healthy living trees seldom fell across the water. By the time a storm and fast currents had undermined a bank, cutting out the mud that buried its roots, the tree no longer flourished. This looked wrong.

Tapping the accelerator gently, pulling on the rudder stick, Mara turned the airboat again and made her way back upstream. The tree was a once-great silver maple, its leaves still green and pliant. Pickerel, a tall stalked, purple-flowering plant, grew on both banks, crushed by the branches on one side. Beneath the water, the blooms were still open.

The tree had fallen recently. Very recently.

Reaching down, she pulled the 9mm from its secure location in the side-wall of the boat. Coasting, barely moving, she approached the maple's root. Fine chips sprayed the surface of the water and across the mud near the root. Fine as dust. Chips a chainsaw made when it cut into mud and dirt in an inexperienced user's hands. Mara edged closer. The trunk was also unevenly cut, as if the lumberjack had little experience, or was in a hurry.

Round-toed boots had trampled the muddy earth, the soles grooved for traction in mud. On the far side of the tree was a smooth scar where an airboat hull had rested.

She wasn't foolish enough to think that Kenno had cut the tree, wasting time here. He had cohorts. They had waited here for him to pass, then followed once the bayou was blocked. Mara could try to get *Jenny* up the bank and down the other side. She had a lightweight block and tackle stored in the aft compartment. Lucien had seen to it that the little craft had more equipment than Mara could ever use or would ever need. Until today. But she no longer liked the idea of following in Kenno's tracks. He had blocked the waterway. There were nastier tricks he could pull.

She turned the boat and sped back downstream. There were other ways to reach Running Man Tree. Mara figured she knew them all.

"You see them?" Miles slowed the helicopter, spotting a fast moving boat below. It was a fishing boat holding two men and a half-dozen cases of Budweiser. No women.

"I can't find anything," Lucien said, his eyes intent on the landscape below. "No trace of Kenno. Once I thought I caught a trace of Cady. She wanted to go to the bathroom, and she was face down in a boat bottom with one hand on Rosemon's foot. Her toes were wriggling. Rosemon's, I mean," he said, laughing. "And of course there's nothing from Roseman, but then, she hasn't been herself since the night Andreu died."

Miles glanced at Lucien. "Want to tell me about it?"

"Could, I reckon. Might some day, over a couple a beers. Your treat."

Miles grinned and finessed the helicopter against the blustery westerly wind. "Of course." The wind died to a soft, five-mile-an-hour breeze one moment, and gusted up to thirty-five the next. It took all his concentration to follow the narrow winding bayou below and engage Lucien in conversation at the same time.

"For the moment I'll say that the DeLande hold over LeMay women has been both financially rewarding and emotionally devastating," Lucien said.

"Spoken like a well-bred cynic."

"Actually, I'm not well bred, I'm a bastard. I'm just well read. All the LeMays are. It's our one concession to modern education."

Miles glanced at Lucien, dividing his attention between the controls, the wet landscape below and his newfound cousin. "Trying to shock me?"

"Did I?"

"Do you laugh at everything?"

"Most everything. Funerals being the exception. Momo boxed my ears till my head spun the last time I forgot myself and laughed during a eulogy."

"Are we indulging in the LeMay concept of discourse?"

"This is a power play, not a dialogue. Something a DeLande should understand."

"I understand it, Lucien. I just never liked it."

"I'll keep that in mind, Eldest."

Miles grinned again and lifted his chin. "Do that."

Behind them, Enoch laughed softly into his mic.

Chapter Fourteen

Jenny and Making Poor Time

Mara tapped the controls, easing between the trunks of living cypress, and the knees that supported the trees' weight in twenty-five feet of mud. The water here was slow moving, the cypress stand perhaps a thousand years old—young by cypress standards. Three thousand years would pass before *old* cypress again lived in these waters.

She bumped between trees. Gray moss hung above like ashen shrouds. Oak and scrub grew up where the water was most shallow, making her passage difficult. There was discernible current to ripple around the foliage. Stagnant water stank, a warm, wet scent. There were few patches of cypress like this left in the Badlands. Too young to be bothered with or too difficult to reach even with the heavy equipment, the rapacious loggers of the last century had left the small stand of trees alone rather than risk the quicksand hidden in their roots.

Cypress grew about three-quarters of an inch in height a year, max. Some years, more than that would die back only to begin again, the living wood growing up beside the dead. A thousand-year-old tree might be no bigger around than a basketball.

The cypress knees that rose above or hid just below the water could be deadly to a boater whose hull was pierced or whose craft flipped over. Probably wouldn't do the tree much good either. Even with the thin layer of ultra-high molecular-weight polymer that sheathed *Jenny's* naval-grade aluminum bottom, hitting a cypress knee could do damage.

Lucien's lessons. How to pilot an airboat. How to survive in a swamp or bayou. How to reach Running Man Tree by one of several paths.

Movement caught her eye. Flash of color to the left. Mara dropped down, finding the form. A man, kneeling in the shadows of a magnolia tree on a tiny island. She shoved the rudder stick hard right, slamming down the accelerator. Cypress knees or no, she shot ahead, Mara's heart in her throat.

She felt the impact of the round before she heard the shots. A hard thump into the side of the boat. A sizzling sound, like bees at high speed as another round missed her head. Dual cracks, like the sharp sound of lightning touching down before the roar of thunder.

At top speed she had little control of the airboat, and less reaction time. But she wasn't waiting around for a shot that intended to kill. Mara knew a warning when it aimed past her. The man could have hit her at any time before she saw him. Her speed had been a crawl, and an airboat announces itself with engine drone for miles. He was there to intimidate, not injure. *Or to cause her to speed into a trap.*

Jenny lifted beneath her, thrown up by some unseen barrier at the surface. Mara hit hard, biting her tongue. Her mouth flooded with the warm metallic taste. Over a thin rim of dirt she lifted again, almost out of control. Mara laughed when they touched down, a wild, defiant sound. Odd laughter. Scary. She swallowed back blood.

Skimming over the water, she flew through tall pointed leaves and the flatter pads of lilies that had been imported decades ago and had taken over. She caught her breath and slowed, her heart a savage throb in her chest.

Ducking, she raced beneath low-hanging boughs. Thin stems raked the prop cage, beating like whips against the tubular steel.

When teaching her to care for the sleek craft, Lucien had called an airboat at top speed a "suicidal head-rush". Mara remembered his laughter as he piloted *Jenny* over open water, the sound wild and reckless. Laughter strangely like her own. She laughed again and swerved into the strong current of the Sabine River, jerked the ear protectors off her head, and guided the airboat north.

Half an hour later, Mara checked the gas level. Still nearly full. Some airboats had a thirty-five gallon tank assuring six to eight hours' running time. Kenno had removed the larger tank, replacing it with a twenty-five gallon one. The result was slightly more speed, but less running time. That had never mattered before. Not untill now. Unable to stand the roar of the engine behind her for long, Mara resettled the ear protectors in place.

Having discarded any thought of safety, she was making good time. Still watchful though, not wanting to rush up on an ambush meant to kill. Especially not wanting to pass one unnoticed and get shot from behind.

The speed of her passage had ripped long strands of hair from her braid. Her dress was limp and damp, heavily wrinkled where the wind had battered it. The weather, so unpredictable, had turned hot and scorching.

Mara passed a stand of blooming lilies, purple on tall stalks. They bobbed in the wash from the airboat, floral heads doing a little dance.

The Sabine River was up and running fast, its current blending with the swamp, making narrow ripples and eddies in the water.

Mara shook her head and wiped away a trickle of sweat. She could *feel* Momo in the back of her mind, hovering and smiling. Mara didn't know how to block her out. Urgency and anger in equal proportions clouded Mara's mind.

Chapter Fifteen

Shadows Within Shadows

Kenno was as lost to them as if he'd never existed. Before now, Miles knew of only one DeLande capable of such total blocking. Himself. He had grown up in a household where most pure-bred DeLandes could be sensed, communicated with, read at all times. There was no privacy, little shielding from another's thoughts or desires or rages. No retreat from curious minds.

When Miles first came into this gift, his mind was like an open wound, tender to the touch, flinching from all contact. Every waking moment was painful as intrusive minds violated his most intimate thoughts. As the innocent ones in that horror of a home suffered and bled.

And then, one particularly bad day, he had run from the Grand Dame and the awful games she had insisted her children play. He had run into an unused wing of the sprawling estate house and hidden in the dusty closet of an old-fashioned, vacant room. Ducked down between the satin of moldering clothes. Crouched among spiders, dead moths, and beetles which scampered over a dozen pair of old formal shoes.

No one could find him. With the pulling to of the door, he shut away his mind. Only he of all the generations of DeLandes had had that ability until now.

Now there was Kenno. An unstable, violent man who, though illegitimate, had the age-old right to replace him—as head of the DeLande family and de facto ruler of the DeLande Estate and finances. Because Kenno was older, he could become the Eldest. Which would strip Miles of his power and return the DeLandes to the abhorrent control and disgusting practices of forced inbreeding and incest that had created them in the first place.

Miles reached down beside the pilot's padded leather seat and the helicopter's lightweight composite door. His fingers touched the cool metal of the Glock 9 mil in its nubuck holster. The one he had placed there upon liftoff from the cabin on Elephant Bayou.

"Deep water ahead," Lucien commented. "According to local lore, the source of Sang Bayou."

Miles looked down, slowed the Sikorsky, banking ten degrees, rolling out and dropping altitude. Beneath him was a strange, wide pool of water with tall banks on one side. The muddy brown or near black water typical of bayous had altered here. Rather than the hue of a dark roux, it was reddish, as if mixed with molten iron. Or blood. Sang Bayou. Blood Bayou.

He glanced in the mirrors, viewing the bayou which snaked out behind him; the water there was brown again, untouched by the reddish brown stain.

"The French called it *Blessure de la Terre*," Lucien said, laughing.

Miles was getting weary of the sound. Though initially it had been pleasant to be around the rare sunny human being who found life so agreeable and humorous, it was beginning to pall. Miles wished for a more unsociable character or even another silent type like James or Enoch.

The pair quietly occupied two of the seats behind him, weapons stowed at their feet and backs. Though Miles was relatively certain that neither man had been in a helicopter before, they had remained stoic and unimpressed with the executive interior and all the bells and whistles the top-of-the-line Sikorsky offered. Dour. Totally unlike the voluble and effusive Lucien.

"Loosely translated it's *Wound in the Earth*," he continued. "Don't know what the Indians called it, they stayed away. I've yet to find a geologist or bayou dweller who can explain the color. One of the Walker's—a Cajun family up towards Starks, Louisiana—stole a dredge and brought it up here. Sucked up about four hundred tons of bayou bottom, all of it brown. Never could find any red. I've always thought the water was the color of spider blood. Rusty, thin and reddish brown."

Miles glanced at Lucien, wondering if his experience with the Grande Dame's black widow spider had somehow been plucked from his mind. If so, he would have to watch these LeMays carefully. They might be even more than they seemed. In Miles' world that was dangerous. Lucien's face was bland, however, his eyes on the water below.

"Running Man Tree?" Miles asked.

"There," Lucien said, pointing.

Miles propelled the Sikorsky forward a gentle nudge at a time. Moments later the pontoons touched down, easing into the bloody-looking water. Using the cyclic stick to attain a gentle forward motion, he felt the bank firm against the front runner. He powered down, bottoming the collective stick, pulling the engine levers to idle before shutting off.

The silence still contained a roar, the sound of the engines an aural echo inside his head. Enoch and James unloaded their weapons and fanned out along the bank. They worked together, movements synchronized and smooth, with a minimum of hand signals passed back and forth. Somewhere, they had received topnotch paramilitary training. As neither could read, Miles wondered who had provided the training, then decided he didn't need to know. Survivalists had claimed patches of land in bayou country for as long as there was memory. Often on DeLande land. They claimed squatters' rights, and were hard as hell to move out once they were entrenched. If there was a camp operating nearby, he didn't want to know about it.

To his right, Lucien had stepped from the Sikorsky and secured a land-line to the front strut. Dragging the line behind him, he jumped through the water, waded to shore, wrapped the free end around the base of Running Man Tree and tied it off.

The tree looked eons old, a weathered-gray forked trunk, perhaps twelve feet tall, like arms frozen in motion. Short stumpy legs were the roots, exposed by erosion. The head of the man was missing, a blackened splinter of charred wood and curled bark where lightning had struck, adding an eerie pathos to the setting. Headless man, running nowhere.

Looking at the tree, Miles accepted that Kenno might be more than his equal. Might be his superior. Once again he touched the nubuck leather of the holster. With quick resolve, he lifted the weapon and strapped its leather traces around his chest. His breathing was shallow as he worked the buckle, his fingers cold.

On the shore, his distant cousins conferred. Blond and untamed, the three moved with the famed DeLande grace from tree to tree, using standard search methodology, cover and concealment. Yet, they made it a dance, the motion of their bodies so smooth and supple. A DeLande gift this lissome strength.

They were heading toward a building at the back of the cleared space beyond the tree. It was decrepit, a ramshackle place little bigger than an old shed. Its tin roof had been rolled back by high winds and lay curled and rusting against an old oak's branches. Gray moss waved in the hot breeze. A black bird with a touch of red on its upper wings surveyed the men below him before uttering a single cry and taking off to the east.

The bank around him was smooth from erosion, the last rain's runnels still marking the soil. There were animal tracks, places where the wind had piled leaves. No sign of an airboat. No sign of humans. Miles knew it was possible to fly low over a boat on the bayou and not see it, hidden beneath the heavy overgrowth. Yet, he wondered if Lucien had a reason for not seeing this particular boat at this particular time. DeLandes were known for looking to the bottom line in all things, and the bottom line for most of them was unheeding, unthinking avarice. Whatever they wanted they took, with no thought for another's pain or needs. His entire life had been one long plot within a scheme within a conspiracy, until he was suddenly made the DeLande Eldest and put a stop to it all. He had thought—he had hoped—he had put all the intrigue behind him, conquered the others, bent them all to his will. Yet, he had no notion how these LeMays related to one another or to his position as Eldest.

If Lucien was working with Kenno . . .

Miles broke into a sweat, his consciousness reaching for Lucien's, meeting only amusement. His fingers touched the butt of the weapon that rested against his shoulder. Lucien laughed softly, glancing at Miles, a mental banter.

Miles positioned his three *cohorts* among the shadows on shore. Further inland, a fourth shadow moved, joined by a fifth in the foliage. Someone was waiting. And somehow, Miles knew it wasn't Kenno. This was a trap.

Chapter Sixteen

No Man is an Island

Slowing the airboat, Mara turned to shore. Around her, deep water flowed into bayou, mixing uneasily, bloody and red with muddy and brown, like an omen. Ahead was the open water at the heart of Sang Bayou, the helicopter resting on its bloodstained surface.

Moving slowly, like a sleepwalker at the controls, she turned off the ignition. Pulled off the ear protectors.

They were here, or somewhere close by. Cady was in pain. Mara could feel her fear like a joint that ached in the cold of winter. Mud was everywhere around the young girl, warm and wet beneath her. Fear and pain, a throbbing pulse in Mara's mind.

Momo had never told her that *listening* would be like this. Half-formed pictures, as if she looked through another's eyeglasses and a kaleidoscope at once. Feelings, sensitive as a boil to the touch, red and tender. How did any of them stand it twenty-four hours a day?

Some rational and dispassionate part of her mind was considering what would happen to this communication when she found Cady. At least it was Cady he had. She was gentle, but she was also determined. Even stubborn. And she knew how to survive alone in the Badlands should she be able to get away. Cady would be ready to help in her own rescue. Cady wasn't defenseless.

Mara pocketed the ignition key, though usually she simply left it in the ignition, ready to go at any moment. Daddy's Colt, she pushed into the waistband of her dress. It was heavy, pulling at the blouse and the skirt both, but it was secure. Lifting the shotgun, she checked to see that it was fully loaded. Three rounds of .00

buckshot. The gun seemed heavier than before, or perhaps fear simply weighted it in her arms. A ten pound gun was a ten pound gun. Even Kenno couldn't change the law of gravity.

Stepping out of the airboat, her foot sank, squelching deep into the mud of the shore. Something rotted nearby, dead fish, and worse, the stench of mammalian decay. Inside her shoe, her toes were flooded with water. With the next step, her other foot was also instantly sodden. Footing would be precarious here. Perhaps deadly.

She should call Lucien on the radio. Tell him where she was, what she was doing—going ashore on a thought, on a whim, on an intuition. She should. Yet Mara would feel foolish if she called him and Kenno wasn't here. There were no tracks in the mud to show he had beached nearby. No evidence her hunch was right. And she didn't like the thought that she was acting on DeLande intuition, following some subconscious trail of Cady's mind like a soothsaying tracker on the prowl.

Clicking off the shotgun's safety, Mara scanned the shoreline as she moved away from the water. To the right it rose sharply in a low bluff some fifteen feet high, muddy and bare of trees, the remnant of the Walkers' folly with dredging equipment.

To the left, thick scrub and low-growing trees crowded against the bank. A narrow animal trail wove inland, deeply scored with hoof prints of deer, paw prints of various critters, and impressions that looked as if they had been made by a small child walking on its hands. Raccoon prints. No human prints at all.

Moving carefully, shotgun braced against her shoulder, Mara followed the animal path, mud to her ankles. The stench of dead animal grew stronger. A soft buzz, the white noise of Momo's old AM-band radio, the dial set between stations, sounded ahead.

Resettling the shotgun, she secured it more firmly, the butt snug in the hollow between shoulder joint and collarbone.

Breath came in gasps between her lips. Sweat beaded on her upper lip. On her nose. Trickled down the thin ridge of spine beneath her blouse.

Movement to the right. A flicker of brown.

Mara whirled, feet slipping in the muck. She went down, landed on one knee, off balance in the mud. In her sights was a small bear, resting in the V of a young sapling. To the side, the bloated corpse of the mother bear lay, black, brown, and red with gore. Flies danced in the air over the matted fur. A family of nutria, one a twenty-five pound monster, fed off the entrails. The smell was cloying and sickly sweet.

The baby bear stared at her, its eyes hopeless and pleading.

"Sorry, sweetheart. Can't help you just now," she whispered. Rising to her feet, Mara walked on. Her knee was stiff where she landed in the mud. Her skirts were heavily caked, making progress slower, less secure. To one side, a vulture landed on the dead limb of a tree, watching the spectacle of fellow scavengers feed.

Before her, the trees opened out. A clearing wide as a house appeared, swamp water beyond. Mara was on a small island. Her heart rate tripled, a near painful cadence against her ribs. From upstream came the faint sound of gunshots. Staccato, then rapid fire, both handgun and shotgun.

The cage of an airboat materialized near the water, the stainless tubular steel blending with the scrub along the shore. It was a big boat, the size tour boat companies used, with one driver's seat high up near the cage and two bench seats in front like church pews for the paying customers.

Footprints sank into the muck, both booted and bare, scarring the muddy landscape.

Cady and Rosemon wore no shoes. Mara didn't know how she knew that, but like Cady's pain and fear, she *knew* it was so. Their footprints led into the scrub, back behind, to her left. She turned. And focused on Kenno.

He was sitting on a stump, his spine to a live oak, its trunk bent, gnarled, twisted with age. A venerable chenier, a shield at his back.

Rosemon was held in his arms, draped across his body, a .45 pressed against her temple. Her eyes were closed. Mara couldn't tell if she was breathing. Her own arms supporting the 12-gauge began to quiver.

He was shirtless in the heat, the lions on his upper arms moving with the play of muscles, maws open in twin silent roars, bright droplets of tattooed blood welling in his skin. His reddish-blond hair was loose, a wild, tangled mass, to his waist. Blue eyes on

Mara. The black crow feather was prominent on his left cheek beside the blazing orb. He smiled, showing white, white teeth.

She suddenly smelled the stench of scorched flesh, heard the sizzling of Kenno's face as it burned beneath the brand she held. Old memories. Old fear.

A gust of hot wind whipped through the clearing, chasing away the scent of cooked meat, replacing it with the rotten redolence of dead bear.

At Kenno's feet was Cady, lying in the mud, Kenno's booted foot square on her back. She was facing Mara with eyes full of tears; her dress was torn, exposing her shoulders. Anger and hatred filled the clearing like the bear's rank scent. The anger was Kenno's, hot as the molten blue of his eyes. The hatred was Cady's.

She was still afraid, yet the fear was mutating even as Mara focused on her. Some strange, unnamed emotion was writhing there, like the coiling motion of smoke or a serpent, spiraling back on itself, taking form and growing stronger. Something powerful and fierce, barbarous and violent. Out of control.

Cady blinked. Pulled back her lips in a silent snarl. *Do something*, her eyes screamed. *I'm ready*.

"Cady, was Kenno alone? Or were there others?"

"Upstream," she grated out. "With Lucien. He's dying. An Eldest killed him."

Mara started, confused for an instant. *Miles killed Lucien?* And then the truth of it filled her. A stranger lay dying, his legs in bayou water, his face in pickerel weed. Miles stood over him, Lucien a pace away. Mara wondered if the man had been Kenno's friend.

Kenno's grin became as ferocious as the lions on his arms. "No greeting for your Uncle Kenno?"

"I have no uncle. He was branded an outlaw and banished, driven out. Dead to us." The quivering in her arms was worse. Mara had been holding the weapon at ready for too long. Moving left again, feet cautious in the uncertain footing, she spotted a young tree with a crooked branch. If she moved in front of the tree, she could rest the barrel of the shotgun on the branch while placing the butt against the trunk. It was the only way to get off more than one shot and still hit her quarry. "You're not my uncle, you're a target."

Kenno pulled Rosemon's head back. Her lips were bruised where he had kissed her or hit her. Perhaps both. Mara hoped that was all he had done. Her mother took a breath, the motion difficult because of the angle of her neck, the cords of muscle and esophagus moving painfully. At least she was alive. Kenno bent and licked her lips, laughter in his eyes.

A hawk called far off, its keening cry a death knell. Rage lashed through Mara.

The world slowed around her, telescoped down to one moment in time, one focus. The hawk cried again, the sound long and piercing overhead.

"Now!" she shouted.

Cady rolled right. Instantly Mara stepped into the protection of the tree's bent branches.

Kenno's arm shifted, steadied. He sighted on Cady's rolling form; his finger tightened. The .45 fired. Mara braced the butt of her shotgun against the narrow trunk. Aimed low, away from Rosemon. And fired.

The place where Kenno's foot had been exploded in a blast of mud. Smoothly, he turned the gun on Mara.

Eyes like spheres of blue sky brought to life stared down the length of his bare arm. The weapon was aimed at her head. Mara's was aimed at his bare chest, inches from Rosemon's breast.

Cady stood behind Mara, panting. She could feel the heat from her sister's slight body. Hear the soft wheeze of her lungs, breathing as fast as Mara's own. "Wipe your hands on my skirt," she whispered, unable to find the breath to speak louder. "Then take the 9mm from my waistband."

It was difficult to hear her own voice, her eardrums deafened by the concussion of sounds. If she couldn't hear her own voice, then Cady's wheeze must be bad indeed. Asthma, conquered in her sister's youth, had returned with her fear.

The fabric of her skirt moved, Cady's hands on the cloth, wiping away mud as Kenno leveled his gun. Sweat ran down into Mara's waistband, puddling against the elastic before being absorbed. Her breath was fast, drying her lips; they cracked in the heat.

She rested the forearm of the shotgun on the crooked branch, easing the tension in her arms. Cady tugged the 9mm from the damp skirt. Mara could feel her movements as she checked the weapon.

"The airboat is on the deep-water side of the island. Key in my pocket. Take it. Go call Lucien. Tell him where we are." The pull on her skirt returned briefly.

Wordless, Cady slipped away, moving fast, from tree to tree, back the way Mara had come.

"Mexican standoff," Kenno growled. Mara could barely hear his voice over the ringing in her ears. When she didn't respond, he moved the weapon quickly from Mara back to Rosemon's temple and continued. "You shoot me, I shoot Rosemon. I shoot Rosemon, you have no reason not to shoot me. What do you think, sweet sister?" he said to Rosemon. "What will your daughter do? Shoot me, hope her spread pattern centers on me and doesn't include your tender flesh? Then hope I don't retaliate by blowing off your head," he concluded, looking again at Mara.

He was right. She had no chance of winning this game. None at all. But then, neither did he. The rage that had shot through her moments before boiled now like oil, so thick and strong she could barely speak for the fury. "You wanted Miles. That what we're waiting on?"

A strand of hair fell over his face, pale against his tanned skin. "Miles Justin DeLande," Kenno snarled. "His head would look nice hanging on my trophy wall. Do you think his skin would react well to taxidermist methods? Or would it rot and turn color?"

Kenno pulled Rosemon closer, his hand in her hair, her eyes still closed, lids fluttering. Mara's mother was a living shield covering more than half of Kenno's body. Mara glanced down. The .00 buckshot had punched several holes in Kenno's mud covered boot. A trickle of bright red trailed out one of the ragged gaps, into the mud. *First blood.*

"I'm the rightful Eldest. As qualified as Andreu. More so than my father." More hair fell forward over Kenno's face, moved by the westerly breeze.

"Some stranger from the Badlands is not exactly Eldest

material," Mara said, wondering when Cady would start the airboat. There hadn't been the familiar roar. The bayou was silent. She licked her lips and tasted the old blood from where she had bitten her tongue, the flesh as ragged there as the hole in Kenno's boot. "You don't even know who your daddy is so you can't exactly claim a strong relationship to the DeLandes."

"You believe that old story about mama being raped by a stranger?" Kenno grinned, strong white teeth a threat. "Ask Momo about it sometime. She knows the truth. Nevin DeLande's my old man. Royal DeLande pulled a fast one on the old woman. Stole Delice one night after Louis severed ties with her. Took Delice right out from under Momo's eyes, Rosemon still asleep in her crib. He gave her to his other son Nevin. This is my dear departed mama I'm talking about, and her protector's brother, in a rather muddy violation of the DeLande/LeMay contract." Kenno laughed, his eyes blazing.

"There had never been a provision for the loophole that was created when Louis left Delice. LeMays were safe as long as a LeMay consort was bonded to a DeLande protector, and though Louis wasn't Eldest yet at the time he took Delice, their bonding satisfied the contract. Now there was no bonding and no contract and Delice was *almost* fair game.

"Momo was in a rage, way I hear tell it. Especially when Nevin rose to Eldest before Louis." Kenno moved his hand along Rosemon's breast, the metal of the weapon in his fist a casual and obscene caress.

Mara was horrified as the old story unfolded. And she knew it was *truth* even as he spoke. Literal and complete truth, not the small lies and half-truths the children had always been told.

"Royal, the old bastard, changed everything. And Momo knows it. She knows that a DeLande patriarch screwed her; screwed all the LeMays. And I'm the result of night-play my mama never forgot, not even when the old woman found a husband willing to take damaged goods. Old Banoit claimed me, but I'm not his.

"That gives me one qualification for Eldest—the eldest living male child of an Eldest. Ask Miles. He'll tell you. Andreu was an Eldest and stood between me and the position of patriarch. And then Andreu's brothers. Now it's just Miles and me. And I'm

104

older. Except for the issue of legitimacy, I fit the qualifications better. And there is some question of Miles legitimacy, as I understand." Kenno smiled, his hand still.

Mara swallowed down her fear, steadied her arms, though the pain in her muscles was a burning ache. The story might change LeMay lives in untold ways. Yet, it was ancient history and had no immediate bearing on the problem of Rosemon and the gun pointed at her. "You didn't answer my question. We're waiting on him aren't we?"

Kenno laughed again. Mara's ears were clearing of the white noise and ringing from the blasts of the weapons. She could hear the derision in Kenno's laughter.

"I always said you're a smart little thing. If Rosemon hadn't been more my type, I'd have taken you instead. But I like my women spirited. Hungry. A bitch in heat, not a brain. When Rosemon was twelve she was so hot, she called men from as far away as Jasper, Texas."

"So I heard."

"Momo told you, huh?" Kenno jerked his head, flinging the strand of hair. It fell back over his face again with the next breath, but the gun at Rosemon's head had dropped for an instant with the motion.

If she could time the stirring of the breeze and Kenno's irritation, Mara could get in a shot while his gun wavered. If. Maybe. *Rosemon dead by her daughter's hand.* The quivering returned to her arms, faint tremors running along the taut muscles. Her fingertips were icy and white.

"The old broad sell all my hunting trophies or did she give them to one of Rosemon's brats?"

It took Mara a moment to understand that the *old broad* was Momo. And that they were back to the subject of hunting trophies again. Kenno had always been an avid hunter, trading hard labor and his skill as a guide to tourist fishermen for the funds to mount his kills each year. *And when he wasn't hunting, he was torturing cats . . .* Mara's chin came up.

"She burned them," she said, watching his face. A peculiar expression appeared there for a moment. "We had a big bonfire with coals made from deer and fox and even that elk you shot in

Canada that time." The expression on his face grew, mutated, moved from a subtle incredulity to a horror Mara understood. And could use.

"Once it cooked down to hot coals, we added wood and roasted a small pig over it," she added, "and had us a party." Mara laughed viciously. At the sound, Kenno's eyes widened, dilating to full black. And he turned the gun from Rosemon to Mara.

A blow took her in the side. Dual shots sounded as she hit the ground. Kenno's handgun. Mara's shotgun. The recoil jolt in her shoulder stunned her. Pain spiraled out, down her arm, around her chest. She lost her breath. Rolled in the slick mud. She hadn't been shot. She had been tackled.

Someone rolled with her. Body to body. Heat, scorching, intense, flared between them. Swelling. Soaring. They rolled through the mud, settled in a depression deep with sediment, his body over hers. The 12-gauge rested between them, its stock crushing her abdomen and hip.

He wrenched the shotgun away. His mouth found hers. Hot and demanding. Just like before, the sensation leaving her blazing with a need she didn't understand. Dimly aware, she pulled him to her. Arms mud-slick across his back.

Enoch?

No. Miles.

Miles . . . Mouth hot. Body to body. *Shots.* Far away. *Shots.*

Lucien.

Mara jerked away, forced Miles from her. Found his black eyes. "Lucien," she gasped. Her brother screamed. The pain in his side was her pain. A sudden blazing, shrieking agony. *Pain. Pain. Pain.* And Miles was gone.

Rolling, Mara struggled upright, to her knees. Hands searching the contours of her body—hips, side, abdomen. She was whole. *It was Lucien who was shot. Not her.* Mara hadn't been certain. She had thought, just for a moment, it was her.

Miles slogged uphill, his steps a wet sound. From above, Mara hadn't seen the slight depression where she knelt now in the mud, her dress around her waist. The brand of Miles' hands, Miles mouth was still hot on her flesh.

Like a torch in the night.

Voices sounded. Guttural. Savage.

She clawed up, out of the hole. The top of the small hill caved in around her, burying her legs. Mara grasped a root and pulled herself up on hands and knees, through mud that wanted to climb with her or suck her back down. Quicksand in the making.

Before her was Lucien. His blood wept into the earth, brighter than *Blessure de la Terre*, the wound in the earth. He gripped his stomach, eyes on hers. Green eyes. Mad as Kenno's, but laughing. Even now, laughing.

"Sociopaths," he grated out. "Every last one of us. Sociopaths, DeLande style."

Beside him was the .44 he inherited from Andreu. It was smeared with blood and mud. Mara's fingers found it, warm still from the heat of his hands. The heat of firing. How many shots? How many rounds left?

She struggled to stand. Had lost her shoes in the mud. Barefoot, Mara stood and searched the small clearing. Rosemon was sitting against the chenier where Kenno had dropped her. Eyes wide and blinking, full of tears, as if she were a child coming out of a deep sleep and bad dreams. Surprise marked her face. Rosemon focused on her. "Mara Noelle?" Her middle name. The one she hated, given to her because she had been conceived on Christmas Day. It sounded lovely on Rosemon's lips. Mara laughed, the sound blending into Lucien's half-mad laughter.

"Yeah, Rosemon. Mara Noelle."

Near her, two forms rolled, covered with mud. One was massive, the mane of his hair clotted with bayou sludge. The other was slight, wiry, graceful, still alive only because the mud made strength relative to speed. Suddenly Miles twisted, stretched, and spun to his feet. Mara's shotgun was in his hands.

Faster than she could see, he chambered the last shell, the sound metallic and sharp in the clearing. Riveting. The barrel aimed at Kenno's throat.

In a single instant, everything stopped. Kenno's struggles. Lucien's moaning laughter. Rosemon's tears. Mara's very heart. The only sound was the harsh grating of the men's breathing.

Miles pressed the barrel against the soft tissue of Kenno's throat. Indenting the flesh. If he fired, there would be nothing left of the column of muscle and tendon and fragile bones. Mara could picture the scene in her mind clearly. And the after-effects of the death that would scar Miles. Warp him. Change him forever.

She didn't know who Miles was, exactly, but she knew that to murder would alter him. Change him much more surely than the death of the man he had killed in self-defense only moments before in *Blessure de la Terre*. To murder would make Miles into someone else entirely. Some*thing* else. She *knew* it.

"Miles . . . don't"

Beneath the mud, his chest heaved. His legs and arms stretched and quivered, rippling with the effort of immobility. A killing moment arrested in time.

"If . . . if you kill him to save one of us the action is defensible," she said softly, "both in a court of law and to the DeLandes whom you rule." Mara took a breath. It pulled at her chest and the shoulder bruised by the shotgun blast. She could feel Momo in the clearing, stirring in her soul, anxious and fretful. "If you kill him to retain the title of Eldest, you will become like the worst of us." Tears gathered and fell, rolling over the mud on her face, cutting runnels through it. Miles made a small sound, low and deep in his chest. Fury and anguish fused in the soft note. Silence followed. The breeze died.

The moment stretched. Mara's tears slowed and began to dry. She remembered the heat that had flowed between them like molten gold, a fiery glowing path of desire, *like a torch in the night*. She willed Miles to remember that passion. To choose against the murder that seemed so necessary. The murder that would set them all free.

"If you kill . . . if you, the Eldest, murder, we'll all be marked. We'll become something different. Walk a different path as DeLande and LeMays," she whispered seeing in her mind's eye a dark future opening from this moment. A changed Eldest, full of something she couldn't name. Something silent and suffering.

Mara pulled back from the pictures in her mind and wiped at her eyes. Blinked into the sunlight and met Miles' eyes for an instant, black on black, like bayou water in moonlight. Horrified, she stared at him. But she *knew*. Mara *knew* she was right.

"That's all I need in my life, he whispered. A DeLande seer."

Mara started. A *seer? What had she said?*

"Take his weapon. It's a few inches from his head."

She saw the gun in the mud, the barrel so packed she didn't think it could fire.

Seer? Seer . . . The word echoed, blurring in memory. The odd sensation of *knowing* vanished. Her own *knowing* or Momo's? Her own mind or the old witch's?

Mara bent, moved forward, and picked up the weapon. She found breath to speak. "I'm not a seer. I'm just smart."

Lucien laughed, the sound raspy and weak. "Kenno's judgment. Smart." His breathing was congested, as if his lungs filled with blood as they spoke. And still there was the laughter underneath, cutting and wry.

"Get up," Miles said softly, his face like stone as he backed away from Kenno. "Get up and get out. You've got thirty seconds to clear this island."

Kenno said nothing, just pushed up from the muddy ground. Hatred, blue and hot as a welder's arc, swept over Mara. Her knees buckled and bonelessly she sank to the ground. Still without a word, Kenno turned and made for the shore, waded in and submerged to his neck. Clothes dragging against his progress, he swam slowly downstream and vanished from sight.

Leaving Miles and the LeMays in the small clearing, silent and wounded. But alive.

Chapter Seventeen

Betrayal

"You let him go!" Cady's voice was thick with anger, the dammed up emotion spilling over as she stepped between the trees at Mara's back. The Colt, extended before her was held in two trembling hands, pointed at Miles.

Lucien laughed, the sound burbling wetly, a half-groan. Mara saw him stir in the mud to her side, but kept her eyes on Cady. Bedraggled, chest heaving, she stepped through the clearing, moving like one of Momo's cats through tall grasses.

"It wasn't my idea," Miles said evenly. His breath came fast, yet his voice was calm, as unconcerned as if Cady held a bouquet instead of a gun. Lucien's laughter became a cough.

Miles tossed the shotgun at Mara's feet, flipped a shell into the air and caught it easily as Cady approached. She hadn't seen him remove the round, hadn't heard the distinctive sound of metal on metal. He tossed it again, his booted feet planted firmly in the mud beneath him. Mud-covered and poised, the raw violence of an instant ago was gone as if it never existed. Yet Miles' eyes were still dark with some emotion Mara couldn't read, couldn't name.

"I had other thoughts," he said. "Your sister made the decision."

"She's a half-breed," Cady said with fierce cruelty. Mara's heart twisted painfully at the words. "She has no say in LeMay verdicts. I'm the one he . . ." She took a deep breath that wheezed in her lungs. "I'm the one he touched." Tears gathered at the corners of her eyes, liquid crystal that never fell. "He put his hands on *me*. *I* should decide. *I* should choose."

Miles stood straight, his eyes on Cady's hands, waiting. The stench of putrefying flesh blew into the clearing. Somewhere close a fish jumped, splashed down again. The hawk she had heard eons ago called again, far off.

"Put down the gun, Cady," Miles said. There was steel in his tone. Gentleness also. "Put it down," he repeated softly. "If you don't, Enoch will be forced to shoot you in the leg, and the thought pains him."

Cady wavered, her eyes on Miles. A breeze tugged at her dress, exposing her shoulders, soft rounded flesh shuddering. Lips trembling she said, "Enoch?"

"I'll try to put the shot in your calf, me sha, but I can't promise to miss bone from here," he said, his voice matter-of-fact. "And I hate like hell to shoot kin, but I can't allow you to kill an Eldest. Momo'd skin me alive."

"But Kenno . . . touched me." The words quavered, rustled with her breathing like leaves in the wind.

"We'll deal with Kenno, me sha. Kenno's a LeMay problem. A LeMay responsibility. And your *sister*," he said with quiet emphasis, "was right about an Eldest killing Kenno. Not a good idea, no matter how personally appealing. Now put down your gun."

The moment stretched out, no one moving, no sound on the island but the hot wind in the trees and the call of the far-off hawk, Cady's wheezing and Lucien's tortured breathing. Slowly Cady's arms dropped, lowering the weapon by degrees until it pointed to the ground between her feet. Enoch stepped around and took the Colt from her limp hands. Her tears pooled in rainbows, bright against the sky blue of her eyes. She dropped her head. Red hair tumbled thick and curling over her face.

Like a dancer moving quickly across a stage, Miles moved to Lucien and fell to his knees in the mud. In a single motion he gripped Lucien's shirt and jerked, tearing the fabric, popping the buttons. Blood and flesh appeared. Mara pulled in a breath.

"I know you want me, Miles," Lucien whispered, his voice almost gone, "but have a care for my clothes. 'Wasted passion don't put potatoes in de pot', to quote Momo."

"You've yet to meet my sister, then," Miles said roughly as he folded over the bloody shirt and pressed it over the wound. "She'd disagree. Besides, you can always steal another shirt."

Lucien chuckled weakly, the sound unlike his usual boisterous laugh. Sickly sounding, softly sucking. Beside Mara, Cady's wheezing worsened. Her asthma had once been brought on by emotionally charged situations, and this one was no exception. Mara had to get her sister away from this place. From the sight of blood and Lucien's distress.

"James has gone for the first-aid kit in the chopper," Enoch said from the side of the clearing. "But this'll help." Loping back, he handed Miles a blue plastic box, a faded red cross on the lid. "Not much left inside but gauze."

"Just what we need," Miles said, smiling. But Mara could read the fear beneath the words. Her brother was dying. He needed help fast.

"Keys are still in the airboat Kenno was using." Cady said. "We can haul him to the chopper in that."

"Good." Miles ripped open the paper packages and pressed yellowed gauze pads to Lucien's chest. Blood welled redly through the cloth. "One round," he said, "just below the ribs, right side. Could have caught the liver, gallbladder, pancreas or bowel. And if the angle is right, the kidney."

Ignoring Lucien's groan, Miles rolled him over and checked his back. "We have an exit wound between two ribs, same side. Which could be good, except it's a little high for my comfort level," he continued, his voice cool and conversational as he wrapped a roll of gauze around Lucien's chest. "Let's get him to the boat, Enoch."

"You act like you know what you're doing," Enoch said, as he holstered his weapon.

"I took an Emergency Medical course a few years back. After I saw my brothers die in a swamp, I thought it might be a good thing to know a little bit more about keeping people alive."

"*After* they died, huh? Good timing, seems like."

Miles' hands stilled on Lucien's chest. "Meaning?"

"Their dying made you Eldest."

Slowly he looked up and met Enoch's eyes. His face gave nothing away, but Enoch flinched and stepped back a half-step before he could stop himself. The potential for violence boiled in the air between them, a turbulence building in the depths of the Eldest's black eyes, a hurricane at midnight. "Have a care what you say, Enoch," he said, his voice so soft it seemed to die on the air and fall at their feet. "Have a care."

Enoch, his hand on the butt of his gun, blinked, and took another step back. He shook his head as if in denial. Confusion paled his blue eyes.

"Help me lift Lucien and position him in Kenno's airboat. Then get Rosemon. We don't have much time. Lucien's loosing blood into his lungs."

"Yes sir," Enoch said, his words thick and slow.

"Mara, take your sister and get back to Momo."

"I won't ride with her," Cady said, her voice sulky.

"Fine. Stay here then," Miles said as he and Enoch lifted Lucien to a sitting position, ignoring his gasps and groans. On crossed arms, they carried him to the airboat. Unexpectedly, Rosemon followed on her own, skirts dragging through the mud.

Moments later, Cady and Mara were alone, the roar of Kenno's airboat receding from shore.

Chapter Eighteen
Blood Relation

Mara stared at Cady as the sound of the airboat faded in the distance. Quiet settled in the clearing, uneasy and edgy, like the quiet of one of Momo's cats before it pounced on prey. Cady stood unmoving, slimed in dark mud, her feet buried in the stuff. Patches of pale skin were visible through the muck. Her eyes blazed, vibrant and hostile, below a caked mop of hair. She stared away, to the place where Kenno had sat. Where she had lain at his feet. With the others gone, her breathing was growing easier. Calmer.

"Do you want to help the bear?" It wasn't what Mara had intended to say; the words simply fell from her mouth of their own volition.

"What?" Her sister—half-sister as Cady had so callously pointed out—turned blue eyes on her. Mara flinched from the naked emotion there. A stark, raw bitterness.

Mara licked her lips, tasting blood and the grittiness of drying mud. She had started this way, perhaps she should finish this way. "There's a baby bear, a bear cub, in a tree, its mother's dead. I thought you might want to help it."

"I wouldn't know about a bear. The only thing I've seen of this island is the mud beneath Kenno's feet, and your back."

Mara said nothing to that, just watched Cady's face, knowing what the young girl wanted to say, what she had to say eventually. And knowing that she, Mara, had to stand and take it, had to listen, and then try to make her sister understand. Moments passed. The normal rustlings of plant life and susurration of water returned to the bayou. A twig fell. A buzzard soared overhead.

Cady's eyes narrowed. Slowly she sucked in a breath. "You let him go. Why?"

"Murder and revenge aren't the same thing as justice." That was what Mara had intended to say originally. That was the meaning and the reality that Cady had to see. Words Momo had said countless times over the years as she settled a dispute between LeMays or between LeMays and outsiders. Murder and 'venge don't be same as justice.

Cady blinked, absorbing the words. Perhaps hearing Momo's voice in her memory as well.

"If Miles killed Kenno in a rage, or cold blood, to protect his position as Eldest, the DeLandes in New Orleans would—"

"Vacherie. They live in Vacherie, not New Orleans," she said. She was always doing that, interrupting to correct or clarify a point. Lucien always laughed at her ploy, telling her she was cute.

Mara shrugged, annoyed by the little habit. "Near enough. They'd know what he had done. Eventually they'd pick it up or they'd hear something and they'd know he killed a DeLande who claimed to be Eldest."

"And so what? What would they do? Turn him in? No. Not the DeLandes. Never one of their own kind. DeLandes are above the law."

"No. They wouldn't turn him in. But they'd change in some way I can't explain to you." Mara stopped, unsure what to say. Her mouth was dry and she swallowed past the parched tissue. "Miles is trying to . . . to change them. To bring some good out of what they are. He's trying to . . . stop the forced inbreeding. Stop the evil things they do to one another and to their children," she said, knowing the conclusions she had about Miles fell more in the area of intuition and guesswork gleaned from a dream about green stone than in fact and specifics and proven truth.

There had been a moment when she looked at him, into the black wells of his eyes, that she sensed something dark, coiled, and deadly. A serpent, patiently awaiting prey? Mara shook away the thought.

"Good guy, is he? Wears a white hat and a silver six-shooter? That why he was groping you in that mud hole while Lucien was getting shot?"

Mara's face flamed. "Do you want to help the bear cub or not?" she asked, ignoring the fact that now she was using Cady's tactic. Changing the subject away from the conflict.

Cady's face twisted, huge tears pooling in the sky of her eyes. Mara plodded the few steps to her and stopped. Put out a hand and touched her face gently. A large bruise marred her chin. Dime sized bruises placed like fingertips peeked through the torn fabric of her blouse, darkened her shoulders where Kenno had shaken her.

"Oh, Cady," she whispered. Moving slowly, Mara pulled her close and cradled her against a shoulder as she had for so many years. Years when Cady had been both sister and child, and Rosemon lay uncaring in some private hell.

Cady shuddered once and fell against Mara, all gangly adolescent bones and bruised flesh and mud. She sobbed, her face pressed into the hollow beneath Mara's collarbone, her arms tight with desperation. Disregarding the pain of her own bruises, Mara returned the embrace. The place where the shotgun had struck when Miles knocked her away from Kenno's bullet, and the bruises from her fall in the airboat, she ignored.

"He . . . he touched me," Cady whispered. "He touched me."

In that moment Mara understood that it was more than just the touch of Kenno's hands that had bruised and terrified Cady. It was the touch of his mind. The things he had *thought* at her. She tightened her arms around Cady, holding the terrified girl close and still. Kenno had bludgeoned her with images, some which Mara caught faintly, as they stood, skin-to-skin. Images of a man or men with a woman. With a young girl. Cady sobbed harder and Mara held her fiercely, letting her sister cry out both fear and fury, absorbing both, letting Cady batter a familiar spirit with her horror.

It was this that Mara hated about the gift that had been bequeathed to her through her blood. Through her heritage. This evil thing Kenno had done.

Contrary to all of Momo's strictest interdictions, he had used the DeLande gift as a weapon. Used it to injure and frighten. Used it in the DeLande manner, as a weapon of power and dominance. Heedless of bruises, the sisters clutched one another.

Suddenly Mara remembered the day Kenno had attacked

116

Rosemon. The look of shock on her face. The blank terror. Kenno had been assaulting her with his mind as well as his body. Mara understood that now. He had been misusing the gift of his DeLande heritage. Abusing it. And he had been furious when he'd looked at Mara, turned his mind against her, and she had not reacted. Too young, she supposed. Her own gift undeveloped.

For a moment, Mara wondered why she hadn't responded to his assault today, in the clearing, when he'd taunted her with his words. Why she hadn't caught some taint from his mind. And then that thought melted away as Cady's misery called to her.

Mara stroked her hair, pulling out leaves, a small twig, smoothing away mud which caked in the heat even as she touched it. And she tried to draw off some of Cady's anguish, wishing she could take it all away and carry it herself. Wishing she had picked up a gun and shot Kenno. Wishing his bullet torn body lay at Cady's feet, his blood soaking into the wet ground. After long minutes, Cady quieted, sniffed and pulled away slightly.

"I'm supposed to be mad at you," she said. In the distance, a shotgun boomed. Cady jerked.

"It's okay. They have to hole the boat so Kenno can't use it again," Mara said. This wasn't some DeLande knowledge she spoke, just bayou wisdom. It was the way one man controlled another in this wet world. Hole his boat, or steal it if you had the time and the means, and he had to wait until someone found him, or risk a dangerous swim in predator infested waters.

Cady relaxed. Lifting red-rimmed eyes, she wiped her nose on the back of her wrist. "We look like mud wrestlers."

"I tossed a few things in my bag. We may not get entirely clean, but we can take a bayou spit bath and be more comfortable."

"You were running away, weren't you?"

"Yes," Mara said, not ashamed, though maybe she should be.

"Are you going to kill Kenno?"

The question shook Mara. *She had shot four men and felt nothing.* "Someone will. But it won't be Miles. The Eldest *can't* kill him. The repercussions would be more than the LeMays would want to consider."

"If Kenno gets back to Vacherie and becomes Eldest, we won't exactly be well off. He intends to bring us to the DeLande Estate and make us part of them. He thinks he can breed up something different if he uses us indiscriminately. Something the DeLandes haven't seen in a while."

Mara stepped away, letting her arms fall to her sides. "Us as in you and me or us meaning all the LeMays?"

"The LeMays. All of us."

"He'd have to kill Momo first."

"That was the idea," Cady said.

Mara bent and picked up a handgun from the mud. It was so caked that she couldn't identify the make. There was a rifle in the depression left by Lucien's body. Mud and blood and a thin eddy of water. She lifted the rifle and surveyed the clearing for other weapons. "Let's go get cleaned up."

"That's all you got to say?"

Mara looked at Cady and swallowed hard. "I'll kill Kenno with my bare hands before I let him touch another one of us. That what you wanted to hear?"

Cady nodded slowly and Mara wondered what the young girl picked up from her mind as they studied one another. Cady's eyes softened. "Yeah. Well. You didn't happen to bring shampoo did you?"

"I have shampoo."

"Good. And Mara? I'm sorry I said you weren't one of us. You're blood. I was mad and when I'm mad sometimes stuff comes out of my mouth that I don't mean."

"You wanted to hurt me. You succeeded."

Cady looked away. "You wanted to save me. You succeeded. Thank you."

"You're welcome."

"We can check on your bear cub on the way out." Cady said, a smile pulling at her mouth.

The cub was too wild and too mature to be held on a lap, too large for the airboat, older than he first appeared. The two girls left him to fend for himself and placed the muddy weapons in the bottom of *Jenny*. Moving quickly, they started the little airboat and turned with the current, heading downstream.

Mara handled the rudder stick, her shotgun on her lap, her body strapped into the pilot's chair. Cady sat in the bow of the boat, cushioned on a life preserver with Lucien's rifle in her hands. They roared downstream, scanning the bayou water and the banks for sight of Kenno.

Only when they were a mile or so from Running Man Tree and felt safe, did they begin to search for a shallow cove to clean up in. Some place where the water flowed quickly enough to keep scum from forming, and slowly enough to allow them to see bottom and approaching predators.

Kenno, they no longer feared. Bleeding, he wouldn't swim long. Not with gators in the bayou. He'd have to hole up and make new plans

The sisters finally found a shallow basin with a sandy bottom, the water so clear they could see the base bubble as a spring-head percolated up. A cooter sunned himself on a stump near the bank, but there were no alligators waiting, nostrils in the air, no snakes draped across branches lazing the day away, and no tall water grass for them to hide in. While Mara kept watch, Cady stripped to the skin, rinsed her clothes over the side, and then slid into the water. The pool was deeper than it looked from the surface, a full three feet of safe water to swim in, and Cady took advantage of the opportunity, washing her hair and scrubbing dried mud from her skin.

Bayou water wasn't always safe for swimming. Every year, one or two reports of snakebite or gator attack came over the maritime radio, as some Badlands dweller was surprised in formerly safe water. Devora, their elder sister, had been part of one year's statistics, her left leg and right arm deeply scarred by a young gator's sharp teeth. The three-footer, eyes bigger than its stomach, snapped, trying to pull her under as she waded near shore and Mara watched, stunned, only feet away from the thrashing beast.

Rosemon had shot the reptile, emptied her gun into its body, one of the few times she had ever used her .38, and saved Devora.

Lucien had a pair of boots made for Devora from the gator's hide, a belt from the paler skin along the gator's underbelly, and a necklace from the teeth. The two largest teeth were studded with fiery garnets. The necklace was a project that kept his mind occupied as Devora suffered.

It took her a year to recuperate fully, and she nearly lost her leg to infection. It was eight months before it was healed enough to put on the custom-made boots. The scars made her siblings wary of the water.

Devora had never been the same after the attack. Always frail and sickly and far too meek, she withdrew even more, became submissive and passive, uninterested in the things she had once loved and could no longer do with ease. Running, skipping, jumping, fishing, writing poetry with the delicate, spidery longhand she had developed. She had to learn to walk again, to write again. But now she limped, the bad knee stiff, often painful, and her writing was crabbed and halting, her shorthand the only writing her sisters could read well. She had become compliant and unresisting, indifferent to her studies except where nursing and physical therapy, herbs and anatomy, were concerned.

Devora had married young into the Mickle Clan and moved to Mickle Toes over on Chope bayou. And unlike her sisters, wouldn't last an hour in bayou country unprotected. And she would *never* bathe in the bayou, no matter how dirty she was.

After Cady finished with her bayou bath, Mara washed up and they both dressed from the supplies in the duffel bag before heading home.

Chapter Nineteen

Sikorsky

Moving swiftly, Miles stowed the weapons and unfolded two blankets. They were tightly woven Olefin, fire retardant, never used, still showing the creases of the original packaging. Shaking one out, he passed it down to the Welch brothers who supported Lucien in the bow of the airboat.

It was a tricky maneuver to pass the injured man up, over the side of the boat, inside the Sikorsky and into a secure position between the front and middle seats. Grunting, they accomplished it by brute force, and wrapped Lucien in both blankets. He was pasty white, his fingertips the gray-blue of a dead man. Miles checked his pulse at his wrist and again in his carotid. Thready and weak at 100. It didn't look good.

Below him, James and Enoch helped Rosemon into the helicopter, strapped her into the front passenger seat and cast off. They were well disciplined and again Miles wondered who had trained and polished the paramilitary precision with which they worked—so smooth each movement appeared rehearsed.

Without words one pushed the airboat into the current of Bayou Sang while the other lifted a shotgun and holed the boat. Before Miles could power up, it had sunk below the surface of the bloody red water and disappeared, leaving a few beer cans and an oily sheen on the surface.

Miles flipped switches, ran a practiced eye over the gauges and dials, and checked his coordinates. "Enoch. Where the hell are we? Still in Texas or in Louisiana?"

"Don't rightly know. You thinking about hospitals?"

"Yeah," Miles said.

"We're within spittin' distance of Starks, which is right on the border. Could be closer to Beaumont than Lake Charles, but I don't think so."

Miles checked his fuel level and the mental map he had of the area. It was going to be close for either hospital.

"Lake Charles control, this is November 11962. Over." Speaking and flipping switches at the same time, Miles powered up and lifted off, leaving the bloody waters of Sang Bayou dripping from his pontoons.

"N11962, Lake Charles. Go ahead."

"Lake Charles, N11962 is an east-bound S-76, thirty miles west of Lake Charles, squawking twelve-hundred, at twenty-five-hundred. We're transporting a gun shot victim. Request clearance and vector to nearest trauma center. Over."

Beside him, Rosemon clawed at the straps holding her in, her fingers working at the clasp. Miles checked the wind speed and direction by the movement of the cypress ripping below him.

He angled his head, trying to get a clear look at Lucien and keep an eye out on the struggling Rosemon at his side. Smart flying meant giving the helicopter his undivided attention. He wasn't flying smart and didn't think he'd be able to. He only hoped he wouldn't have to restrain Rosemon if she panicked and tried to jump from the helo. Miles had never lost a passenger, and didn't want to start today.

She unhooked the belts strapped around her and tossed them aside. Miles grabbed her arm and held her. For an instant she met his eyes, her own tortured, fear-ridden.

Below the fear, something else stirred in the smoky depths of her gray-blue eyes. A faint hint of determination. It was that determination that caused Miles to drop his hold on her arm. Her lips curled slightly. Turning, Rosemon slipped back to Lucien, wedged on the floor.

"Nearest trauma center would be Saint Patrick's or Lake Charles Memorial Hospital in Lake Charles. Do you copy?"

"Give me GPS of Saint Pat's, Lake Charles control. And the phone number direct to the emergency room," he said, reaching for the abandoned clip-chart at his side.

The tower complied, Miles writing down the numbers as he flew.

"Weather over Lake Charles is clear, wind two-seven-zero at fifteen," the dispatcher said, telling Miles the wind was at 15 knots out of the west. "Lake Charles would appreciate word from you when you reach Saint Pat's."

"Will do. Thanks, Lake Charles, you've been great," he said into his mic.

"Pleasure's mine, 11962. How 'bout letting us know how your patient fares."

"Will do. November 11962 out." Miles clicked off, ending transmission with Lake Charles tower, and dialed in to the hospital's emergency room. As he worked, he positioned a mirror and watched Rosemon with her son.

She had squeezed across Lucien and turned to kneel, facing the front of the helicopter. Her lithe body was crushed between the side door and the bench at Lucien's head. Like a petty dictator, she pulled the Welch brothers out of the middle seats and pushed them to one side of the cramped confines as she removed the Olefin blankets. Directing Enoch and James by commands and hand signals, she had each man take one of Lucien's legs and prepare to lift. As they got into position, Rosemon opened the fully stocked bar and pulled out a bottle of vodka.

She looked at home in the helicopter, as if she'd flown in it before. *Rosemon was Andreu's woman. The woman of an Eldest,* he remembered. Her previous presence in the Sikorsky was a given. Andreu would have come to her in the helo, and together they would have traveled wherever they wished.

Rosemon broke the seal on the bottle and poured the spirits out over her hands, washing mud and filth and imported liquor into the carpet. She scrubbed her hands, working the vodka under her nails.

Leaning over the arms of the seats, she ripped Lucien's makeshift bandage loose, and poured the vodka into the bleeding hole in his side. And plunged two fingers into the wound.

Her face was a mask, devoid of all emotion but the determination he had seen as she moved from her chair to her son. Rosemon twisted her hand as if searching for the source of the bleeding that was stealing Lucien's life. Coated to the wrist with crimson, she ignored Lucien's cries of pain as he struggled against her hand, cries Miles could hear even over the engine sound and his head phones.

Rosemon paused, and smiled. It was a peculiar smile. Serene, almost. She closed her eyes, lips moving in words Miles couldn't hear.

Blood pumped up out of the wound in Lucien's side, thick red gouts of it. And then it slowed. Pumped a final time. And stopped.

Miles watched, his eyes moving from the skyline to his gauges to the scene behind him. The wind buffeted the craft, the gusts far greater at his current altitude than at ground level. He compensated, his eyes on Rosemon's face.

She was a healer. Rosemon was a DeLande traiteur. Miles had never seen one at work before. Never watched the melding of hands, mind, gift, and purpose that could work miracles. He shook his head. Healers—*traiteurs*—were rare even among the DeLandes, a talent and gift that required total empathy and immense power. Hers was the mind that had cried out to his, grasping with a brittle and powerful and wounded spirit. She had seen him as he searched for the DeLandes from the Bell Jet Ranger. And she had been Andreu's woman . . .

Suddenly Miles realized that Rosemon had been in contact with Andreu's mind the night he died. He didn't know how he knew, only that it was fact. Rosemon had experienced the bite of the water moccasin as it attacked Andreu's throat. She had known the agony, the awful burning pain of acid-like snake venom, the fear as suffocation commenced and the tissues of his brother's breathing passages swelled shut. And the death throes. Just as Andreu had experienced death, Rosemon had. And lived beyond it.

Miles had watched his elder brother die. Helpless, miles from any assistance, in the depths of a bayou backwater, he had stood by and watched him suffer and die, his spirit blinking out slowly. He had closed off his own mind from Andreu's pain. Watched as Richard, his other brother, did the same, leaving Andreu to die alone and without solace. But Rosemon had been there, pinned by the strength of Andreu's mind and her own empathy. And it had broken her.

With her free hand, she directed the Welch brothers to lift

Lucien's legs and milk the blood down into his torso, their hands pressing and sliding down the long length of calf and thigh from foot to groin. She made a fist, indicating that each man should make one, and press it into Lucien's groin area over the major artery that feeds each leg, preventing blood from returning to the extremities. Enoch and Lucien complied, positioning and re-positioning until Rosemon was satisfied that the blood flow had been slowed.

Miles grinned and accelerated the Sikorsky to full power. Rosemon had blocked the bleeder and fashioned makeshift compression trousers. Her actions might—just might—keep Lucien alive to St. Pat's.

Below, swamp and bayou and islands of higher ground swept past. Highways and secondary roads with their plodding automobiles and slow moving cycles. The Sikorsky roared and rocketed forward at full power. With the wind at thier tail, the big bird could do a bit better than 150 miles per hour. They would be in Lake Charles in just minutes.

"Saint Patrick's, Emergency, Burgess speaking."

"Burgess, I need to speak with your doctor on duty. I am a Sikorsky helicopter en-route with a GSW, ETA ten minutes. Do you read?" Miles said into his mic.

"Hold on. Doc, we got an inbound with a gun shot, can you take it?" Miles heard Burgess ask. A moment later a different voice came on line.

"This is Dr. Thibodeaux. Understand you are inbound with a gunshot victim. Are there any trained medical personnel aboard your craft?"

"Affirmative. I'm an EMT, but I'm flying this thing in. No EMS equipment aboard. Repeat, no EMS equipment aboard." Miles watched as, with her free hand, Rosemon counted out Lucien's pulse. Her eyes were closed, lips moving quickly, her fingers at his carotid. Reading her lips, Miles compared the count to the second hand on his watch.

"We copy that. Can you give us a report?"

"Affirmative. Victim is a twenty-two year old white male with a single gunshot wound to the upper right quadrant, forty-five caliber weapon fired at approximately fifteen feet. Entrance wound is just below the bottom rib. We have an exit wound same side, approximately two inches from the spine, between the last two ribs. Pulse is approximately one hundred and steady. Patient has lost a great deal of blood and appears to be in shock. Patient is in makeshift compression trousers. Copy?"

"We copy, but say again. Makeshift what?"

Miles glanced behind him again. "Patient is in makeshift compression trousers, like a MAST effect," he said, meaning the anti-shock trousers developed by the US military. As best he could, Miles described the position of Lucien's legs and the Welch brothers' fists. "Patient's mother has placed her fingers into the wound and appears to have blocked off the artery. Copy all that?"

"Copy. Unbelievable. We're on the west side of the city with a helicopter pad on the roof marked with a great big blue H inside a red triangle. Landing lights are on. What's your ETA again?"

"Estimated time of arrival is five to eight minutes. Lake Charles in sight."

"We'll be waiting. Saint Patrick's clear."

Miles clicked off, watching Rosemon in the mirror at his head. She was still counting Lucien's pulse, her face serene as a painted saint's in some dusty cathedral. Her lips moved erratically now, as Lucien's heart reacted to the stress and blood loss. It was well over a hundred, by the movement of Rosemon's lips, and Miles knew that had she not been with her son, Lucien would probably already be dead.

Ahead, chemical plants with burning towers of bright yellow flame gave way to the white-capped surface of Lake Charles, the water dazzling in the light of the setting sun behind him. The city named after the lake sparkled just beyond, as he descended. Neon-lit riverboat casinos rested at anchor in the muddy brown water near shore. The light was changing as he flew, going from bright afternoon glare to the softer sheen of early dusk. Miles hoped he could spot the hospital quickly. Hoped he could set the big Sikorsky down in the blustery wind.

He glanced again at Rosemon. The doctor was right. His brother's woman was unbelievable. Correcting for wind shift, Miles did his part and flew with all the skill at his disposal. If Lucien died, it wouldn't be for lack of speed.

The hospital roof and its well marked landing pad were visible as he slowed the helicopter's forward momentum, a great blue H on the flat top of St. Pat's. Miles checked his wind conditions and decided on an easterly approach pattern, directly into the wind. It was gusting now, strong drafts buffeting the helo. The landing would be tricky. Approach and touchdown weren't helped by the presence of huge metal housings on the north side of the deck, possibly the heating and air conditioning units that serviced the hospital.

On the west side was a roofed structure with open double doors. A mass of people and a stretcher sheltered within the doors—the trauma crew and support team waiting.

Carefully, as gently as his sensitive hands could, Miles maneuvered the big craft toward the deck, raising the nose, slowing the rate of descent. An updraft caught him; he compensated. The Sikorsky rocked, a sickening motion Miles felt in the pit of this stomach as the rotors dipped toward the half wall.

Delicately, he eased over the wall surrounding the landing pad, the blue H within its red triangle only feet below him. With a last smooth touch, he positioned the helicopter and set her down. Instantly powering down to idle, he cut power to the huge rotors and began cooling off the engines. The rotors still turned, but the people standing beyond the double doors didn't wait.

Green, white, and plum clad hospital personnel streamed from the building as James Welch leaned over and opened the side hatch. Miles ripped off his head gear and the straps that held him in the cockpit. Opening his door, he watched from the pilot's seat as the Sikorsky cooled down from its frantic flight and he was finally able to shut down the roaring engines.

Around him, the hum of the helicopter went silent, a silence suddenly filled by the clamor of human voices. While the doctor on the radio had been a man, the one that met them was a woman dressed in scrubs overlaid with a long-sleeved paper apron. A plastic face shield dangled around her neck. Gruff as any general, she directed the removal of Lucien's body to the stretcher, keeping his legs in the air, pressure on his femoral arteries, and Rosemon's hand buried in his torso. Working around Rosemon, the doctor ordered Lucien strapped into an actual set of military anti-shock trousers, his legs Velcroed into place and the thick lining of the pants inflated to prevent Lucien's desperately depleted blood flow from returning to his legs.

To either side, others worked at finding veins for IVs in his gray-skinned arms. The babble of voices was frenzied and hurried, yet beneath the seeming confusion, was an order born of long practice.

"Got one," someone yelled. "Blood's going, opened wide. RL ready for next site."

"No luck over here. Ouch. That's my foot."

"Sorry. Watch out. Dirty needle. Thanks."

"MAST trouser completely inflated, Doctor Kinsey."

"Great. I need that other line. I'll take a jugular if you can find one. It'll be faster than putting in a line." Dr. Kinsey stepped to the head of the stretcher and checked Lucien's pupils with a penlight. Her lips pursed and fine frown wrinkles surrounded her eyes as she worked. With her stethoscope, she listened to Lucien's breathing and her frown increased. Dr. Kinsey didn't like what she heard.

"Okay, lady," she said, snapping the ear pieces from her ears and turning to Rosemon, "You're his mother, right? I'm going to slip my fingers into the wound and you're going to remove yours. Ready?"

"No."

"No?" The doctor stopped, her hand poised over Lucien's wound. Around her, activity slowed and it was obvious that the medical staff were preparing to deal with a difficult family member. Miles grinned again and ran his fingers through his hair. The wind billowed around the crew assembled on the upper level of the deck.

"Look, lady, you probably saved his life out there, but now he's where we can help him. He's going to die if—"

"The artery is clotted over," Rosemon interrupted, "just behind where my fingers have it pinched off. If I move, the clot will break free." Her hair whipped in the wind, a blond mass of tendrils caked with dried mud. Her eyes bored into the doctor's, intense and unyielding. "I can't guarantee you can find it and tack it shut before he bleeds to death. It looks like I'll be going to surgery with you, doctor."

"Lady, you don't know what you're doing. I don't want to call security—"

"No, you look," Rosemon said, gray eyes like twin torches. "I do know. I'm the only thing keeping my son alive and I'm not moving until you have his belly open and a set of clamps ready. I'm doing my job. I suggest you do yours."

The doctor's eyes sparked with anger, but before she could speak, Miles laughed, attracting her attention. He held her gaze with his own and smiled. When he spoke, his tone was almost cajoling, deliberately soothing. "She has a point, Doc. Wrap her in one of those paper aprons and haul her in with you. What's it gonna hurt? Break a few rules to keep a patient alive.

"It's not like you haven't always wanted to break a few rules around here," he added, reading the set of her mouth, the perpetual dissatisfaction in her eyes. A rebel in green scrubs. "Now's your chance. Besides, if she's right, you save a life and a lawsuit here today."

The trauma team waited to hear the doctor's reply, a watchful stillness in the windy air. The nurse who had complained about her foot being stepped on grabbed an IV line and thumbed a valve open. She had successfully started a line in Lucien's neck. But she didn't speak, just watched Dr. Kinsey's face.

The doctor's eyes moved from Miles to Rosemon and back again. Finally, she said, "Okay, guys, let's go. I want six units typed and matched with two more units O-neg waiting in surgery when we get there. Blood gasses, H and H, a seven, all STAT, and a cath UA. We need to see if his kidneys are compromised.

"Good going on the IVs. Let's get him intubated." She turned back to Rosemon. "You pass out in surgery, don't expect one of us to move you to the side. I'll walk all over you till I'm done. Understand?"

Rosemon nodded and smiled, her shoulders visibly relaxing.

"Let's move. Lady, you keep up with us." Dr. Kinsey's voice faded as the trauma crew wheeled Lucien into the elevator on the other side of the double doors and prepared to descend into the hospital.

Just as the doors shut, Rosemon looked up and smiled again, her gaze directed at Miles. Her lips moved silently. The unspoken words shocked him to his soul.

He leaned against the fuselage of the Sikorsky for balance and stared at the seam between the doors where Rosemon had vanished. The roof beneath his feet seemed to sway and buckle. The wind tore the air from his lungs, leaving him strangely weak.

She knew. How . . .

Andreu. Andreu must have told her. Only the DeLandes knew the name he had called himself as a child. Personal. Secret. His covert ambition when he was growing up in that awful place, back when there were several brothers and their offspring between him and the position of Eldest. The name that marked his private ambition still.

Three words. "Thank you, Peacemaker."

James chuckled, breaking the spell Rosemon's words had woven. Laughter bouncing off the metal housing into the wind, he said, "That's one tough woman. I wouldn't want to piss her off."

Privately, Miles agreed, taking a deep breath and centering himself.

"I remember her before her man died. A ball of fire. Sexy as hell and—"

"We still have problems, boys," Miles said, cutting in, uninterested in hearing of Rosemon's passions and the effect she'd had on young men growing up around her. He knew about DeLande women and how they worked. He didn't need to hear it from these backwater boys. "Cops."

"What about 'em?" Enoch said. "Cops never give me no trouble, Eldest."

"Well, this time's different. We aren't in the Badlands where you can just disappear. Lucien's going to be in this hospital for some time, even if Rosemon has worked a miracle or two with her hand rammed down in his gut. Cops aren't going to like us bringing in a gunshot victim, and unhappy cops want answers."

Enoch shrugged again and levered himself up into the Sikorsky. With his butt resting in mud and gore and vodka, and his feet dangling, he fished a crumpled pack of Marlboros out of his T-shirt pocket, passed one to James and lit his own from a battered Zippo lighter. He didn't offer a smoke to Miles, and Miles didn't consider it an oversight of manners. Enoch was DeLande enough to know Miles didn't smoke. He tossed the lighter to James and exhaled, eyes wily and intent on Miles'. A strange smile quirked at the corner of his lips.

"What you got in mind, Eldest?" James asked, cupping his hands around the Zippo's flame and inhaling. Smoke blew out from his nose, whipped away by the wind.

Miles fought a smile and a strange sense of relief at hearing the title. Both had called him Eldest, even after hearing Kenno's claims. Perhaps *because* of hearing Kenno's claims. "A simple story. Covers most of the bases. I'm a tourist. Wanted to do little sightseeing, a little fishing. You guys offered to guide me for a price and Rosemon came along for the ride. First time in a helicopter."

Miles pushed away from the fuselage where he had recoiled when Rosemon spoke the silent words to him. "You told me about *Blessure de la Terre* and I agreed to the trip." He stayed next to the helicopter, his body protected from the wind by the open pilot's door, spinning a tale. "When we set down in *Blessure de la Terre,* we startled two gator poachers. They shot first. We shot back, hitting one, and lifted off. Came straight here. What do you think?"

"Lame, Eldest. Totally lame." Enoch blew out a double stream of smoke from his nose. There was covert laughter in his eyes, now, and the smile was full, amused. "Cops'll laugh out their butts. But," the brothers exchanged a glance and James shrugged, "it covers all the bases. I reckon it'll do if we can get to Rosemon and Lucien before the cops do."

"You'll have to live a while in the Badlands before you can really lie," James said, inhaling deeply on the cigarette. His eyes were on the double doors where Lucien had disappeared, his voice the laconic and terse tone of a man who seldom spoke, but who had things on his mind right now.

"You should hear Old Banoit. That old coot can spin a tale, can't he, James? Maybe you could pay for lessons." Enoch laughed at his own little joke, liking the idea of an Eldest taking lessons at a Badlands dweller's knee.

Miles kept to himself how little extra time he wanted to spend in the Badlands. He had other plans for the rest of his life. Like living to a ripe old age in some sort of safety and comfort.

Meanwhile, he needed to win the loyalty of the Welch brothers. Or at least their compliance.

Climbing into the cockpit, head over his shoulder, "We have work to do, then. Let's get to Chenault Field and get the helicopter cleaned up and refueled. The cops can track us down there and take our statements." He slapped on the headphones and strapped himself in. The brothers ground out their cigarettes beneath their heels in mirror-like motions, climbed aboard and slammed shut the doors.

As Miles powered up, he glanced into the mirror still positioned to the back and said thoughtfully, "You boys ever stayed at a really nice hotel? Room service, a workout room, sauna, a fully stocked bar by the bed?"

James looked up and spoke above the whine of the engines. "HBO and Playboy?"

"Air conditioning and a heated pool?" Enoch added hopefully.

"Whatever you want. I'm paying."

"Eldest, you DeLandes sure do know how to have a good time," Enoch said. "I can't remember when we had such a interesting day." He pronounced it "in-ter-es-tin'" and smiled when he said it. "Throw in a couple loose women and we'll be happy men."

"I'll buy you new clothes, feed you and get you a room. You pick up your own women."

"Rental car?" James inserted into Enoch's bargaining, his voice slow and deliberate.

"A sporty one," Enoch said. "Each."

Miles groaned softly, hoping the sound was covered by the Sikorsky's roar as he lifted off. "You boys have a driver's license? Either of you?" he asked into his mic, as the brothers slipped the headphones on.

"I got one," James said after a long moment, as if he had to think carefully to recall the words and then force them down to his tongue. "Still got a few good points on it yet. I think."

"In that case, one car, a four door, no bells and whistles."

"Done," both men said.

"I've always wanted me a pair o' them Dockers. How 'bout you James?"

"Oh, one other problem," Miles said, grinning wolfishly in

challenge. "We're nearly out of fuel."

The brothers exchanged a look and then grinned back, finding Miles' eyes in the mirror. James reached down and twisted open the bottle of vodka left by Rosemon. Tilting back his head, he lifted the bottle to his lips and drank. A dozen long swallows and the level in the bottle went down considerably. He passed it to Enoch who finished it off. Without asking permission, they both lit up and blew gray smoke at him, their satisfied expressions seeming to say: If we're going to die young, it'll be drunk, with a couple of good smokes under our belts.

Miles didn't argue with their thinking. He hid his amusement and turned back to his controls and the low fuel gauge. He had enough to get where he wanted to go. He just hoped there was enough left to set her down slowly instead of at the speed of gravity.

He had found the key to the Welch brothers' hearts and loyalty—money. *One set of LeMays down. A couple of dozen more to go.*

He wondered what it would take to win over Mara. And wondered if he really wanted to try.

It was after dusk when the girls approached Momo's cabin, still bedraggled, only half clean and wearing mis-matched clothes. The cabin was dark but for a candle in a front window, its glow brightening the outline of the front door. Cady called out, "Hello the house," in proper bayou tradition as they beached *Jenny* and tied her down. And though they were anxious to hear about Lucien, they gathered up the gear and damp clothes and the guns which Cady had cleaned on the last leg of the ride back home. Together, through the falling dark, the sisters ran for the house.

Momo was waiting for them on the front deck, sitting in the dark in a rocker she had pulled through the door. Her face was emotionless. In her arms was a shotgun she couldn't have fired from the rocker. Beside her was a box full of mewling kittens and a lazy mother cat, gray-striped and watchful.

Cady placed a greasy bundle of newspaper in Momo's lap, and Mara added an open bottle of Co'Cola, one so cold a frost had formed on the outer glass. Cady hadn't eaten since breakfast, and so they had stopped for boudin balls at the Old Ferrar Place on the back leg of Elephant Bayou. Whole hog, rice and spices, crispy hot, fried in bacon drippings and served up with homemade pepper sauce and onion rings, it was a treat they hadn't been able to pass up. Even worried about Lucien, the ten-minute stop was one they'd deemed necessary. Bacon grease smeared fingers and coated their lips. The aftertaste of peppers still burned like the coals of an old fire.

Momo didn't speak, the planes of her face catching the light, hollows shadow-filled. She was *listening*, her lips slightly parted, skin slack, dark eyes half-lidded. She turned her head, seeming to focus, yet Mara knew Momo wasn't seeing them. Not really.

"Momo," Mara whispered. Carefully she settled at Momo's feet. It was a sign of the old woman's preoccupation that she didn't notice the blue jeans Mara wore, or that the sister's feet were bare and dirty. Momo was busy elsewhere.

Cady leaned over her and tore open the greasy paper on Momo's lap. A tendril of steam wafted up, carrying the scent of grease and pork and strong spices. Momo dropped her head, looked at the food on her lap, and sighed, a soft breathy sound, as if she hadn't exhaled in hours. And she breathed again, deeply, the wind whistling through her nostrils in a two note tone.

Settling beside Mara, Cady stroked the mother cat in her box and silently counted kittens, lifting them, mouthing the numbers. Over the bayou, the last traces of daylight tinted the horizon a dull plum with violet clouds. Bats chased mosquitoes. An alligator roared far off, its demand echoing across the water. On the bank across from the cabin, an egret settled for the night in a pile of driftwood, nesting. Temporary shelter. A stellar moon was rising through tree branches, close and huge and hazed by thin clouds.

Momo blinked. Focused on the cold Co'Cola and the cooling boudin balls. Slowly she shook her head as tears appeared and glistened in the hollows of her eyes then fell, dripping against the paper.

A shiver started between Mara's shoulder blades, traveling though her like fear. Like the need to fight or to run.

Without comment, without wiping the tears on her face, Momo lifted the bottle of Co'Cola and drank it down in a long series of gulps. She tossed a whole boudin ball in her mouth, chewed twice and swallowed. Only when she had eaten two more and half a dozen onion rings did she speak.

"*Vin, se' plait,*" she muttered in Cajun, her words slurred and soft as her breathing. Shoulders drooping, she slumped in her rocker, and Mara caught the shotgun before it hit the deck. Cady caught the empty bottle and ran for the cabin and the wine Momo needed, returning almost instantly with the bottle and three juice glasses which she handed to Mara.

Pouring Momo a glassful, Mara placed it in her hands. They were cold, even in the heat that made the girls' skin prickle with sweat. Gently Mara wrapped Momo's fingers around the glass and helped to lift it to cracked and wrinkled lips. Momo sipped once before draining the glass. Mara filled it again and this time, Momo's fingers gripped the glass with a life of their own. Mara added a swirl of wine to each of the other glasses, her own hands shaking.

What had she seen?

Cady took her glass, frowned at the meager measure and drank it down with Momo's abandon. Mara sipped at hers, throat closed in fear. All she could see was Lucien's blood swirling in the muddy water where he had lain.

Momo licked a drop of wine from her lip and said, "Lucien, he nearly die, two hour pass, him on table strap down, tube in he lung. Rosemon keep alive, him, her hand in he belly." Momo bent down and lifted the mother cat to her lap, as if she wanted the heat and the mellow purr against her hands. The cat licked at a knuckle and snuggled down in the folds of Momo's skirts, her nose shoving at the greasy paper. "Rosemon help him. Heal he kidney. Doctor . . . not understand."

Cady snuggled a kitten in her lap and stroked the small form, appearing engrossed in the shape of feet, the texture of softer-than-soft kitten fur, but really waiting with Mara for Momo's verdict. It was her decree, made generations ago, that no LeMay would allow an outsider to know just what talents a LeMay had. It was family business. Sometimes Badlands business. But never the business of outsiders, their LeMay gifts. That was the code. Like never to hit. Never to touch within bloodlines, brother to sister or parent to child. It was the only thing that passed for law here—Momo's edicts, Momo's rulings that kept the DeLande curse at bay.

"Him back now. Heart beat, lungs breathe. Blood in he veins. And Rosemon actin' like she don' know how Lucien kidney got scar on it and how he blood vessel got seal off. She actin' good. Rosemon be back now from dark, gray place, place with de shadows, where she been so long. I rule it good, what she done and Lucien alive. I rule it good."

Momo drank her wine, more slowly now. And Mara sipped her own, feeling the awful tension slip from her with each swallow. Knowing this awful day was almost over.

"You in jean, Mara. Go get clean, both you. Turn generator on and wash hair, wash you dress. Bed for you. Eldest's men done gone, all but one. Dey take Lucien new boat back through the bayou to airport. De one man lef' be with Albert and Alain. They watching bayou upstream and down so we sleep like lamb, be safe. Mara. No jean. I rule."

Mara stood and finished her minuscule amount of wine. "Yes, Momo. You coming inside?"

"Soon. Soon," Momo said, nodding and beginning to rock. The treads rubbed across the rough boards in a steady rhythm, deep and slow. "I watch sky for omen and porten', call out to Jesus, he good *maman*, and God. I come to bed soon."

Cady and Mara went into the silent cabin, blew out the candle and started the generator, driving back the night and the shadows that lurked in the corners, waiting for the unwary.

Chapter Twenty
Saint Patrick's

Miles walked the plum colored hallway, boot soles squeaking softly on the waxed floor. Behind him was the nurse's station outside of ICU, ahead of him was the waiting room and Rosemon. Florescent lights cast a sickly white glow on the floors and the second-rate artwork hanging on the walls, making the colors appear washed out and dull. Or maybe it was third-rate art. In some circles Miles was considered a bit of an art snob.

In his private suite on the DeLande Estate there were two un-catalogued masterpieces by Matisse, three early Picassos, as well as half a dozen of Bonnibelle Sarvaunt's sensual works. All were gifts from the artists, some which had been in his family for decades.

Miles hadn't spent a great deal of time in hospitals, but already he didn't care for the ambiance, the stink of body wastes and deodorizers, the decor which somehow just missed being either cheery or restorative, the harried expressions on the faces of the staff. Somehow there was an air of both desperation and unconcern in the overly busy professionalism. It had been a long time since his being a DeLande hadn't mattered. Here it didn't. Not yet.

Dark had fallen and rain was on the way as a thin veil of clouds grew thick and tall, obscuring the stars. He wanted to be at home in bed, swathed in his own eight-hundred-thread-count cotton sheets, luxurious and smelling faintly of herbs. Barring that, Miles wanted the casino hotel room, the impersonal decor of the penthouse suite, doors locked and soft music playing to mask outside sounds. Perhaps a glass of wine or a snifter of brandy to soothe his spirits.

Instead he had institutional smells and lighting and the feel of sickness in the air. And a healer awaiting him. One his brother Andreu had almost killed. One who, he feared, knew far too much about him and his private fears and solitary needs.

The waiting room was large and L-shaped, recently redecorated with new wallpaper and the almost pleasant hint of fresh paint. He stopped in the doorway, allowing his eyes to adjust to the dimness. Someone had turned off the harsh overhead lights, leaving the room lit by the red glow of a Coke machine and the shimmer of outside illumination. Upholstered chairs and two long couches followed the contours of the walls, making several small conversational groupings, each with little tables placed to hold tissues or drinks or books. Beside the Coke machine was a six-foot wooden table and chairs all neatly pushed into place but for one. The remains of a snack rested at the empty seat, crumpled paper and scattered cracker crumbs caught the light from the hallway. A Coke can glowed like fresh blood. Beyond the wide window at the far side of the room, lightning flickered from cloud to cloud, flashing strobe-like. In its glare, he saw her.

She faced the window, her back to him, sitting on the couch with her bare feet up on a coffee table. She hadn't turned, yet he knew she was conscious of him. As the lightning faded, her eyes, reflected in the window glass, met his.

Slowly Miles crossed the floor, a strange awareness flooding through him. And though she didn't move, her eyes tracked his progress across the room. And he knew . . . he *knew* that she felt the strangeness too, as if the air was alive with the lightning that sparked again, causing his skin to lift and a feather-light tingle to rest at the base of his skull.

He reached the couch, passed around the arm and stopped. She had changed. Somehow Rosemon had found a shower and washed away the mud and the gore that had splattered her. She wore a scrub suit and her wet hair was braided, woven across her head like a crown.

"I brought you a few things," he said, placing a mauve-striped duffel bag beside her feet. "Dresses. A skirt. Blouses. The Welch brothers said you wouldn't wear trousers or jeans though I'll buy those for you as well if you wish. Toiletries provided by the hotel.

I'll get better for you tomorrow."

"Not trying to buy me, are you Eldest?"

Miles was shocked by the words, opened his mouth to deny any such attempt. And then Rosemon smiled, amused, just a bit tired, more than a little self-conscious. The skin at the outside corners of her eyes wrinkled delicately.

"Because if you are, you'd have better luck with that." She pointed to his left hand, which held white paper bags of food in steaming paper cartons. "I'm famished."

Miles grinned back, settled on the couch beside her and opened out his feast. He had no idea what the boxes contained. He had tipped a bellboy a hundred to race out to the casino on the lake and pack him a picnic of the very best. The cost of the meal would be added to his room bill, and in return Miles knew he was expected to lose a small fortune at the gambling tables. The losses suffered by the Welch brothers would have to be enough. Except at the roulette wheel, Miles never lost while gambling. He didn't really know how to lose.

He opened cartons of roast beef and steamed jumbo shrimp, roasted new potatoes coated liberally with herbs and garlic, steamed, cold asparagus spears, grilled mixed vegetables and ranch dressing. Yeast rolls and creamery butter and a whole pecan pie finished the meal. Briskly Rosemon tore off a large piece of yeast roll and stuffed it into her mouth, followed it with a shrimp dipped into hot sauce he had missed seeing, and then ate the rest of the roll. She ate quickly, using her fingers and licking them clean between bites, the motions swift and economical, unselfconscious in her hunger.

Taking a roll himself, Miles went to the machine and bought two Cokes without asking her preference. He licked his fingers clean on the way back to the couch.

With the exception of the roast beef and the pie, they ate the meal without utensils, as if they were at a picnic and the night sky their entertainment. The storm grew, lightning brightening the heavens, gusts of rain lashing at the window and running down like liquid diamonds. Thunder, explosions in the air, shook the building, vibrating beneath their feet.

They watched the storm as they ate, Miles' feet propped beside hers on the coffee table. It was a peculiar sort of camaraderie, considering he didn't know the woman. He felt completely at ease once that initial sense of strangeness passed.

When the feast was done, even the pie mostly gone, Rosemon looked away from the light show and met his eyes. Held his gaze.

Unlike Mara and Cady, her eyes were no true color. Neither blue nor green nor brown nor even gray, but a mottled hazel with flecks of all colors buried in the depths and folds of iris. And there was one odd wedge of clear and purest blue in the outer corner of the right eye. Two centuries ago, Rosemon would have been burned at the stake for having that marking. "The evil eye," they would have called it, the sign of the Devil. And Miles wasn't so certain they would have been wrong.

"When I was thirteen, there were two men of the Idlewild clan at our door. They had guns and too much liquor, which no Idlewild carries well, being part Irish and part American Indian. One held a gun to my stepfather's head, another held a gun at Momo, and both men were prepared to use them. They wanted me," she said, her tone pensive.

"I had been foolish, as most young girls are, I suppose, testing my powers and charms. But I had more to get into trouble with than most young girls. And I had been searching for men, any men, for months. They weren't the first to try to take me. But they were the last for many years.

"They shot into the cabin roof. Beat my mama, Delice, until she bled from the mouth and nose. And I watched it all from the clothes chest where Momo had shoved me. I knew I was to blame."

Miles listened silently, with all of his senses, with his ears to the story she told, with his DeLande gifts to the rest, feeling the ebb and flow of tension in the taut body beside his, tasting her misery, watching the emotions of the moments she recreated. The tears and the anger and the fear she had experienced in the dark and musty place where they had hidden her away. He knew about safe places. He understood guilt and its power.

"And then, just when one of them pulled back the hammer and shoved the gun into Old Banoit's temple, Momo started laughing. I don't think I'd ever heard laughter that sounded like that. Wicked and judgmental and just so . . . amused. As if the whole thing was one great cosmic joke that only she and God understood. And the helicopter came across the treetops and settled into the cove where we lived at the time.

"The Idlewilds had never seen the like of Andreu and his men. All armed, churning out of the helicopter like soldiers overrunning some small village. The helicopter like some huge, black, roaring bird, making the water chop and the air wet with spray, and so loud no one could hear themselves speak." Rosemon smiled, a faint movement of muscle and tendon and flesh that somehow exposed all of her longing and need and the excitement of that moment. Her breathing was shallow, and her smile widened.

"And Andreu, like some green-eyed god, striding in the front door of the cabin just as the Idlewilds fairly flew out the back." Dimples appeared, unexpected things, on either side of her mouth. "He held out his hand to my mother, Delice, and lifted her from the floor, dried her eyes and mopped her bloody face with his handkerchief. Silk it was, I still have it somewhere. And handed her to Old Banoit like she was a queen newly rescued.

"Me still watching all this through the clothespress door. Still scared. More scared by then, I admit it, of this new threat. But intrigued. *God, how intrigued.*" The dimples deepened.

"And then he bowed to Momo and kissed her hand. Really kissed the back of her hand like those French men on old black and white movies. 'Bout took my breath away.

"Outside his men had gathered, standing guard around the house, six of them including the pilot. He'd shut the noisy helicopter down and I could hear again. I knew where each man was, even the Idlewilds, making tracks upstream to safety and the bâteau they had beached there. It's one of my talents. Men, I mean." Rosemon glanced at Miles under lowered lashes, her eyes laughing and provocative.

He offered a wry smile back, not doubting her claim. Passion was thinly buried in this woman, fire and fury and a need he could scarcely comprehend.

"If there's a man anywhere around I always know where he is and what he wants. I just know." She shrugged.

Miles was drawn to the story, scarcely able to speak. Unable to

141

respond except to nod and stare into her most peculiar eyes. As she surely knew.

"He spoke to Momo, kneeling there beside her rocking chair, still holding her hand, his voice so low I couldn't really hear it. And then he stood up, walked over to the clothespress and opened the door, took my hand and pulled me out of the linens and directly into his arms."

Rosemon's smile faded a bit, winsome, a little lost. Miles had no doubt that she was aware of his every reaction. That she played to his feelings like a skilled actress telling her own story to an audience of one, holding him in the palm of her hand. Yet, there was some other emotion just below the surface of her skin, some shadow that Miles couldn't name without opening himself to her— and that he was afraid to do. Mortally afraid.

He had a sense of her now. The empathy with which she healed. The sheer power of the woman. DeLande, yet not DeLande. Something more, as all the LeMays were something more.

"He took me straight away to the helicopter and up into the air, holding me on his lap, his arms around me. Took me to New Orleans where a limousine met us. And then to an apartment he used when he wanted privacy.

"I was willing. More than willing by then, you can imagine. And he bonded me to him. Mind and heart, and, I thought—until you came and managed to get my son shot—my soul. I thought that when he died, I was supposed to die, too. I wanted to. I nearly did.

"You reminded me that I have a place. Children. Andreu's children. And Mara."

Miles blinked at the name, unable to hide his response and the vision it invoked, Mara, skirts rucked up, Enoch's hands beneath, the man's mouth on hers.

Rosemon laughed. And laughed again at his blush as he looked away. He was the Eldest. He had more actual power than any man in the country save a very few select and senior men in congress. And the President, of course. Over some of them, he had political clout. And here he sat, food smeared on his hands and mouth like a four-year-old, sitting in the dark with his brother's woman, being manipulated like a child. And he had a feeling she was teasing him.

Looking at her eyes, Miles was certain of his conclusion, detecting humor there, lighthearted and not unkind. He shook his head, finding words at last. "She's . . . interesting. Your Mara."

Rosemon laughed, a full throated, deep sound as she shook her head. "*Interesting*, Eldest? Just *interesting*?"

Miles grinned again, fighting the temptation to run his fingers through his hair as he used to do when he was very young and nonplussed. Might have anyway but for the grease on his hands. "All right. More than interesting. Perhaps a great deal more than interesting."

"Andreu chose her for you. From the beginning."

His smile disappeared. Standing, Miles stepped to the window, stared into the darkness and the storm-lashed trees far below. An ambulance moved slowly past, red lights flashing. A sedan followed close. An accident in the home perhaps. Or a sudden illness. Stroke. Heart attack.

Andreu chose her for you. From the beginning.

Miles moistened his lip, tasting yeast and the sweetness from the pie. Stuck his hands into his pockets. "Why?" He could feel her smile. Feel the dimples form. Feel her surprising tenderness.

"For you. For his first born."

Miles clenched his hands. Stared down into the darkness which was surely brighter than the depths of his own soul. *". . . his first born."*

He took a breath, painful past the lump in his chest. "How do you know?"

"That he's your father? Or that he intended my daughter for you?"

"Either. Both." Miles raked his hands through his hair, heedless of the meal he had eaten with his fingers and the grease that coated them. Heedless of the impression of youth the gesture implied, the impression he had worked so hard for the last few years to dispel. No one knew his paternity. *No one.* Not even the Grande Dame, his mother.

"He asked me if you were his."

Miles turned at that, startled. Rosemon hadn't moved, was still sitting on the couch, legs stretched out, bare feet on the coffee table, crossed at the ankles. Her fingers were intertwined across her stomach. Deceptively relaxed.

"We met before, though I doubt you'd remember, being so young. Barely five. Andreu wanted to know for certain just whose child you were. He—none of you—could have asked for paternity testing. And Andreu wanted to know. The Grande Dame didn't." Gently, as if she wanted to spare him pain, Rosemon asked, "Are you aware that she had seduced three of your brothers in the months before you were conceived? And that she was sleeping with all of them? Her own children?"

Miles blanched, to hear his mother's *sins* spoken of so calmly. In such a gentle tone.

Rosemon smiled again and shook her head, her expression wry. "I've changed too much, then. Aged. This is the first time I've ever had an attractive young man think I'm gentle. Or anything close." Without pausing, she went on, "Yes, the Grande Dame was and is a sick woman, even considering the history of the DeLandes. She's sick in spirit and mind and heart. She has the morals of a gutter dog and the face of an angel."

Miles glanced back.

"Yes, I've met her. That's a story for another time. Right now, it's you I'm concerned for. Do you want me to continue?"

"Yes." The word was little more than a whisper.

"Then come back here. I can't see your face for the darkness and the lightning. And I need you to understand what I have to say."

Like the child he felt, Miles returned, sat gingerly on the couch and waited.

"You were wearing a little sailor suit, navy and white with a nautical tie knotted around your neck, and you were running around the lobby of some hotel in New Orleans. I forget which one. Already you'd broken a vase and scattered fresh flowers and water over the carpet and no DeLande could control you at all. Or wanted to. The concierge was furious and not doing a very good job hiding it.

"You looked up as Andreu and I came through the doors, and you ran for him, your arms wide, laughing with abandon, your little mouth open and black eyes shining. So beautiful. Like a cherub. An angel all light and dark at once, power and innocence both shining from you. And then you spotted me. Altered your course and flew into my arms instead. Andreu was quite miffed, let me tell you."

"The lady in pink," Miles breathed. "I remember. That was you?"

"Perhaps I wore pink that day. I can't recall."

"You picked me up and held me. I thought you were the most beautiful woman I had ever seen."

"Yes," she said, though Miles didn't know to what she might be agreeing. Perhaps all of it.

"I knew instantly that you were Andreu's. The son of an Eldest. And one he couldn't claim. I told him so, that you were his. And he nodded, lifted you from my arms and kissed you as he handed you to the nanny who suddenly appeared at our sides. I never saw you again until today. But Andreu planned Mara for you. Even if you never did become Eldest in your turn. She was bred for you."

The storm was losing some of its strength. The rain was less powerful, trickling down the window now instead of beating against the pane. Lightning flashes were fewer and from some other part of the sky, hidden behind the building.

Rosemon took his hand and held it. Hers was warm, the skin like silk. Miles returned the pressure. "Lucien is your half-brother. Today you saved him, Miles. And Cady and me . . . from a danger greater than you can possibly know."

Rosemon took a deep breath, the sound shuddering and hollow. When she spoke again, her words were formal, stately, like the pronouncement of royalty. "I and mine are yours to command, Eldest. In both honor and thanks. Whatever we have that you might desire is yours because of what you have done today."

"Like a vassal in a medieval play?" Miles couldn't keep the fear from his voice, nor the misery. He understood what Rosemon was offering, and it wasn't some easy sexual surrender or a simple gift of the moment, that he might abuse or misuse or worse. It was a gift far more complex and absolute than that. And it had to do with the missing records of the Eldest, which he did not have and might never find.

Dispirited, he rested his head back against the couch and closed his eyes. He wasn't aware of falling asleep. Nor of the gentle pressure of Rosemon's hand holding his. Nor of the healing she shared with him in his dreams.

The overhead lights came on, brighter than lightning. Miles jerked up from the couch, a hand covering his eyes. *He was in a hospital . . . Lucien and Kenno and Rosemon . . .* Blinking through tears into the light he focused on a form in the doorway. Female. Not Kenno.

Rosemon gripped his free hand. "*The doctor,*" she said *sotto voce*. A warning, a signal in her tone that Miles didn't understand. Fear flowed from her in a sudden wave as she clutched his fingers and stood beside him.

Miles wiped his eyes and blinked as the problem, and Rosemon's fear, clarified for him. She was a DeLande traiteur in the presence of a doctor, immediately following a healing. It had happened in the past, according to the official DeLande annals. And never with any good result.

"Dr. Kinsey, how is Lucien?" he asked.

"Better than he has any right to be," she said, standing beside the Coke machine hands on hips. Her face was tired, deeply lined, hollows beneath her eyes like bruises. She was angry. A pulsing, trembling anger vibrating into the room. Miles went very still.

"By all rights he should be dead. At the very least he should have lost a kidney. Instead, I have a mostly conscious patient in recovery with a kidney that appears to be functioning properly. A kidney that had nice new tissue along one area where there should have been nothing but a hole where a bullet went through. I should . . ." Dr. Kinsey raked her fingers through her hair and for a moment, Miles thought she might kick the Coke machine in her frustration. "I should have had to reattach the renal artery and vein. I didn't. There should have been a hole in the diaphragm and a shattered rib on the other side. There wasn't. The bullet appears to have passed though the diaphragm without leaving a hole, missed the lung and left the body with no further damage. And that's *just not possible.* None of it."

Dr. Kinsey stared from Miles, who had crossed the room while she spoke, to Rosemon standing frozen in front of the window, behind the scant protection of the couch. Miles stepped to the Coke machine and paid for a drink, popped the top, and passed it to the doctor. "So. You're saying the surgery went well. Isn't that great, Rosemon? Lucien's doing fine."

"Well, hell! It went bloody damn near perfect. A first-year surgical resident could have performed it with one arm tied behind his back. Blindfolded," she added. "Dr. Thibodeaux in ER could have performed it and I could have gone on home. It's just—"

"Wonderful. We think it's just wonderful, don't we, Rosemon? Dr. Kinsey must have done a fine job on him." Miles willed Rosemon to speak, say or do almost anything. Her mouth opened, sheer terror on her features.

"Don't try to placate me with that, mister. It's not just wonderful. It's impossible!"

Miles started laughing, soft chuckles making their way up from some perverse part of him, some dark place bequeathed him by his more than perverse mother. "The miracle of a mother's love— though I've never experienced such an emotion. Looks like it's your lucky day, Doc. And Lucien's, of course." Dr. Kinsey glared at him; Rosemon snapped her mouth shut and glared at him too.

"A miracle. I'm sure that's just what it is, Dr. Kinsey. Drink up, drink up. It's a miracle. A time for celebration. Right, Rosemon?" The lady in question lifted her brows, an unwilling smile hovering, as if she might—just might—approve Miles' course of action. Brazen it out, admit nothing, all in true DeLande style. His family had brazened out all kinds of awful peccadilloes and scandals and never admitted to a thing. For centuries.

Dr. Kinsey looked from one to the other of them, and drank down a large swig of the drink as commanded. She stopped suddenly, stared at the can in her hand, looked back at Miles and finally to the machine. "So how did you know I liked root beer?" she demanded.

"Lucky guess." He grinned unrepentantly. Behind him, Rosemon smothered a nervous laugh that came out mostly through her nose.

Dr. Kinsey narrowed her eyes again, her mouth firm, her expression perturbed and just a little bit bemused, as if she thought they might have been making fun of her in some obscure manner. Setting the mostly-full can on the table, she glared at Miles, ending the conversation as she had started it, by walking out. At the door she paused and, without turning, said, "He'll be coming to his room in half an hour. You can see him as soon as he's settled." The surgeon took off down the hallway, none of her questions answered, none of her suspicions confirmed. A most unhappy woman.

Rosemon's laughter escaped in little puffs of muffled hilarity from between her fingers. Miles turned, one brow lifted in patently false innocence.

Rosemon slid to the couch as if boneless. Perched on the edge, she kneeled, arms braced on the back, as Kinsey's footsteps receded. Quiet but for her giggles, she collapsed into the cushions stifling the sound. When she raised her head from the seat again, her cheeks were pink, her strange eyes sparkling. Miles knew then exactly what Andreu had seen in her. The thought stopped him. Andreu who had been his father. To cover his reaction, he bought two more Cokes, his hands busy at the machine.

"Andreu said you were daring and arrogant, but he never mentioned audacious, reckless, and impudent, to boot. That was wonderful! Just absolutely wonderful! I'd never have had the guts to just . . . what were the words you thought? . . . brazen it out? Never. I'd have hemmed and hawed and stuttered and tried not to explain and gotten all tangled up in my explanations and lies. But you? You just ignored it all and looked . . . *naive*. Didn't you?" she almost shouted the last three words. "You looked virtuous and harmless and *totally* unassuming. Very Un-Eldest."

Miles handed her a can and shook his head, not in denial but in deprecation. "I guess I did, sort of. I didn't think it through actually. It was more a reflex than a plan."

He had learned to lie with a straight face from the time of his first sentence; to lie well was a DeLande survival mechanism, falsehoods the only way to hide the darkness in the heart of the family. Truth could never be shared with outsiders, never be hidden from another DeLande. It was a fact of his upbringing.

An unwilling smile tugged at Miles' mouth, as he watched his brother's woman. She didn't know how to lie at all.

Rosemon opened her drink and sipped, the occasional giggle escaping as she did. "She'll ask again, you know."

"It's likely."

"She'll ask *me*."

"And you'll tell her what a wonderful surgeon she is and how grateful you are that she saved your son's life. You'll gush, and you'll bat your eyelashes at her and think innocent thoughts. And she'll go away no more satisfied than tonight."

"I'm not much good at innocent thoughts," Rosemon said, a decidedly wicked gleam in her eyes.

Miles reclaimed his seat on the couch, a few extra inches farther away than before. "Try," he said, voice still wry. "Practice. Work on it, Rosemon. Think of it as a challenge,"

"I never thought I'd see the day when a DeLande counseled innocence."

"Be a good girl, Rosemon. Drink your drink."

"Yes, Eldest," she said with false docility. "And again, my thanks."

Miles wasn't certain he wanted her thanks, especially considering the devilish gleam he had spotted in her eyes while she was teasing him. Troublesome women he had enough of in his life. He didn't need another. Shaking his head, he rested it again against the couch.

Suddenly the vision of Mara in Enoch's arms appeared, fresh and potent in his memory, as intense as his own reaction to the original scene had been. And he remembered the feel of Mara's flesh beneath his hands, mud-slick and heated. Had he been alone, he might have groaned.

Chapter Twenty-One
Lightning and Mickle Toes

Mara struggled against the hand holding her prisoner, the awful weight of a body; hot and sweat-slick above hers. Fought hard, wrestled her way up out of sleep and whispering nightmare dreams, visions of mud and blood and a maggot-crawling carcass. Dreams interspersed with black-on-black eyes and the unfamiliar passion of hands and mouths and a burning heat. Waking, she found she was in her own bed, pinned beneath Cady's sleeping form, the too-soft feather mattress having rolled them together in the collapsed center and risen around them.

Gasping, pushing away the evil dream of a bayou-isle horror, denying the strange heat that possessed her, Mara crawled out from beneath Cady's weight and off the bed.

Lightning cracked, shivering the air, throwing the cabin into a camera-flash of light, blue and flickering. Making her way to the sink, Mara pumped water into the blue ceramic basin, dipped in a rag and washed her sweaty throat and face, along her arms and up under her T-shirt. The tepid water was cooling, touched by the wind through the open doors.

Damp gusts carried the smell of storm and rising water. A spray of rain wet the floor boards at the front of the cabin. Dark descended—the pregnant, waiting dark between daylight flashes.

Rain beat against the metal roof, roared water-on-water on the bayou out front, tapped on the windows and ran down, making the glass waver as if alive. Mara drained the water from the sink, the soft gurgle lost below the storm.

A piercing crack, keen and caustic, sounded overhead: the soft warning that presaged a shaft of lightning close by. Very close. Instantly the world was shot through with bright blue, so intense it obliterated shadows, lighting the cabin and the world outside like an artificial sun at midday. A prolonged flash, hovering on the edge of pain. The hair on her head crackled and lifted, quivers raced along her skin, pinpricks of pain in the damp where she had washed.

Momo grunted, the sound she might make if hit with a fist in the stomach. Mara whirled. Found her in the blue blaze of light.

Momo stood before the open door, empty only an instant past, wreathed in a burning flare of illumination, limned in a silver-blue glow of storm-light. Her arms were raised above her head, hands fisted in defiance of the wildness just beyond.

Mara blinked against the glare. Thunder exploded around her, an earthquake's strength, shaking the cabin. Glass rattled, slipped and fell, shattering. She gripped the table behind her, dropped to the bench, bruising her thigh. The rocking chairs moved in the dying light as if tipped, each one, by a separate hand. Momo's skirts billowed out, black in the silver light. Mara pushed away, took a step toward the open door. In that instant, the rain stopped. The silence was exotic and almost foreign after the storm's roar. The light outside hadn't completely died and seemed to brighten in the peculiar silence, glittering along the bayou, idling, star-dust-bright on the twigs and branches on the far bank, a sluggish, melancholy glow, as if lightning were trapped in the water that raced by, clung to the foliage, dripped from the eaves.

She pushed upright, rubbing the tender place, palm against bare leg. She watched Momo stare down the strange light. Thunder rumbled in the distance, afterimage-sound like the afterimage-glimmer. Water dripped in a thousand muted sounds. Mara crossed her arms, gripping opposite biceps as if cold, and indeed, the skin there was prickled and icy, hair still raised in alarm.

The air was thick and hard to breathe. Her lungs ached with in-drawn breath. Time seemed shattered, like the glass at her feet, into a thousand glittering shards.

Momo stepped back from the odd light, the glow following her into the cabin. Blue all around, brightened on chair and cupboard. The wind died. The silence was unnatural, as the world held its breath. And the glow grew stronger, coming closer, filling the windows and doorway. The screens covering the openings burned bright, the hot blue blaze of lightning. Appearing out of the night, it stood before the cabin.

A round blue-bright ball, large as the full moon on a cloudless night, the result or perhaps the source of the strange, outside glow. Sizzling energy coruscated across its surface, boiled within. It moved.

Mara caught her breath. She had read about it, heard accounts of it; never thought to see such a thing. It moved though the screen, throwing sparks of peculiar brightness, white-hot.

Feet moving slowly, Momo stepped back, and back, away from the ball lightning. It followed her as if pulled by her upraised arms across the room. The air snapped and sparkled, potent energy.

Mara felt smothered, the air so thick she couldn't draw it in. It burned at her nostrils, tingled on her tongue. Her eyes ached, smoldering dry.

Momo turned to the side. The seething globe wafted past her, radiating a frigid heat that churned and broiled and left Mara both frozen and blistered. The glowing sphere moved through the cabin, wavered once as it traversed the length of the kitchen table, only feet from Mara. It slipped out the back door with a final flare of brightness, a scent of molten metal.

Darkness descended, utter and complete, a silence marked only by an occasional drip, the relic of the storm. Retinal images burned in the night, red-light visions of Momo and the lightning against Mara's eyelids. She heard Momo grunt again, and the soft whisper of a cushion as she sat. A light splatter of rain fell, feather-light on the bayou outside, strengthened and settled into a steady cadence of delicate sound. Thunder rumbled, very far off.

Fingers shaking, numb and trembling, Mara lit an oil lamp. A match flared, sulfur smell of smoke. Her eyes watered. Her skin was tight and aching and Mara knew she was burned. Lightning-burned. It still hurt to breathe. Perhaps she was burned inside as well, lungs lightning-scorched.

She adjusted the wick and placed the clear crystal globe on the heavy, blue crystal base. Adjusted the wick again as the flame steadied.

Momo was sitting in the padded rocker, the chair covered with the same over-bright blue as the antique chairs gracing either end of the kitchen table. Her head was back, mouth open, eyes closed. Her lids quivered, their thin skin traced with blue veins.

Mara lifted the spectacles beside the lamp and carried them to Momo; placed them in her open hands. Momo didn't, or couldn't, respond. With sudden understanding, Mara found two glasses, stepping gingerly past the shattered one on the floor, and filled both with water from the pump, its metallic sound grating in the silence.

Mara held a glass at Momo's lips, tilting it, letting water slip inside. Momo swallowed and swallowed again before lifting a hand to grip the glass and drain it dry. Mara gave her the other glass and watched while she drained it as well, though a little less desperately.

Mara refilled both glasses and drank one herself, placing the other full one at Momo's side on a small table. It was still covered with a crocheted doily, placed there to impress the Eldest DeLande. The spectacles were now on Momo's face, and her withered chest lifted and fell with a smooth rhythm, a little fast perhaps, but not the urgent pace of over extended exhaustion Mara had expected. Taking the seat beside Momo, Mara sat, sipping her own water. It burned cold on her tongue, settling queasily in her stomach. She had to force herself to finish the glass.

Finally Momo spoke. "Evil got skin on it face."

Though she couldn't see how that comment could relate to the vision of ball lightning, Mara waited, patiently.

"Evil. It got a name."

"Lightning?" Mara asked.

"No, Mara. Lightning not evil. Not good. Lightning just lightning. Even ball like you see. Just lightning. Maybe cause by water all round. Trap it and throw it back up." Momo shrugged, the motion saying she had thought about it, guessed about it, but didn't know, and didn't really care.

"But lightning and storm . . . both portent. Strong portent. Prove change to come, Mara." Momo lifted her head. Lamplight, as always, obscured her eyes, glimmered on glass lenses and gold wire. "Change for you, I be thinking, Mara."

153

Thunder crashed nearby one last time, a punctuation mark after the storm, quick and unexpected—a shocking sound in the silence that followed the violence of the storm and Momo's casual words. The cabin shook as the final echoes rumbled away. The flame of the lamp quivered, tossing shadows.

The quiet in its aftermath was paralyzing, assaulting their ears with mute vibrations and swirling around their bodies like a voiceless wind. Rare drops still landed with loud splats outside the doors. The cabin creaked, settling itself after the buffeting wind.

Mara opened her mouth to speak. The radio crackled, the white noise of a transmission being received. The storm returned via the tinny speaker, a sound of thunder and rain. And the scream.

"Momo! Momo! Help me!"

Mara raced to the radio. Turned up the volume. A gunshot sounded, the booming blast of shotgun. Another. And again the scream.

"Devora."

It was Cady beside them, sweat-sheened in the lamplight. "That's Devora's voice."

The transmission went silent. "Kenno," Mara said. "Get the guns."

Cady moved. Bare feet flying.

"Watch out for broken glass! Beside the cupboard," Mara said as she ran to the clothespress. Hands flew as she pulled out two pair of jeans, two clean T-shirts, underwear, socks, and from the floor beneath the bed, two pair of sneakers. Throwing off the sweaty T-shirt and boxers she slept in, Mara dressed.

Behind her, Cady slapped the guns on the table, metal clattering on wood. Momo rocked, with a steady soft sound of treads on floor boards.

Not bothering to tie her shoes, Mara raced for the table and gathered her two weapons, the Colt and Winchester, secure in her hands. She had been taught that guns were tools, her mind was the weapon. Her mind made the decisions about the gun's use, her skill made the decisions possibilities, and her body followed through. The hickory stock and grip were a commitment and a pledge.

"Meet me at *Jenny*. Clothes on the bed."

Cady's pupils were so wide their blue irises appeared black. "She never learned about guns. She never learned about self-defense. She's helpless."

"No. She has us. Dress."

Cady sighed, the sound frightened.

"Momo, we need help. Where are Albert and Alain and the man Miles left behind? You said they were upstream and down, keeping watch."

Momo nodded. "Water rising. They forced back, to high ground." She looked up, spectacles flashing. "You alone, Mara. High water make it hard to find Mickle Toes. Fast water, high wind make *Jenny* . . . not safe, I be thinking."

"So say a prayer for us." Mara swung around and ran to the back door, glass crunching once beneath her sneakers.

The air outside was wet and cool, a breeze shaking droplets loose from tree and eaves. The ground squelched and gave, mud soaking through her canvas shoes.

The lean-to had kept the engine dry, though there was a sheen of rain water in the shallow bottom. Mara stowed the weapons in the side pockets, checked the gasoline and oil and tossed several floatation cushions into the bow.

Devora had never learned to swim. Since the gator attack, she feared water almost as much as she feared fire. Devora was afraid of a lot of things. She had no survival skills at all. None. And she was pregnant.

Mara refused to think about the gunshots. Devora's awful scream.

Tossing the single tie-down free, Mara turned the key and *Jenny* roared to life. The running lights came on with the flip of a switch. Cady clambered aboard, stowed the guns, two boxes of ammunition for the hand guns, and then returned to land. Bending, she shoved off, into the bayou, jumped in and sat on the low seat, tailor-style, facing Mara as she strapped herself in. It was too dark to see her sister's eyes, even in the glow from the pole light mounted beside the engine cage. Cady's face was a skull, white and shadowed. *Jenny* rocked and moved from shore with the current. Water was high and fast. Debris swirled past. Mara tossed Cady ear protectors, turned on the handheld maritime radio and pressed the accelerator gently. *Jenny* pushed forward through the water and the blackness.

It was difficult to travel on the bayou at night even with a full moon and no need for speed. It was downright stupid to do so on a cloudy night after a storm when flotsam and churning water made the bayou perilous. It was clearly suicidal and just about impossible at high speed. Mara gunned the engine at her back and shot forward.

Cady swiveled, re-secured her seat-belt, and scrabbled in the side pocket, one hand holding tight to the gunwale. The flashlight came on in her hands, its flare bright against the hull, almost lost on the muddy water. The thin beam showed whitewater at the shoreline where rivulets had become torrents pouring into the bayou. Twigs, branches, whole trees lay tangled in the water's path or tumbled along in the turbulence.

The sturdy craft plowed through and over a small pine, its stump hitting the bottom. Cady bounced and lost her grip on the flashlight. It tumbled across the bottom, blinding Mara. A moment later it was back over the water lighting misty shapes just beneath the surface while red and green dots danced on Mara's retinas.

She knew this part of the lake, the curving leg of the Elephant. Could navigate it in her sleep, even with the water high. She needed to reach the northernmost leg of the Elephant and enter the swampy marsh separating Elephant Lake from the parallel Chope Bayou. Chope, as in bottle, an apt description of the wide runnel of water. The bayou didn't roll free and deep but thinned out, wide and shallow as marsh, the water bottled up, often emptying into or joining with other bayous or small lakes. Mickle Toes was north on Chope Bayou, hidden in one of the marshy coves to the east. Momo was right. It would be hard to find in the night, with high water. But Mara kept hearing in her memory Devora's scream and the sound of the gunshots. Devora's scream . . . so like the sound of her voice the time the gator nearly took her under.

Mara had been there, watching her sister splash in the water, laughing and giggling, chasing polliwogs as they darted past. And then Devora made a "whuffing" sound and fell, landing neck deep, braced on her arms. Mara stood, attentive, immobile, staring as her sister was dragged into deeper water, screaming. Screaming. The water billowing up clouds of thinned-out red.

Rosemon had appeared, thigh deep, firing the .38 in sharp cracks, stinging smoke puffing from the barrel. She yanked Devora out by one bloody arm, raw flesh hanging. Threw her to shore, delicate limbs cart wheeling, blood flying in spirals through the air.

All the while Mara stood there and stared, transfixed. Doing nothing.

Jenny swerved out of the Elephant's leg and into the belly of the beast, bumping over something half floating, half sunk. Both girls held on as Mara pushed the little craft north through the current, moving fast in the dark of night. Overhead, the moon tried to peek through the clouds, creating a bright spot in the sky, doing little to light up the earth.

Minutes passed, the wind ripping at their braids, occasional splatters of rain from the clearing sky stinging tender skin. They were both getting wet, though Mara's back was dry, protected by the seat. Cady looked bedraggled, her braid half undone, wet golden hair plastered to her scalp.

They entered the northernmost leg of the Elephant, and though Mara didn't want to, she slowed the airboat, eyes straining into the night. The north leg was stumpy compared to the other legs of the lake, ending in a shallow place of tall grasses and lilies and tangled brush. In dry times the area was above water, the soil rich and aromatic. When the water rose, the plant life disappeared beneath the surface, a twisted mass to threaten fisherman's propellers and snare plastic bait. The foliage was no danger except where deadwood floated. Mara didn't want to flip over and be forced to spend the night in a tree.

She eased the airboat through the tops of tall grasses, watching for open water on the far side. Pygmy Bayou traveled east and north and, in high water times, like now, opened into Chope Bayou. A shortcut to Devora.

Sudden rain pelted them, a heavy drenching. Lightning split the sky, dividing night from false day, and Mara gunned the engine over the last few yards of dangerous passage. Cady shouted, pointing. Mara swerved. A form thrashed in the water so close it brushed *Jenny's* sides. *Deer? Caught in the storm?*

Pygmy Bayou opened up before them, rain battering its surface into whitewater. And then they were through the shower into mist, tendrils of fog twisting past. Mara adjusted the speed to a steady race. Cady swept the bayou with the light. They were both shivering, night wind on wet flesh and clothes.

Half an hour later, they entered Chope Bayou. Like the northern leg of Elephant Lake, Chope Bayou was shallow and dangerous. Much more so because Mara came here so seldom. It wasn't exactly safe for a female alone to encounter a Mickle male. It was rash and reckless to actually enter their territory unless one intended to stay on as wife to one man or another.

Moving slowly, easing the boat through the tips of tall grasses and dwarf sweet-gum trees, she scanned to right and left, memorizing her path. They might have to make their way back with speed, either to outrun Mickle men or to get Devora to safety. And if she was hurt, speed would be essential.

Long minutes later they spotted lights ahead. Windows of ramshackle homes lit by lanterns marked the first landmark near Mickle Toes. It must have been after two, far too late for lighted windows. When they passed, the night was darker still. Mickle clan used a different channel on the maritime radio from the LeMays. If Devora had managed to send out her mayday to the Mickles as well as to Momo, then the Mickle clan would be gathered. The airwaves would be crackling and full. The LeMay channel was silent.

Mosquitoes gathered, attracted by the running lights, their speed slow enough to let them keep pace. There hadn't been time to put on repellent. Cady and Mara would be eaten alive. They sped up again, trusting in luck and Momo's prayers for safe deliverance.

Off to the left were more houses, these also well lit. No john-boats floated at deck or dock. No pirogues or bâteaus waited on land. The Mickle clan had taken to the water.

Finding the entrance to Mickle Toes was easier than expected. All seventeen houses in the odd-shaped cove were lit up. Boats were gathered, tied off Devora's and Charlie's dock, pulled up on land at either side of the cabin or floating in the cove. The scent of gasoline and tobacco and fresh perked coffee drifted on the cold air. Men's indistinct forms stood about on Devora's front porch deck, back-lit by windows.

Mickle Toes was a mosquito-infested, swampy marsh except in high-water times like now. A backwater place full of uneducated, unread, surly near-hermits about whom there was much rumor but little concrete knowledge. Gossip insisted that Mickle men seldom bathed, never shaved, and practiced ritual slaughter of wild hogs in the new moon. The sacrifice was rumored to be to some pagan god who—in return for the fresh pork—made the Mickle men all but irresistible to women. The only verifiable fact about the Mickle men was that no girl child had been born into the clan in over one hundred-fifty years. Wives were imported from other clans each spring when the Mickle men went courting.

Women had always been scarce in the Badlands. For over two hundred years, Texas and Louisiana had driven criminals, convicts, and the unwanted into the swamp. Only in the twentieth century had more modern practice of law taken over the old ways. Until then, men who survived the law, the gators, snakes and quicksand, were adopted into one clan or another and many stayed on, marrying and raising families in the back-water. In those days, women for all the clans were imported—though "stolen" might have been the more correct term. Every spring men from each family grouping would go hunting and bring back girl children. Nice, healthy, beautiful girl children who would act as servants until they grew old enough to marry into the clan.

The race of the girls wasn't important. Anglos passing through, heading west, would wake up from a night's sleep and find young girls missing. Black slaves from nearby plantations were removed from their families and their masters. Indian villages would loose some girl children by theft, others by barter. The resultant mixed race of Badlands dwellers was considered by some to be the most beautiful people in the world. Honey-colored skin, flashing black eyes, bone structure provided by the best genetics, the finest that could be stolen.

Mickle women were still in short supply. Their men still went hunting each spring, taking a rumored yearly bath in bayou water, shaving for the first time, sometimes even washing their clothes. Then they would descend on the rest of the bayou looking for wives. Teenagers rebelling against parents, unhappy spouses, the lonely and the unfaithful, were all targets for the Mickle men.

Thanks to the hog god, many women went voluntarily, married into the clan and stayed. As had Devora when she was fourteen years old. And she had been happy.

Cady shut off the flashlight and pulled her rifle from the side pocket, passed Mara's Colt up to her. The shotgun would have made more sense against so many, but the Colt could be fired from where she sat. Cady stuck a second clip into Mara's T-shirt pocket. It rested, cold and metallic against her breast through the wet fabric.

There hadn't been time to find bras. The sisters would look like contestants in a wet T-shirt contest; not the best attire when paying a visit on the Mickle clan. And with *Jenny's* roar, it wasn't as if they were making a covert approach.

Torches and guns were aimed their way. Mara slowed to a drift, the hull still moving through the water.

"Hello, the house! We're LeMay clan," she shouted over the engine's roar. "Heard there was trouble in Mickle Toes. Our sister is your healer, Devora, married to the Mickle clan by choice. Her man's name is Charlie. May we approach?"

On the deck-porch of Devora's house, a man gestured them forward, rifle in the air. Seconds later, *Jenny* was grounded, the ignition key in Mara's jean pocket. Her shotgun in one hand, the Colt in the other, she led the way up the back stairs.

Men with two-inch long, untrimmed beards stepped from her path, making a space on the stairway. They were packed so close she could smell them. One opened the back door for the two girls and stood aside. Mara carefully did not make eye contact with any of them. The men stood silent along the walls inside Devora's house. Too silent. Waiting. Mara stepped in, Cady close on her heels.

Herbs dried in bundles were tied to the kitchen rafters. Fresh herbs grew in pots beneath south-facing windows. Canisters, two deep were ranked on one shelf, neatly labeled and dated in Devora's own personal code, the shorthand she had learned when the gator attack left her unable to write for several years. Basil. Colt's foot. White Willow bark. Marigold. Dandelion leaves. Dandelion roots. Dandelion flowers. Rows and rows of herbs.

Crystal and china were neatly in place over the sink. A bowl of fruit was centered on the six-legged table.

In the next room, drying blood puddled on the floor, dark and thick. A body lay on planks stretched across the back of sturdy chairs, laid out according to the old custom, a white sheet at the feet for covering between the viewings. Charlie. He had been cleaned up and shaved, dressed in clean clothes. His wound, wherever it was, had been bound so it wouldn't leak. There were gold pieces on each eyelid, a bunch of flowers on his chest. Two women stood at the bier, silent and wary. Mara glanced at them and then away.

The eyes of the men were steady. Probing. Focused on the LeMay guns as often as on the girls, evaluating and watchful.

Devora was nowhere to be seen.

Finally an older man stepped forward, an old 30.06 across his chest, cradled in his arms. "You LeMays?"

"Yes," Mara said. Cady stood at her left, watching the men, leaving the talking to Mara. The cabin was thick with the scent of herbs and men and the underlying tang of blood.

"You bring guns into a house of mourning."

Mara lifted her brow. "So do you," she said pointedly. "We came to offer help. Devora is our sister. She called us on the radio. There were gunshots." She offered nothing else. She had no intention of making this a one-way information exchange.

After a moment, the man tilted his head. "A boat like yours took her away." Mara closed her eyes. Pain flashed like lightning from her chest, settled in her palms and the base of her throat. She opened her eyes as he continued: "Close as we can figure, it was one man. Come in silent. Poling most likely, through the storm. Nobody saw him. Heard the shots, though, and the screaming. And the boat taking off. Some of our men gave chase, but we couldn't keep up. Fast boat."

Somewhere, Mara found the words and the breath to speak. "Our sympathies on the death of Devora's man. Charlie was good to her."

The man nodded. "You know who took her?"

"Yes, I think so."

"You . . . going to bring her back?" The question surprised Mara, or perhaps not the question, but the way it was asked.

Thoughtful, as if there was more he might say. And then Mara remembered. Women were valuable to Mickle men and Devora perhaps most of all. She was the clan's folk healer.

"We'll bring her back to Momo LeMay. When she is well, she can decide if she'll come back to Mickle Toes. *She* will decide," Mara stressed.

The man said, "There's many of us who might court her. If she was willing."

Mara understood. Many of them, like the man before her, authority in his voice, his heart in his eyes. Blue eyes, strong chin and jaw on an olive-complexioned face. Black hair, broad shoulders, younger than he had looked. *And clean*, her mind registered. Good-looking, if rough and uneducated.

"Devora's choice. But if she chooses, it'll be after the baby comes, and no need for stealth. Charlie was good to her. Mickle men will be welcome in LeMay territory."

The man nodded, silent, as if that was his most common method of communication. "Mickle help to bring her back. If you need it, ask freely."

Mara said, "Thank you. Safe passage for LeMay women back to Elephant Lake?"

"Done. And then there's this." The man stepped forward, offering a square of folded paper.

Mara slid the Colt's safety on and placed it on Charlie's bier, near his booted feet. She took the paper, unfolded it one handed and studied the strange words and markings.

Brovil

¿

Sasim 3 days 8pm

"We found it on Charlie. Ain't his writing. Could be hers, I reckon, if she was scared. We figure it was left by the man who took her. You know what it means?"

"No, but . . . Brovil could be a place, spelled phonetically. The question mark and Sasim . . . I don't know. But it's her writing, I'm sure." Mara held the note so her sister could read it. Cady dipped her head once, briskly. Rain water dripped from long tendrils of hair with the motion. Her T-shirt was nearly transparent with damp. "Looks like we have three days to figure it out." Three days while Devora would be at Kenno's mercy.

"Wee Boy, Curtis, follow the ladies back down the exit from Chope Bayou. Make sure they ain't molested."

"Mickle men might want to court more'n Devora," a voice said from the kitchen.

Mara looked back. It was a tall, slender young man with hair to his shoulders and dark shinning skin. Bold eyes, tip tilted and wide, were watching her. He was beautiful as some dark elf out of legend.

"My sister is promised to the Eldest DeLande," Cady said, "according to our custom. She's not available." Mara should have known Cady's silence wouldn't last.

"What about you?" the boy asked.

Cady shrugged. "We have to find our sister first. And Momo decides everything else."

It wasn't a bad answer, especially for Cady. Mara picked up her gun and thanked the man who had spoken for the Mickle clan. Proper etiquette demanded that they at least exchange names. Mara was glad the Mickles didn't know that. All things considered, she had no desire to be on a first name basis in this crowd. Contrary to one rumor, they were all clean. In accordance with another, they were all beautiful. Somehow, that seemed dangerous.

A path opened up to the kitchen and out onto the porch. They were dismissed. Mara and Cady walked through the opening and down the stairs. Wasting no time, they stowed the weapons and made their way out of Mickle Toes in the wake of Wee Boy and Curtis' boat.

They hadn't accomplished much. Charlie was dead.

And Kenno had Devora.

The radio crackled softly. "Old woman. You hear me?"

Momo picked up the handset and pressed the transmit button. "Kenno. You got Devora," she stated flatly.

"Yeah. I got your girl. Killed her man." His voice slithered over the airwaves and shivered against her skin.

"You hurt her, I make sure you pay."

"Fat pregnant females don't interest me, old woman. It's Mara Noelle I want. She shows up where I told her, then I'll let Devora go. She don't show up, I'll cut out Devora's baby and send it to you in a bucket." The transmission went silent.

Fingers trembling, Momo replaced the handset.

Chapter Twenty-Two
Old Banoit and *Queen Fisher*

The girls were cold and hungry when they beached *Jenny*; dawn was brightening the sky, pushing aside the clouds with a soft lavender hand. Momo stood on the back porch, two cats at her feet, tails twitching and voices raised in rough meows.

Exhausted, the sisters joined her. "Show me Kenno note."

Mara dug it from her pocket and watched as Momo unfolded it. Adjusting her spectacles, she read. "Brovil. Huh. Mus' mean Breauxville, up past Calcasieu Lake."

Cady settled on to the porch step and pulled a cat to her. Instantly it began to purr, its voice a contented rumble.

Momo handed back the note. "Go to Breauxville. Kenno there. Take Devora back."

The shivers, which had never really left Mara's skin, intensified. "I heard what he said to you on the radio."

"You go bring her back," Momo demanded again.

"Okay. Yes, ma'am," Mara said, praying that Momo had made coffee and boiled water for a bath. Or better yet, had turned on the generator so the water heater could steam water for a shower.

"Devora with Kenno now, in storm. Pass Sabine Point. Wave bad." Momo shook her head sadly. "Wave make her much sick. Maybe this bring on her baby.

"You pack now. I call Old Banoit. He take you in morning to Gulf, in deep water to Breauxville. You save Devora and her baby before Kenno kill them. *I have spoke.*"

Mara had been on Old Banoit's boat. Every LeMay had—the girls being taken for a ride, crashing through the waves on the gulf,

165

sunbathing on the deck, the boys put to work hauling nets laden with shrimp, stripped to the waist, sweating with effort, muscles burning from constant activity. For the girls it was a vacation, for the boys it was an education in the importance of a work ethic almost extinct in the U.S. On Old Banoit's boat there was no such thing as equality of the sexes, a fact which the LeMay girls appreciated and about which the boys griped. Not that it did any good.

A day trip on Old Banoit's *Queen Fisher* had always been a pleasure for Mara. But not today. Perhaps not ever again. Momo handed her a duffel packed with skirts, T-shirts and even a pair of blue jeans which Momo had folded herself and tucked inside. It was that fact which frightened Mara most: Momo, telling her without words that she could wear the formerly banned, unfeminine skin-tight jeans.

And then there was the money.

One thousand dollars in crumpled twenties and fifties and tens. And a credit card in Mara's name, right there on the front in raised plastic letters—Mara N. LeMay. A Gold Card. As if Momo had been planning this, expecting this for some time. All that money was then strapped to Mara's waist in a leather security pack, the fastenings checked by Momo as they stood together on the deck out front of the cabin.

The world was clear and new, fresh as a storm-washed day should be. But the perfectly circular hole burned through the screen at the front door and back told a different tale—a tale of change and fear. And Momo packing denim jeans, sending her away to rescue Devora.

Mara was cold. She hadn't been warm since the ball lightning had come through the door and hovered in front of Momo as if conjured there. She had shivered through the rest of the night and into the morning as she lay curled against Cady's warm body in the soft feather bed. The shivers had not stopped as the muted diesel sound of *Queen Fisher*'s engines rumbled up Elephant Bayou and idled in front of the cabin.

Momo handed Mara's weapons and two boxes of ammunition to Old Banoit, and passed over Mara's duffel bag, and gave last minute instructions to the Cajun shrimper. Out front, two LeMays-by-marriage loaded *Jenny* on to the deck of the big boat, helped by the waterlogged man Miles had left behind.

Mara ignored it all. She was leaving the Badlands, that oft-contemplated but never before possible journey. And still she shivered, violent tremors that seemed more like premonition than some simple and ordinary reaction to a rare cool morning.

Nauseous with fear, she stared out at the boat: tall central beam with winch at bottom and block and tackle at peak, decks swabbed clean. *Queen Fisher* was a deep royal blue with white trim, both named and painted in honor of Momo.

"Mara." The voice was sharp, demanding and censorious at once. Momo gripped her arm and shook her hard. Stern eyes glared from behind smudged spectacles. "Mara. You not cold. I tell you dis. *You not cold. You not sick.* Devora cold and sick. Not you."

Mara blinked. Momo shook her again. With the touch, the cold seemed to fade away, slipping from her pores like some glamour or sorcery instantly dispelled. Heat from the sun had warmed her clothes while she stood watching Old Banoit's men work. It seeped into her skin, as if it had been stored in the cloth, waiting for her use. Delicious warmth.

The sickness was gone as well. *Could it have been Devora's feelings she was experiencing?* Mara no longer *knew* what emotions and perceptions were her own. If Momo was right, she now had an awareness of passions not her own, an intuition about, and a response to, sensations that weren't hers. And who was she to doubt Momo? Momo the witch.

Instantly a vision of Momo, arms uplifted, guiding the blue globe of lightning through the house, was imprinted on her eyelids. Mara thought the image might remain there forever as if tattooed on her brain.

Momo turned and stared into her eyes. Lips tight with consternation, the woman shook her again. "I no witch, Mara," she whispered, voice harsh as a bird's croak. "You listen good, Mara Noelle. Some peoples stand on de side of good. Some peoples stand on de side of evil. Light and dark, dis you know?"

Slowly Mara spoke, "Yes." Her lips cracked as she formed the single word, cracked and bled where the heat from the lightning had scorched her skin. She tasted the blood, salty-sharp, like pain. "Yes," she said again. "I know. Some people are evil, some good."

"Most not aware of evil and good. Not *know* it. You understand? You know dis?"

"They just . . . go with the flow? Situational ethics." Clearly Momo didn't understand, and Mara licked away more blood, wetting her lips. "They do the right thing if it feels good and if it's easy enough to accomplish. But they don't suffer for it. They don't . . . take a stand. They just go with the flow," she repeated.

"Yes. Like raft on bayou. Let water take dem where it will, use pole to push away from problem but not to steer. Like dat, yes. Dere peoples like dat.

"And den dere peoples like Momo."

Mara cocked her head, listening with all her being. For once willing to be LeMay in the fullest sense if she could understand this one thing. This one valuable thing. This was important, these words Momo was speaking. Vastly important though Mara couldn't have said why she knew it. She stared through Momo's smeared glasses and met the black eyes beneath.

"Momo stand on de brink of abyss, all her life. Look down at dark. Guard between good and evil. Between light and dark. Fight darkness, in prayer." Her hands made grasping motions, fingers joining together in circles. "One link in long chain.

"Evil got smarts. Purpose. And sometime take flesh and bone of it helper. Evil got skin on it face now. Evil got Kenno."

The shivers returned, but now they were the ordinary shivers of simple fear. "You mean like . . . like he's possessed or something? Like in the *Exorcist*?"

"Some like, yes. You go fight. Choose good. Choose light. Momo be dere when you need. Put word in you mind. You listen for Momo. You fight Kenno."

She turned to Old Banoit. "Take Mara in de boat. Take her far as you can. She Momo's arm now. Momo fist."

Old Banoit grinned, exposing a semi-toothless, dark cavern. With a single motion he lifted Mara into his arms and lowered her over the side of the deck. Another's arms took her then and settled her in the slatted seat in a bâteau. It was leaking slowly, two inches of water sloshing in the hull. Old Banoit stepped down and took the oars. With strong strokes he rowed to the royal blue boat idling on the bayou. Beside Mara, a man bailed water out of the boat bottom. Mara didn't look at him. Didn't look back.

The cold had reclaimed her.

She was leaving the bayou. Leaving Momo. Leaving the Badlands. And the first step of the journey was in a leaking boat powered by a worried old man. Mara shivered again in the midday heat.

Chapter Twenty-Three
Decisions and Destiny

Queen Fisher toiled the long length of Elephant Bayou south to the Sabine River and into the wide basin of Sabine Lake. Sports fishermen and water-skiers dotted the placid surface. Barges and tugs, shrimpers and sporting craft, gave a wide berth to the rare larger vessel, salt-stained and heavy laden, carving north from the gulf and ports around the world. Sunlight sparkled on eddies and ripples of current. Diesel fumes and the pervasive scent of shrimp tainted the air, underlaced with the odors of strong detergents and the briny breath of gulf water.

The boundaries of the lake were mutable, banks giving way to marsh and bog. Most of the land around them, to either side of the lake, was inches underwater, tall grasses and the wide leaves of water lilies thrusting up from muddy bottoms into sunlight. In some places, soil met the air, black and rich and wet, covered with a profusion of bracken, climbing vines, and storm twisted trees. Stumps, remnants of a ravaged cypress forest stabbed the air in the distance.

Noon came and went, the sun beating down, unforgiving of tender skin and lightning scorched flesh. Mara sat, legs curled beneath her, in the bow, facing south, wind in her face, ignoring Old Banoit and her kin. The shrimpers should have been plying the waters, nets spread, buoys floating behind. Instead the crew mended nets, unknotting and re-tying, and repaired equipment. One shrimper even sat in the stern, sanding a small door, brass hinges glinting where sunlight caught the shining metal. They should have been making their living, not providing water-taxi service for a teenaged girl to some strange place . . . yet they worked uncomplaining, moving to the beat of a radio station that played zydeco and blues until they chugged through the Sabine Pass and into the Gulf of Mexico, where the music faded into static and the only sound was the throb of engine and the splash of water on hull.

They were making good time. Better time than the average shrimpboat, their speed enhanced by the modern, energy-efficient engine insisted upon by Momo when she bought the boat for Old Banoit years ago, and upgraded several times since. *Queen Fisher* was the flagship of old Banoit's fleet of twelve shrimpers, the first and the best. Sleek for a shrimpboat, powerful and fast. The canny Cajun had taken Momo's gift and built an empire beginning the day of its delivery. He and his men worked hard, sharing the profits from each catch; back-breaking physical labor that had made old Banoit rich.

But today they rested, doing chores most often left until stormy weather, carting Momo's girl-brat on some errand. Uncomplaining. Mara had the feeling that each man would have opened a vein at Momo's command and bled for her, with as little complaint. She curled tighter into herself, the wind of their passage in her face.

The gulf had no current, little swell of tide, unlike the Atlantic, yet the waters still responded to the thrust of trade winds, the violence of storm and the pull of the moon. The storm of the night before had left swells rolling on the water. *Queen Fisher* lifted and fell with the slow, regular movements. Again and again. To fight the queasy sensation, Mara sipped continuously from a bottle of water and kept her eyes on the horizon as the big boat turned east and moved along the coast.

There was nothing here, the world as desolate and empty as a blank and rotting canvas. The gulf to her right. Marsh to her left. The occasional boat in the distance. The call of gull overhead. The rare flight of brown pelican, the sun beating down, a merciless blaze of heat.

And some strange town ahead, unknown and unfamiliar. If Momo was right, Kenno would be there holding Devora captive. The obscure danger of the man was multiplied by the presence of

171

his hostage.

And Momo had sent her. Momo could have sent all of Old Banoit's sons and nephews, the shrimpers working in the stern or laying in the sun. Momo could have sent her own kin, the LeMays, rough men, ready with guns. Mara's uncles and cousins like Albert and Alain. They'd have made a party of it, like the yearly LeMay fais-do-do, a drunken revelry while they found, stopped, and killed Kenno. But Momo had sent her.

Mara.

Once again to be the arm of Momo's judgment.

But this time there was no glowing brand and stink of hickory smoke. No angry crowd demanding judgment and penalty. No special instruction, *Place brand here, Mara. Press firm.* No planned punishment. Just Momo's order, *Go to Breauxville. Kenno there. Take Devora back.*

What was she to do? Kill Kenno? Mara shivered. She didn't want to kill. But she had shot four men and felt nothing. That was her heritage. A heritage that seemed curse only, offering no solace at all.

The afternoon sun was setting behind *Queen Fisher* when Old Banoit turned the shrimper and headed north, plowing a watery trail between warning buoys. Fishing boats and shrimpers crowded the safety lanes, returning with a day's catch; the radio crackled and spat with news and greetings. Mara could hear the timbre of Old Banoit's voice as he identified himself and asked for the town marina. Breauxville Marina.

Mara, her skin blistered by last night's lightning followed by a day in the sun without sunscreen, shivered steadily now. Never warmed. Breauxville. Kenno. *Why was she here?*

Breauxville was several miles inland along Branle-bas Bayou, a deep, straight placid run of water whose name meant "clearing the decks". Branle-bas was part of the water system that created Grand Lake and White Lake, and existed solely for the fishermen and their kin and the old French families who lived further upstream in Breauxville.

The fishermen lived near the mouth of Branle-bas on a spit of land higher than the surrounding marsh, a cluster of houses and bars for the men and warehouses for the day's catch. It was a nameless, unincorporated town of unpainted clapboard houses just off Highway 82 where trucks rumbled all through the day and night, heading north and east and west to satisfy the palates of the nation's seafood lovers.

Queen Fisher crossed under 82 and chugged slowly past the cove.

With dusk falling, Old Banoit headed north and east for the town Devora's note had named as Kenno's destination. Alone on the bayou, they moved slowly, running lights on as mosquitoes collected near warm flesh and water fowl settled for the night along grassy banks.

Breauxville Marina was in good repair, well lighted and marked with warning buoys and "No Wake" signs. Dry storage was in a three-story-tall metal building to the left of the marina. Covered docks for boats of all sizes lay to the right. Centered were the temporary docks where expensive fishing boats rocked slowly while their owners ate in the rustic building just beyond. It blazed with light, a white painted building with open rafters where waitresses served fried catch-of-the-day and tall drinks to rich men on holiday.

The scent of frying food was a delicious, mouth-watering temptation riding the wind out over the water. Mara, stubborn and fearful and queasy with the roll of *Queen Fisher,* had eaten nothing all day. Now her stomach clenched, empty and demanding its share.

She stared in the windows at the raucous crowd. Tinny chords of the house band drifted down to the marina. A red-headed girl delivered a tray of plates, laughing and teasing as she passed out the orders.

Old Banoit chugged up to the public dock still speaking into his radio. Two of his men jumped free, tied off *Queen Fisher* and grinned up at Mara. They wanted food as well, she could see it in their faces. And perhaps they wanted to talk to the pretty red-head still preening to the crowd before the windows.

"Mara."

She jerked, startled, a hand coming up as if to ward off a blow. Old Banoit took her fist into his hand. Warm and callused fingers held hers, his leathery face crinkled at lips and dark eyes with a smile. "I no hit you, Mara. An' I no like leave you here. But Momo say dis de place fo' you destiny. You and Kenno. You got money?"

"Yes."

"We not dock here tonight. I make berth back at Hameçon. You see? We pass it, downstream."

Mara nodded, watching the red-haired waitress flirt with her patrons. She laughed a lot, serving the men with an ease and speed that was amazing.

"Mara? Kenno no here now, but he come soon. You unnerstand? I make berth fo' you *Jenny*. Make rent another boat fo' you. Fast boat if you think you need. An' hotel in Breauxville. All you do is give you credit card to Marina Manager, Bill Lephew and you got new boat. Give credit card to owner Patty Gueymard, Auberge Breauxville. Suite there fo' you. You got license to drive car?"

"No. No need to."

"You need car you talk Bill. Banoit take care dat fo' you. You need Ol' Banoit, you call." He pushed a folded slip of paper into Mara's now-warm fist. "It how you get Old Banoit at he office. I call Momo fo' you or any place. I no like leave you here alone, Mara. I no like."

"She won't be alone."

Mara whirled. Old Banoit just blew out a lusty, resigned breath, full of French passion. Mara laughed out loud.

"You sleep last time I look. Why you not stay sleep?" Old Banoit asked.

"I slept because I was bored. I thought I hid pretty good though. How'd you find me?" Cady asked, running her fingers through her hair. Not waiting for an answer, she continued, "God, it was hot inside. Mara, you're blistered. Hope you brought some aloe. So. Where are we staying tonight? I always wanted to stay in one of those fancy hotels with a bar downstairs and a cafe and a workout room." She shook out her skirts as she chattered, the men on the deck and the dock watching with slow smiles of appreciation. "Can we see a movie, Mara? Hope you packed enough clothes for me too. 'Course if you have one of Momo's credit cards, we can go shopping."

"Take her back, Banoit." Mara interrupted.

"No, Mara. You can't send me back. I won't go!" Cady

stamped her foot. It was an unpleasant reminder of Mara's own temper.

"She can't stay. Momo'd skin me alive if she knew—"

"Mara!"

"Momo know. Raise Old Banoit on radio while we still in Elephant Bayou."

Both girls looked at him, their argument suspended. Banoit's strong yellow teeth caught the sulfur glow of the marina lights. "That why you so easy to find, Cady, girl. Momo say you gone. Say Mara make decide you stay or go. Mara destiny, Mara decide." Banoit shrugged, a Gallic gesture, full of shoulder rolling indecision. It was obvious he didn't want either girl to stay in Breauxville.

"So part of my destiny is to take care of Cady," Mara said flatly.

"I can take care of myself. I brought my gun."

Mara ignored her sister, focusing narrowly on the old Frenchman who had married Rosemon's mother when Delice's DeLande protector left her.

"And if she gets hurt?"

Banoit nodded slowly. "Destiny strange thing, MaraNo. All thing you do, all thing you think, all thing you decide, come together. Shape future for you. Sometime fo' other peoples."

"And *your* destiny?"

Banoit patted the hand he still held.

"Mara, I'm not going back. You listening to me?" Cady asked.

"Old Banoit widower, long time past. Five sons and good life behind. Delice man die, her alone, yes?"

"Yes," Mara said.

"Storm come, hurricane from Gulf. Should go panhandle, Florida, hit there. 'Stead it hit Port Arthur, Sabine Lake. Square." He socked his palm with his fist to show the impact of the hurricane.

Mara had heard it before, all her kin had. It was the love story of Old Banoit and Delice, and the way the old man got *Queen Fisher*. They had heard the story a hundred times. But never from Old Banoit.

"Banoit have eye on Delice long time, but her done took, got man, DeLande Eldest. Love him. Want to grow old with him though he treat her not good time-to-time.

"Storm come. Banoit boat name *Jacinthe Des Près*, Blue Bell, dock for storm in mouth of Neches River. Old boat. Old engine. *Ah . . . que decier, ah . . . que prend l 'eau.*"

"Leaky," Cady said. "It leaked."

"*Oui*. Old Boat. Banoit wait on board for storm surge. It too big, Banoit plan to cut lines, ride surge up River Neches. Make decide, yes?" He settled dark eyes on Mara. "Make decide. Part of destiny, Old Banoit."

Caught up in the story, she whispered, "Yes. I understand."

"Storm come fast. Middle night. Water rise, and rise, and still rise. Wind carry man off, he stand against it, yes?"

"Yes." Cady said softly. "It was . . . violent. Dangerous."

"Pump go steady but water rise in *Jacinthe Des Près.* Storm pound old boat . . . Radio cracklin'. Old Banoit hear woman voice." He smiled. "Delice. Call for help. Say roof gone, two wall come down.

"One hand on board. Banoit son, Pierre. Good boy. Good . . . good boy. He . . . follow Banoit anywhere. He destiny . . . to follow.

"Banoit take ax to moorings. Pull *Jacinthe Des Près* into storm. Make mouth of Sabine River when storm surge lift old boat and carry her. Up river.

"Engine strain. Leak fast, hull full of storm, yes. Somehow Pierre and Old Banoit make mouth of Elephant Bayou. Cold. Wet. Boat creaking like old woman bones. Groan. Banoit know she not last long. Yet . . ." He shook his head, his eyes trying to tell Mara more than simple words.

"Found Delice cabin. Delice tie girl child and boy child to pilings. Tie herself. House gone. Storm like some *furie diabolique*."

Mara could picture the scene. The old boat riding low in the storm-tossed water. Branches, beams, debris beating against the hull. Thunder a continuous rumble. Pilings of deck or house thrusting up through the wild water. The small bodies tied there.

"Pierre . . ." Banoit gripped her hands, holding both of them now, too tight, bones grinding. Cady slipped closer. Banoit's men were there now as well, listening to the old, old tale. Banoit's throat worked, eyes damp with tears. "Pierre tie heself to line, jump into storm. Swim to piling. Cut girl child free. Swim back to boat. Get her on deck, under Old Banoit's feet. No help. Banoit fight storm and surge and old engines. No can help Pierre.

Pierre jump back in storm, bring back boy child. Put beneath Old Banoit's feet. They silent. Big tears. Or maybe storm so loud no can hear when they cry.

"Pierre tire, now. Fall. But jump back into storm. Save Delice, but no strength for to get her up. Banoit tie off wheel. Run to help. Find Delice in water, pull her to deck. Reach for Pierre . . . Pierre gone."

Banoit shrugged, as if to say, *"You see. Destiny. Make decide to save Delice. Pierre die."* Instead he said, "Banoit destiny to mourn. Have Delice, have new boat from Momo. Have riches. Rich man is Old Banoit. And he destiny to mourn."

"And Pierre's destiny?"

"To follow Old Banoit. To be love for all time. To die young. A hero." Banoit shrugged again, a different shrug this time, one full of pathos and suffering.

"She can't stay. Take her back with you."

"I'm staying." There was a soft metallic click, the sound clear in the grease-scented silent air.

Mara looked at Cady, who stared at Old Banoit. "Want to lose another son?" Cady stood pressed against one of Banoit's men, the feeble light glinting off the metal barrel of a small hand gun. Blonde hair lifted and fell in the breeze. Mara saw another man start, tense, and pause. Indecisive. A strange tension filled the air on the deck of the *Queen Fisher*. Part fear. Part wary amusement. This was a LeMay with a gun. Everyone knew the LeMays were more than a little crazy. "I haven't studied anatomy yet. Momo says I'm too young. So I have no way of knowing what I'll hit if I pull the trigger. So what do you say? Do I stay in Breauxville or do I bloody up your deck?"

"I'm not . . ." The man in Cady's arms cleared his throat and tried again. "I'm not Banoit's son," he managed. There was a peculiar smile on his face, as if he was uncertain if he should speak, remain silent, or give way to hilarity.

Cady jabbed the barrel deep into his side, deciding for him. He remained silent, eyes now pained. "So that makes you more dispensable to him. Maybe I'll have to shoot you twice."

Conversational tone, little girl voice, grown up words.

LeMay crazy. Mara could see it on every face.

Would Cady shoot?

Mara had.

Banoit met her eyes, a message there. Mara almost smiled. "So stay. You die, Banoit can tell his little destiny tale to Momo, and I can mourn for the rest of my life. Right?"

Banoit nodded. "You make decide, Mara."

"No way. Not so easy. You guys," Cady said to Banoit's hands, "unload *Jenny*. Mara, get out on the dock. Banoit, up to the fo' castle. I'm not stupid. I let Pierre-the-second here go when I'm satisfied that I can stay."

Mara sighed, picked up her duffel and tossed it to the dock below, jumping down after it. "My guns, please." She held up her hands for the shotgun, which slapped against her palms. Propping the Winchester on the duffel, she lifted her hands again for the Colt. *Jenny* splashed softly into the bayou behind *Queen Fisher*, settling like a lady into a rainbow of fuel-splattered water.

"Power up, Banoit. Cast off, ya'll. And be so kind as to stand aside so I can reach the dock. Thank you all."

Queen Fisher's engines rumbled. The mooring lines slipped free and Banoit's hands landed on the deck at bow and stern. The destiny of Old Banoit pulled from the dock, an inch. Two. A foot.

Lithe as a swamp panther, Cady ran, jumped, and landed lightly. Big grin on her face for an instant before she turned back to the boat. "I need my rifle, please. I was using it for a pillow." *Queen Fisher* idled. A moment later the classic little Remington was tossed through the air. Cady caught it one handed. "Oh, and tell Old Banoit neither weapon was loaded. I'm not that crazy."

"Not loaded?" Mara said, the words explosive.

"Shhh! Of course they were loaded, I'm crazy, not stupid. But they don't need to know that. What good is an unloaded gun? I'm hungry. We eating here?"

"Jesus, Mary and Joseph," Mara swore.

Unrepentant, Cady laughed out loud.

Chapter Twenty-Four
Lessons not Taught

Jenny was guided by a tousle-headed boy, who pulled the bow line up under the covered moorings to 27C, her berth number. A cabin cruiser of mammoth proportions was docked at her port side, open water was to her starboard side.

Hungry, muscle-sore from lack of movement all day, tired and worn, Mara and Cady made their way up the incline from the covered berths to the rollicking activity of The Lizard Spits. Spits was a haven for rich fishermen who wanted to let their hair down and act like good-old-boys for a spell, drinking and celebrating being away from the wife and kids and office, smoking *ceegars* when the mood struck, telling tall tales about the one that got away—fish or woman—and acting like kids again. Spits served great food, huge drinks, and offered a complementary taxi service to all the best hotels in town for its more inebriated clientele.

Mara and Cady parked their weapons at the front desk—it being impolite to bring guns into a fancy eating establishment—and took a booth along the wall. And ate.

There were eateries all over the Badlands. Private homes—bayou cabins—where the woman of the house would fry up almost anything on hand and sell it to passing boaters. Truly delicious food. But for sheer selection there was nothing in the Badlands to compete with The Lizard Spits. The two girls ordered an appetizer of fried delights, a combo of fried cheese, fried vegetables, fried octopus, onion rings, fried apples, fried fish strips, hush puppies, salt and pepper fish strips, buffalo wings, and little hot pepper and cheese pastries called mini-quesas. The sisters emptied the basket of goodies and a liter of wine and a carafe of ice tea within minutes.

And all that was before the meal came. Hunger and sun-scorched torment were so strong, Mara never once thought of Devora in Kenno's power. Worn and weary, she simply ate and watched the crowd, her mind empty.

The fisherman's platter was a delight of fried flounder, fresh-water bass, fried shrimp and stuffed deviled crabs, fried oysters, cole slaw, scallops, and all the french-fries, hot sauce and hush-puppies they could eat. Which was everything in sight.

Mara learned several things during the meal: She could hold as much food as one of the pot-bellied businessmen at the window tables. She looked far older than her actual age—as no one behind the bar asked to see the ID she didn't have. And she definitely did not know how to flirt.

All through the meal she watched the red-headed waitress tease her way through her customers, pocketing the highest tips, luring the highest-paying customers, tempting fate again and again—and walking away unscathed, the cash tucked into her bra. Flirting, it seemed, was an art. One of which Mara had no knowledge.

Momo had given her long lessons they'd shared over the last two or three years, yet flirting was one thing she had left out. The old witch had made certain Mara had a rudimentary understanding of physics, biology, some self defense, chemistry, the French language—Parisian style, not Cajun—world history and geography, and social mores from around the world. Momo had even shared her most explicit vision of sex education. Yet never, not once, had the old witch mentioned flirting. Momo had made certain Mara watched old videos of *Tom Jones*, and read *Catcher in the Rye*, had provided materials on the effect of hormone levels in developing embryos of rats and monkeys, and found a copy of *Lady Chatterly's Lover*. And once, on a particularly memorable occasion, she had shown an X-rated film about a homesteader and his family of daughters when visited by a band of traveling randy, naked, gorgeous Apache warriors. But no flirting. None.

So Mara watched.

A lifted brow was meant to tease.

A toss of long red hair conveyed sauciness.

A wrinkled nose meant, "You're cute, but try harder."

A glance under slitted lids said, "Better keep trying."

Pursed red lips meant, "Only if you're really lucky . . . and available."

And a shaken head meant, "Sorry, fisher-boy, I saw the tan line from your wedding ring." *Shame. Shame. Shame.*

It was a new kind of study for Mara, and for Cady as well. A lesson in sexual "come-hithers". The sisters shared comments and observations, conclusions and opinions, and decided they definitely needed red lipstick and skin-tight jeans. First thing in the morning.

When thoughts of Devora finally intruded, they glanced at one another, but did not mention her. Instead they kept their attention and comments on the food, the ambiance of Spits, and the raucous music. For just this little time, they needed to put aside the sound of gunshots and screams and the memory of Charlie's blood on the floor.

Breauxville Auberge was a white-columned beauty just outside town, a Georgian ante-bellum plantation home built in a square, a spectacular two-storied Bed and Breakfast with a wrap-around porch. It was situated on acres of ancient oak and azalea, the foliage dark and shadowed in the moonlight. A bronze plaque out front proclaimed it to be on the Historical Society's list of local landmarks.

Wide unpainted cypress boards planked the porch, oiled and waxed to a dull, muted shine. Turned oak balusters lined up like soldiers along the edge, lips and rims bloated by dozens of layers of white paint. Rockers moved slowly in the night breeze, ruffled cushions fluttering.

As the taxi pulled away and silence settled around them, the two girls climbed the stairs to the entry vestibule, which protruded on to the porch. In the distance an owl hooted. Answering calls came from nearby like a reverse echo. Mosquitoes and moths buzzed around the porch lights—huge brass cages of leaded glass, wired for electricity. The brass knocker was the shape of a lion's head, growling, holding in its mouth a brass ring. Cady lifted the knocker.

"Wait."

She looked over her shoulder and paused, the brass ring ready to pound.

"You remember how The Lizard Spits' manager looked when we tried to bring our guns inside?"

"Yeah," Cady said, impatient.

"And how the taxi driver made us lock them up in the trunk?"

Cady nodded, listening closer now.

"Well, maybe they don't use guns here like we do in the Badlands, and maybe it would be a good idea to leave them on the porch, in the shadows, until the people inside are asleep and then come back for them," Mara said.

"And how do we get them back outside in the morning?"

"Windows."

Cady considered a moment before gently replacing the lion's ring against its resting plate. She pulled her small .32 out of her waistband, and, reversing the weapon, gave it to Mara butt first. Bending, she lifted the Remington and handed it over as well. Laden with the weapons, Mara stepped to a wicker settee against the house wall and placed each underneath in the darkness puddled there.

"Good," Cady said, and banged the brass ring down three times. Moments later, a form darkened the leaded side lights, the wide door opened and Mara gazed inside.

A mirrored ebony coat rack and settee, some six feet wide and at least twelve feet tall, sat to the side of the door, umbrellas and carved walking sticks in the tall ceramic pots to either side of the cushioned bench. A delicate little loveseat upholstered in dark melon-colored velvet faced the coat rack. Beyond the vestibule, inlaid parquetry and vibrant oriental rugs graced the floor, while deep persimmon walls were a backdrop for gilt framed still-lifes and black and white family photographs. The foyer was two stories high with twin suspended curving staircases climbing its height to a wide landing on the second floor. Urns of exotic flowers rested on antique tables beside tasteful vignettes of old family heirlooms. A stack of dark leatherbound books. An old mandolin and case. A pair of gold spectacles. Small inlaid boxes. It was all an exquisite backdrop for the woman at the door.

She was elegant in the way a princess is elegant, one born and bred to the position through generations—tall and graceful, silver hair swept up in a soft chignon, black silk charmeuse blouse, black raw silk slacks, ballet slippers and pearls and a welcoming smile creased into wrinkles that somehow added both beauty and character to a perfectly oval face.

Instantly, Mara stood straight, lifted her chin and scolded herself for not rebraiding her hair and applying make-up in Spits' ladies' room. Cady's back straightened as well, and her sister couldn't quite muffle an awed gasp at the sight of the woman.

"*Bon soir*. Welcome to Breauxville Auberge," she said, her tone gracious, with a light French accent. "I'm Pat Gueymard and you must be the Misses LeMay?"

Cady opened her mouth but no sound emerged. Mara stepped forward into the odd little silence. "Yes, thank you. I'm Mara and this is my sister Cady. We appreciate you opening your home to us this late." The words were formal sounding and not too garbled. Mara was intensely grateful that the guns were hidden away instead of in their hands.

"Come in, please." The welcoming smile offered no judgment, no criticism of two disheveled girls with a single faded duffel bag between them. Mara hefted her duffel, smoothed the wild strands of hair back from her face and tried not to stare at the elegance of the inn. "I've placed you in the Aube Room as it has two beds and a small sitting room as well as its own bathroom." Elegant brows, thin and silver, lifted. "I understood from your grandfather you would need a secure location for the weapons you brought?"

Both girls halted, Cady's shoulders lifting, a bright embarrassed flush brightening her face as she turned accusing eyes on Mara. Old Banoit had been very thorough. Subduing an uncomfortable urge to giggle, Mara handed over the duffel and smiled back at Pat Gueymard. "Thank you, Mrs. Gueymard. My . . . grandfather suggested the weapons should remain out of sight until such time as your other guests were abed."

The lie flowed easily from her lips. Cady's eyes widened, impressed with the improvisation. A sudden flowering in their blue depths warned Mara that the lesson had taken instant root, but she was too far along in the game to change tactics now. "Would now be an acceptable time to bring the weapons to you?"

"Of course, my dears. It is, after all, nearly midnight." Mara winced, further embarrassed at the late hour, and went after her weapons.

Behind her Cady said, "Our other baggage will be delivered tomorrow, and I do hope you'll forgive our bedraggled appearance. We spent the day on my grandfather's, ah, yacht."

Lifting the guns, Mara straightened. *Yacht?*

"This is a beautiful home, Mrs. Gueymard," Cady continued. "I've always loved silk rugs and little Duncan Phyfe tables. And I adore this bizarre hat rack. It looks like it was made for this spot."

"It was. By Benjamin Latour, one of the *gens du couleur libre*, who was a master craftsman and wood carver before the War for Southern Independence. After the war, he made the piece you mentioned as well as several of the tables in the foyer. When he . . ." The delicate French accent faded as Cady and Mrs. Gueymard chatted their way into the foyer.

Burdened with the weapons that clanked barbarically in these elegant surroundings, Mara followed.

Chapter Twenty-Five
Family Obligations / Family Sin

Miles left the Welch brothers in the casino and took the transport skiff—a twenty-foot refurbished tug—to the hotel. Enoch, following a disastrous run of bad luck, was steadily winning back the bankroll Miles had staked him at the craps table. James was holding his own in a private poker game. Well dressed in double-breasted American-designed suits they had conned out of him, each man had acquired a blowzy female and an instant aura of charm reminiscent of Old West gamblers. Neither man needed Miles.

Bored with the decadence and the neon affluence, he had politely turned down the offer of a late dinner with the casino's principal investor, a well-known former talk-show host, pleading exhaustion. The night was balmy, the briny scent of Lake Charles somehow fresh, even tinted with the excess of chemicals wafting across the lake from the little towns of Westlake and Sulfur. The chemical plants lit up the horizon, festival-bright in the thick night air. The artificial breeze created by the slow passage of the tug ruffled his hair, and blew back the lapels of his Armani suit jacket as he studied the lights reflected on the lake.

The DeLandes were shareholders in several chlorine plants in the area and, as Eldest, Miles should make it a point to announce himself and perhaps take the company presidents to lunch. One of the dry, dull meals where production figures and future plans, labor disputes and the increasing cost of doing business, took precedence over more civilized conversation. So far he had avoided that fate, spending his daylight hours in the hospital at

185

Lucien's side and holding Rosemon's hand as she worried over her son. Including the Welch brothers' exorbitant expenses and the cost of Lucien's surgery, Miles' visit to Lake Charles was costing a fortune which he couldn't even consider tax deductible.

Perhaps in a day or so Lucien might be recovered enough for Miles to do a little business and satisfy the bevy of accountants who would review his trip for write-offs. As it was, staying in touch with business concerns by fax, phone and email was the best he could do.

The slow moving tug landed at the dock. Tossing a twenty-dollar chip to the "Captain", Miles bounded off the boat and whistled his way along the boardwalk toward the hotel. The entire voyage from casino to hotel lasted less than three minutes, a watery concession to Louisiana's off-shore gambling laws. By moving the floating casino a few yards from the bank and tossing anchor in Lake Charles, the law's minimum requirements had been satisfied. Tourists could gamble away their vacation funds and locals could lose their livelihoods.

Miles reached for the double handles into the casino hotel and stopped, his motion arrested by a sudden thought. He knew how to satisfy the accountants and turn this trip into a profit. His lawyers would be delighted. Smiling, he entered the lobby, held a short conversation over the house phone with the former talk-show host and entered the brass and walnut elevator for the short ride to the penthouse suite. Using the electronic card-key, he entered his rooms.

It was the scent that warned him. Feminine and earthy in the darkness beyond the door.

Miles twisted as the weight descended. A soft whoosh of sound close by his ear. Instant pain, intense and numbing, flowed from shoulder to fingertip.

The door slammed shut. Blackness descended.

Wounded, he crouched, trying to picture the room as he remembered it. Recklessly he moved forward to where the chair—barrel shaped and deeply padded—had rested in the maroon carpet.

His fingers touched the upholstery. His assailants hadn't over-turned the room, but knowing that was little help. DeLandes seldom traveled with weapons, and he was unarmed, wounded and alone.

Body bowed and coiled for powerful release and instant action, Miles explored his shoulder. Dry. No blood on his fingertips, or wet and slick on his clothes. A blunt object then. Aimed at his head. *To stun or kill?* He regulated his breathing. Slow and easy.

Feeling, sharp prickles of pain, tingled in his numb hand. A dull ache in elbow and wrist.

Kenno?

No. The perfume. Feminine. Somehow familiar. The sound of breathing intruded on his assessment of his situation. Stealthy movement pinpointed one intruder. A shadow shifting in the darkness. He could pick out no others. The lack of other sounds convinced him there was only one. Silently Miles slid forward. Slipped into the chair. Eased his body down so the cushions' escaping air made no sound.

Lifting his wounded hand he draped it across his lap. Crossed his legs, propped his chin on doubled fist. And waited.

Arrogant, yes. But if his attacker wanted him dead, he—she?— would have shot first and played parlor games later. At the moment, the arrogance of his pose was the only weapon he had.

Another movement in the darkness, cloth against cloth. A faint click.

Light flooded the room.

Miles smiled. "Your aim always was off."

"Damn you!" she hissed. She stood in the shadows by the door, shoulders hunched, fingers like claws.

Miles made a soft *tsking* noise and shook his head, the skin of his jaw moving on his fisted fingers. "Silly games are beneath you, Angelique." He dropped his hand from chin to lap and surreptitiously touched the other. It was warm, which he knew was a good sign, but it ached as if the bones were broken. His pulse was a dull throb of monotonous agony along the limb. "Besides, why just injure me? Why not go for gold and use a gun?"

She curled her hands into fists, bared her teeth. Red hair threw golden sparks in the dim light, tousled and savage. "I hate you!"

"Angelique, I'm tired. All I want is for you to go away so I can shower and go to bed."

"Alone?" Suddenly her face changed, fury giving way to

187

something more dangerous, slit-eyed and feral. "Poor Miles, always sleeping alone. Even as a baby. Run, baby Miles. Run away and hide." She laughed and he steeled himself for her taunts. "How long has it been for you? How long since a DeLande touched you skin-to-skin, mind-to-mind?"

Angelique lifted a hand, delicate, manicured, fingers flaring like a fan before she touched a button at her throat. "You remember what it was like, don't you, Miles?" She said, her voice a deep vibration, fraught with invitation. "Remember the heat?" Her fingers pushed at the button, mother of pearl in red silk. It slid loose. Fingers moved to the next and the next, smooth white flesh flushed softly pink appearing in the widening gap.

Miles noted for the first time the red silk oriental pajamas she wore. Delicate cloth embroidered with gold strands. Most redheads couldn't wear scarlet. But Angelique could—and did—do anything she wished. Tension built in the air between them. Pressing against his throat. Breath came slow and harsh.

Desire radiated from her in waves of heat. His skin flushed and warmed. His pulse slowed to a heavy surge. His eyes were riveted to the curve of her breast. The last button was released.

"Name me the next Grand Dame, and I'll be yours, Miles. All yours."

Suddenly Miles laughed, the sound raw and explosive, shattering the spell she wove. "All mine?" He laughed again, the tone strained and relieved at once, and deliberately cruel. "Hell! You've shared yourself with so many men . . ." his gaze flicked over the exposed flesh and back up, meeting her eyes. The glance was insulting, deliberately brief. "If you notched each one of them into your bed post there'd be nothing left but a pile of splinters. You're used goods, girl."

White teeth shining, red lips pulled back, Angelique growled and rushed him. Metal flashed in her hand.

Afterward, Miles could never remember the exact sequence of events. The guttural scream. The battered-in door. The crush of bodies. Stumbling, shouting. Sound of blows falling. Sight of welling blood.

And Enoch's eyes, a pale-pale blue as he held the blade at Angelique's bared throat, her pulse pounding above perfect breasts. An odd hush, almost peaceful, in the room. Angelique's eyes were wide and pleading, Enoch's full of fury, his teeth bared. Peculiar stillness swelling.

That he always remembered. The silence. Taut and twisted, vibrating and cloying. The sound of his own laughter still echoing in the suite.

Enoch's eyes demanding. *Kill her? Tell Me! Kill her?* Basic, the demand. Life or death. Harsh, the silence.

Slowly Miles uncrossed his legs. Looked from Angelique's eyes, where terror dawned as she realized her danger, to Enoch's, waiting. To James' muddy gaze above a long slash from ear to chin at jawline. *Superficial*, Miles' mind informed him.

Leaning forward, he rested his elbows on his knees, pleased that the injured arm responded almost normally, though the pain had not abated. He clasped his hands and studied the tableau.

"We could kill her, I suppose. But then we'd have to pay for a new carpet. And I'd have to explain to the police why I allowed my sister's throat to be slashed."

Enoch blinked. The fury faded to a type of . . . horror. *Sister.*

Miles tried for a smile and failed. "Enoch and James Welch, may I introduce Angelique DeLande? My sister."

James' eyes flashed to the wild red hair and exposed skin, bare breasts now heaving under the blade in Enoch's hands. The discarded scarlet blouse in a silken heap.

And still the silence. Shocked now, as the men realized a seduction of sorts had been planned. Or a killing.

"Yes," Miles acknowledged, "she didn't care which. One or the other. The seduction might have gained her the family position of Grande Dame, a position of power among the DeLandes almost as important as that of Eldest. What I don't know is what she could have gained by my death."

Angelique's eyes flashed, light glinting in their depths. She hissed her refusal to respond to that statement, words that were really a question. A demand for information.

Enoch's mouth thinned. He pulled back on her hair, his fingers tangling in it. The blade pressed into her skin, drawing a thin line of red against the perfect flesh. A trail of scarlet trickled to her collarbone. She swallowed, sweat gleamed with the pull of muscles. Finally she hissed, "I *will* be Grande Dame. If not through you then through another. We have a deal, she ground out, And he *will* have me in his bed."

"Another?" Miles asked, brows raised politely.

"Yesss," she hissed again. "Kenno."

Chapter Twenty-Six
Longing for Feather Beds

Mara turned on the firm mattress and shoved a pillow between her knees. On the feather bed at Momo's, her knee bones never touched, the down supporting the joints of back, hip, shoulder and knee so perfectly. She never woke up sore or bruised. The commercial mattress of the inn was not proving so accommodating.

While the bed was less than welcoming, the shower and bath in the adjoining bathroom had been pure heaven. Unlimited hot water on demand, without boiling pots on the gas range first, or waiting for the small electric water heater to reach optimal temperature for a quick shower, had beaten the stiffness from shoulder and back, and the whirlpool bath had soothed her burnt skin. Absolute bliss, even without the aloe Momo hadn't bothered to pack.

Little water blisters pebbled her nose and cheeks. Mara knew she might peel as the burn aged. Even the deep skin tones bestowed on her by her American-Indian father and the mulatto several-greats grandmother couldn't protect her from the foolish hours in the sun.

Mara hammered the pillow as if it was the cause of her discomfort, and rolled over on to her back, pulling the sheets and quilt with her. A draft of cold air slithered down her body from the air conditioner vent beside the bed, billowing the lace curtains and casting amorphous shadows about the room. Uncomfortable bed, silly little light, unfamiliar air conditioner, bizarre shadows. Mara knew she would never fall asleep. It was her last thought until Cady woke her, shaking her shoulder just after dawn.

"Get up," she demanded with a far from gentle shove. "I smell breakfast cooking, and coffee. I could eat a snake, raw."

"How appetizing." Mara rumbled into her pillow. Rolling over stiffly, she added. "And Mrs. Gueymard looks like just the type to keep a nest of snakes out back for her guests' bizarre tastes."

Cady giggled and ran a brush through her hair. Long crinkled waves left by her braid separated into individual blonde hairs and stood out from her head with static electricity. The younger girl moved with a lithe grace as she brushed and chattered, commenting on the glass knickknacks and the framed art works and the old books on the shelves.

Mara tuned her out, stretching against the stiffness, pulling against tight muscles as she headed for the hot shower and the relief it promised. There was something almost obscene about Cady's resilience and grace after a night on a hard mattresses.

Half an hour later, the girls clattered down the stairs, tiered skirts fluttering, hair neatly braided with long tails dangling. Following their noses, they found the dining room. Mrs. Gueymard had coffee in carafes, surrounded by a breakfast fit for royalty.

A crystal bowl of cubed fruit was the centerpiece, the brim of the bowl curving up like petals of a huge flower. Watermelon, honeydew, strawberries, cantaloupe, fresh wedges of pineapple and green slices of kiwi filled it.

On a bread warmer were half a dozen types of muffins: bran, cranberry, blueberry and peach that Mara could recognize. China cups, sterling silver tongs and cutlery immediately reminded the girls of their manners.

"Good morning Mrs. Gueymard," they chorused.

"Good morning, girls." She looked as picture perfect as the night before, dressed this morning in shrimp colored cotton knits, a more delicate strand of pearls around her neck, her lips the exact shade of the blouse. Mara was impressed.

"We have decaf, dark French roast with chicory and roasted pecan, or tea if you prefer. Juice is on the sideboard—orange, pineapple, and a delicious new one I'm trying, strawberry-kiwi-passion fruit juice. Bacon is fresh off the griddle, with scrambled eggs and grits coming right up."

"Yesss," Cady said. "But pecan coffee sounds, well, kinda

nasty, begging your pardon."

Mara could have kicked her sister. Momo would be horrified. Mrs. Gueymard just smiled.

"Actually, Cady, they take a rich coffee blend and add the flavoring to the beans. I think you'll like it."

"I'd love a cup," Mara said before Cady could respond, and shot her sister a murderous glance behind Mrs. Gueymard's back.

Cady grinned and stuck out her tongue. "I'd like a cup as well, if you please," she said the instant her tongue was back in place, all propriety. "And eggs and grits sounds wonderful." She stuck out her tongue again as their hostess offered a steaming cup to Mara.

"Thank you. I'll just have muffins and fruit if you please," she said, irritated yet trying not to laugh.

"Help yourselves, girls. We don't stand on ceremony at Breauxville Auberge, and you may eat anywhere. The front porch is pleasant this time of day," suggested their hostess. "If there is anything you need, simply ask. Now, I need a moment in the kitchen and the eggs will be right out. After your breakfast, I'll be glad to answer any questions you may have about Breauxville."

The muffins were pure heaven. Even Lillybloom couldn't hope to achieve the light, delicious texture of the bread and its sweet fruit. Cranberry was the best, Mara decided, and the pecan flavored coffee was anything but nasty. Truly delectable, in fact. They went back for refills so many times that Mrs. Gueymard gave them a pot for the table. Between them, the sisters finished it off.

Complimentary newspapers were delivered partway through breakfast and by the time the girls were drinking their last cup of coffee, nibbling at crumbs and giggling over comics, the other guests began arriving.

Sleepy-eyed, middle-aged and overweight, they settled at various tables in the breakfast room and on the porch, slurping coffee as if it held the prescription for eternal youth. The couple at the table beside them hid behind separate newspapers, drank coffee in silence, and ate one handed. Not once during their meal did they speak, even to ask for butter, or sugar, or honey. Between them was a strange tension, like anger or dislike or boredom. Still without speaking, they rose from their cleaned plates and re-entered the house, the man trailing silently behind his wife.

Cady leaned over and whispered, "If that was marital bliss, give me a DeLande protector any day."

Mara, disturbed by the lack of attention or even interest between the couple, almost agreed. When Andreu had been home and anywhere near Rosemon, they talked and teased and chattered incessantly, touching often, sharing long glances. They seemed happy together, as if they had been made for one another.

Mara pursed her lips, wondering if marriage was really so bad, or if the couple beside them had simply quarreled. She remembered quarrels between Rosemon and Andreu too, loud, noisy arguments and the occasional broken dish. But they had been the preliminaries, always, to long hours spent behind Rosemon's closed door, giggles and thumps and strange noises coming through the walls.

Momo had chosen Rosemon for Andreu. Bred her for him and raised her to be sensuous and earthy, dependent and tender. A being created solely for him. Mara, on the other hand, had been raised to be independent, protected from most forms of sexual awareness. Had been encouraged to explore the bayou alone, led to be stubborn, inspired to be feisty. More than once instructed to be cruel.

For Miles? Mara shivered in the early warmth.

Mrs. Gueymard opened the door and stepped out on to the porch, her eyes going to the gardens, and cloud-free skies, before finally settling on the girls. With her ubiquitous smile, she asked, "May I join you?"

Mara quickly stood and indicated the closest chair. "May we get you some coffee?" Mrs. Gueymard sat and stretched out her legs, in a very unladylike pose. "Thank you, no. I'm supposed to serve you, remember? Besides I drank several cups while the guests ate. Your room was comfortable, I hope?"

"Yes, very," Mara lied as she retook her seat.

"Loved, absolutely loved, the whirlpool tub, and have every intention of loving it again tonight," Cady said.

"Ben told me you would be staying several nights, but never indicated why you were here. Sightseeing?" Mrs. Gueymard probed kindly. "The inn has several bicycles available if you would like to hire them out for the day?"

"Ben?" Cady asked.

"Ben Banoit? Your grandfather?"

"Ben is his first name? Neat. We just call him Old Banoit. Right, Mara?"

Mara smiled at Cady's ingenious response. It beat answering with the truth. *No, not sightseeing. We're here to kill or be killed by our uncle who has kidnapped and very likely injured our pregnant sister Devora.* Mara's pleasure in the morning faded. Devora and she had never been close, not since the gator attack. Devora had grown timid and subdued, avoiding the water, reluctant to touch a gun, and for reasons Mara had never bothered to explore, had become deathly afraid of fire, black crows, blue-bottle flies, and a myriad other insignificant little things.

Yet, Kenno had her. There was no chance he would leave her uninjured, unmolested, no matter what he promised to Momo. Mara remembered the screams of a dying cat . . . Was he hurting her now? Was she hungry? Was her leg hurting, the one the gator had injured? It ached sometimes. "I think the bicycles sound like fun," she said to stop the thoughts chasing around in her mind. "Cady and I don't get much opportunity to ride these days."

"Shopping is first thing on my list. I need everything," Cady said. "Jeans, shoes, lingerie, at least two party dresses. Do your bikes have baskets?"

Mara stared at her sister. She knew Cady hadn't forgotten Devora but had no idea what the younger girl was up to.

"We have bicycles with baskets. And several stores will deliver your purchases to the inn, if you like, for a small fee. Most shops open at ten, so you have a few hours yet. I'll make you a list of the best boutiques in town, though jeans are best purchased at Wal-Mart which is quite a ride. You might prefer a taxi, but I'll see if I can find a map marked with the locations of shops. And if you do get fatigued, Bluebird taxi will deliver both you and your bikes back to the door."

"Wal-Mart. That's like a big superstore, right?" Cady said.

Mrs. Gueymard looked surprised. "Well, yes. It is."

"Neat. I think the taxi is a great idea. Thanks for the bikes too. We can use them while it's still cool this morning, then switch to the taxi."

Mara nodded, forced the wavering smile back on her face and stood. "Thank you so much for the lovely breakfast, Mrs. Gueymard. And, yes, we'd like the bikes for sightseeing this morning. Have you ever heard of Sasim? S-A-S-I-M," she spelled.

"No . . . I can't recall the name. Is it in town or a shop? Or perhaps one of those nail places you young girls frequent?" Mrs. Gueymard's eyes dropped to Mara's hands, the nails cracked, rough and bayou jagged.

Mara resisted the urge to hide her hands. "We aren't really sure. A friend mentioned the name. We'll ask around. Would half an hour be acceptable for the bicycles?"

"Certainly, girls. Go change and I'll see you shortly."

Cady followed Mara into the house. "Change? Change into what?"

"I suppose jeans or something. What did you wear when you learned how to ride a bike?"

"A pair of Lucien's old trousers tied up with a rope, and some of your old sneakers."

"Really?" Mara paused partway up the stairs. "Momo made me learn in a dress. Gosh awful trying to ride a bike when you can't even see your feet."

"Why'd you get so upset out front? Was it because Mrs. Gueymard called Old Banoit, 'Ben'?"

"No! Why should I care what she calls him? I was—"

"Because I think she's got a crush on him."

"What? Who?" Mara asked, thoroughly confused.

"Mrs. Gueymard and Old Banoit. I think she's got the hots for him. You hadn't been so upset, you'd have seen this look in her eyes like she's just dreaming about him."

"Old Banoit smells like shrimp."

"Not when he cleans up. And he cleans up real good. I even saw him shaved once. He had false choppers and he was wearing cologne."

"Cady, you have some weird ideas, girl."

"So why were you upset?"

Exasperated, Mara turned on her sister. "Kenno has Devora. Kenno is probably hurting Devora. Devora is probably scared witless. And we're making plans for a shopping spree! I think that's reason enough."

"You don't have to get so huffy. Devora's not stupid. She'll be fine."

Mara was stunned by her sister's callous tone. She looked at Cady as she spoke, watched the younger girl's fingers smooth back her braid and rub across her chin as if searching for traces of bacon grease. But her fingers trembled and she was unable to meet Mara's gaze.

"You're afraid of him, aren't you? Because of what he did to you when he had you on the island."

"He said he wouldn't *hurt* her. Besides, what can we do about it? Kenno isn't here yet. Old Banoit said so. So. Lets find this Sasim and go shopping." Cady put her hands on Mara's shoulder, turned her and pushed. "Change. We have orders." Silently, Mara complied.

Miles smiled grimly and lifted his sister into the Sikorsky. The engine whine was loud enough to preclude conversation, but nothing could hide the peculiar light in Angelique's eyes, or the way her hip curved against his chest, or the feel of her breast against the side of his hand. Or the waves of desperate sensuality that rolled out from her, inexorable as the tides. Wanton needs and a hedonistic anger all directed at him, and beneath it all, fury at herself for being so easily snared. She had planned her violent seduction without thought or knowledge of the Welch brothers. Planned it meticulously.

And Miles still did not know how the Welch brothers had arrived on the scene so quickly. The skiff could scarcely make the round trip in the time between his last sight of them, and when they broke down the door to his room. Yet the question—how they had known of his danger—was not one they had answered. *Danger. Peculiar, personal, sexual danger . . . Would he have succumbed?* No. Never. *But would he have wanted to?* Angelique laughed deep in her chest. He could feel her amusement in his bones.

She was right. Kenno *would* take her to his bed.

Dumping his sister onto the floor of the helicopter, he tossed a blanket over her squirming body, as much to hide her bound hands and feet as to provide a minimum of comfort.

He slammed the door shut on her furious face, stepped back and waited for lift off. The pilot and the guards had their orders. Take her to the little "guest" house near Lebeau, drop her off with two of the guards—who had orders to "keep her happy"—and make the return trip to Lake Charles for the flight back to Elephant Bayou with a miraculously improved Lucien. They would log a lot of air-time in the next twenty-four hours.

Rosemon and Miles couldn't keep up a pretense about Lucien's extraordinary recovery much longer. Dr. Kinsey had hounded them with her questions and suspicions, while Mile's platitudes about the healing powers of a mother's love had already worn thin.

They would transport him back home first thing in the morning. Miles, who didn't usually tire his employees—especially the pilots—would fly the return trip.

And he would see Mara.

Meanwhile, he had the free hours required to seal the DeLande Estate investment in Lake Charles' newest floating casino, the triple-decker floating monstrosity to be built to order in the state's newest shipyard near Morgan City, and delivered within the year. It was a sure investment. As every gambler eventually realizes: the house always wins. The DeLandes had never invested in casinos, bingo, or night clubs, yet, Miles would do many things to keep the estate's pencil pushers happy.

The Sikorsky, its wheels down for a land based take-off, rolled out to the open space specified by the tower and took off. She was a beautiful sight to Miles, black finish gleaming in the sunlight, the DeLande bird of prey painted in red on her sides above the insignia, and duplicated on her underside. No such bird existed. Never had. But then, no such family as the DeLandes had ever existed either. He wondered if Mara would be fool enough to consent to join it.

Chapter Twenty-Seven
Muscular Complications

The sun beat down on the girls as they peddled their unsteady way down the road to town. Neither of them remembered riding a bike to be so difficult. Calf muscles bunched and strained, the hard, anatomically incorrect seats bruised, and the sun glaring down on them multiplied their discomfort. Instant and prolonged misery.

Riding in tiered skirts did the rest.

Mrs. Gueymard watched them go down the drive, shaking her head. Mara knew they would long be remembered as two of the inn's most eccentric clients.

After the first half-mile, Cady developed a rhythm that smoothed her bicycle's movement. Mara couldn't determine why she was unable to do the same. The topography of Southern Louisiana was perfect for long-distance rides. Except for man-made hillocks, sculpted drainage systems, and deliberately bermed earth, it was flat.

Seldom was there more than three feet of vertical lift above sea level anywhere. When the bayous and rivers flooded or storm surges came ashore—which was fairly regularly—the earth was submerged beneath feet of water. In years past, homes were built up off the ground on brick pilings in a style appropriately called the "Tidewater" style of architecture. The arrival of Texas sized and Texas born termites ended the reign of tidewater homes with their wooden floor systems, and created the trend of slab-built homes—ugly, squat, flat looking things with engineer designed roof systems created to withstand hurricane winds and large volumes of torrential rain.

Mara knew all about the architecture of the state, and architecture in general, that being one of the things Momo felt she particularly needed to learn. Back home on the shelves were dozens of books on the subject.

Understanding the reason for changes in building styles did nothing to ease the cramp in her legs. At least if there had been a hill or two, she could have jumped off and walked the bike to the top. The idea of coasting downhill seemed positively wonderful.

By the end of the second mile, when the town came into view, Mara was more than ready for a rest. They drank from a fountain in the shade near the modern Holy Epistle of God church, and walked the rest of the way in, pushing the bicycles, catching their breath. Breauxville was a quaint little town: old French houses surrounded by wrought-iron fences and lush gardens so full of bougainvillea and lantana, old-world roses and ornamental trees, that it was like looking into mini-rain forests contained in the enclosed spaces.

The homes were Italianate, Georgian, or French country with tall narrow windows and operative storm shutters, odd little Baroque or Rococo twists in the bizarre shape of a rare window, the fluted columns across a stately porch, or the gingerbread scroll work. Black-painted wrought iron in the shape of javelins, axes, or roses—or once in the shape of crossed six-shooters—made up the fences and the balcony railings. Wicker swings, settees, tables and rolling tea trolleys abounded.

Ferns and pansies bordered old, cracked slate walkways, green with mildew.

Birds sang so loud it was a chorus, and at one home, white geese walked across the lawn or floated in a small pond, squawking and quacking and generally making a green gooey mess of things. It looked as if they had been there for years, and as if the owner of the house hadn't. Men in tennis whites or golf clothes or more rarely in business suits climbed into expensive cars, picking up the phone before pulling out of the drives. Nannies dressed in pink pinstripe or teddy bear prints walked with strollers, while slim and well-toned housewives jogged with weights in hand. Teenagers roller-bladed with hockey sticks down the center of the streets, while younger kids played with basketballs or dolls or rode bikes with an ease Mara envied.

Closer into town the homes were older, smaller, vaguely Spanish in style with deep-set arched windows and slate or tile roofs. Narrow, tall and elegant, they were set close together, separated only by overgrown ornate iron gates that revealed hints of secluded gardens and splashing fountains at the back. The streets were narrow here, the sky completely obscured by over-arching oaks.

Mara had never seen anything half so lovely.

Through the old leaded windows priceless antiques inlaid with mother of pearl, ivory and extinct woods radiated a luster that spoke of tender care for centuries. Heavy draperies closed off other homes creating an oasis of privacy in the center of city life.

Some six blocks in, the streets widened into a boulevard, the median planted with annuals and greenery. A statue of Ponce de Leon on horseback paused in mid-stride in a luxuriant hedge of hibiscus. Scarlet blooms moved in the breeze, brushing the horse's withers. Across from the statue, separated by a roadway, splashed a fountain, water erupting from the spout of a cavorting dolphin. Beyond from the intersection was a grand domed edifice fronted with enormous Ionic columns, plaster scroll work and weathered marble facing. Government buildings of one sort or another lined up to the right, stately and official. But none of that was of interest to the girls.

West of the main intersection, which appeared to mark the center point of the old town, was the business section. Old buildings with quaint signs stood side-by-side with newer, less refined structures, modern neon signs garish and out of place. In the opposite direction was the commercial part of town.

They turned their bicycles east.

It was early yet for the boutiques to be open, their solid wooden doors still shut and locked against the night. Yet, the girls could see wide, square windows which displayed various wares, with shop names stenciled in gold leaf at the tops. They were elegant and sophisticated, expensive and genteel, every one. One after another they extended for blocks: jewelers, antique galleries by the dozen, dress shops, hat shops, lingerie shops, specialty shops strictly for shoes. Overhead, balconies extended, providing partial protection in the event of rain. Old-fashioned gilt signs advertised coffee houses, bagel bakeries, tobacco shops and artist's studios above street level. It was opulent and extravagant, rich and wasteful, and beyond anything the girls had ever seen.

"Jesus, Mary and Joseph," Cady breathed.

"Uh huh." It wasn't much to say—far less than the sight warranted—but it was all Mara could think of. Finally she said, "Sasim could be a shop."

"Could be. It'd take us a whole day just to walk down this street and look at the shop names. And I still need some clothes."

"We're here to save Devora."

Cady propped a hand on one hip. "Are you still talking about that little scene with Mrs. Gueymard?"

Mara frowned. "Well, it was pretty . . . ah . . . cold hearted."

"Look, I know what Kenno is. You understand? I *know!*" Cady's eyes blazed.

Mara looked away, knowing that what her sister had suffered had been because of her, in her place, a substitute. Like Devora was suffering now because of her.

"But we do have to buy some stuff, and we have to search the town to find Sasim. Now we have a reason that Mrs. Gueymard will accept as perfectly normal for us to be looking around. All I had to do was sound just like a silly, empty-headed teenager. Right?"

Reluctantly, Mara's frown smoothed away. "Guess you have a point."

"And it's not as if we'll find Kenno by sitting still, watching the breeze in the trees at Mrs. Gueymard's. We have to *look* for him. I still want the jeans, but I know we have work to do. Besides," she added with a wicked little smile, "Kenno said he wouldn't hurt *her*. It's you he's after."

A bitter laugh, a single note of pain, escaped from Mara. "Thank you so much. That makes me feel *ever* so much better."

"I'll take this side of the road, you take that one. Anything that looks like that funny upside-down question mark or Sasim, holler. Okay?"

Mara sighed. "*Oui, mon capitaine.*"

Cady raised up on the pedals of her bike. "Race you to the end."

The wealth of shops was beyond Mara's wildest expectations. The commercial section of town was four blocks long with side streets of positively exquisite little specialty stores, boutiques, bakeries, and studios. Even with the gold credit card emblazoned with her name, most everything was out of Mara's price range. And not one of the shops boasted a question mark or the name Sasim, though they searched almost without stopping until nearly noon.

Early on, they did stop and purchase sunglasses, wide-brimmed Panama hats, sunscreen, and water bottles at a little place called *Ban-de-Soleil*. In gold lettering on the front window was the name of the shop and a stylized sun bonnet, exactly like Momo's gardening hat—which she called her *ban de soleil*. The hats the sisters came away with looked nothing like Momo's sun bonnet, with its eight-inch slits in the forward facing brim, each with its own smooth strip of wood inserted to help the bonnet hold its shape and keep off the sun's heat.

Instead, the brims of the new hats were wide all around and woven of some slick-feeling plant. And they were lightweight as well, unlike Momo's heavy head-wear.

At the shop next door they purchased oversized cotton T-shirts and biking shorts, scandalous tight little things made from a stretchy fabric called Lycra that pulled on tighter than a second skin and molded to the shape of buttocks and thighs like paint. The sales girl assured them that the little pieces of apparel were what everyone wore when bicycling, but the LeMays knew what Momo would say to that.

The fact that she was nowhere near to complain made the fashion statement a guilty pleasure.

Separately and together, they peered into jewelry shops where antique settings sported polished gems, and globes of amber preserved gnats or tiny flowers, and in one a dragon fly, one wing bent beneath, trapped forever. Silver candlesticks older than Momo, violins with worn necks and bows without horsehair strings, old gold spectacles, tiny watercolors, Italian blown glass, bits of Venetian lace and delicate silk corsets, old books with rotten leather bindings, were displayed up and down *Rue Souhaiter*. Fancy street. A street of dreams.

And an entire store devoted to Elvis paraphernalia. Momo liked Elvis. On a whim the sisters bought her a pin of the younger Elvis, hips jutted forward, guitar slung around his waist. It was blue, and Elvis wore blue suede shoes. They knew Momo would like it.

Mara paid for the Elvis pin with cash, pocketing the receipt and replacing her sun-glasses as she stepped back into the humid heat. Warm black waves swayed above the asphalt—simmering and shimmering summer temperatures. A dizzying, torpid fever.

Catching the doorjamb, she leaned against the wall of the shop; rough old-brick scratched through the cotton of her T-shirt.

Devora . . .

Nausea` rose in the back of her throat. *Devora with Kenno.*

Cady was not the only one who knew what Kenno was. Mara knew too. She *knew.* She had stared into the blue flame of his eyes through waves of hot coals. Heard the sssshhhisst sound as his skin sizzled. Seen the hatred. The sun suddenly became too much, and the trappings of wealth all around grew cloying. She hadn't known people really lived like this. *And meanwhile Devora was suffering.*

"MaraNo?"

"I'm okay. I'm okay." She smiled weakly at her sister. "Let's go."

Tired, sick at heart, Mara turned her attention to the churches which were scattered haphazardly, at least one in every block. Two were still in use. St. Lawrence's, a Roman Catholic church established in 1756, and the Church of God our Father of Prophecy and Love. The cornerstone of the Prophecy Church had been laid in 1812 in the old church of St Luke. Mara had a feeling the original St. Luke parishioners were rolling in their grave at what the modernist church members had done to the building.

Inside, Prophecy had torn down or covered over all the old plaster and put up wall board, destroying or hiding any frescos, decorative scrollwork, and the elegant columns holding up the vaulted roof. They had dropped in a low ceiling of panels held in place with metal strips. Electric musical instruments littered the podium at the front of the church while huge black speakers were stacked to left and right. Microphones were everywhere and tambourines were slotted next to hymn books on pew backs. The color scheme was a vibrant orange and burnt persimmon, and the place smelled of mold and sweat and some musk-like scent underneath it all. Clearly a place of worship taken over by the hoi-poloi.

St. Lawrence's, on the other hand, was unchanged from the date its cornerstone was laid. Scents of sandalwood, camphor, tallow, paraffin, old smoke, and the odd, delicate hint of lemons pervaded the dark and somber place. Gilded and painted statuary, holy water in a basin and antique tapestries carefully restored, caught the wavering flames and seemed to move in the damp, chill air. Marble worn by the footsteps of centuries covered the floors. Niches, shadowed and still, held statues of the saints in Grecian-style robes, faces turned to stare at the crucifix hung above the altar. An ivory Christ bled there, agony etched on his face and body.

Mara shivered, staring at the vaulted ceiling lost in shadows. Echoes whispered of forgotten prayers and death and time that rolled on and on.

Devora was not there. Devora was nowhere.

Quietly, without speaking to anyone who might have helped them, the LeMay sisters left the church. The others were little more than historic monuments, an admission price charged by the city for their upkeep. As neither was called Sasim, the girls pressed on, returning to the more secular pleasures of *Rue Souhaiter*.

When they had seen every store front, looked at every sign and occasionally lusted through a shop window, they chained their bikes to a street lamp and ate a late lunch at a croissant shop. Rich white cheese slathered on croissants, fresh basil leaves and bean sprouts, tomatoes and sliced cucumbers, were smothered beneath mounds of thin-sliced highly seasoned pork. Yet, the meal became a guilty pleasure. The moment it was delivered they knew, somehow, that Devora was hungry. And afraid. The knowledge—or the fear—kept them quiet as they ate, served by a pimply faced teen in jeans and polo shirt.

Over coffee, Cady said, "He said he wouldn't hurt her."

"But he never said he would feed her."

"We have to eat. We can't help her if we're prostate with hunger."

"Prostrate. Not prostate. Prostate's a gland," Mara said with a half-smile.

"I know. I just wanted you to relax. Besides, Lucien once said an army fights on its stomach. Did you know he learned all about fighting?" Cady patted her mouth with the paper napkin and passed the bill to Mara. "Besides those automotive courses and finance stuff we all had to study, Momo made him analyze the fighting strategy of Napoleon and Genghis Khan and even the American Indians."

"Why?" Mara asked, only half listening. She was stunned at the prices in this town. The shorts and hats had been bad enough, but twenty dollars for two sandwiches was beyond understanding. Clothing and supplies might be pricey in the Badlands, but food was cheap.

"Maybe he was supposed to be here instead of us."

Mara shrugged, and paid the waitress. "Things don't happen unless they're supposed to happen. Remember? Momo's maxim number twenty-four."

Cady had an amused gleam in her eyes. "So we were supposed to enjoy a really good meal and buy these neat biking shorts?"

"I don't think that's what the old woman meant, somehow."

"Old woman. That's what Kenno called her."

"She's a hundred and twelve. What else would you call her?"

"She's got a name."

"So do you, Turtle Knees."

Cady dissolved into laughter, rocking back on the spindly metal legs of her chair.

"No one's called me Turtle Knees in years."

"I've been gone for years."

Cady's smile faded. "Yes. You have. And I've been looking after Rosemon."

Mara looked out the window. Shoppers, many obviously tourists, cameras hung at neck, paraded past, packages in hand. The older couple who had shared the front porch with them at breakfast walked down the street on the far side. Still not touching. Not speaking. Each only half aware of the other, faces frozen in disinterest.

"Do you hate me for it? My being at Momo's?"

"No. Well, sometimes. When she was really bad. But most of

the time, no, not really."

Mara focused on the store front behind the passing couple. A map hung on the wall near the window of the store. It appeared to be a parish map. Something tickled at the back of her brain. Something she should know. Mara pursed her lips. "I didn't go because I wanted to."

"You didn't?" Cady said, surprised.

"No. Momo said I had to go. Said if I didn't, I'd hurt Rosemon, someday. Hurt her bad."

"Why would she say that?"

Mara looked back from the map and studied her sister's face. Such beauty. Lightly tanned skin, hair a thousand shades of copper and gold. Eyes so blue they rivaled the sky for purity. So unlike her own black hair and eyes and dark, dark olive skin. "Because she didn't have to be that way."

"Huh? Who?"

"Rosemon. And don't say 'huh'. She didn't have to be lost in another world. She could hear us, I know it, and see us sometimes. But she wouldn't snap out of it."

"Why do you think she could hear and see, Mara? I took care of her for years. She was lost. Blank. Not really there."

"I made her cry once. She wouldn't have cried if she couldn't hear what I was saying."

Cady leaned forward, the question in her eyes, on her parted lips.

"I was going through the chest on the floor beside her bed."

"The locked one?"

"I picked it with one of her hair pins."

"Show me how someday?"

"You want to hear this?"

"Sorry," Cady said.

"Anyway, I know she was watching. I put her in the chair by the dressing table so she couldn't help but see. And I picked the lock. And went through the stuff in the chest."

"And?" Cady sat closer to the table, eyes wide.

"Photos. Pictures of her and Andreu. Ticket stubs. Our birth certificates."

"Yours, too?"

"Yeah."

"And?"

"Andreu is listed as my father."

"No!"

"Yeah. I held it up at her and accused her of keeping me from my real father." Mara looked away from the fascination in her sister's eyes. Back at the map across the street. The tiny tingling was still there, in the depths of her mind. She had studied maps when Momo introduced her to geography. *What about the map . . .* "I called her a whore and . . . other stuff . . . for being Andreu's woman. And for sleeping with my father. She cried."

"Jesus, Mary and Joseph!"

"Momo would skin you alive if she knew how often you say that."

"My life is in your hands."

Mara smiled then and looked back at Cady. "So I know she can—could—hear. All those years. That's when Momo moved me to her cabin. So I couldn't hurt Rosemon even more."

"So she knew Rosemon could respond if she wanted? That's what you're saying?"

"Momo is Momo. She knows stuff the rest of us can only guess at. Come on. Let's walk across the street. There's something I want to see."

Leaving a generous tip, Mara and Cady crossed the street. Together they studied the map, a crinkled weathered parchment, sealed within a glass-fronted case. It was an old map, from the early 1800s. West of Louisiana and east of the Mexico territory was a wide strip of land marked the Badlands. Her home was famous even then as a dangerous place to live.

Further east was Calcasieu and Creole and a small star for Moyen, Breauxville's ancient name. And below Moyen was a peculiar mark, like a question mark. The map mark for Hameçon. A fishing village even then, named after . . . a fish hook.

Chapter Twenty-Eight
A Place Which Doesn't Exist

Hameçon was too far to ride on the bicycles, and with an afternoon rain threatening, the girls had other considerations beside their own desire to search through the town immediately. A taxi took them and their bikes back to the inn and waited as they unloaded their few purchases and changed back into the tiered dresses that Momo approved. Guilt at wearing their skimpy new clothes was beginning to spoil their day.

The driver, an old Cajun named Joseph, balked at having two handguns, a rifle and a shotgun loaded into his trunk, throwing up his hands and shouting, "No. *Bon Dieu*. No. I don' have gun in my cab. No. Take you away. Guns and criminals, I don' transport. No. No. No. *Sa c'est de la couyonade*."—*That is foolishness*, in Cajun.

Cady's judicious use of a twenty-dollar bill convinced him to put aside his concerns and open the trunk though he muttered imprecations and threw them evil looks. Another twenty convinced him to wait, meter running, as they bought new jeans, running shoes, more T-shirts, and waterproof jackets at Wal-Mart. They were even able to stock up on ammunition, and promised themselves a return visit to the superstore when they had Devora safely back. There was a whole section of maternity clothes and baby items that she would simply flip over.

Dressed for hunting, they clambered back into the taxi and rode through the rain to Hameçon. The tires sang a soft note against the wet asphalt. Joseph, taciturn as a Mickle man when he wasn't shouting and calling on God, ignored them and their purpose, content to have their money. It wasn't until they were nearly into

Hameçon that he asked them their destination.

"Where you go in fishhook?"

Cady jumped at the word. Mara pulled her attention from the wavering, wet, unpainted houses to either side, back to Joseph's old eyes reflected in the rearview. His bottom lids drooped like a Basset hound's, red inner lid exposed. "We're looking for our sister. At a place called Sasim. You know it?"

He shrugged. "There a whore house for the young men. Call it *San Souci.*"

"She's . . . Devora's no whore," Cady said. "She's a widow. And she's pregnant. Like this." Cady held her hands far from her stomach, showing a belly near to term.

"*Mais no.* Madame Collette no let her girls work *enceinte.*"

Cady slumped back against the seat, defeated. Mara hadn't expected anything better. Yet her eyes burned as if she had held them open too long, as if they had dried out from a day in the sun. A bar, half of its neon sign extinguished, slid past, followed by more houses, rot showing on unpainted fascia boards, muddy yards eroding, running into the street. Rusted cars on cement blocks stood in weeds. The road beneath the tires of the old cab was rutted and uneven, full of holes the state had never bothered to patch.

"There an old church.—San Simeon. Your sister go there maybe?"

"San Simeon," Cady shrugged, "Why not."

"It an old place. Bats in it belfry," Joseph cackled. "Holes in it floor, *mais yeah*. It flooded so many time the priest one day walk away. Say, 'The devil got Sam Simeon'. Dat back in," he scrunched up his face, "1920 for sure."

"Flooded. That means it's on a bayou," Cady whispered grabbing Mara's wrist. "Kenno would set up in some place near water, some place where he could come and go as he pleased, and have more than one way out, like a muskrat den with several entrances."

"Which bayou, though?" Mara whispered back. "It's not like we're back home where we know every inch of the waterways. Kenno's been gone for years. He's had time to learn anything he needs about this place."

"You whisperin' 'bout dat bayou out to San Simeon? I say it

Bayou Deces. Dat bayou flood church and holy ground. Float off de dead parishioner casket, time and time and time, I guar-an-tee." Joseph cackled again. "And the rich men's moved the church to Breauxville, called Moyen long time back. Think San Simeon wash to de Gulf. But dat ol' church, she stand dere still. Cats, dey prowl and bats dey live and mouse and polecat, too. But de roof still stand mostly. I take you to San Simeon, yes?"

"Please," Mara said, pulling her wrist away from Cady's fierce grip. "Take us to the old church."

"Yeah, I do dat fo you. An' I wait for you. Take you back to de inn, you and you sister *enceinte* if it be you find her dere."

Cady checked her watch, suddenly excited, but Mara wasn't foolish enough to think Kenno would be there waiting for them. They were twenty-eight hours early. Even if this were the place, Devora wouldn't be there yet.

The old church was constructed of sun-baked clay bricks, the mortar worn away, the bricks cracked and crumbling, damp from the recent rain. Once, there had been a thick layer of stucco on the outer walls, now only small patches still adhered to the brick, the rest washed away by flood. The walls stood in a copse of ancient oaks in the curve of Bayou Deces, moss hanging like shrouds over tumbled gravestones and a fallen stone wall.

The church was one great room surrounded on all sides by a wide portico, six Spanish-style arches to front and back, eight on either side. The portico had a flagstone floor with arched niches for statues long removed. Openings for massive doors hung empty, even the hinges scavenged away, and tall, narrow windows that held no glass.

Birds and squirrels had nested in the niches, spiders had strung webs across everything. Illegible graffiti scored the brick and broken bottles littered the ground. One whole wall of the portico, the one that faced the bayou, was blackened by smoke, the remains of a camp fire cold at its base, fresh deadwood stacked nearby. Cigarettes, beer cans, a broken bait box, tires and an old couch huddled beneath its protection.

When Joseph had claimed the roof still stood, he had been overly optimistic. Inside the church, debris littered the flagstone floor, pouring through holes above. Dust sifted down where the roof still stood. Rain dripped where clouds and a weak sun peeked through. Something skittered through the rubble. It wasn't safe to enter by day. It would be twice as dangerous at dusk. Mara checked the shotgun's safety, carrying it barrel down, pointed at the earth. No one was visible here.

"You think this is the place?" Cady asked.

Mara shrugged, stepping carefully out of the central opening back into the dim confines of the portico and out into the church yard. Birds sang. Squirrels ran along the oak branches overhead, shaking the long moss. Spiders wove sticky webs attaching trees to church. A black snake sunned himself on a slender twig.

San Simeon had been spared the worst of the rain, the storm passing to the north and east. Mara studied everything left behind by the shower, not certain what she looked for. There were hundreds of tracks in the soft ground, half washed away by the recent rain, but nothing that looked familiar. There were places along shore where boats had been beached and then pushed off. Two looked like airboat tracks, smooth and wide. But airboats were as common as johnboats in bayou country.

Back through the cans and a pile of what looked like women's clothes, Mara wandered to the cemetery. Tilted stones, broken and cracked, empty crypts, lids shattered or pushed to one side, comfirmed Joseph's comment about repeated floods. Caskets held air. Put enough water over even the best and heaviest crypt slab and the air trapped in the coffin beneath still wanted to get out. Had to get out. Fact of nature. Under the right conditions, the trapped air would blow the crypt lid off and the casket would float merrily down the bayou, coming to rest in the branches of a tree, on someone's front porch or perhaps tilted over a cow pasture gate. Wonderful sight to greet the day with. Worse yet if for some reason the casket didn't stay closed.

Weaving her way through the cemetery, Mara touched a gray marble headstone, a rose almost worn away at its arched top. Stepped carefully through the broken lids of crypts side-by-side. Husband and wife? Children lost in some plague of tuberculosis or polio or influenza? Blackberry brambles, the fruit hard red buds, climbed over another crypt and the brick wall beyond. A muscadine vine trailed up a nearby pecan tree. And then she saw what she had been unconsciously searching for—a bare heel print near a grouping of purple flowering plants. It was familiar, this plant. And one had been carefully dug from the ground. Run-off from the rain had filled the hole where the roots had been.

"Cady, come here!" Mara shouted

Crashing through the underbrush, jumping across gravestones and open crypts, Cady joined her, her handgun pointed at the ground by her side. "Find something?"

"I think so. Look. It's that weed stuff Devora took a planting of from Momo's garden. Major Something."

"Vinca Major." Cady grinned, triumphant. "Periwinkle. Keeps away insects, she said."

"And look here. A bare footprint, do you think? Devora?"

"Of course. Who else would dig up a weed, or go looking for it in the first place? Only Devora, because she wanted to keep away flies. And maybe she put some into a can or cup she found lying around here so it would work longer."

"Maybe. Maybe not," Mara said. "It's a pretty purple flower."

Cady snorted, clearly disagreeing. Mara didn't respond. She wanted this to be the place, too. But if it was, why didn't Devora spell it right? And why *Brovil* and a *fishhook* instead of the real name? It was one of the problems Mara had been worrying through for hours. And she still didn't have an answer, except the possibility she didn't want to consider, that Devora had been badly wounded. Injured, Devora's own personal code—the one she had developed when the gator attack had left her with limited use of her right arm and hand—could have been illegible.

"Mara," Cady shouted, "it *was* Devora and I can prove it."

She looked up and spotted her sister standing over a marshy place near the water's edge. Mara stepped quickly through the broken marble to the muddy bank, following Cady's gaze. Overhead, a breeze shook the tree tops, sending down a splatter of water. Drops pelted her shoulders.

"Sweet Sedge," Cady said. "Somebody dug up Sweet Sedge."

There was a clump of a reed-like plant, half in, half out of the water. It had sword-shaped yellowish-green leaves with crimped, wavy edges, and dense greenish-yellow flowers packed on a blunt spike. A sweet scent wafted up from the plant, minnows fed among its roots. And a fist sized-section was missing from the center. Someone had been harvesting herbs. *Devora.*

"Okay. She's been here. It's the right place." Sudden tears stung Mara's eyes. The taste of blood was a faint metallic flavor in her mouth where she had bitten through her cheek. She'd been tasting blood a lot lately. Maybe it was an omen, as Momo might say. Maybe it meant death. Angrily, she dashed the tears away with the back of her hand and turned from shore.

"Let's go."

"Mara?" Cady stopped her with a touch. "MaraNo, don't. She's a prisoner. She left the only clues she could think of for us. Clues Kenno wouldn't recognize."

Yes. And if I had gone with Kenno in the first place, Devora's man would still be alive and she would be home making baby clothes. But Mara said nothing. Just pushed past her sister and returned to Joseph's taxi. Stowing her weapon in the trunk, she threw herself into the back seat and slammed the door.

At the back of her mind, memories twisted, as kinked as the muscadine vine wrapping around itself as it climbed the graveyard tree. The sounds of screaming from the day the gator attacked and pulled Devora under. The screams over the maritime radio when Kenno took her. The screams of the cat Kenno tortured the day she first saw him. Not once had Mara helped. Not once. It wasn't a thing she could speak of, let alone explain. It was her guilt, her crime, and hers alone the blame.

Joseph crushed out a cigarette beneath his heel and climbed behind the wheel, exhaling and filling the sun-heated cab with smoke. "Where you go now?" he asked.

"Back to the inn. And how much is this ride going to cost me."

Joseph shrugged, a broad, uncaring lift of shoulders and both palms. "It will cost what it will cost."

Mara snorted, and didn't care how unladylike and childish the sound was.

More sedately, Cady climbed into the back seat, closing the far door. Joseph cranked the engine and, with a deft twirl of the wheel, spun the cab toward the road. Sunlight, hidden behind puffy clouds and the dense foliage of live-oak, broke through, blinding and sharp.

214

Mara turned back to the old church for a last look. The bricks glittered in the slanted light, the holes where windows had been were dark sockets. And the old sign . . . "Stop!" she screamed. "Stop! Let me out" Her hands scrabbled for the handle and wrenched.

The cab lurched, tires grinding on the gravel road. "Stop!" she screamed, blinded by the sun and fast tears. Before the taxi rocked to a full halt, Mara was out and running. Tears fell in earnest now, stinging her sunburned face as she ran. Her breath came short and her ribs ached, a stabbing pain. She reached the tall stone seen from the cab.

Brambles cut her, unripe blackberries flying, as she shoved the stiff weeds away from the arched brick gateway marking both the entrance to the church and the boundary of the cemetery. Water collected in the foliage drenched her as she exposed the words carved into the old stone. The blackberry bushes had hidden it from one side. The glaring sun had exposed it from the other. Old, old brick and mortar crumbled beneath her wet fingers. "The name . . . the name of the church . . . San Simeon. The Church of Saint Simeon, but the letters are worn away," she gasped as Cady joined her, her handgun drawn.

"Jesus, Mary and Joseph, you scared me. I think Joseph pissed his pants."

"Look! It's worn away. All that's left is S-a, S-i-m. Sasim. Sasim. Cady, look."

"I see it. Wipe your nose. Jesus, Mary and Joseph, my heart's going ninety miles a minute. I thought you'd found a body, for God's sakes. And look, you cut your damn hand."

"Don't swear," Mara said, laughing through her tears. "Don't cuss."

"Blow your nose. It's gross."

"I can't. I don't have a hankie."

"Don't look at me. I just grabbed my gun, which, by the way, will only make Joseph even more mad than he is now when he realizes I didn't put it in the trunk. I kept it in my waist band. And don't look now but here he comes."

The old cab backed recklessly up to the girls and halted. "You want Joseph cab, you get in. We go," he shouted through his open

215

window. "I no stay with crazy teenage girl who jump from moving car. My insurance go t'rough de roof!"

"Don't worry," Mara whispered as she wiped her face, bloody hands, and nose on her T-shirt hem. "He won't take off. We owe him too much money." Turning back, her fingers traced the worn letters cut into the stone, leaving smears of blood from the cuts. Sa Sim.

Joseph gunned his motor. Cady pulled her toward the cab and pushed her inside, slamming the heavy door. Joseph accelerated too fast, slamming the girls back into the seats. The cab fishtailed on to the main road, leaving Sasim behind. They had found it. Relief flooded through Mara, so strong she didn't even care that she had ruined a perfectly good, brand new T-shirt. The pale pink cloth was smeared with the blood still oozing from wounds on her palms. Wounds that were only now beginning to hurt.

"Bet Kenno told her what to write and she just spelled it like he said. She never asked him how to spell Breauxville either. And Sasim the same," Mara said.

"Yeah. She never could ask a question if she didn't understand something. Why start now?"

"We'll get her back."

"And Kenno?" Cady asked. "What about him?" A hard rain beat against the cab for a moment, even as sunlight sparkled on the falling drops. Tires whirred against the bumpy road.

Hameçon came slowly into view, drab and steaming dry in the late-afternoon sun. Finally, Mara answered, her smile faded from warm to something colder, relentless. "It's like Old Banoit said, Kenno has his destiny, his choices." Her voice was hard as iron on stone. "We have ours."

"What's that thing Momo says? The one she keeps misquoting. About every action having an equal and opposite reaction?"

Her voice still hard, Mara smiled and quoted, "Every action, it have a consequence. And every inaction de same, only sometime, de worse."

"Dat so," Joseph said, his voice ominous. "Dat so."

The girls stopped once more in Breauxville for supplies Mara thought she might need, Joseph pulling the cab into the parking lot of Cabal's True Test Hardware Store. Through the wide front windows, it looked like old McHenry's General Store back in the Badlands, but the prices advertised on the signs hanging here were cheaper and the store's proprietor didn't look the type to keep a loaded sawed off shotgun below the counter. He actually wore a smile. In fact, the residents of Breauxville didn't seem to keep guns around much at all, though the Wal-Mart had a nice selection available for sale.

Life in the Badlands had led Mara to believe that danger existed around every turn, every bend of bayou. But here, for the residents of this old town, life was easy, safe. She had a feeling most of the delicate-looking females she passed as they drove didn't even know how to use a gun at all. Like Devora who had believed herself safe while living with the LeMays. Safer still in protected seclusion in Mickle Toes.

And even if she'd had a gun back at her cabin, would Devora have been able to use it? Would she have been able to kill Kenno to save Charlie? Mara didn't know, anymore than she knew if she'd be able to kill Kenno to save Devora. If it came to that. There are some things you don't think about. Can't think about or plan for or—

"You going in or we just gonna sit here?"

Mara stepped from the cab. With a heavy heart she pushed open the front door to Cabal's and entered, a cowbell clanking merrily over her head.

Miles concluded his twelve-hour session with the talk-show host and his group of investors. It wasn't his meeting, but it was his money—or rather DeLande money and DeLande power—they would be using in this new partnership. As the meeting progressed, and attention had shifted from man to man, they had turned more and more often to Miles for comments and suggestions. As he had been bred to do, he had eventually taken over the meeting. It was a DeLande trait, this power over others. This control. The ability to read men and make money.

In true good-old-boy-style he clapped each man on the back and clasped each hand, smiling, always smiling, and with each flicker of eyelid, each hesitation, learned more. Miles didn't particularly like the men he was doing business with. Didn't particularly trust

them either. But it wasn't necessary to trust or like them. He just
had to know more than they did. To that end, he had already set in
motion a few fail-safes, one of which had been to pass along the
names and pertinent information about the men to his
investigators. In less than a week, Miles would have a full file on
each of them. He would know it all, from the mundane like what
banks they used, their net worth, where their kids went to school
and what charities they supported, to the more interesting, like
what they ate for midnight snacks and who they slept with when
the wife was away. Controlling men in the short term was a
common DeLande talent, a family gift. Maintaining that control
long-term meant much more.

As the conference room at the hotel cleared, Enoch and James
stepped in. Both men wore somber expressions and the suits he
had acquired for them on the first day in Lake Charles. With a nod,
Miles indicated that he understood there was a problem. With a
glance, he suggested they wait by the window.

They stood, silent and observant, in postures similar to soldiers
standing easy. Backs to the view, feet spread, watching the last
men depart. Though they might not have intended it, the subtly
menacing stance sped up the departure, the last three men leaving
together as if for mutual protection. Miles smiled. It was a tactic he
would remember next time he was in a hurry.

What?" he said when the door closed behind the last investor.

As usual, Enoch spoke for them both. "Kenno took Devora,
Lucien's sister. Killed her man. MaraNo and Cady went after them
to some place called Breauxville. Know it?"

Miles rested a hip on the table, one leg swinging. "Yes. Nice
place. How long's Mara been gone?"

If the men noticed Miles' reference to Mara they didn't
comment. They also side-stepped his question. "They got a note
from Kenno. He's expecting them to meet him at a place called
Sasim at eight tomorrow night," Enoch said.

"And you found out all this by . . ."

"Old Banoit. Called us on ship-to-shore soon's he found out
from Momo where we were. The old woman said Mara had to go
off alone, handle it by herself. Well, she's done most of what
Momo wanted. Time for family to step in. James and me are

heading out."

"I thought Momo ran things in the LeMay clan."

"She does. Up to a point."

"Which is . . ."

Enoch didn't reply to that question either. "You in or out?"

"Let's put all the cards on the table, here. What you really want is the Sikorsky and a pilot crazy enough to fly you into a danger zone."

James smiled, a lazy twist of his lips. "This Eldest is near 'bout as smart as the last one."

Miles shook his head and stood, adjusting his lapels and cuffs. "On the contrary. I'm not really very smart at all."

"Oh? Why's that?" Enoch asked, shoving his hand into his trouser pocket.

"I'm going to fly you into Breauxville and help you against Kenno."

"Well, every Eldest has his weakness," Enoch said. "Andreu's was Rosemon. Yours is Mara."

"Enoch?"

"Yeah?"

"When this is over, she's mine," Miles said.

"Wouldn't have it any other way Eldest. Wouldn't have it any other way."

Chapter Twenty-Nine
Reinforcements

The arrangements to fly out in the morning were not complicated; Miles delegated the care of the Sikorsky and the Cessna to the men who had flown in from the Badlands, and the purchase of the necessary supplies to the Welch brothers. Miles, taking time to relax, changed clothes and headed over to St. Pat's. After all, he was the Eldest.

In jeans, boots, and an old work shirt, he was himself again. Just himself, not Miles Justin DeLande, the Eldest. It felt good, though he was experiencing the sensation less and less since the death of his elder brothers. The office of Eldest was a pervasive thing, slowly seeping into his veins and tissues and taking over until it was near to impossible to find himself in among the changes in his life.

Miles pushed through the doors of St. Pat's, smiled at the blue-rinsed woman behind the reception desk and took an elevator to the surgical wing. The smells no longer bothered him, the decor no longer grated on his nerves, the people in scrub suits and white no longer looked both harried and somewhat threatening. Many even knew him by name.

"Evening, Mr. DeLande."

"Hey there, Mr. DeLande. Your friend was up walking earlier."

"Thanks for the pizza, Mr. DeLande. It was delivered a couple hours ago and we've been eating on it since."

"Hi! Great pizza! Thanks."

Miles smiled, having forgotten he had ordered pizza for the entire surgical wing. He wasn't above using DeLande funds to grease his way out of a sticky situation. Lucien's amazing recovery had become such a sticky situation. He tapped on the patient's door and entered.

"Well, well, well. Rosemon, look who's here. Brother-mine who buys pizza for the fiends in this torture chamber but forgets to provide any for the patient."

Lucien was sitting up in an ugly brown recliner, his knees tucked under an open-weave blanket. Though his words were petulant, a grin split his face and he held out a hand to Miles.

"Business keeping you running?"

Miles took the hand and gripped it, finding a sudden solace in the touch of skin-on-skin. Before he answered, he reached past Lucien, picked up the phone and dialed a number from memory. As it rang he sat down on the bed.

"Pizza Hut, how may I help you?"

"This is Miles DeLande. That order called in earlier? I'm ready for it now."

"Yes, sir, Mr. DeLande. It'll be delivered in half an hour, sir."

"Thank you." he hung up the phone.

"Pizza?" Lucien asked, his grin widening.

"Pizza. But if you get sick on the stuff, it's your problem."

"After a few days on the gruel and dry toast they feed the patients in this place, I think I can handle it."

"Good, because we're taking you home tomorrow."

Rosemon, who had been sitting in the far corner of the room, her back to the window, stood up and stretched. Fingers interlaced, she tried to touch the ceiling, her wrinkled dress falling in soft folds from her waist. "What's the matter, Miles?" she said when her hands pointed at the floor again. "Getting tired of trying to convince the surgeon Lucien is just an ordinary patient?"

"That too, I must admit, but there is another problem—Kenno." He had spent hours with Rosemon over the last two evenings, talking about Kenno and his threat, and the danger to her daughter.

"Mara?"

"No. Devora. Kenno has her. And he killed her husband."

"*Tcheue poule!*" Lucien swore, calling Kenno "chicken-ass" in slang Cajun. "Rosemon, she's pregnant. Like six months or so."

"Seven," Miles said.

Rosemon squeezed shut her eyes and lowered herself back into her chair. Lucien dropped his feet to the floor, hands on the armrests.

"He left a note, from what I understand, for Mara to meet him at Breauxville, at a place called Sasim at eight P.M. tomorrow night. Momo sent Mara and Cady there alone."

"That interfering old—" Rosemon began.

"James and Enoch and I will fly you home to Momo's in the morning, and then find them. We'll get Devora back." He didn't add "I promise". He had met Kenno face to face.

"I won't be much help," Lucien said. "But—"

"No, not from a sick bed you won't. You're not going, son. I'll see to that," his mother said.

"Miles—"

"Don't look at me. This is LeMay family business. Besides, you're right, you wouldn't be much help. You would probably just get in the way," he said, thinking over Rosemon's muttered comment about Momo.

"Why did Momo send her off, Rose?"

Rosemon took a deep breath and opened her eyes, their peculiar irises accentuated in her anger. "Because she's the *Great Momo*, in charge of everyone's life and keeper of *destiny*. So certain her visions and dreams are images of absolute truth." Her lips turned down. "She'll put my daughters in danger because once upon a time she saw a vision of Mara killing Kenno in defense of Devora and Cady."

"A vision?"

"Yes. With fire and gunshots and an old deserted church. She had it when Mara was just a baby, before Cady was even born. That's why she keeps her close, so she can make sure Mara is ready to face him.

"But her visions aren't always right, you see. Sometimes she sees things one way and they work out differently." Rosemon leaned forward. "She had a vision Kenno would rape me on a dock in the bright of midday. And Lucien would shoot him. Run him off. And instead of warning me about it, she sat at home and waited. For days, she waited," Rosemon said, voice laced with bitterness. "And when he attacked me, it was the bright of day on a dock, but it was Mara who saved me, not Lucien. And Kenno wasn't shot. She was wrong. And now she's sent MaraNo out after him . . ." Rosemon paused. "I'll kill the meddling old witch myself if my daughters are harmed."

The door opened and a young girl in polo shirt and jeans poked her head in. The distinctive scent of pizza floated after her. "Pizza delivery."

Miles stood, took the brown box and bag of salad and colas, tipped her handsomely and pushed the door shut behind her. Moving with the economy of grace and effort which was a DeLande trait, he cleared off the rolling bedside table, poured cola and opened pizza boxes.

With no further comment, Miles, the Eldest DeLande, served up dinner for his half-brother and Rosemon. Behind them, the moon rose slowly over the city of Lake Charles.

Later, Lucien in bed with a painkiller, snoring softly, Miles and Rosemon walked the hospital halls. Rosemon, as graceful as any of his sisters, moved fluidly beside him, floral dress whispering along her limbs. Miles paced beside her, hands in his pockets, little fingers dangling outside.

"Tell me about Mara? And about her father."

"Wondered when you would ask."

"Didn't want to pry."

"Course you did. But you were hoping I'd just offer to tell, so you wouldn't have to."

"True. But you haven't been very agreeable."

Rosemon laughed, the sound echoing hollowly. TV sets blared from rooms ahead and behind them. Nurses were talking somewhere, voices low. Miles waited.

"Mara was Momo's creation from the beginning. Saw her in a dream when I was just a girl. When Andreu claimed me, she insisted that part of the payment for me was his approval that Mara be allowed to be born. A child by me, but not from him." Rosemon's perfect lips pursed. "Andreu agreed, providing he chose the man for me. I didn't know it at the time, of course, and wouldn't have approved had I known. I loved Andreu. Couldn't have imagined wanting another man." She clasped her hands behind her back, eyes staring straight ahead and into the past.

"After Devora was born . . . She was such a delicate little thing. Prone to fevers and chest congestion, earaches all the time . . . Not near as strong and robust as Lucien. Anyway, when she was born, Andreu disappeared.

"Understand, he did that often. The position of Eldest is very demanding."

Miles smiled at the floor in front of him. "I've noticed."

"And I knew that. I never begrudged him his time away, or even his 'real' family back at the estate. Sometimes he would leave me and be gone for weeks. But this time he was gone for far longer. On Devora's first birthday, he had been gone for ten months. No card. No letter. No little gift left at the post office up to McHenry's General Store. Nothing from him at all.

"And then this man appeared in the Badlands. Word was he'd killed a man up Lafayette way and was on the run from the law. And word was, he was the most beautiful hunk of human flesh ever to appear in the Badlands. Even better looking than a Mickle man all cleaned up, and I found that hard to believe."

They passed a nurses' desk, her voice falling silent. Moments later, she picked up the narrative.

"I had been the most beautiful woman in the Badlands for all of my life until I swelled up like a watermelon with Devora, and got all puffy and stringy-haired, and waddled, breasts wagging like a cow's dugs."

Miles laughed glancing at the woman beside him, elegant, even in a peasant dress. Sophisticated though unschooled, naturally beautiful and self confident.

"Thank you," she said, interpreting the glance. "But I was. And by the time the weight was off and my hair and skin back to normal, Andreu was gone. And I was angry.

"So I put on my best party dress, left the baby and Lucien with Mama and Old Banoit—my *beau-pere*, my step-father—and I went to see for myself if this Cherokee chief was so wonderful."

"Cherokee?"

Rosemon shrugged, the motion smooth and earthy and dainty all at once. "Or Apache or Cheyenne. I wasn't there to talk, understand."

Miles laughed again. "Forgive my impertinence for asking."

Rosemon shrugged again. "The affair was . . ." She stopped, standing still in the empty hallway, a slight flush lighting her cheeks. "Intense. And marvelous. And far too short." She started moving again, her eyes meeting his once before sliding back to the hallway floor. "Two days after I told him I was pregnant, he went into Orange to pick up some supplies for us and the law took him. He'd left me his guns so there wasn't any thought of fighting. And that was the last I heard of him. Ever."

"You think Andreu arranged it?"

"The next day he flew in, laden with gifts and toys for the children and perfume for me and money. *Lots* of money. The *very next day*. And when I finally got the courage to tell him about the affair and *me bébé*, he already knew. *Mais oui*, he knew—" she said, her slight Cajun inflection growing strong with her memories. "I realized then that he and Momo had planned the whole thing so I would have Mara. So Momo's visions would come out right.

"Only, they made a single mistake. They never planned on me falling in love with the man," Rosemon smiled softly, her tone wry.

"Things were never the same between Andreu and me after that. They were good, mind you. Very good. But something had been lost between us. Something innocent, I suppose. Something pure."

"And you never heard from the man again?"

Rosemon shook her head, a wisp of blonde hair falling forward from the braid she wore. Miles almost reached over and tucked the strand back behind her ear. Stopped himself in time.

"What was his name? The man, the Indian who was Mara's father?"

A soft smile crossed her face as she said his name. "Samuel Grayfeather. I called him Sammy. He hated it."

"And what did he call you?"

"Rosey. And I hated it." Her smile widened.

Miles made a mental note. Samuel Grayfeather, arrested in Orange Texas nine months before Mara was born.

"And Mara?"

"Born in August, black-eyed and brown skinned and squalling like a banshee. Momo standing there, white dentures gleaming, saying things about destiny and dreams, and waving her *gris-*

gris—charms—and me wanting only to sleep.

"She's passionate, *ma bon pichouette*, my Mara Noelle, no matter what Momo says about her being cursed with no feeling. She's passionate and fiery and so strong willed. She's everything her father was and more."

"She doesn't want to be bound to me."

Rosemon laughed then, a tinkling sound. "And you want the Eldest's Legacy. The files and secret wealth that are traditionally passed from Eldest to Eldest." She fixed her eyes on him, the blue wedge of iris catching the light.

Miles ran a hand through his hair. This woman was a strong DeLande; there was no option but total honesty. She would discern anything less. "That too. That and Mara."

"Like my daughter, do you?"

He was silent, watching his silver boot tips flash as he walked.

"Sparks flew, did they? When you met."

"You could say that."

Rosemon's voice dropped, a strange timbre hidden there. "Wanted her? Needed her? Thought about taking her on the floor?"

The breath caught in Miles' throat.

"What exactly do you think a DeLande-LeMay bonding is, Miles? Some psychic hocus-pocus with the blood of dead chickens and drugs and spell casting?"

Unwillingly, he smiled again at the picture she had drawn. For it was exactly what he had suspected.

"Bonding is mating, Miles. Pure and simple. The perfect man for the perfect woman, minds wide open and bodies ready. 'DeLande-type mind to DeLande-type mind' is the way Andreu explained it to me. And you can fight a perfect mating, soul-to-soul and body-to-body if you want. Mara can fight it. But you'd both be fools."

Miles fought down his body's reaction to her words, the rush of heat. The sudden need. "And the Eldest's Legacy?"

"I have it. I've been sleeping over it for close to twenty years."

At his blank look she rephrased.

"Books, Miles. Books. The Legacy is under my bed."

The heat leached its way out of him leaving him cold, fingertips icy, an oxygen deprived gray beneath his nails. He had to force himself to breathe.

Rosemon turned and watched him, her peculiar knowing smile in place. Miles was suddenly aware that he had stopped walking.

"Tell me about them. Why do you have them?"

A nurse slipped between them in the hall, curious eyes shifting from one to the other. Miles began walking again, caught up with Rosemon where she had paused.

"I have them because Andreu knew they would be safe with me. The Grande Dame couldn't get them there. So far as I know from the single time I tried to read them, the Legacy is history, Miles. History and fairy tales all mixed together, like *Revelation*, *c'est vrai*. In the Bible. Symbolism and such like. I didn't understand one word in three." She smiled, softer this time. "But *you* will understand them. You will, when you read them."

"Are they . . ." Miles stopped, uncertain how to ask. His boots scuffed against the polished tile floor.

"Yours? Oh, yes. You may have them whenever you wish. But remember this, young Miles. You must be prepared to safeguard them and use them wisely." Her smile widened. "Andreu never looked into them, you know."

Miles looked up, startled.

Rosemon quirked a brow. "You heard me right. He was afraid of them," she said softly. "Deathly afraid."

Chapter Thirty
Strategy for Sasim

Mara tossed and turned, the sickle moon shining through the inn's window. Waxing or waning? She didn't remember. Her bones ached against the hard mattress. Her burned skin tingled. Her mind flashed from possibility to possibility, from old Spanish-style church to bayou water, to Miles.

He had been in her thoughts for hours, intruding where he shouldn't, interfering with her ability to plan. Confusing her. She had met him once. Kissed him once. Big deal. So what? Yet her mind couldn't put away the feel of his hands or the taste of him, fiery and sweet. The touch of his soul as she first saw it, like warm green stone cracked and wounded. Had it been real, that touch of his soul? Or a dream.

She was supposed to be DeLande—in part. And DeLandes were supposed to be able to . . .

Mara tossed the covers aside and rose from the bed in one lithe motion, padded silently to the window. Pushing aside the thin gauze, she stared out at the trees and the azaleas below her, hands against the window glass. Overhead, a vent began blowing cool air which quickly became cold, chilling her skin. Somewhere beyond her room, a clock sang out a dozen notes, then chimed two A.M.

Tentatively, Mara reached out to Miles. Uncertain, embarrassed. Hating the blood and genes that made her want to do this. She . . . *reached.*

Nothing happened. No change. No warmth. No green stone beneath the palm of her mind. Nothing.

Disappointed and uncertain why, Mara returned to bed, the

sheets icy and damp from her sweat. The bed unwelcoming and unforgiving.

It was early when Cady and Mara left the inn, packed lunches beneath their arms, their weapons and supplies loaded into Joseph's cab. The sun was up, an orange ball floating above the horizon, peeking through the boughs of leafy trees. It was going to be a scorcher, the humidity already so high their T-shirts stuck to their skin and loose tendrils of hair hung limp.

And Joseph's air conditioner on the blink. Without a greeting, Joseph drove down the drive. "My day off. I take you to de marina. You all on you own after dat. You hear?"

"We hear," Cady said.

Mara was silent. Gravel and shell crunched beneath the wheels. Joseph's nose whistled when he breathed. *Had it done that yesterday?*

Mentally, she went over the supplies in the back of the cab. It was almost certain they had forgotten something. She only hoped that what they had would be enough. And then, suddenly, a chill crawled over her skin. Thick as old blood. Icy as the moon on glass.

Cady looked at her, eyes wide, face pale. "What is it?" she whispered.

Mara took her hand, her own sore from the splinters she had suffered at the old church the day before. "Kenno. It's Kenno. He's hurting Devora. He's . . . hurting her." She *knew* it. Knew it in the way the DeLandes knew. The way LeMays knew. Gut deep and mind sharp. He was hurting her. Hurting her bad.

Cady clasped her hand, nails cutting Mara's skin. "He's . . . he's . . ." Cady groaned softly and bent double, forehead to knees. Her breath came in gasps, her hand clammy. When she spoke, her voice was almost lost in the crevice of her knees. "He's hurting her. Like he hurt me, only worse. A lot worse . . ."

Mara gripped harder, bruising Cady's flesh. Her own skin crawled, though the images were indistinct and out of focus. DeLande-type images. Mind-to-mind. A picture of a thigh, a man's hand on it. A glimpse of arched neck. A woman's pleas and tears. Big rounded belly beneath a faded dress. A man's laughter and his fist coming down.

"I'll kill him. I swear. I'll kill him."

The words were low, grating. Mara realized they were her own.

Miles watched as the medic lifted Lucien and placed his stretcher on the floor of the Sikorsky. He had checked out AMA—against medical advice. It had cost Miles close to seven thousand to secure his freedom—the cost of the surgery and the room and the intensive care—with more bills to come. But there wasn't a choice. They had to leave today. Mara was in danger. Kenno had Devora.

Enoch and James helped Rosemon into the back passenger seat and strapped themselves into the bench seat at the rear. Miles would be flying the Sikorsky this morning, and his men would be heading back home to the estate, the pilot taking them in the Cessna. Miles tossed a casual salute to the attendants—EMTs by the patches on their uniform shirts—and jumped into the helicopter. Twenty minutes later they were airborne, making a wide turn over Lake Charles, heading west.

Mara and Cady stood in front of the old man. He was older than Momo. Had to be, the way his neck wattled down to his collarbone, the way his eye lids drooped, the way his fingers trembled. And he was slow. He had been thinking for five minutes as he tied off the feathers on a lure.

The girls waited, however. They had it on good authority—Mrs. Gueymard—that no one knew the bayous here about better than Sylvester Thoreau. Sly to his friends.

Finally Sly tied off the last knot, his fingers grabbing the loose thread on the third try. Satisfied, he leaned back, smacked his lips and looked at the girls. "Joseph and Mrs. Gueymard say I should take you where you want to go on bayou. You say you want to go San Simeon, I take you. Fifty dollar. Plus gas."

"Done, if we leave now," Mara said.

"Yeah okay. We leave now. But, *'tite ange,* she don't look too good."

Mara looked at *'tite ange.* Cady. The *little angel.* Pale, tear stains harsh red on her white skin, she trembled almost as bad as

Sly. "She'll be fine." And she would be as soon as there was something to do. Some way to occupy her mind. Some way to block out Kenno and the sound of his laughter. The sound of Devora's screams. They had faded from Mara's mind quickly, but Cady was still in contact with her sister on some level. Mara did not envy her the touch of Devora's mind.

Sly stood, his head no higher than Mara's shoulder, and walked to a small skiff moored at the dock near the gas and diesel pumps. He climbed inside, his weight rocking to counterbalance the motion of the boat on the water. "You in my bâteau or follow, 'eh?"

"We'll follow," she said.

Sly nodded once, quickly. Reaching back, he gripped a rope with a wooden handle and pulled once. A small, two-cycle motor roared, blue smoke pouring out for a moment before the action smoothed. Mara prodded Cady to follow, sprinted toward slot 27C and strapped in. Sly's rippling wake was rolling against the banks by the time they pulled into the bayou.

The little breeze of their passage was a welcome relief. Mara tossed Cady sunscreen, ear protectors, and one of the wide-brimmed hats they had purchased the day before. And then, when she refused to respond, handed her the Colt and her own little handgun. "Clean, lock, and load, Cady, girl. Kenno's coming. We need to be ready."

By the time they caught up with Sly, Cady was dry-eyed and determined, preparing the weapons for firing.

Sly left them on the bayou bank, fifty dollars richer, plus ten dollars for gas. It was an outrageous fee for the four-mile trip but at least the girls now knew two ways to reach San Simeon. *Sasim.* One on winding little roads, one by winding little bayous.

After the old Cajun was gone, happily counting his money, little engine putt-putting along, Mara and Cady turned *Jenny* and explored upstream and down for half a mile each way. They were looking for places Kenno might have hidden Devora. They were looking for possible problems and any conceivable obstacles to the plan they had worked out. It was a simple plan. Shoot Kenno. Take back Devora. Get her to a doctor. Easy enough.

Upstream, there were three cabins grouped close together, four boys fishing from the dock in front of them. The houses were fifties-style: asbestos siding on the exterior, rusted tin roofs, insulated electrical wires running from poles to meter boxes on the sides. All were on stilts. A boat was half sunk in sand on shore. A yellow school bus rusted beside one house in a rutted drive. Pit-bulls were chained to posts in the shade. Clothes fluttered on lines. Dirty upholstered sofas and chairs slumped on the front porches. All the luxuries of home. The boys waved as they passed by.

Further upstream were sunken docks and several deserted homes, siding falling off, holes in roofs, the result of hurricanes or financial ruin. A hawk sat high on a dead tree branch watching for rats or snakes in the undergrowth. It cocked its head at them, unafraid. Blue herons nested in tall grasses, ignoring the hawk. Here, Bayou Deces had split, a tributary some of the old timers might have called a "ditch" flowing sluggishly south.

The sisters followed the ditch a ways, finding nothing but marshy land and dozens of young gators. The ditch made the land on the far side of Bayou Deces into narrow islands, which fit well into their simple plan to take Devora back. After a short discussion, they explored the island created by the splitting of Bayou Deces, and then the land around the church, out to the road. With a little refining, it would work.

Back at the old church they unloaded their supplies and searched the grounds for any sleeping homeless or last night's drunken fishermen and party-makers. Finding nothing new beneath the porticos except a stained mattress and three used condoms left behind by an amorous couple or two, they went to work.

Using *Jenny*, Mara made several trips back and forth across the bayou, searching out places with easy to reach sturdy, low branches She chose a camouflaged spot on high ground and dropped off the flotation cushions in the scrub, along with a water cooler, and one of the flashlights recommended by the manager of Cabal's Hardware the day before. Young persimmons, heavy with unripe fruit, hid the location from the water and the church, yet allowed a good view of both from between leaves. The rest of the supplies they had purchased from Cabal's she left in various places along the shore. She off-loaded five, five-gallon plastic containers, the weight ripping at her shoulders, and positioned them at the sturdy low branches. And she added 150 feet of coiled nylon cord. It was backbreaking work.

The deadwood pile under the portico on the bayou side of the church had been depleted the night before by the lovers who believed so strongly in safe sex, but didn't believe in cleaning up after their activities. For the girls' plan to work, they needed the wood, so Cady gathered fresh deadwood from the graveyard and along the bayou bank, replenishing the pile. When she finished long after noon, the pile was higher than her head.

By unspoken consensus they broke for lunch, unwrapping grilled chicken sandwiches and crisp apples provided by the inn. Feet dangling in the bayou water off the stern, they ate in companionable silence, and washed the meal down with IBC Root Beer kept cold in the second cooler.

Mosquitoes, gnats, and flies pestered them, though few braved the layer of poison the sisters had smeared on. Sunscreen and bug repellent made a nearly impenetrable film. Sweating always weakened the protection, however, and the girls carefully reapplied more as the day's heat continued to build.

After lunch, they switched places. Cady worked on *Jenny*, repositioning and restowing gear and creating an open space for the inflatable mattress they had purchased for Devora. Satisfied, Cady cranked up the airboat and motored across the bayou, upstream and down, from sturdy branch to branch, and back to the location where Mara had left the cushions, stringing the trap the girls had envisioned.

Starting on the shore across from Sasim, Cady slid washers over the one hundred feet of thick nylon rope and draped the cord from limb to limb. Every twenty feet—at the location of each container—she cut a thinner cording and tied an eighteen-inch long stringer to a washer, careful to make certain the metal ring still slid easily on the larger rope. The lower end of each stringer, she tied to the handle of a container. The trap was designed like a trot-line but was created to work on the surface, not underwater. Cady, whose nimble fingers tied fine taut knots, was the perfect one to construct it. When she was done, she piled brush over the containers, hiding the bright red.

Mara watched as she cleaned up the shoreline in front of the church and dug a shallow trench, lining it with the abandoned clothes she had found the day before. As the day's heat increased, the stench of urine and old beer grew stronger.

By mid-afternoon, the preparations were finished and the girls were hot, tired and miserable. It would have been wonderful to make the trip back to the marina for an early supper in the air conditioned comfort of The Lizard Spits. But they had agreed they had to wait out the day in place. There would be no respite from the heat and pestering insects.

They had claimed the ground around San Simeon and prepared it for their own purposes. Any interloper, whether fisherman, drunk looking for a dry place to sleep, or lustful teenagers hoping to use the mattress they had left behind, would be summarily sent packing. If a polite request didn't do the trick, then Mara's shotgun would certainly accomplish it. There could be no bystanders to get in the way when Kenno came calling.

Raiding the cooler, making periodic trips to the woods for nature's necessities, they checked over each other's work, further refining the plan and the phrasing that would trigger it. Searching for loopholes and errors, timing it down to the smallest detail, they worked away the afternoon.

Chapter Thirty-One
Plans of His Own

Miles loaded the weapons into the Sikorsky, handing them up to Enoch who secured them for flight. Though he knew soldiers carried loaded weapons on helicopters during war-time as a matter of course, he wasn't happy about their presence on board while he was flying. He wasn't happy about loaded weapons at all.

Miles had hunted with his brothers for years and could shoot the black eye out of a squirrel at a hundred yards, yet he had never grown to love weapons and ammunition like many other Southern boys. He preferred antique cars, powerful aircraft, fast horses and a life of affluent routine.

Enoch took the last box of ammunition and turned on his haunches, stowing it away. James also squatted, one hand holding the floating helicopter away from the deck-porch in front of Momo's cabin, a half-smoked cigarette between his lips. He blinked against the smoke curling around his face, eyes watching the placement of each weapon.

Behind Miles stood Rosemon, hip-shot, pink dress limp in the heat. A black crow perched on the eaves, head angled in curiosity, red eyes glittering.

Rosemon's hand touched the skin above his elbow, fingers cold in the heat. "Miles."

He paused, squinting in the sunlight even behind the aviator glasses he wore.

"This isn't your fight. You can just drop Enoch and James off, if you want. Wait for them to bring the girls back."

Beside him James nodded. Enoch watched the tableau, no

emotion apparent on his face. Turning, Miles took Rosemon by the arm and led her to the far side of the deck. Flowers grew in wild profusion from the bank beside the cabin down to the water's edge.

There wasn't time to be polite, or to word this a better way. Gruffly, he said, "I know you loved Andreu, but you knew he wasn't a saint."

Rosemon lifted a shoulder. Soft perfume, perhaps hers, perhaps from the living bouquet below him, scented the air. "There were parts of himself he didn't share and places where I didn't pry."

Miles released her arm. "Enoch once made a comment about how it was convenient that I learned a few lifesaving techniques *after* my brothers died. Do you want to know how they died? And why?"

"Yes," Rosemon said, her eyes wary.

"They were killed trying to track down my sister-in-law Collie. She killed her husband, my brother, Montgomery, in self-defense after she discovered he had molested her daughters. They intended to rape her, kill her and parcel out the daughters when they were done. And they expected *me* to help."

Rosemon's eyes clouded over. She stared at the garden as if it scented the air with poison. But she didn't deny or disagree.

"I went along for the ride because I didn't have the guts not to. Collie laid a trap with snakes. Water moccasins. It was one of those snakes that took Andreu in the throat and killed him, nearly killing you.

"That made Richard the Eldest. And he went after Collie with dogs. Deep into bayou land down in the Atchafalaya River basin. Her alone against dogs and us. When we had her within sight, Richard told me to shoot her."

Miles stopped, his eyes staring as blankly as Rosemon's. He was glad of the anonymity the dark lenses provided. "I shot her."

Rosemon lifted her hands and clasped her upper arms. It was a curiously feminine gesture. Self protective and tender.

"I put the round in her side where she might live through it. Not many vital organs. And still she kept running. I think she might have stopped, given up, but Richard kept shouting to her. Telling her what he was going to do to her children.

"Richard was a monster, Rosemon. Vile and foul and perverted.

And when I looked in Kenno's eyes the one time, the barrel of my gun pressed into his throat, I saw Richard's soul.

"I can't walk away. Not this time. I can't stand by and watch someone else stand up to him. Watch someone else protect the innocent."

Silence settled between them. The silence of bayou. Birds chirping, fish splashing, gators roaring in the distance.

"What happened? To Collie?"

"She's happily married to a lawyer in New Orleans, pregnant with another of my nephews or nieces."

"And Richard?"

"Someone else killed him. Someone else saved Collie. Not me. Understand?"

Rosemon nodded and dropped her arms.

"I didn't try to save her. I would have let him hurt her like he planned. Kill her, do what he wanted to her children, and not ever have lifted a hand or said a word to help. And I guess I loved Collie DeLande more than I loved than anyone else on earth."

Rosemon looked away and sighed. "Be careful, Eldest. If you die and Kenno lives it'll be . . . the beginning of the end for LeMay clan."

Taking those words as dismissal, Miles walked back to the helicopter and the two men waiting there. Pausing, he turned back to her. "We'll get them back, Rosemon."

"If you find them," she said softly. "And if your own demons don't stand in the way."

The words hovered uneasily in his memory as he powered up the Sikorsky and prepared for the flight to Breauxville.

As the big bird lifted from the water, pontoons dripping, Momo came out on the deck. Eyes black as crow feathers fixed on him. Her hands gripped the twin necklaces she wore around her neck; her mouth moved as if speaking, sound and meaning drowned beneath the engine roar. Along with Rosemon in her pink dress and the cabin itself, Momo vanished behind the bulk of the fuselage as Miles accelerated east.

It had been a long day. It was going to get longer.

Shadows grew as the afternoon advanced. Widespread shadows

of live-oak. Tilted shadow of tombstone. Moving shadow of a bird in flight and moss in the breeze. The heat, bearable only in the shade of the old church, broke toward seven o'clock as clouds crossed the sky. Distant thunder boomed, lightning cracking from black clouds in the south as a storm moved along the coastline.

A few splatters of rain fell on the bayou and grounds around San Simeon. Several more fell though the roof. But the storm passed them by.

Kenno didn't come early. No airboat engine sounded from upstream or down. And perhaps because of the threatening storm, no one came to the old church to disturb the peace or their plans.

The sun brightened with color as it fell, its light diffused through cloud and mist into a soft orange-pink glow. It lit the old brick like orange flame and revealed pale pink buds on an old climbing rose they hadn't noticed.

Cady checked the weapons once again, sighting down the barrel of her Remington, mumbling about light and shadows and how she wished for a scope. At a quarter after seven, she stood and walked to *Jenny*, started the little airboat's powerful engine, and idled slowly downstream across the bayou to the thicket where her cushions waited. On the way, she paused at each of the submerged containers and carefully opened each lid. With a last acceleration, she drove the airboat up on the band of the narrow island and shut off the motor. Mara watched as the younger girl pulled bracken and dried water grasses over the engine cage and settled down out of sight, then finished her own last-minute preparations.

Destiny. The result of decisions and lack of decisions. Cady had determined to come to San Simeon. Mara had not sent her home and because of that she was in danger that Momo had never foreseen, never predicted. By placing her sister across the bayou out of harm's way perhaps Mara had saved her from some of the peril they faced.

Listen to my voice, Momo had said. *Listen to my word.* And the old woman had sent her on to confront Kenno at Breauxville.

For ill or good Mara waited.

The sun lowered itself into violet clouds like some exotic queen on to velvet cushions. The shadows lengthened, thinning out and elongating as they darkened. The church threw back the light as if flames danced across the old brick.

Just before eight, an airboat engine sounded in the distance, faded out, grew stronger, negotiating the curves of the bayou from downstream. *Kenno*.

Furious, Miles circled Breauxville and Hameçon, the Sikorsky low on fuel again, the vibration of the big helo's engine having sunk into his bones. They had searched for three hours for the two missing girls. The only possible guides—two old black Cajun men—had taken sudden riches and gone fishing at noon. Joseph and Sly had disappeared to their favorite fishing hole, some secret place where the catfish grew to six feet and the crappie fairly jumped on to the shore so anxious were they to be caught. It was rumored that one man kept a still there as well. They always returned from fishing considerably liquored-up.

And so no one knew where the girls were. Not Old Banoit who had been fishing the waters of the gulf south of Hameçon. Not the French woman who ran the inn. No one. And it was nearly eight P.M.

Chapter Thirty-Two
Fears as Strengths

Mara stepped slowly toward the shore, shotgun hanging from one hand, the Colt hidden on the portico. The airboat engine roared around the bend powering a small, black-painted craft up the bayou. Kenno, in black denim jeans and white T-shirt, sat on the driver's seat, the safety straps dangling below him to the hull. Devora sat beside him, his arm around her big belly, her body shielding his. The westering sun caught red stains on the hem of her dress. Her face was white, too white, bruises like a mask around her eyes. Her dress was ripped, fluttering in the breeze of their passage, molding itself to her belly.

Kenno had hurt her. Hurt her bad. What was it he had said to Momo? Something about big-bellied women holding no interest for him.

Devora trembled, the muscles of her legs quivering visibly even at a distance. There was a gag in her mouth. It too bore traces of red captured by the sun. Her lips were swollen and blistered. *Jesus, Mary and Joseph, what had he done to her?*

Kenno guided the airboat down the center of the bayou, hands sure and steady. His hair was pushed back behind his shoulders, a mane of gold and red. Beside his eye, the black crow-feather brand stood out sharply in the rose light. With a final burst of power, Kenno beached the boat near where Devora had dug up the water plants.

His back was to Cady. Devora's head was close to his. Like back at *Blessure de la Terre*, he used the helpless as a shield. Tears trickled down Devora's face, pain and desperation and profound

240

fear etched deeply.

He cut the engine. Exhaust fumes billowed a gray fog. A heavy silence descended, settling on the water like a bird nesting for the night. Kenno's eyes burned into Mara's. Even in the falling light they were bluer than any noonday sky. He smiled. Devora's eyes widened in alarm.

Warm steel touched Mara's neck. Pressed gently.

Devora's silent warning had prepared her. Mara didn't flinch though fear jetted through her. She had never expected Kenno to come alone. He had never worked solo before, why should he change tactics now?

"Drop it," a voice said softly in her ear.

"You want me to drop a loaded gun?"

The barrel against her neck nudged firmly.

"How about I just lean it against this tree?"

When the voice didn't answer, Mara rested the butt of the gun on the ground and settled the barrel into a deep ridge of bark. Its safety was off.

"I wasn't sure you'd come, niece," Kenno said. "I thought you'd continue to hide behind the old woman."

"Unlike you, I don't hide behind the weak and defenseless."

Kenno laughed. "That old woman isn't defenseless! She's a hundred-twelve-year-old stick of dynamite. But I've got you and sweet Devora here and the latest unborn LeMay trying to be born as we speak. I have the last say in what will or will not be."

Mara glanced quickly at Devora. Her eyes were closed, breath coming in deep gasps. The quivering in her limbs was greater now and her hands clenched the side of the seat where Kenno held her. A slow dread forced its way through Mara's skin and down into her bones. It was too early for the baby. Two months too early. With Devora in labor, there would be no help from her. The scent of gasoline permeated the air. Mara fought against panic racing in her veins.

"You have me. Take me and leave Devora," she said, her voice steady despite her fear. "I'm the one you want. Devora is useless in bayou country. Can't fish. Can't row or pole a boat." Mara's voice changed slightly for emphasis. "Devora *passes out at the sight of fire*. Just *rolls forward and falls,*" she finished, glancing at Devora, hard. Her sister's eyes widened.

The smell of gasoline grew. Kenno smiled, started to speak. Mara interrupted.

"I'm the one who held a gun on your spine and threatened to cripple you. I'm the one who pressed the brand into your skin." She remembered the awful heat, the blaze of fire. The iron red hot in the coals. Kenno's eyes like dual blue flames searing into hers. Daring her. Not believing she would have the guts to follow through.

"I'm the only one who . . ." She remembered the sound of skin as it sizzled. The stench of seared flesh. The ghastly scream. As she paused, Mara knew Kenno lived the moment again with her. The moment that had bound them together, eye-to-eye, soul-to-soul, tormentor to the tortured. His lips bared. Teeth grated. Slowly he stood.

Mara steeled herself. ". . . the one who made you scream, and piss your pants, and cry like a child. *I* marked you. *Me.* Not her. She's useless to you, She's afraid of fire, for God's sake." Devora's eyes widened, her trembling grew. She slipped from Kenno's grasp as he rose, sank to the seat.

The shot rang out, crisp and piercing. Kenno stumbled. A red cavity exploded in the flesh below his collarbone.

Mara dived for the shotgun, rolling across the trench she had dug. Her palms slapped against the hickory stock. She came up to one side of the tree. Two shots sounded so close they overlapped—Cady's last shot and an explosion from where Mara had just stood. Pain splintered across her hip. Mara went down, wrenching her knee. Raised the shotgun and whirled. Fired.

The man before her jerked and fell, a circular crimson pattern materializing on his chest. His eyes met hers, surprised. He fell in a loose heap. Gasoline fumes choked.

Mara came to her feet. Kenno held a gun pointed at Devora. He laughed. The sound was lost beneath the damage to her ears, the perpetual thunder of the weapons' discharge.

With a whoosh and a pop the bayou exploded in heat and light. Flames roaring over the aural resonance.

Devora fell forward. Over the gunwale. Hands out-stretched toward the burning water.

Mara lifted the shotgun. Centered it on Kenno's chest.

For a single heartbeat, he stared down the length of his arm through the sights of his barrel. Focused on Mara.

In the next instant, fire and flame erupted downstream and up. A trickle-blaze ignited at the shore beside Mara, raced up the trench through the whisky-soaked clothes she had placed there. Kindled in the deadwood on the portico.

Sparks glared and spewed. Heat blistered the air. Firewood crackled. Kenno's eyes glowed an indigo laser. Mara could hear his laughter as he switched his aim to Devora sprawled on the muddy bank.

Mara fired. Kenno rocked back. His weapon flew up, out of his hand. Steel caught the light from the flames.

Mara ran for Devora who crawled up the bank, fingers like claws in the mud.

Kenno's airboat rumbled to life. With a wave of sound that buffeted the flaming water, the shallow draft boat pulled from shore and turned in the midst of the conflagration. The propeller beat into the flames, driving the boat downstream, forcing the flames higher. Red plastic containers—which had held the gasoline safely at the edge of the waterline—dangled, burning, on a rope along the shore, dripping water and flame, igniting the leaves in the trees.

Kenno was a black statue against the brightness, standing above the flames, hair seeming to blaze.

A line of fire snapped from the water just before him, tossing flames like a whip. He tried to duck, but the cord strung across the bayou caught him across the face. Sent him flying up from the airboat. Flipping through the air, blood spurting in a crimson spiral.

An awful scream gurgled as he fell through flame into the gas-soaked water. Thrashing. A diving torch. Alive and burning.

His hair erupted in a mad inferno.

On the far shore, Cady dropped the gasoline-soaked rope that had rested below the burning water until Mara's command. Lifting her Remington, she aimed at the water. At Kenno's thrashing figure.

Mara beat the flames from Devora and lifted her, carrying her to the far side of the old church. Eased her down on the cool, cool stones.

Behind them a shot rang out. As the round hit Kenno's gas tank an explosion rocked the world.

Chapter Thirty-Three
Flames and Destiny Intertwined

Miles spotted the fire, banked the Sikorsky and descended, too fast. The cyclic stick was wet with sweat in his palm.

It was a bayou on fire. Both banks, and a building beside the shore. Black smoke mushroomed into the air.

By the movement of the smoke, he calculated wind speed and direction, though that would change with the rising heat. As he dropped, there was movement on the water. A boat, flames licking at its sides, raced through the fire. It exploded in a fireball of flame and billowing smoke. Miles squinted against the sudden glare.

Small fires kindled, licking along the banks. Wet foliage steamed. Little blazes blossomed here and there. He looked for a place to set the aircraft down. He had to land on the bayou; he was rigged for water and there wasn't time to lower the land-gear. Upstream looked like the best bet. He banked and turned into the last rays of sunset, scarlet across the sky.

Even as he gauged the distance in the failing light, the fire below him began to die. Patches of black oily water looked like deep holes in the flames.

Smoke, rising air, and unexpected down drafts made any landing perilous. Shadows like the black pits of hell smothered the landscape. The landing lights were worthless. Beside him in the passenger seat, Enoch swore steadily. James, behind, was silent.

And then, they were past the fire, water white-capped beneath them, beaten by the rotors. The pontoons touched down.

The helo was prepared for most eventualities; there was a sea anchor on board. Shouting directions to the Welch brothers, Miles concentrated on powering down while the brothers searched for it. It was a big sucker. There weren't but so many places it could be hidden. A splash, sounding over the cooling engines, let him know their success.

He hoped the water wasn't too deep in the bayou. He hoped there were no water moccasins or gators. He hoped the Welch boys could swim.

"Get to shore," he said over his shoulder. "See if that's Mara and Cady. I'll swim out as soon as the helicopter's secured."

Two somewhat more prolonged splashes let Miles know they had understood. Moments later the Welchs crawled on to shore, weapons held over their heads.

The shutdown was the fastest Miles had ever attempted, slamming switches and securing the controls. Then the silence. The Sikorsky's vibration had seeped into his bones, he'd been flying so long. Though she was silent, he could still hear the sound of her engine in his mind.

Sunset blazed like fire across the horizon. Black night was close. He really didn't want to attempt a takeoff in the dark. But he didn't really want to stay put for the night either.

Smoke and the smell of gasoline crawled upstream, blanketing the water like black fog. The ghost noise left over from the hours of flying grew stronger. From out of the sunset an airboat appeared, her running lights blazing red, green, and white, flying full out into the night. The last rays of sun caught the yellow bands of the prop cage. *Jenny.*

Miles flipped a switch. The Sikorsky's running lights went off and back on again. Once more. The airboat slowed, circled the helicopter to draw off the last of its momentum and eased close to the pilot's door.

Cady, blonde hair tangled and wild, cool blue eyes too wide, too calm, shut off the engine. "What took you so long?" Her voice was rough, her face smoke-darkened.

Miles, his pulse fast and irregular, rested a booted foot on the pontoon. The silver tip caught the crimson sun. "Mara? Devora?"

"Downstream."

Miles tossed her a tie off. "Secure me to shore."

Moments later he stepped on to Mara'a boat and sat in the bow.

An inflated air-mattress cushioned his body. Smoke, acrid and stinging, replaced clean air.

"Don't puncture Devora's mattress with your fancy boots. Hold on."

Before he could reply, *Jenny's* engine roared again and he was flying downstream inches above the water. Fires burned everywhere in piles of mostly dry deadwood along the shore. Fresh smoke rose and coiled, mating with the low, dark cloud hanging in the branches.

To the left was a building, partly illuminated by a strong torch sitting on a low wall, but mostly by a bonfire on the porch. Backlit figures shoveled aside the piled wood. And then *Jenny* hit the shore at full speed and careened across the earth toward the porch.

Cady had stopped the airboat. The shock of the landing was the worst he had ever experienced, traveling from pelvis to skull in an instant, yet he was beside Cady as she dived from the boat for the porch. In the sudden silence, he could hear a woman's voice.

"It's too early. It's too early. It's too early . . ." Over and over like a litany cried to the heavens. And then he saw them in the flare of the torch's beam.

Mara, blood pouring down her thigh and puddling on the flagstones, knelt beside a body lying on its back, big rounded belly straining the cloth of its dress. Blood-splattered fabric was up around her knees. Dirty blond hair spread out like a veil on the stones beneath her. *Devora.*

Miles knelt and put his hands to the belly. It was hard and firm with a contraction, and seemed to move beneath his hands. Without asking permission he re-positioned himself between her knees. "I need to check you, Devora. I'm going to touch you down here."

"No. Don't touch me." She drew her knees together and rolled to the side, protecting herself. She pulled away from him into Mara's arms. "Please don't let him touch me," she whimpered.

"It's okay, Devora-sha. It's okay. He's the Eldest. Like Andreu. He won't . . . hurt you," Mara whispered. She met his eyes, her own like black diamonds in the dark. Her misery flooded over him.

And then Miles realized that some of the blood stains on Devora's clothes were old, caked and crusted over. *Kenno had tortured her. The son of a bitch.*

He broke off the thought. "I have the Sikorsky up stream a ways. The hospital's not ten minutes by air." It was the one advantage of his fruitless hours of searching by air. He knew where every building in the parish was.

"Enoch, James," he shouted. The brothers stepped around the wall of the porch. Water from their swim trickled from their legs but the fronts of their shirts were dry, almost crisp, from the minutes spent fighting the fire. "Let's get Devora into *Jenny*. Then we can get her to a hospital." Enoch and James knelt on either side of the moaning girl.

"Hands go here, here, and here to lift her. Cady, help Mara. She's bleeding. Okay, on a count of three. One. Two. Three." The men lifted Devora and carried her to the mattress. Pushing Cady's hands away, Mara settled beside her. James and Enoch took off jogging through the trees heading upstream, rifles dangling beside them.

Miles settled on the pilot's seat beside Cady, after he'd pushed the small craft back into the water. His eyes sought out Mara. Blood and smoke were streaked across her face. Her hair was singed on one side, skin blistered and peeling. "Kenno?" he asked as Cady reached for the ignition.

"Dead. I put a bullet in his head." He didn't know who answered. Didn't care. Pulling a handkerchief from his pocket, he folded it and pressed it against the wound in Mara's hip.

Chapter Thirty-Four
Bonding... Soul-to-Soul

Mara sat on the floor of the helicopter, Devora's body supported against her own. The girls were cushioned by the air mattress the Welch brothers had used to lift the pregnant girl up into the helicopter, and by the fire retardant blankets Enoch had found. As she held her sister, listening to her quickly exhaled breaths, Mara watched the brothers strap in, pull beers from a cooler and settle back. Cady was in front, beside the Eldest. Beside Miles.

The vibration in the floor and walls grew. A low whine intensified and amplified, and with a sickening lurch, they were airborne into black night over black water.

Devora moaned, her good hand gripping Mara's so tightly their bones creaked. Her bad hand was cradled in James' massive paw. "It's gonna be fine, Devora. It's gonna be just fine," he crooned softly, beer-scented breath like a warm breeze. "Eldest'll get you to a hospital. And then Enoch and me'll get Rosemon for you. You just hang on now. That's right, you breathe."

It was the most words Mara had ever heard him say at one stretch. Heck, it was probably more words than she had heard him say ever, all other monosyllabic comments combined.

"I'm . . . I'm having this baby. Right now," she panted. "Right now."

As if in answer, the Sikorsky shot forward and banked. Over its roar, Miles shouted "Don't let her push, Mara. Make her just breathe."

"Easy for you to say, Eldest," Devora shouted back. "It's not *you* having this baby. Ungnnnnn . . . !"

The flight to the hospital took hours, Mara was sure of it. Hours of Devora's blowing and groaning, and finally actually cursing, though Mara had never heard her sister say anything harsher than "dang it" in all the years of her life.

"Mara," she panted as they landed. "MaraNo, listen to me."

"What, Devora?"

"I want you to come into the delivery room with me."

Mara's mouth opened silently. Visions of blood and babies covered with blood and Devora maybe bleeding to death swamped her. She swallowed hard, the action painful on her smoke-dry throat. But before she could respond, James spoke.

"Devora, Mara's a little young. And she's green just thinking about it, so I don't reckon she'd be much help."

Mara wanted to agree, but failed in the attempt. In her mind, her sister was splitting apart like a ripe fruit, a baby clawing its way out.

"I've helped a time or two with deliveries. It'd be an honor to assist Charlie's son into the world."

Devora laughed, the sound ragged and thin as torn paper. "Deliveries of what, James Welch? Puppies? Cattle?"

"Pigs," he said with a smile in the darkness, white teeth shining. "But they was right sizable pigs."

Devora laughed again, the sound cut off in mid-peal as a contraction hit. When it passed she said, "Fine. But if you try to name my *daughter* Porky, we'll fight. Understand?"

"Your *son* will be named Charlie after his daddy," James pronounced firmly.

"Daughter. And her name will be Charlene."

"Son."

"Daughter. How much longer to the hospital?"

"It's in sight now, Devora. They'll have a stretcher waiting," Miles said over his shoulder. Mara realized she had been hearing his voice over the engine drone and their conversation. Steady, demanding tones. He must have been talking to the hospital.

And then the helicopter was down, the landing hard and noisy as metal creaked and protested.

"Sorry 'bout the rough landing," Miles said. "We got fog coming in, the landing pad was partly obscured, and pontoons were never intended for concrete."

Red and blue lights were flashing through the windows, a misty radiance. The engine's pitch changed again, dropping off sharply.

The door behind Mara gave way and other hands took Devora from her arms, lifted the pregnant girl down with the blankets beneath her. James, still holding her hand, jumped down and followed, glancing back only once to wink at Mara. Cady and Enoch followed the knot of people. Someone closed the doors to the helicopter, shutting out sight and sound and the single glimpse she had of nurses and medics entering a wide door beyond the landing pad.

Alone in the back, Mara pulled a clean blanket close to her, wrapping it around herself to stop the shakes. The air mattress was warm beneath her, the Sikorsky finally silent. Miles' voice came from outside, the words indistinguishable. She hadn't heard him leave.

Like a child, Mara curled up on her side, knees to her chin, eyes blinking in the night. Her fingers, still sore from the thorns of the day before, traced the bloody place in her side. Her wound was minor; a jagged stick or a stray bullet had plowed a ridge through her flesh. The bleeding had stopped.

Outside the windows, above her head, the lights flashed less frantically, the reflections dwindling. Her fear, so strong she could taste it, began to ebb, until she blinked and saw Kenno at the back of her lids. *Burned black, a bloated corpse floating on the bayou.*

Mara's shivers grew worse. Tears coursed down her face—tears of exhaustion, tears of grief. She saw him with each blink. Kenno, his hair flaming. Heard his cry above the roar of the fire and the airboat engine. She wondered what his death at Cady's hands would mean to her own destiny and Momo's predictions. Exhausted, slumber beckoned like a siren, lulling her into the deeps, and unexpectedly she was asleep.

Light invaded the helicopter, soft as lamplight with a delicate yellow tint. Outside sounds followed—buzz of insect, call of mourning dove—and the briny scent of rain or fog. The door closed, cocooning her in silence again.

The blankets were scratchy. Sweat pooled beneath her breasts and trickled slowly across her back at an angle, from shoulder blade to kidney. She could smell herself—smoke, bug repellent, scorched hair, gasoline fumes, and somewhere the faint tint of burned flesh. A weight settled beside her, the mattress complaining in rubbery squeaks.

"You'll roast in that thing," he said.

"I'm trying to confine the odor to one place."

Miles chuckled. At the sound, little tremors ran from the pit of her stomach out and down. She liked his laugh. It was soft and somehow . . . real. Slowly, Mara sat up and pushed the blanket away from her face.

She could see him in the darkness, right arm resting on right knee, left leg outstretched near hers. Left hand buried in the darkness close by.

"I think this blanket gave me a rash."

"Probably. They feel like grain sacks." He continued, as if the two subjects were related, "Your sister is in hard labor. They just took her back to the labor room."

"Where was she before?"

"In the delivery room."

"Seems backwards."

"Could be. I haven't been in one in twenty-three years."

Mara laughed. "Are you making small talk to relax me?"

"Is it working?"

"Yes."

"Then that is it absolutely. I want to relax you."

Mara could pick out his eyes, black as her own. And hair . . . so different. While hers was black like the midnight sky, his was like the sky before dawn. Dark, but suffused with strange lights. She wanted to touch it. See if it was as soft as it looked. She clenched her fists.

The hand across his knee lifted; the pale, long-fingered hand stroked the side of her face. She caught it, almost pushed it away, threaded her fingers through instead. His hand was warm and dry.

"I hardly know you," she whispered.

"You know me. You know all about me."

"The green stone?"

He inclined his head, agreeing, his hair seeming to catch the light and throw it back in sparks.

"Cracked and mended and cracked again?"

Miles lifted their hands and kissed the knuckle above her thumb. A strange heat suffused her in the darkness.

"I don't want the DeLande gift," she whispered. "I don't want to be like you."

He smiled again, teeth flashing. "You don't have to worry about that. You don't have a gift like mine. No one does." His lips moved to the knuckle above her index finger, his breath warm on her skin.

"Momo says my mind is opening up. Expanding."

Miles shrugged, the motion as elegant as a movement in a formal dance. "Perhaps Momo sees your potential. What you *could* be. But I am an Eldest, Mara-love. I see what *is*. And you have a gift, yes, but for now it's sporadic. Strong one second, closed up like a fist the next. If you're close to someone, or want—perhaps need—someone, you can make contact. But almost any child can do the same, DeLande genes or no DeLande genes. And I have no idea if it will grow or simply die away."

Mara-love . . . The words burned in her mind. "Momo says . . ." Her voice quavered and stopped. His lips parted and he placed them on the inside of her wrist. Above the pulse. She could feel the warmth of his flesh and breath. "Momo says I have no emotions."

"Trust me," he whispered, the words against her flesh like warm green stone and heated mist and far off lightning, "you can feel."

She laughed shakily. "Are you doing that . . . to me?"

Miles shook his head, eyes dancing and piercing as onyx honed to a point. "You knew all along you could feel. And tonight something happened. And it convinced you. And you mourned."

It was no surprise that he knew. That he could feel what she felt, know what she knew, understand what she understood. He was the Eldest; such things came with the genetics. Andreu had been the same, knowing too much, his eyes missing nothing. Without thinking, she said, "I killed a man."

Miles nodded, unsurprised.

"I shot four men in the last few days and felt nothing. Nothing at all. But tonight," Mara pulled away her hand, "tonight I killed a man, and it wasn't Kenno. I killed a stranger. A hired hand. And I saw his eyes. The surprise, the dismay. Isn't that a strange thing to see in the eyes of someone dying? Dismay. Not fear or anger, or some stronger emotion. Just this mild trepidation." She pulled her hand from his.

Miles left his hand hanging in the air between them, waiting. His eyes never left hers. Never wavered.

"And that's when I knew Momo was wrong about me. It didn't bother me when I shot those other men because it wasn't *real*. They didn't die. But now . . ." Fresh tears made a new path through the salt and smoke on her face. She swallowed and the motion ached deep inside.

Miles' hand slid up the length of her neck and cradled her head. Palm against her cheek. Long, long fingers curling back and up, settling against her nape. And when he pulled her forward, she didn't resist. But he didn't kiss her. Just touched his forhead to hers and held her close, mouth to mouth, breath to breath. The ache he had started was a deep pulse low in her belly. Heat settled all along her skin, electric, like that faraway lightning in his eyes.

"Cady killed Kenno, then?"

"Yes," Mara whispered.

"You smell like smoke."

Mara nodded slowly. His head moved with hers.

"And gasoline."

Mara smiled, the motion bringing her lips to within a hairs breadth of his.

"And . . . ginger ale."

She laughed, a soft explosion of sound. "And you smell like sweat."

"Yes, I do."

"I also smell like burned flesh. Kenno's flesh."

"Yes. You do." The words softened the light in his eyes, like the fog outside the windows softened the hospital lights. The darkness she had sensed in his soul moved in the depths of his eyes, coiling and intent. Fear, sudden and fierce, swept over her. Mara put a hand against his chest as if to push him away. His heart beat against her palm, strong and pure. Miles smiled, a dark angel, beautiful and deadly.

He kissed her. Gently. Lips just touching. Breath intermingled. Gazes locked. The kiss deepened. Slowly, Mara lifted her hand to touch the soft hair, fine as spun silk. Warm skin, warm as cracked green stone. The heat spiraled out from her and caught him. Warm spirit and soft breasts and aching, anguished need. Miles' hand slid around her, pulling her close, tight against him. His other hand lifted her T-shirt and feathered across her bare stomach, lips across her throat, her pulse pounding against his mouth. When she sighed, he raised her shirt and lowered his mouth to take in a firm breast and pointed, tight nipple. Heat exploded through her and Mara arched closer to him. "No," she whispered. "No."

"Yes, Mara love. Yes. Now and always." She felt his hands everywhere, his mouth on her skin. She should stop him. She should. But his passion and his need beat at her. And when he slid the last of her clothes away she reached for him and pulled him to her.

Far away an old woman rocked, the sound like a drum on the polished plank floor. She smiled, lamplight on her lenses.

Below her, gators thrashed, throwing up white water in the black of night. Tails beat the pilings holding up the house, in an uneven cadence. Outside, a crow uttered a long piercing cry.

Chapter Thirty-Five
Courting the Three-Footer

Mara rested her head back against the rough bark, the sun on her face like a caress. Her legs were stretched out into the sun, skirt pulled high, toes wiggling, casting long shadows. The three-foot catfish made a shadow as well, fins slowly moving, brushing the sandy bottom. He was so still she could have captured him by hand, curled fingers stabbing through the water. But she didn't. There were rules to this game.

It had become a contest of wills between them. She, patiently waiting, believing in the tantalizing flavor of the tasso ham baiting her trot-line hooks. He, disdaining her strategy.

Together, they had whiled away a month as the last of the summer flowers in Momo's garden withered and browned in the heat and the bayou levels dropped from lack of steady rain.

And the LeMays healed. Slowly. As if the heat baked the misery from their souls.

Mara bobbed her pole. It was baited with ripe tomato, a sliver of red pepper, and a chunk of fatback. "Take it, fish. You know you want it. You know I'll have you eventually; all it takes is the right bait. Why not end the misery now and I can eat well for a few days?"

He flipped a fin at her, unimpressed.

In the distance a gentle pulse beat the air. The steady throb of a giant heart. Or a Sikorsky helicopter. Or both.

The sound grew, a constant tempo, until she could make out the rhythm of dual rotor blades, and the black bird blocked out the sun. Miles.

The helicopter dropped lower and lower, blades generating an artificial wind, swirling the tree tops, stirring the hot air. Miles slid open the door and kicked out a rescue ladder, body lithe and nimble, graceful as a wild animal. He climbed and down landed on the muddy bank.

He had chosen the far bank, across from her. Unmoving, she watched him signal the helicopter away. The scent of aviation exhaust was overpowering as the Sikorsky lifted.

Slowly the sound faded.

She'd have to have a word with Cady. No one else would have told him where to find her. Cady was altogether too bossy these days, taking the job of aunt to the newest LeMay far too seriously. Growing up too fast, too soon.

Miles tilted his head, silence settling down around them. "Good afternoon, Mara Noelle."

A long moment later, she said, "You scared off my fish."

"I'm sorry." He stood there, hands in pockets, little fingers dangling outside, tall and lean and unconcerned that bayou mud coated his expensive boots. Utterly beautiful. Eyes like an angel, or a devil, or perhaps both. Light and dark. Good and evil.

"You tricked me."

"Maybe."

"Bonded with me without telling me what you planned."

"Guess I did."

"It shouldn't have happened."

"Yes, it should. We were bred for it to happen. Created for each other."

"Words an Eldest would speak," she spat. "Excuses for taking what you wanted."

Miles looked at the dark water between them, his eyes unreadable.

"I won't be your slave, Miles Justin."

"I don't want one. I just want you."

"That why you left us at the hospital and just disappeared? Without a word."

His face changed. A faint tension appeared there, beneath the skin. Or perhaps she just *knew* it. *Felt* it. He had been right, she had no real power yet, not as LeMays and DeLandes defined it.

But sometimes things came to her like a glimpse into another land. Another heart.

"I had to go home. To the estate."

Mara said nothing. Tapped her pole, trying to entice the fish back out for a nibble. She was certain that was his shadow beneath the fallen log and pile of brush. She waited.

"My sister Angelique got away."

"She was a prisoner or something? A DeLande hostage?"

"Something like that."

"How cozy and homey-sounding."

Miles grinned. She could see it out of the corner of her eye. "Did you think I wouldn't come back?"

"No. I knew you'd be back. I just hoped you would wait a while longer."

Miles ran a hand through his hair, ruffling it in the slight breeze. She could feel the softness there, silken and fine. Or perhaps she just remembered. It was impossible to distinguish between the two sometimes. Between memory and longing.

"You wanted me, Mara. I knew it. You knew it."

"I wanted you. I didn't want the bonding. I didn't know the two were the same thing." She looked at him, met his dark eyes, felt the pull of them. "You knew. Rosemon had told you. So you took what you wanted. Just like any other Eldest. Just like Andreu."

This time, Miles flinched, lips tightening. "For us there can be nothing else. You know that."

She didn't know if he meant for the two of them and the bonding in the helicopter, or for Eldests, who had too much power and were tainted by it. Who took whatever they wanted because they were hardwired to do so. After a moment, she said, "Devora had a boy."

"Of course."

"Four pounds. He came home last week. She named him Charlie, after her husband."

"How is she?"

"Grieving. Recovering. She and the baby are with Rosemon and Lucien and Cady. They called you on the maritime radio, didn't they? Told you where I was."

Miles didn't answer, just stuck his hand back into his pocket, and stepped through the mud to a higher spot. He leaned against a tree, his face in shadow. "Should I have courted you, Mara?"

"Yes."

"I could do that now. If you'll let me."

"To what end, Miles?"

He crossed his arms and slowly squatted, though for him it was a dancer's movement, with a dancer's grace. He smiled, the tension back in his face. "You could come to the estate. To live."

"Another DeLande whore?"

"Another DeLande wife. Mine."

Mara couldn't help the peculiar thrill that shot through her. Fish stuck a nose out from beneath the log, whiskers quivering. "I'm only seventeen."

"Eighteen soon. Very soon. Happy birthday."

Mara smiled, said nothing.

"I have a gift for you."

"Courting already?"

"Trying to. You still have your gun?"

She lifted the weapon a moment. "Badlands are dangerous, Miles. Predators everywhere." She held his gaze a moment. "I always have my gun."

"Well, I found the original owner."

Mara looked over at him, not following his meaning. Then her hands dropped, lowering the Colt and the pole in nerveless understanding. The weapon banged on the root where she sat. The bright red bob on the mid-point of her line tilted to the side in the water as excess line coiled around it.

"He's in jail. Doing thirty years for murder one. He's been there eighteen years."

Mara pressed her lips together. Lifted the pole. It wasn't what she wanted to hear. Wasn't what she had believed all these years.

"My lawyers and investigators think he didn't do it. They've managed to convince a judge or two. There'll be a retrial in about three months."

Mara smiled. "Pretty impressive, Eldest." She meant to sound aloof, but even to her own ears there was a secret joy in the tone.

"I have a more personal gift for you, if you'll let me swim over." He looked at the water. "Wade over, I mean."

259

"Can't. Leaches," Mara lied, smiling. "And you'll scare away my fish again."

"Ahhhhh." He studied her silently as the fish nosed out from the protection of the log. "You cut your hair."

Lifting a hand, she touched the short locks feathered close to her head. "Momo did it. Most of it was scorched on one side."

"I like it."

"It feels weird. Light." She moved her head from side to side to show the weight was gone.

"What if I don't want to live at the estate?" she asked suddenly, surprising herself.

He managed not to smile for which she was grateful. "We can live anywhere."

"What if I want to wait a few years?"

A smile swept across his face, heavy-lidded and sensual. "You have beautiful legs, stretched out in the sun. I remember the way they felt under my hands."

"Unfair, Miles. You're cheating again," she said, flipping her dress down over her knees.

"Yes. I'm very unfair. Downright sneaky, in fact," he said, laughing. "But be honest. Do you think you want to wait for me? For us?"

The fish swam out, slimy skin glistening in the sunlight. His shadow was long and leaner than he. He'd be good eating.

"No, probably not," she said finally. "It depends on how good a job you do courting me."

Miles laughed out loud. Fish darted away, leaving a trail of silt floating in the slow current. Mara blew out a disgusted breath.

She had a feeling she might never catch this fish.

About the Author

Born in Louisiana and raised in the southern states, Gwen Hunter now lives in South Carolina. Her novels have been published around the world in at least twelve countries and seven languages.

Please visit her website, www.gwenhunter.com, for the very latest news and contact information.

Printed in the United States
66478LVS00006B/142-165

9 781933 523118